Becoming
Jinn

Becoming Jinn

Lori Goldstein

Feiwel and Friends
New York

For Marc, for being right.

A Feiwel and Friends Book
An Imprint of Macmillan

Printed in the United States of America by R. R. Donnelley & Sons Company, Harrisonburg, Virginia. For information, address Feiwel and Friends, 175 Fifth Avenue, New York, N.Y. 10010.

Feiwel and Friends books may be purchased for business or promotional use. For information on bulk purchases, please contact the Macmillan Corporate and Premium Sales Department at (800) 221-7945 x5442 or by e-mail at specialmarkets@macmillan.com.

Library of Congress Cataloging-in-Publication Data Available

ISBN: 978-1-250-05539-2 (hardcover) / 978-1-250-07916-9 (ebook)

Book design by Ashley Halsey

Feiwel and Friends logo designed by Filomena Tuosto

First Edition: 2015

10 9 8 7 6 5 4 3 2 1

macteenbooks.com

Zar Sisterhoods

1

A CHISEL, A HAMMER, A WRENCH. A SANDER, A DRILL, A POWER SAW. A laser, a heat gun, a flaming torch. Nothing cuts through the bangle. Nothing I conjure even makes a scratch.

I had to try, just to be sure. But the silver bangle encircling my wrist can't be removed. It was smart of my mother to secure it in the middle of the night while I was asleep, unable to protest.

Though my Jinn ancestry means magic has always been inside me, the rules don't allow me to begin drawing upon it until the day I turn sixteen. The day I receive my silver bangle. The day I officially become a genie.

Today.

I slam my newly acquired accessory against my bedroom closet, leaving a rounded indent on the wood door. The pristine, gleaming metal mocks me. For the rest of my life, I'll go where I'm told, perform on command, and do it all without question.

Screw that.

Barefooted, I can't kick the pile of tools without impaling myself. I settle for shoving the saw, but in the blade, a flash of gold reflects back at me. I've ignored the unusual sensation of hairs tickling my bare shoulders all morning . . . the new *tap, tap, tap* of my nails against the conjured metal . . . the hem of my pajama pants now flirting with my calf. Ignored just in case. Just in case this bangle wasn't here to stay. But even my talent for denial is no match for my curiosity when it's been piqued.

Standing at the bathroom mirror, my breath catches in my throat.

The deepening of my olive skin, the angling of my cheekbones, the lengthening of my torso. I've seen them all before. On my mother, who wears them like she owns them. Unlike me, who wears them like a rented Halloween costume.

I lay a finger on the bangle and push, watching it spin around my wrist. Somehow this thing stimulates my body to reach full maturity. As an inherently attractive species, this tends to make us Jinn . . . well, hot. I'm pretty sure it's less a quid pro quo thing (thankfully, otherwise we Jinn would be the most shallow of species) and more an ancestral one, but then again, I'm not privy to the inner workings of the Afrit, the council that rules over our Jinn world.

I run my tongue along my bright white teeth and give thanks that my birthday falls during the summer. Not that I think the HITs (humans in training, aka teenagers) I go to school with would likely question this new and improved Azra Nadira staring back at me. Guess there are benefits to not being popular. Unlike other newbie Jinn, I certainly won't need to change schools or even incite hushed rumors about plastic surgery. For me, one or two fibs about a to-die-for stylist and an oh-so-talented makeup artist will do.

Laughably out of character, of course, but, again, there are benefits to not being popular.

Inspecting all the ways my body has been altered while my mind was unable to resist, I note a distinct lack of curves remains. Seriously, a little *va-va-voom* here or there (and by "there" I'm talking to you, status quo B cup) was too much to ask?

I upend the basket next to the sink. A pair of nail clippers clanks against the marble counter, landing in between dental floss and a barely used compact of blush. I drum my nails, now as luminous as ten perfectly polished pearls, against the cold stone and brandish the nail clippers like a sword.

I knew this was coming. *Click.* I grew up knowing this was coming. *Click.* But still a part of me believed something would stop it. *Click.* Maybe my mother would finally realize I was serious. *Click.* I've been begging her to find a way around me having to become a genie since I was old enough to understand what the word "destiny" meant. *Click.* Maybe the Afrit would decide my well-honed lack of enthusiasm was an insult to the long line of Jinn from which I descend. *Click.* Maybe they'd take one look at me and realize that, for the first time in Jinn history, powers should skip a generation. *Click.*

I turn on the faucet and watch with satisfaction as the tips of the long nails that replaced my short ones overnight swirl around the basin and disappear down the drain.

A lock of my newly long hair falls across my eye. With a puff, I blow it aside and drop the clippers on the counter. Peeking out from under the overturned basket is the pointy end of a pair of scissors.

Running away was never an option. *Snip.* I found that out when I was ten, twelve, and fourteen. *Snip.* My Jinn blood is the equivalent of a permanent tracking device. *Snip.* And now it's not just my mother who can find me anywhere, anytime. *Snip.* The Afrit will be watching. *Snip.* If I refuse to grant wishes, if I screw up, if I expose our Jinn world to humans, I will be extracted from this human life I'm pretending to live. *Snip.* I'll be tossed in a cell deep inside the Afrit's underground lair where they sit, rubbing their hands together and cackling as they toy with us Jinn pawns. *Snip.* It's not a death penalty. *Snip.* As much as it may feel like it is. *Snip.*

A blanket of dark espresso hair surrounds my feet. I've sheared off the three inches that are new since yesterday and then some. The color, which morphed from mouse to mink while I slept, is an exact match for my mother's. That can stay. The sheen helps the choppy bob I've given myself look halfway decent.

They can make me grant wishes, but they can't dictate what I'm going to look like while doing it.

I splash water on my face and feel the length of my eyelashes. The gold flecks of my eyes have consumed the hazel. The new color is an exact match not only for the color of my mother's eyes but for the color of all Jinn's eyes. And I can't have that.

Lucky for me, my learning curve with this conjuring thing has been fast. One crooked wrench, one inoperable lighter, and one unrecognizable reciprocating saw preceded the plethora of tools turning my bedroom into a hardware store. And in all fairness, the mangled saw stems less from my lack of skill and more from my ignorance as to what a reciprocating saw actually looks like.

Just as I did when conjuring each tool, I steady my breathing, tune my ears to the beat of my heart, which pumps my Jinn blood at a rate closer to that of hummingbirds than humans, and close my eyes. In my mind, I form the perfect image of a pair of transparent contacts tinted dark brown.

An icy tingle snakes through my body. I shiver. My body craves heat. In all the ways I take after my mother—in all the ways I take after all Jinn—an intolerance for cold is the one that bothers me the least.

I concentrate until a bead of sweat forms on my upper lip and the slimy lenses float in a sea of saline in the palm of my hand.

Good-bye gold. Good-bye Jinn.

I plant my face an inch away from the mirror. With my index finger on my top lid and my thumb on my bottom, I create a larger bull's-eye for the brown contact. My first attempt sends the lens down the drain. After conjuring another one, I force myself not to blink. I'm successfully affixing the lens to my eyeball when I notice my fingernails are once again long. And red.

My hair shoots past my chin, flies down my neck, and leaves my collarbone in the dust. Post-bangle, pre-haircut, it barely skimmed my shoulders. It now lands mid-B—*Wait, is that now an A?*—cup boob. The gold of my eyes deepens and shimmers until my irises resemble balls of compacted glitter.

Apparently the Afrit *can* dictate what I look like. I dump the contact lenses in the trash and poke my finger in and out of the intricate carvings etched into the bangle. I wouldn't be surprised if one of these indents housed a tiny spy camera and the Afrit were really just a bunch of pervy Peeping Toms.

I dive into my bed and burrow under the soft down of my comforter, grateful for its instant warmth. Ignoring the sound of the dog barking outside, I drink in the sweet smell of the lilacs in perpetual bloom in our backyard and catch a faint hint of sea beneath the floral perfume. Our house is close enough that, when the wind blows a certain way, we can smell the ocean. It doesn't happen often, mostly because the windows are usually shut to seal in the warmth and the curtains are usually drawn to seal in, well, us.

I will myself to fall back to sleep. Even if I can't sleep, I can still choose to skip today.

All I have to do is stay in bed. All I have to do is not open my eyes. All I have to do is pretend. Fortunately, being skilled in pretending is another way in which I take after my mother, another way in which I take after all Jinn.

Turning toward the window, I breathe in the lilacs. Along with the fragrance comes the pollen. Along with the pollen comes the coughing. Along with the coughing comes the involuntary opening of my eyes.

Who am I kidding? I can't skip today. I don't have that kind of control. The bangle assures that I never will.

I crawl out of bed and shed my pajamas, dropping them on top of the drill. Of course the black tank top I pull over my head and down my newly elongated torso is too short. As I move, the hem plays a game of peekaboo with my belly button, an unintentional homage to the midriff-baring genies of fairy tales and fantasies.

I rummage through the top drawer of my bathroom vanity until I find an elastic and the pair of bug-eyed sunglasses my mother bought for me last year. I gather my hair into a ponytail and hide my gold eyes behind the tinted shades. It's summer. Well, almost summer. In New England, summer doesn't debut until July. And only if we're lucky. June is always a tease. Still, with tenth grade in the rearview mirror, I can camouflage my new look this way until school starts again. By then, no one will remember what I used to look like.

As if that's a valid concern. I could walk into calculus tomorrow with rainbow-colored dreadlocks and half the class wouldn't even blink an eye.

Being invisible is a trait I've learned all on my own.

2

The smell of chocolate fills my nostrils as I head down the stairs. The bracelet slides easily around my wrist but is in no danger of falling off. It doesn't have to be tight like a handcuff to achieve the same effect.

I linger in the kitchen doorway. My mother gathers her long hair with one hand and secures it into a bun with the other. The silk of her emerald kaftan glides across her body, accentuating her graceful movements and making them appear all the more effortless. She leans over our farmhouse table and pushes back her sleeves.

I wrap my hand around my silver bangle. It is identical to the one around my mother's wrist except for the color. Hers, like that of all retired Jinn, shines a deep gold. The same color as her—now, our—eyes.

"Happy birthday, kiddo." As she takes in my appearance, she shakes her head. "Nice touch with the sunglasses. Very movie star incognito. But the way you're strangling those pretty new locks is criminal."

I lower the shades so she can see my eyes rolling. Flipping the end of my ponytail, I say, "How else am I supposed to explain the sudden change in length? I'm not the type of girl to get hair extensions. I don't want people to *think* I'm the type of girl who would get hair extensions."

"Because they'll think you're vain? Or be jealous?" My mother laughs. "Believe me, they've been jealous all along. Yesterday, even I would have sworn you couldn't look any more beautiful." She smiles. "But I'd have been wrong."

Despite or maybe because of what I've seen in the mirror, I dismiss her compliment. It's actually my mother who has the capacity to stun. I've spent fifteen, no, sixteen years looking at her, and her beauty still catches me by surprise.

She returns her attention to her pastry bag and with a gentle squeeze pipes the second "a" of my name in gold icing. *Azra.* The letters shimmer atop the chocolate-frosted cake. I know from previous birthdays how sugary the combination is, but nothing's too sweet for us. Salt, we are sensitive to, but the amount of sugar we eat would incite comas in humans.

She underlines my name with a squiggle of gold. Then she pipes that loaded "16" underneath. The exclamation mark she adds causes me to use my long fingernails to scratch at the skin underneath my bangle.

"So," my mother says, "just in case your stubbornness kept you under the covers for the better part of the day, I scheduled the party for tonight."

The groan that escapes my lips is a reflex. She knows I don't want this party because she knows I don't want this birthday.

At least the guest list is short. It's not like I have any friends from school. Having to hide who we are from humans means our social circle consists solely of fellow Jinn.

My mother wanted to invite all five of the female Jinn who make up her Zar, the lifelong friends she calls her "sisters," and their daughters, who, once we all reach sixteen, will officially make up mine. But I negotiated her down to just Samara, my mother's best friend, and her daughter, Laila, whom my mother has been desperate for me to make my best friend since we were born. They're the closest I have to a family.

My mother then makes me promise to be good, like I'm turning six instead of sixteen.

"I'd appreciate it if you could dial down the attitude for the party," she says. "Laila hasn't turned yet. Let her be excited, okay?"

She sinks sixteen candles into the smooth icing, and I promise to try. But I know it's a promise I won't be able to keep. The only way I could is if the wish I make when I blow those candles out comes true and this band magically falls off my wrist. But I know better. Birthday candles, eyelashes, shooting stars, that's not how wishes are granted. Being selected by the Afrit, that's what makes wishing so.

Even if I don't get a birthday wish, I should be able to spend the day however I want, wherever I want. Sun, sand, and a book. Maybe mussels for lunch. Considering we live less than ten minutes from a four-mile-long sandy shoreline, that's a wish even a newbie genie like myself could easily grant.

"If the party isn't until later," I say, "we can spend the whole day at the beach, right?"

"We could," my mother says, "but I think we need to start practicing."

The perfectly decorated cake leaps from the counter, beelining for my head. My instinct to duck kicks in a second after my instinct to throw my hands in the air. The cake freezes, hovering three feet above the hand-painted Moroccan tile floor.

I walk a circle around it, amazed not that the mass of chocolate is floating but that I'm the one making it float. Unlike the magic I've been doing upstairs in my room, this just happened. It was automatic. Something engaged even before my brain could.

I admit it. Having powers doesn't suck. If only they didn't come with being told when and how to use them.

"Who needs practice?" I say with confidence, despite the quiver in my hands.

Crumbs fly and chocolate icing splatters the dark cherry cabinets as the cake plummets to the floor. The three-second rule doesn't even get a chance to be applied, for the cake reassembles in perfect form in less time than it takes to blink.

My mother smiles and places her hands on her curvy hips. "Practice? Certainly not me."

No, my mother doesn't need practice. She's been doing magic since before I was born. Since the day she turned sixteen, probably even earlier. The rules were different back then.

I wipe the single leftover dollop of brown off the kitchen table. As I suck the icing from my finger, my heart pounds. I have no idea how I summoned the magic that suspended the cake in midair or if I can do it again. I'm as curious as I am terrified to find out.

3

"Now, Azra, now!"

At this moment, my mother is the one terrified. With good reason.

Flames from the inferno I ignited lick the shelf above the fireplace, threatening to consume her collection of Russian nesting dolls.

"Concentrate like I showed you!" My mother springs back from the stone hearth as a flickering yellow flame paws at her foot. "Like you did before." She positions herself behind her favorite pumpkin-colored armchair, more willing to sacrifice it than her hand-beaded slippers. "With the cake."

"I am," I grumble, even though I'm not. We've been at it all morning. My mother's aggressive agenda has taken the magic right out of these lessons. Memorizing the periodic table was more fun than this.

Her worried eyes dart toward the mantelpiece, and the rosy-cheeked Russians dance over our heads, landing safely on the couch.

"This isn't working," I say, upending the empty bucket in my hand. I release my grip, and the metal pail falls to the floor with a hollow clank. The drops of water I've managed to conjure are less than the amount of saliva I could summon sans magic. "How about we compromise and I turn the faucet on with my mind?"

An ember hurtles past the hearth and lands on the antique Turkish prayer rug. My mother stamps it out and shakes her head. "Come on, Azra. Dig deeper than your surface instincts. This isn't hard."

"For *you.*" The frustration in my voice just slips out.

And an admonishment stabs right back.

A *zap!* ten times stronger than a shock from a shuffle across a wool rug pierces the back of my neck. The source of my electric jolt materializes a second later. Yasmin, one of my Zar "sisters."

Having arrived via Jinn teleportation, she quickly drops the red clay pot she's holding onto the coffee table and shouts, "Lalla Kalyssa, watch out!"

Sable-black hair flying behind her, Yasmin rushes to the fireplace, nudging (more like *shoving*) my mother aside. With less effort than it takes to inhale deeply, Yasmin conjures a wall of water that douses the sizzling fire. The charred logs eke out a final hiss as she dissipates the resulting smoke before it fills the room.

"*Phew!*" she says, tossing her long hair off her shoulder. "Good thing I apped when I did."

This is my first time sensing an apporting Jinn. Turns out, it's less like being licked by a puppy and more like being stung by a wasp.

Or in Yasmin's case, a swarm of wasps.

By mutual unspoken agreement, we haven't seen each other in months. For me, these few seconds are enough to reinforce why.

"I mean," Yasmin says, thrusting back her shoulders, "someone could have gotten hurt."

The muscles in my jaw tense, preventing me from returning her condescending smile. Though, since it's always condescending, I should just call it her smile.

My mother straightens her kaftan. "Thank you, Yasmin. Azra was just about to conjure the water. And if not, well . . ." She twiddles her fingers. "I would have never let her get hurt."

"Oh, yes, of course." For once, the patronizing tone is missing from Yasmin's voice. She blinks her thick eyelashes and lowers her gold eyes. "I didn't mean to imply you couldn't have conjured the water, Lalla Kalyssa."

"Lalla" is a term of endearment and respect often used when speaking to a female Jinn one is very close to, kind of like how humans refer to family friends as "aunt" or "uncle" even though they aren't related by blood. I almost believe Yasmin's usage is sincere.

Almost.

"Anyway . . ." Yasmin waves her silver-bangled hand. "My mom wanted me to return your tagine."

Running a finger along the conical dish, my mother says, "The original this time. Not a conjured replica. Thank her for that." She floats the red-glazed tagine straight from Marrakesh, which she swears is better than any magic can create, into the kitchen. "And thank you for bringing it, Yasmin. Though I did expect you yesterday. I had planned to start cooking Azra's special dish this morning."

Back straight as a rod, Yasmin places a hand on her heart. "My apologies, Lalla Kalyssa. I forgot you like to spend all day cooking. Like a human."

She smiles, and I expect to see fangs. She's always seemed more serpent than genie.

She slithers closer as her almond-shaped eyes scan my body. "At least your bangle didn't do much to improve—" She covers her mouth with her hand. "Sorry, I mean change your appearance, Azra." She flips her hair. "We had to move states."

This bangle may change a lot of things, but it doesn't change this: Yasmin getting under my skin in less than five minutes. This time though, instead of scratching and walking away, I burrow right back under her perfect complexion.

"Really?" I raise an eyebrow. "I thought it had something to do with a sloppy lottery rigging. Right about the time you started granting wishes . . ."

Yasmin's flared nostrils are at odds with her syrupy tone. "Having trouble with the H_2O?" She kicks the empty bucket with her foot. "Don't worry, sweetie. Sometimes the Afrit wait months before assigning wish candidates. Me getting the hang of this in a day was probably a fluke." She snorts. "Took Farrah weeks."

Fluke? Sweetie? That's. It. So what if Yasmin's been an official Jinn for almost a full year? Older means older. Period. Not wiser. And sure as Jinn not better.

Narrowing my eyes, I glare at my silver bangle. My heels drive into the wood floor as I squeeze my eyes shut and focus on the *thud thud, thud thud* of my heart. The harsh squawk of a blue jay in the front yard. The traces of my mother's vanilla perfume. The weight of the humidity in the air. Instead of letting it all distract me, I do as my mother instructed and absorb these elements of nature that surround me, welcoming them, internalizing them, commingling their energy with my own.

The sudden shock of current that shoots through my body ends in my fingertips. Water sloshes over the side of the pail, puddling around my bare feet. And Yasmin's.

"Azra!" Yasmin leaps back. "These are *lea-ther!*"

My mother's fleeting smirk doesn't escape my notice as I shove my trembling fingers into my pockets. Still, I'm a bit surprised to hear her unsubtle sayonara.

"No harm done," she says, drying Yasmin's gold gladiator sandals with a swish of her hand. "There, you're good to go. Thanks again for returning the tagine in time for Azra's birthday."

As if this reminds her, Yasmin tips her head in my direction. "Oh, yes. Happy Birthday, Azra." She squares her shoulders and snaps her heels together. "See you later."

And she's gone. Disappeared. Like a snake down a hole.

The mutual unspoken agreement between my mother and I is not to acknowledge that Yasmin, like her mother, Raina, makes her skin as itchy as mine. Instead, she eases over to me, extracting my fists from my pockets. "Better than picturing a wrench, isn't it?"

She's referring to the way I conjured the tools earlier. Simple visualization is, according to my mother, the equivalent of a cheap parlor trick.

"Inelegant," she says.

"But effective," I say, nodding to the box of tools at the front door, poised for donation.

"Maybe, but we Nadiras are better than that, Azra. That's textbook stuff. If you know how something looks and works, you can conjure it. The more intimately you know the item, the better you do."

Hence my perfect hammer but my unidentifiable reciprocating saw.

"But," she says, "we are not sideshow freaks. Our ability to harness the light and energy of this world allows us to manipulate the environment in ways two-bit charlatans can't even fathom. We can access laws of nature that humans don't even know exist. Until you ground all your magic in nature, your skills will be limited."

My instinct is to dismiss her, but the tingle in my fingertips won't let me.

She tucks a loose strand of hair back into her impromptu updo. "At least one benefit of Yasmin's visit is we learned all you needed was a little encouragement."

"Encouragement, condescension, fine line," I say.

"Whatever works," she says with a teasing glint in her eye.

A childhood of watching my mother perform magic made me fear I wouldn't be any good at it, certainly not as good as her, someone who long ago earned the nickname "model Jinn" from her Zar sisters. But she's always said that being descended from a long line of Jinn means magic lives inside me. Once I received my bangle, all I'd need to do is access it. Or as she's been insisting all day, *allow* myself to access it. I hate proving her right.

Fanning her face with her hand, she says, "How about you prove just how encouraged you are by putting out the rest of the fires? I fear I'm on the verge of perspiring."

I've never seen my mother sweat, literally or figuratively. But if she were going to, today would be the day. The house is stifling, even for us.

My magically ignited fires churn in the rest of the house's nine fireplaces. Nine because we live in Massachusetts and hate to be cold. Nine because my mother, though no longer a wish-granting Jinn, still has her magic and can install fireplaces at will.

Though my hands still shake, all I have to do is think of Yasmin's smug face and I'm able to conjure water instantly at the dining room fireplace. I make my way to the second floor, extinguishing all the flames that have transformed our house into a two-thousand-square-foot sauna.

My bedroom being last, the air is thick with heat. I raise the double-paned glass window all the way up before kneeling in front of the fire.

"I'm flying, Henry!"

I jerk upright, dousing myself and the hearth with my conjured water as the sound of the little girl from across the street penetrates my bedroom. I cross the room and pull the curtain aside.

The open back of the Carwyns' small SUV is crammed with beach chairs, towels, one, no, two coolers, and an overflowing bucket of plastic toys. Mr. Carwyn, a bit rounder and grayer than the last time I saw him, shoves a bright green tote bag in between a large umbrella and a thickly folded plaid blanket as his six-year-old daughter, Lisa, soars down the driveway.

Head bent against the wind, arms straight out behind her, Lisa makes airplane noises as she circles the car. A shiver travels up my spine as she yells again to her older brother, "I'm flying, Henry!"

Ducking his head to get a glimpse through the open back, Henry yells, "Jumbo jet or single prop?"

"Jumbo!" Lisa comes in for a landing next to his passenger-side door.

The top of Henry's sandy-brown-haired head pokes out of the car. He leans down, picks Lisa up, and hauls her into the backseat. "I thought you looked like a 747," he says.

A tired-sounding Mrs. Carwyn calls from the front passenger seat, "Ready, Hank?"

Mr. Carwyn's grunt precedes him slamming the cargo door shut. He steps back, his flat palms aimed at the car, ready to shove the door closed again should it fail to latch on account of the family of four's mountain of gear.

Mr. Carwyn's halfway to the driver's seat when the door begins to rise. All four Carwyn heads face forward, away from me.

Should I? Can I?

The "can" overcomes the "should," and I test out my range. *Click.* The latch catches. Henry turns around. My heart catapults to my throat. But there's no way he saw. Heard? Doubtful. Even so, he wouldn't know what he heard.

Henry pushes a rainbow-striped beach chair to the side and cranes his neck to see out the back. He cocks his head and smiles. At me? Can he see me? Just in case, I smile back. We haven't talked in a while. Not that when we do talk we say all that much. But still, some days, he's the only one in school I have more than a "hi," "hey," or "'sup?" conversation with.

The thumbs-up he gives his father answers my question as the SUV then backs out of the driveway, headed for a day at the beach. There was a time, long ago, when I would have been strapped into the backseat, Henry on one side of me and Jenny on the other.

Before I release the curtain, I let myself seek out the "A+J" scrawled in the bottom right corner of the garage door. Faded as it is, I'm probably the only one who knows it's more than a series of black scuff marks.

I know because I wrote it. I'm the "A," and Jenny was the "J."

For the first nine years of my life, Jenny Carwyn was my best friend. Jenny and I were born on the same day but not in the same place. As Mrs. Carwyn gave birth in a sterile hospital room ten miles away, my mother expelled me out into her jetted bathtub, surrounded by her Zar sisters.

Our entries into the world marked one of many differences, but Jenny and I were inseparable from the moment we became mobile. Before I could even talk, Mrs. Carwyn would find me on their doorstep, having somehow escaped my mother's eye long enough to wander across the street.

Jenny, too, would have turned sixteen today.

"I'm flying, Azra! I'm flying!"

I close my eyes and see Jenny's fingers wrapped around the metal chain next to me. Higher and higher, we rode the swings on the set in my backyard, me promising her that just a little more and we'd be able to touch the tulip-shaped cloud in the sky.

"I'm flying, Azra!"

She was. She did. And then all that was next to me was the metal chain.

The day she died was the day I realized magic couldn't fix everything. It was the last day I wanted to become a Jinn. A Jinn like my mother. A Jinn like my grandmother. A Jinn like my great-grandmother. On and on, generation upon generation, we become Jinn. In exchange for granting wishes to humans, we receive powers that allow us to do the impossible. Though there are some things even our magic cannot do.

We cannot bring someone back from the dead.

This I learned the day Jenny fell from the swing in our backyard. The day I begged my mother to use her powers to save my best friend. The day I lost my best friend was the last day I had a best friend.

"Azra," my mother's voice floats up the stairs. "How about a break from all this, kiddo?"

A break. From all of this. If only there was one. If only I could find one.

Even though my mother always insisted there was no way out of me fulfilling my destiny, when I was younger I thought maybe she was forcing me into this like other parents force kids to take piano lessons.

I steal a last glance at the "A+J." Henry, barely a year older than Jenny and me, tried to take her place over the years, but I wouldn't let him. Couldn't let him. Though it surely would have been better for both of us if I had. But for the past few years, at least he's had Lisa, whose resemblance to Jenny both comforts and unnerves me. For the first time, I wonder if Henry feels the same.

At the brick hearth, I steady myself against the mantel, allowing my thumping heart to retreat to its normal rhythm. I lay a finger on the oval pendant hanging from a silver chain around my neck. The cursive *A* engraved on the front stands for the first letter of the name I share with my grandmother on my mother's side—the necklace's original owner, whom I've never met. Like a security blanket, my *A* has always calmed me. I was so young when my mother first looped the chain around my neck that I don't remember it.

Leaning over the terra cotta bricks, I wring the water out

of my shirt and clutch my *A* once more before heading back downstairs.

When I enter the living room, my mother points to the bookshelf. "Up there," she says. "Happy birthday."

A box wrapped in silver and gold is nestled in among the tchotchkes. Painted tribal masks from Ghana, onyx candleholders from Mexico, baskets of yarn from Ireland, the objects cramming the shelves are a tangible history of my mother's life. Being Jinn has allowed my mother to see the world. Traveling to even the farthest reaches is only a matter of a blink and a nod for Jinn.

My hand reaches the box without me having to stand on tiptoes even though it's on the highest shelf—something I couldn't have done yesterday, but then again, yesterday, unlike today, my mother and I were not yet the exact same height. My tank top rides up, fully exposing my belly button.

"Tell me," my mother says, waving her hand and drying my damp shirt, "because, knowing you, it could go either way. Is the midriff baring an unfortunate side effect of your metamorphosis or an intentional display of contempt for this whole thing?"

I run the tip of my red nail along my exposed stomach, working to bury the ache that always comes with thinking of Jenny. I issue a wry smile that lets her think it's the latter. I wish I would have thought of that. *I wish.* Rolls off the tongue. So easy to say. Takes so much to do.

Inside the box lies a deep purple tunic with pinstripes of gold so thin the effect is subtle, not flashy. I rub the soft linen between my fingers. "It's . . . it's beautiful. Thanks, Mom. Really."

My sincerity throws her. "I can make it black if you want."

"No, I like the purple." The understated nature of the shirt—a departure from the bright fabrics of her wardrobe but in line with my monotone collection of blacks, whites, and grays—proves she knows how hard all of this is for me. As does what comes next.

"I know I said we'd wait until tomorrow," she says, refolding the shirt. "But if you want, if you're not too tired, we can give it a try."

"It" can only mean one thing—the power even I couldn't help but crave.

"Ready to app, kiddo?"

THE RIDES I'VE HITCHED WHILE MY MOTHER APPORTED US BOTH ARE nothing like doing it myself.

I do as she says and stand as still as stone. I'm so attuned to the beating of my heart that it pounds in my ears as if playing through earbuds. I close my eyes and picture the space around me in such detail that I could paint it if I had any artistic talent, which I don't. I envision my destination, focusing on one item I know to be in that location, clearly drawing it in my mind. Eventually, my mother says I won't need a specific object to latch onto. The name of the place itself will be enough, which is how we accomplish long-distance apping to grant wishes around the world in locales we've never been.

My mind zeroes in on my old single-speed bike.

Then it's pulse racing, head spinning, adrenaline skyrocketing. *Rush, rush, rush.*

Unlike the chill that accompanies conjuring, apping sears my insides as if they were made of fire. Light-headed, I plant my hand on the wall of the garage.

I'm in the garage. I *apped* myself to the garage.

What's that sound? That big ole creak? The door to the world just opened, and I'm standing on the welcome mat.

It may only be the garage, but it's a start.

As I app back into the living room, I work to erase the grin that's plastered itself to my face. I convince my mother to conjure us a pint of mint chocolate chip ice cream, and I produce the two spoons.

We're halfway through the container when my skin prickles and a purring fills my ears. It's less a shock and more like the vibration from a pumped-up stereo bass.

The next instant, Hana apports into our living room. Her orange-red hair echoes the fierce flames of my earlier fires, but she's the gentlest of my soon-to-be Zar sisters, except for Laila, of course.

"Happy Birthday!" Hana gushes, with her arms flung wide.

Is it my own arms at my sides that makes her change course? Because instead of hugging me, she pulls her elbows in and takes my hand, giving my arm a shy, tentative tug.

Am I Hana's Yasmin?

As she greets my mother with a kiss, I can't help but think magic lessons aren't the ones I need.

Though we've e-mailed a few times, I haven't seen her since she became Hana 2.0. Body taller, hair redder, lips fuller. What I'm thinking about her, she says about me.

"You're gorg, Azra!"

Except I wouldn't use "gorg" without the "eous." Ever.

She walks a circle around me. "Hmm . . . though it's all actually pretty subtle, isn't it? Thankfully for the rest of us."

My mother and Hana laugh. Unsure if I should join, I issue an awkward half smile. Which results in . . . crickets.

Hana clears her throat. "Just wanted to swing by and give you this."

She holds out a kitschy, tarnished-gold, Aladdin-style lamp, complete with the stereotypical long spout and curved handle. "Congrats! You're the new keeper."

Pop culture has turned genies into a joke. Oil lamps, serving a master, flying carpets, three wishes—none of it's true. Jinn live in houses, not lamps or bottles. Jinn do not fly on a carpet or otherwise. The Afrit assign wish candidates to Jinn. The candidate gets but one wish. The idea of three stems from humans who were greedy and Jinn who were pushovers.

"Keeper?" I ask.

Hana purses her lips. "Oh, right, you haven't been to most of our parties, have you?"

I skipped Yasmin's sixteenth birthday bash. Our other Zar sister, Mina's, too. But what about Farrah's and Hana's parties? I don't recall getting an invite to their birthdays.

Hana and I stare at each other as we each realize this at the same time.

Again, crickets.

"Yasmin started it," Hana says. "She found Mr. Gemp—"

"Gemp?"

"Genie lamp."

"Right."

"Anyway, Yasmin passed it to Mina when she turned sixteen. And Mina gave it to Farrah, who gave it to me, and now, well, now it's your turn." She pulls the lamp, still held in her outstretched hands, closer to her chest. "You don't have to take it if you don't want to. I know it's silly. It's just—"

"No." I pluck the lamp with more force than I intended. I'm really going to scare the poor Jinn. "I might have a wish or two I'd like granted," I say softly as I stroke the side of the lamp.

Hana and my mother laugh again. This time, I join in, even though, in my heart, that wasn't a joke.

There's talk of how Hana's finals went (straight As, as usual) and the summer internship in the costumes department of her local theater she nabbed (with her mother's magical help, of course), and I zone out. Second to Laila, Hana's the one I'm closest to. But closest to and close aren't the same thing.

We just don't have much in common.

"Get your family's cantamen yet?" Hana asks.

Other than this.

"I made these killer flash cards for mine."

Why am I not surprised? Then again, considering the size of my family's genie handbook, that might not be such a bad idea. The Nadira cantamen codex is so big, if I dropped it, I'd surely shatter a toe. Or Yasmin's.

I grin slightly at the thought.

Hana mistakes my look for excitement. "I can help you if you want."

"That'd be lovely, Hana."

Though the words left my mother's lips, not mine, when Hana hugs me good-bye, she whispers, "I told the others you'd come around." She releases me, waves to my mother, and says, "See you later!" before apporting.

That makes two "see you laters." From my soon-to-be Zar sisters. On my birthday.

And it clicks. "You didn't."

"Didn't what?" It's too late for my mother's innocent eyes. Hiding this is the reason—well, part of the reason—she was so quick to shoo Yasmin out the door.

"Seriously? You invited all those GITs to my party?"

My mother gives me a blank look.

"GITs," I say. "Genies in training. HITs are tricky enough. But teenagers with powers?" I shudder.

I was trying to be funny more than bratty. My mother's, "Don't start, Azra," as she leaves me for the kitchen means my ratio was off.

Through the open doorway, I watch her place the red tagine on the stovetop. Like always, my mouth waters.

Her chicken tagine with tomatoes and sweet caramelized onions has been my favorite for as long as I can remember. It's one of the few meals she insists on making without the assistance of magic. "Some things turn out better without magic," she once told me when I was little. "Making something with your hands instead of your mind can be satisfying, even rewarding," she said as I stood on a chair watching her slice the juicy, red tomatoes grown, more or less naturally, in our backyard.

Using my powers of levitation, I steal an orange cherry tomato, a new variety for us this year, from the bowl on the counter as she grinds the cinnamon with a wave of her hand.

Okay, so she uses a little magic.

Before popping the tomato in my mouth, I say, "You should have asked."

She sighs. "I did. You said no."

"And so you invited them all anyway?"

My mother shakes the excess water from a freshly washed bundle of cilantro and ignores me. Again.

Testing my levitation skill with something heavier, I float Mr. Gemp her way. "This will be their fifth."

"Hmm?" She swats at Mr. Gemp.

"Birthday party. Their fifth. Guess I should consider myself lucky I only have to make it through this one."

The unexpected crack in my voice makes me lose control of the lantern. My mother's eyes meet mine as she catches it and sets it on the table.

She begins methodically stripping cilantro leaves from their stems. "My Zar should have never let this go on for as long as we did." She pauses. "*I* shouldn't have."

Leaning against the side of the refrigerator, I think of all the parties I missed. Theirs and mine. I haven't had a birthday party with my full Zar since the year after Jenny died.

"Then again," she says, "I haven't been able to force you to do anything in years."

As I wiggle my wrist, the bangle bounces against my skin. *Except for this.*

She gathers the cilantro leaves into a neat pile. "I thought it'd be better if you came around on your own. All of you. But Laila will be sixteen soon, and your Zar will become official. You girls need to cement your bond now. Besides, there's a lot you can learn from them."

I turn the oven on from across the room. "I've got this."

"I wasn't referring to magic," she says curtly. "But fine, if you're already an expert on what you can do, what about the things you can't do? Crystal clear on those, I assume?"

Having grown up in a house where meals cook themselves, high heels pop out of nowhere, and walls swap paint colors in an instant, the list of things we *can't* do is short.

"I can't grant a wish for a human not assigned to me by the Afrit." I repeat what I learned practically at birth.

From here, I have a perfect view of the Carwyns' garage out our living room window.

"I can't heal humans." A lump finds its way to my throat. "And I can't bring someone back from the dead." I repeat what I learned when I was nine.

My mother's face falls, but I keep going. "We live here. *Alone.* While—"

In an instant, she's at my side. The scent of cilantro clinging to her combined with the way she strokes my back causes the lump in my throat to swell. I fight back the water my tear ducts are conjuring without my permission.

"I get it, Azra," she says gently. "The Afrit's rules stink. But you can dislike what you have to do without disliking who you are. And who they are. Your sisters. It's precisely the restrictions the Afrit have placed on us that make your Zar sisters that much more important. They fill the hole."

My face grows hot, and my teeth clench. The hole? Try holes, plural. Like the hole left when I had to stop befriending humans because my lies about the nine fireplaces and perpetually blooming backyard lilacs were no longer cutting it. Like the hole left by the Jinn father I've never met. Like the hole left by Jenny.

My mother's Zar sisters may be enough for her, but the Jinn girls who will make up my Zar have a heck of a crater to fill.

My mother squeezes my shoulder. "You need them, kiddo.

Learning to access your magic is only part of granting wishes. There's a lot more to becoming Jinn."

Swallowing the fight rising up in my throat, I force myself to say the one thing I've wanted to say since I woke up this morning. "And I . . . I have to, right?"

Though she manages a weak smile, the creases around my mother's eyes show her exhaustion. Whether she's tired or just tired of me is unclear.

"Look, Azra, here's the thing. This may not be the life you want, but it's the only one you've got. Making the best of it, not the worst, is up to you, but it's a long road to take all by yourself. Life is compromise, after all."

Compromise? Really? That's what becoming Jinn is?

My knuckles turn white as I ball my hands into fists. Without a word, I peel out of the kitchen and march toward the stairs. Until the bangle taps against my leg, I forget I don't need the stairs anymore.

I app myself to my room, relishing the internal burn as I collapse on top of my white comforter. I flick the bangle with one finger, letting it ride circles around my wrist.

Compromise suggests a concession on each side. But we're the ones who have to give up everything. We live without the rest of our families, in our little Zar enclaves, churning out the next generation of Jinn. Being able to conjure chocolate truffles doesn't make up for that.

My mother doesn't understand. She can't understand. Yes, the same restrictions apply for her, but that wasn't always the case. She grew up with her mother and her father. She had male Jinn in her life, even . . . even my father. It wasn't until around the time I was born that the Afrit ordered all male Jinn to leave the human world. Even if she only had my father for a short time, it's more than I've had.

I bury my head under my pillow until the smell of browning chicken wafts through my open door. I sit up. My mother's cooking without magic for me. *She's trying.* My birthday present, the purple shirt neatly folded on my dresser, further chastens me. I *know* she's trying.

And the truth is, unless we want to bring the wrath of the Afrit down on us, neither one of us has a choice. On this long road, all we really have is each other.

Mr. Gemp materializes out of thin air on my nightstand.

I swear, sometimes it's as if my mother can read my mind. Because we don't just have each other. We also have our Zar sisters. At least we're supposed to.

Open. Close. Open. Close.

I toggle the lid, but nothing escapes in a cloud of blue smoke. I pick up the lamp to move it to my bookshelf and notice the top isn't fully closed. Something's caught in the hinge. Not a magical genie—at least not yet.

Rolled up inside the lantern is a photograph of six tween Jinn. Along with our shiny hair and penchant for sugar, we inherited our closest Zar relationships from our mothers: me and Laila; Mina and Farrah; Hana and Yasmin. I always thought Hana got the raw end of that deal. Which everyone else must think of Laila.

Laila, sweet, blond, petite Laila, who, even in the picture, is a head shorter than the rest of us. Standing in front with her skinny arms spread wide, the tip of one finger in front of me and the tip of the other in front of Yasmin. The mortar in our bricks then and now.

My mousy self-cropped hair and slouch is countered by Yasmin's cascading jet-black curls and arched back. With her long skinny nose raised in the air, all that's missing is the pointy black hat. Again, then and now.

Hana. Next to me, with her fiery-red hair grazing her shoulders and mine. She was in her eyeglasses-wearing stage then. As if she needed them to prove how smart she is.

And in the middle, Mina and Farrah, as close as Siamese twins. Born with a noisemaker in her mouth and party streamers around her belly, baby-faced Mina stands in her signature stance of hands tossed high in the air. With her boundless energy and vivacious personality, she'd match, hoop for hoop, any dolphin at SeaWorld. Next to her is square-chinned Farrah, whose quick, sharp movements and cuddly nature always reminded me of a rabbit. Her foot's caught in mid-tap and her finger tugs on a strand of hair as she works to cover what she's always thought was a slightly too-big forehead.

Laila, Yasmin, Hana, Mina, and Farrah. My Zar, who stopped inviting me to their birthday parties. But who, apparently, are still coming to mine.

I wonder if they feel as conflicted about that as I do?

Even before I flip the photo over, I know the date it was taken. The day I turned ten. The first birthday I didn't share with Jenny.

I remember the present Laila gave me: a framed picture of Jenny and me kneeling on the grass outside her house with the tiny Laila standing on our backs. Henry took that photo.

I remember the awkward looks on Hana, Mina, and Farrah's faces as Laila gave me that present. None of them acknowledged Jenny's absence then. None of them had acknowledged Jenny's absence in the year before then. Though Jenny had been as much a fixture in my life as they'd been, when she was gone, it was like she never existed.

But mostly, I remember Yasmin. Walking in on her reading my diary later that day. Seeing the guilt turn to hurt on Hana's freckled face. Watching Mina mistakenly snip Farrah's dark brown bangs too short. Feeling Laila's warm fingers interlacing with mine, holding me back as much as holding me.

"*None of them!*" Yasmin read, stomping her foot and treating my words like those of a petulant child instead of a grief-stricken "sister."

> *Not Hana, not Mina, not Farrah, not Yasmin. None of them came. None of them said they were sorry. Not right away and not in the months since. She was my best friend. I thought she was their friend too. They acted like it. Are they acting with me too?*
>
> *Laila's the only one who cares. She's the only one I need. I'd trade all the rest to have Jenny back. I'd trade all the rest to have Jenny back for a single day. Let the Afrit take them. They deserve that and more.*

Even Yasmin's voice trembled as she read that last line.

Each one tried to apologize. The heart-shaped pillow embroidered with my and Jenny's initials that Hana made me still sits on the chair next to my window, though Mina's collage of all the guys from *One Tree Hill* has probably been recycled into toilet paper or coffee filters by now. The mix CD Farrah gave me, bursting with the falsetto of all her favorite boy bands, is tucked away somewhere on my shelves. Yasmin's card? The one where she listed all the reasons not to befriend humans? I read it and burned it.

Maybe in her own way she was trying. They all were. But I couldn't. My tenth birthday is one of a handful of times my whole Zar has been together in the years since. The more our mothers pushed, the more we pulled away.

Sometimes, Laila and I were a team. When Yasmin pulled a new prank on a human, we tattled together. But when Hana staged one of her runway shows, making each of us model ensembles she put together from clothes conjured by her mother, I hit the pavement alone while Laila hopped right up on the lighted catwalk our mothers' powers built. Mina and Farrah morphed from infatuated preteens to full-blown boy-crazy Jinn, sneaking into clubs to see emo bands that I mistakenly thought had something to do with an annoying character on *Sesame Street.*

By the time I was ready to forgive, they were past wanting me to.

But maybe the genie lamp my mother just sent up here shows they're ready to try. Which leaves me as the only one who is not.

As usual.

Before I can talk myself out of it, I'm pulling my favorite pair of jeans out of my closet. Though they weren't when I bought them, they are now low-rise. Ultra low-rise. And cropped. The hem falls mid-calf.

The sudden commotion from downstairs means someone's already here.

Unfolding the tunic as I dart across the hall, I slip it over my head and rifle through the hangers in my mother's closet. The pair of white linen pants I find toward the back fits perfectly.

In my bathroom, I braid my long hair and even dab on some blush and lip gloss. Purple lip gloss. I make it match the color of the shirt from my mother. Groomed and dressed like this, I have to admit my magical makeover isn't half bad.

I'm almost out the door when I turn back around. My mother's right. This *is* a long road. Maybe I *can* dislike what I have to do without disliking who I am. And who my Zar sisters are (Yasmin being the obvious exception).

Using my powers, I center Mr. Gemp on my nightstand and fling the cantamen my mother brought up earlier to the floor, parking it under my bed. Amid the dustballs, the ratty old thing should be right at home.

Life is compromise, after all.

Laila's eyes threaten to pop out of their sockets as I enter the living room. Samara, her mother, smothers me in an embrace. As usual, her golden hair smells like apricots. Now taller than she is, I nuzzle into the soft waves and let her hold me. I've known Samara my entire life. Before I found out she too was a Jinn, there were times when I wanted her to be my mother. That I still do on occasion is a source of continuous guilt.

"My little Azra," Samara says, releasing me. "You are breathtaking. Not that you weren't always gorgeous. But now . . . let's just say you might break your mom's record for most invites to prom." She calls out to my mother. "What do you think, Kalyssa? Will you be upset if your daughter outshines you?"

"Lalla Sam, stop it." I sink into the couch. "There's no danger of that."

My mother joins us in the living room, a tray with bowls of hummus, roasted eggplant, and pita bread following her.

My newly inspired resolve to give this a chance receives its first positive reinforcement when my mother, upon seeing me in the purple tunic, smiles warmly.

Laila still hasn't said a word. I feel her eyes on me and turn to her. "What?" I instantly regret the harshness of my tone.

Weakest. Resolve. Ever.

That we aren't the best friends our mothers want us to be is entirely my fault. Still, we've grown up together, and she's the closest I'll ever come to having a sibling. When we were little, I liked having Laila around. Especially after Jenny was gone, being with Laila made me feel like I wasn't alone.

"It's just . . ." Laila starts. "This is what I'm going to look like?"

But ever since we started needing bras and deodorant, I've been alone again. Because Laila can't wait to be a genie.

"Awesome." She runs her fingers through her already long hair. "Only a few more weeks to go."

Seeing what magic managed to do to me, I'm not sure I want to stand next to Laila, with her blond curls and pale blue eyes, after she turns sixteen, especially if Samara's voluptuous figure is any indication of what's to come. As Samara bends over the coffee table to dip a slice of warm pita into the hummus, I get an eyeful of Laila's future.

I used to think the Afrit were huge fans of that silly old TV show and decided humans deserved their genies sexed up: lipstick-wearing, midriff-baring, cleavage-daring.

But the attractiveness of our species is simply genetic. We are all descended from Lalla Mimouna and Sidi Mimoun, the first Jinn power couple. Legend has it that Jinn were once spirit creatures, made of smokeless fire. These spirits inhabited a plane between the air and the earth and embodied the purest elements of the natural world. In return for corporeal form, the spirits agreed to use the magical powers nature bestowed on them to serve humans for the "greater good."

Guess "pure" translated into "hot" when those spirits got legs. Then again, Jinn are particularly clever. It wouldn't surprise me if the bargain with nature included an eye-candy clause and we Jinn actually are the most shallow of species.

Samara wipes a glop of hummus off her heaving bosom, which causes Laila to turn to me. "Did you need a bigger bra?"

Everyone's eyes fall on my chest, which I am too easily able to cover with my arms.

"I sure hope I do." Laila pulls out the collar of her cotton short-sleeved sweater and studies her breasts.

Samara's deep, sexy laugh precedes her reply. "Oh, you will. Runs in our line. Always has."

Laila pats her boobs and beams.

Though our birthdays are less than two months apart, Laila has always seemed younger. Her being short—and anything under five feet four inches is short for a Jinn—doesn't help that. That'll likely change when she gets her bangle. But she's also seemed younger because she's so eager. She's been excited for her sixteenth birthday as far back as I can remember.

One December, when we were ten, we were celebrating Christmas. We celebrate all the religious holidays on a rotating basis. Some years it's Christmas, some years it's Hanukah, some years it's Kwanzaa, some years it's Las Posadas (my favorite because it involves whacking piñatas), and so on. But that year, it was Christmas's turn. Our moms were huddled together in front of the fire having one of their marathon talks, and Laila and I were rearranging the decorations on the tree.

Laila tore off a piece of the silver tinsel and broke it in half. She tied one strand around my wrist and the other around her own. "There," she said, "now you grant my wish, and I'll grant yours."

She wanted me to pretend first. Not because she wanted to make a wish so badly but because she wanted me to get the chance to grant one first. She was being her usual kind, generous self, letting me be the first to role-play as a genie. To Laila, being able to grant a wish was far more of a thrill than being able to make one.

Six years later, this fact still separates us. The only thing that's changed is my need to pretend. Now I can actually grant wishes. Somehow, everything I've done today makes this prospect more, not less, frightening.

"Dinner should be ready by the time everyone else gets here," my mother says.

Samara snorts. "Oh, Kalyssa, you and your tagines. Tell me, why tagines? Why are tagines the only dish you make the human way? The very, very slow way?"

My mother looks at me. "I just think it tastes better that way."

Her concession to make my favorite meal without using Jinn magic is the closest my mother can come to granting what she knows has always been my wish.

Samara swishes the wrist of her gold-bangled hand. "Yes, because it makes you starving. Hunger makes everything taste better. If I had your talents, there's nothing I wouldn't conjure rather than cook."

"Well," Laila says, drawing out the word, "perhaps if you spent half as much time practicing conjuring food as you do purses, we'd end up with something edible."

Samara flutters her thick eyelashes at her daughter. "I'll let you perfect conjuring food, sweetheart. Until then, we'll have to settle for raiding the kitchen for more snacks."

Laila hops off the couch and grabs my hand. "Want to help?"

Maybe maintaining my resolve is getting easier, because I kinda do. Let's say it's that and not the fact that my stomach is rumbling, begging for more than just the mint chocolate chip ice cream I fed it today.

"Sure, in a minute," I say, which elicits an approving nod from my mother. She follows Laila and Samara into the kitchen while I roll up the sleeves of my tunic.

The house still radiates warmth from the morning's fires. I kneel on the couch and lift the window behind it as the Carwyns' SUV pulls into their driveway. Lisa pops out first, a pink-and-white-striped beach towel tied around her neck like a cape. Mr. and Mrs. Carwyn exit the front seats. Henry is the last to appear.

He waits until his sister has completed her circuit of figure eights across the front lawn and unties the towel. He shakes it, folds it in half, and adds it to the bag his father unloads from the back of the car.

It's a normal Saturday in the Carwyn household.

Mrs. Carwyn carries a red-and-white-checked doggie bag. The styling is instantly recognizable as that of the seafood shack that makes the best fried clams and oysters in our coastal town. The Carwyns must have spent the day at the beach followed by dinner at the Pearl. They spent my birthday the way I wanted to.

Before the family enters the house, each member leaves a pair of sandy flip-flops by the hose on the side of the garage. The four pairs sit there, each representing its owner: mother, father, daughter, son. When my family returns home from the beach, there are only two pairs of flip-flops. And they aren't even sandy. My mother vanishes the sand before we get in the car.

I'm still staring at their house when Henry emerges from the garage. He turns on the faucet and uses the hose to wash out a bucket shaped like a sandcastle. The patches of sun-bleached white on the blue plastic make me certain it's the same one Jenny and I used to play with.

Henry leans over to pick up a pair of flip-flops and his glasses slide off his nose. He digs them out of the slightly too-tall grass and tucks them into his back pocket. The post-beach, sun-touched pink of his cheeks and windblown tousle of his light brown hair suit him better than the fluorescent lights and prison gray walls of our French classroom. He looks directly at me. I freeze. The day at the beach and dinner at the Pearl was surely his family's way of trying to forget what today would have been for Jenny.

I flop down and hide behind the couch cushions. I can't think about that on top of everything else. When my rapid heartbeat slows, I inch back up and peer over the pillows. Henry is turning off the spigot. He wipes his glasses with the end of his shirt before he returns them to their perch on the bridge of his nose. He wasn't wearing his glasses. He couldn't have seen me. I sit back up. He looks right at me. And waves.

Though I'm technically an adult, at least in the Jinn world, my childish response is to duck behind the cushions again.

"Azra!" My mom enters the room with a bowl so full of chips

that she needs to levitate the top ones to prevent them from cascading over the side. "It's freezing. What are you doing with that window open?"

Henry's still standing there when I shut the window. I turn around to see a bottle of wine hovering above the coffee table.

"Care for a glass?" Samara says.

Four wineglasses swoop into the room, landing underneath the bottle of wine just as the cork shoots out of the neck. The red liquid flows in an arc into the suspended stemware.

I grab a curtain in each hand and draw the fabric over the front windows.

It's a normal Saturday in the Nadira household.

6

Wine is delicious.

Samara persuades my mother to allow Laila and I half a glass each, a small indulgence to celebrate my entry into Jinn adulthood. She presses my mother on why human rules should apply. "It's bad enough they have to go to their schools, why should they have to do everything like them?"

This marks the first thing I have no objections to all day.

Traditionally, along with sweets, Jinn love alcohol. My mother has never allowed me a single taste before today. By the time I finish my glass, I have an inkling why. The warmth of my cheeks penetrates my whole body. It's like apping in place. Which, apparently, I'm not allowed to do.

"No apporting," my mother says.

I make a face. Normal high school kids get the lecture about not drinking and driving.

"I'm serious, Azra," my mother says. "I gave in, at least do what I ask, okay?"

I mumble a "fine" and lick the last red droplet clinging to the rim of my glass. Laila places her own empty glass on the table. She drank as fast as I did.

The knock on the door prevents me from angling for a refill.

Laila climbs across my lap and scrambles over the arm of the sofa. She seizes the doorknob but doesn't turn it. Instead she waves me over with her free hand. "Come on, Az. Let's open it together."

The alcohol appears to have dulled my groan reflex. If my mother knew that, she'd probably change her tune and make me use wine instead of milk in my morning cereal.

Positioning myself by the door, I let Laila fling it wide open. I stumble back when, instead of the members of our soon-to-be Zar, before me stands Henry holding a string in his hand. I follow the string up to the balloon it's tied to, the balloon that reads, "Happy Sweet Sixteen!"

Ah, Henry doesn't know that for me, the only thing sweet about turning sixteen is the slowly digesting wine in my stomach.

Suddenly, the hair on the back of my neck prickles, and my "thank you" lodges in my throat. The room hums with static electricity. Thanks to Yasmin and Hana's earlier visits, I know exactly what this means. Laila begins to move out from behind the open door, but I shove her aside in the same instant that a glass shatters behind me.

Samara's shrill voice cries, "Azra, app, appi—"

I'm already launching myself out the front door. I collide with Henry just as eight assorted Jinn materialize out of thin air in my living room. I slam the door shut and pry myself off of Henry's chest. I search his eyes, whose same greenish hue as Jenny's leaves me momentarily speechless, for any sign that he caught a glimpse of the swarm of teleporting Jinn.

I can't read the look on his face. Surprise? Fear? Amusement? Amusement, yes, he's tickled pink, and not just from the sun. From me.

"Sorry," I say. "Laila was . . . changing."

Henry's grin widens as he looks at the door and then back at me. He inches forward, eyes narrowing, head tilting.

I inch backward, shoulders hunching, knees bending.

With Jenny gone, Henry might be the only human able to tell that my change in appearance is from more than a full day at a high-end Boston salon.

"Is something . . . different?" he asks.

"Spa day," I say without hesitation as I sweep my long braid off my shoulder. "Mom's idea of a birthday present."

My lies flow as easily as water from a faucet, but this time, with Henry, as I slink into the shadows being cast by the fading sun, it's not just to hide my new look; it's also to hide my guilt.

Skepticism radiates from Henry's nod as he rests against the weathered gray shingles to the left of the door. He squints and then points to my shirt. "Purple?"

"Another birthday present."

"It's nice. That was Jenny's favorite color."

I flatten my palm across my chest. How could I forget? Did my mother remember? That I'm sure she did makes my heart grow heavy.

"Nice that you're having a party," he says.

A party Jenny can't have. The only sound is that of the foil balloon brushing against the door frame.

Now my heart may as well be made of lead.

Henry clears his throat. "Haven't seen Laila around much. I'm glad you two are still close. And that was her mother? Sam? What was that she was saying? Appy . . ."

Pushing past the knot in my stomach, I issue what I hope is a breezy laugh. "Oh, that was just Lal—" I swallow and laugh again. "I mean, Aunt Sam trying hard to be funny. 'Appy Berfday.' Working on her cockney accent, I think."

My body had sprung into action even before Samara had finished her warning. Which makes me wonder why none of our Zar sisters managed to detect the presence of a human before appearing. Was Henry too far from them or were they too busy horsing around to take notice? My mother said the more attuned we are to our senses and to our surroundings, the better and farther out the detection works.

I notice Henry eyeing the small gap between the front window's curtains and snatch the string from him. "Thanks for this."

Running his hand through his hair and leaving several tufts standing upright, he says, "Oh, sure, but that's just my cover. This is your real present." He digs into the front pocket of his jeans and pulls out a small silver key. "Here."

Instead of taking it, I slide farther into the shadows. "What's that for?"

"My parents finally put a lock on the fence gate. I figured what with it being your birthday and all, you might need your escape hatch."

The string slips through my fingers, but Henry catches the end before the balloon races for the stars.

"You knew?" I say, sounding as dumbfounded as I feel.

Seeking refuge in the Carwyns' backyard during the Zar

gatherings held at our house started a couple of years ago and by now has become my routine. Sneaking away even for a few moments helps prevent the sheer quantity of Jinn-ness from suffocating me.

I had no idea that Henry had been *watching* me.

He gently places the key and the balloon's string in my hand. "If I had as many aunts and cousins as you, I'm sure I'd need a break too."

Our eyes meet, and I immediately lower my golden gaze.

"Hey," he says, "don't look so worried. I haven't told anyone. But I did keep a lookout to make sure you didn't fall in the pool or freeze to death."

I had no idea that Henry had been *watching out* for me.

"Figured your family was coming tonight. Now if you need to go on the lam, you can. And, as always, mum's the word."

Still in shock, I stammer out, "You . . . you won't say anything?"

He shrugs a yes. "Can't have sisters and not be good at keeping secrets."

A smile tugs at the corners of my lips. I'm good at keeping secrets. Sharing them is a new experience. One, at least with Henry, I like. He's become the older brother Jenny would have deserved.

The front door I'm leaning against flies open, and I tumble backward over the threshold and into the living room. I tuck the key into my pocket before facing my own version of sisters.

Steam threatens to billow off my searing hot cheeks as I'm flanked by Yasmin, Hana, Mina, and Farrah. Who just happen to be decked out in genie costumes. Exposed belly button, gauzy harem pants, tiny hat with sheer headscarf, the whole ridiculous nine yards of flowing fabric. And Henry's *right here.* Are they crazy? At least I can count on Laila to help . . . *Oh, come on.*

Laila bounces down the stairs in her own sparkly pink ensemble. She flips the scarf off her face as she rushes to hug Henry.

"I haven't seen you in forever!" Laila says as she lets him go.

He hovers in the doorway. It's not often that humans see six GITs in one place. Add in that five are half naked, and Henry's face turns as red as mine feels.

He shoves the end of his T-shirt into his jeans. "Of all the days for my Batsuit to be at the cleaners."

No one but me laughs at his joke. It's possible no one but me *gets* his joke.

"Wouldn't have pegged you as a costume party kind of girl, Azra," Henry says. He nods to my mother, who enters the room from the kitchen. "Didn't mean to crash the party, Mrs. Nadira."

"Oh, Henry." My mother maneuvers herself to block his line of sight into the house. "You're welcome here any time."

As much as she wants to mean this, she can't. The five scantily clad teenage Jinn behind her and the five grown Jinn levitating place settings in the dining room that I can see out of the corner of my eye are proof of that.

I move past my mother to steer Henry back onto the front porch. I stand with my hand on the edge of the door and lower my voice to a whisper. "Thanks for the key. Odds are, I'm going to need it."

But, I realize, I don't. Even if I could manage to escape my own birthday party, I woke up this morning with my own way to unlock the gate.

"In that case," Henry says, "I'll keep an eye out. I can't wait to see your costume."

I snort. "Don't hold your breath. Unless you want to leave me that Batsuit. I could probably use the armor."

Henry laughs as he walks backward down the steps. "*Bonne fête,* Azra."

"Happy Birthday" in French.

"*Au revoir,* Henry!" all five of my Zar sisters chirp.

He raises his hand high in the air and waves to them over my head as he mouths "good luck." Before I get to say good-bye, the door propels forward, throws off my hand, and closes with a bang in the face of the still-waving Henry.

My open jaw clenches shut as I turn around to see the smirk on Yasmin's face.

"What was that for?" I demand.

Yasmin twirls a long, raven-black curl around her finger and shrugs. "Some guests don't know when it's time to leave. They need a little prodding."

"He *was* leaving. And he wasn't *your* guest."

Looping her arm around Laila's waist, Yasmin says, "Your house is my house. After all, we're sisters, Azra."

Like I need reminding.

Hana slides next to me and hooks her arm through mine. She whispers, "Wow, Azra. Those eyelashes. All day, I've been plotting how to pluck them off one by one and glue them to mine."

With her glossy, tangerine-hued hair and teasingly freckled cheeks, Hana's exterior reflects her spirited interior. She has all of Yasmin's strength with none of Yasmin's edge.

"Don't let her spoil your day." Hana pecks my cheek, and I realize maybe it's not so bad to be reminded of the sister part.

By the time us six GITs enter the dining room, our mothers have already expanded the table, conjured a mismatched array of plush, rainbow-colored chairs, and set out so much food, we'll be eating leftovers for a week.

More than six months have passed since the twelve of us have been in the same room together. Now, with all of us daughters except for Laila having transformed into full Jinn, it's like a room full of lead actors and their stunt doubles.

My mother takes a seat at one end of the table and gestures for me to perch myself at the other. I scoot in right before Samara and snag the chair she was angling for in between Laila and Hana.

Samara gives me a wink before rerouting herself to the seat at the head of the table. To her left is Lalla Nadia, whose auburn hair is a shade deeper than her daughter, Hana's. Nadia simultaneously dims the brass chandelier and lights what must be at least fifty candles spread out around the room.

Yasmin's mother, Lalla Raina, whose glossy black hair skims her hips, is seated to Samara's right. She levitates the wine bottle and begins pouring white wine in everyone's glasses, including those set in front of us girls.

My mother clears her throat. "Do you think that's wise, Raina?"

The shrug dripping off Raina's shoulders is an exact replica of the one Yasmin just gave me.

"What's the harm?" Raina says, eyeing the other mothers.

Lalla Isa, Farrah's mother, and Lalla Jada, Mina's mother, shoot a look across the table at one another that's the equivalent of one of my best eye rolls. Nadia nudges Samara's elbow.

The frequency of the Zar reunions that used to bring our entire group together has dropped in the past couple of years. I was naïve enough to think I was the reason.

I may be a reason but I'm not *the* reason.

Raina's brows dip down over her wide-set eyes. "They're all adults, except for little Laila here. And it's not like they're going to be driving." She fixes her gaze on my mother. "You'd know best, Kalyssa, but that's the humans' biggest concern, isn't it?"

Yasmin, seated directly across from me, is already sipping her full glass.

No one else dares lay a finger on their wine stem.

Usually flapping away, Mina's delicate pink lips hang open. Her thumbs hover over her phone, frozen in mid-texting mode. The soft candlelight highlights the red tones in her rich mahogany hair as her eyes, lined with shimmery ice-blue eyeliner, dart from Lalla to Lalla.

Next to her, a jittery Farrah magically changes the color—pink then blue then yellow then green—of the rhinestones in the headband holding back her pin-straight hair. Dark brown with caramel highlights, her hair is the shortest at the table. The sharp angles hit her shoulders and the long bangs she leaves free of her headband graze her eyelashes, a style that no matter how cool it looks would have me scratching my eyes out.

The wine bottle travels in front of Samara, who stops it and says, "Considering our higher tolerance, a glass can't hurt, can it, Kal?"

My mother plasters on a smile. "Certainly not. It's a celebration."

Samara then fills her glass without using magic. She's clumsier without her powers and accidentally knocks over the bottle as she rests it on the table.

Wine streams toward my aqua place setting. Instinctually, I douse the yellow tablecloth with some conjured seltzer water and then evaporate the liquid, leaving the fabric bone-dry and without a single splotch.

Samara claps. "Kalyssa, clearly you're an excellent teacher. I'm going to have to bring Laila over here for your tutelage."

My mother holds up a hand. "It's got nothing to do with me. Azra's gifted. She was far more advanced when she woke up this morning than either of us were after a week. Probably a month."

This is the first I've heard of this. My mother seemed pleased with my skills, but all day, she simply nodded each time I made something appear or disappear, or blow up or knit back together. She's probably exaggerating, like when she said I had a talent for gymnastics. She kept on encouraging me even though after every class she had to employ the power to heal fellow Jinn that comes with her gold bangle and stitch up an open wound on my forehead or mend a broken toe.

Isa waves her hand. "Well, naturally Azra's gifted. She's your daughter, Kalyssa."

Now Jada and Raina share a look, and Nadia's the one clearing her throat.

Boy was I *na-ïve.*

Nadia swivels her head to address the entire table. "And that's wonderful news for the girls' Zar. Strength in numbers."

Over the rim of the wineglass she's already drained by half, Yasmin narrows her eyes at me.

She's giving me attitude? After what *she* just did? The gate key calls to me from my front pocket. Pushing back against my desire to flee, I change the subject and say to Yasmin, "You shouldn't have done that to Henry."

She points at her ample chest and widens her gold eyes. "Me? What did I do?"

"You slammed the door in our neighbor's face." I look at my mother. "Our *human* neighbor's face."

Though I'm more concerned with her insulting Henry, I say the second part because I know it will rankle our elders.

My mother chokes on her chicken. "Using magic?"

Though Yasmin's only response is to lower her eyes to her plate, I nod vigorously. It's followed by an equally strong nod from Laila and, to my surprise, from Hana.

Raina puts her fork down. "Did he notice?"

Sitting up straighter in her chair, Yasmin says, "Certainly not. I'm no amateur."

"Well," Raina says, "no cause for alarm. Besides, what good are powers if you can't have a little fun every once in a while? Especially with the humans?"

The tip of my mother's knife spears a cherry tomato. Seeds spurt past her plate, creating a polka-dot pattern on the tablecloth.

Raina's, and now Yasmin's, dismissiveness of humans has always been a source of contention for my mother.

Samara quickly intervenes. "I'm the last Jinn to put a damper on fun, but, really, Yasmin should be setting an example for the other girls considering how long she's been doing this. She knows the importance of not exposing our magic."

Remaining true to the way their Zar has always functioned,

Lalla Isa and Lalla Jada let the stronger personalities dominate the conversation.

The same way Laila, always the peacemaker of our Zar, chimes in with, "Plus, it wasn't very nice."

Raina and Yasmin snort at the same time. My mother smiles, but her nostrils still flare. Raina is my mother's least favorite "sister" even if she would never admit it. And Samara is my mother's favorite. Like mother like daughter, generation to generation.

7

Our mothers have retreated to the living room where they're indulging in wine and ancient history as they flip through a collection of photo albums. Nostalgia seems to have eased the tension that hovered like a rain cloud over the dinner table. Well, nostalgia and the wine.

Yasmin, Hana, Mina, and Farrah ducked out to the garage, claiming they had a surprise to work on.

This leaves Laila and me in the kitchen cleaning up my birthday dinner. Serves me right. I wanted today to be like any other day.

Laila stacks a plate in the dishwasher. "Show me more."

"More what?" I pretend to be ignorant though I'm actually impressed she contained herself for so long. This is why she volunteered us for kitchen duty.

"Anything. Everything. I can't wait to see what I'll be able to do."

I gesture toward the living room, where our mothers are

debating who had the cutest pregnancy belly. "You know what you'll be able to do. You've seen it with them our whole lives."

"But they're so high level. I want to see what *I'll* be able to do."

My eyes float back before I can stop them.

Laila's face reddens. "Oh, it's okay. It's not like I expect to be as good as you. I really just want to watch you in action." She clutches my hand. "Az, this is what we've been waiting for our whole lives."

"We" is not the right pronoun, but I can't tell her that while she's looking at me with such affection in her eyes. She squeezes my hand. Maybe when we were younger I deserved Laila's friendship, but why she's stuck by me all this time, I don't know. I haven't been all that friendly the last couple of years. Still, she's here. And not because she was dragged, unlike me the last few times my mother apped us to her house.

"Okay," I say to Laila, setting two empty wineglasses on the counter. Recalling the fruity taste of the red wine we had earlier—and picturing what I know of the wine-making process, which consists of a single image of bare feet stomping grapes, I close my eyes until it feels like icicles are stabbing my insides. When Laila yanks my arm, I open my eyes to see our glasses filled with a deep red liquid that I hope tastes like wine and not feet.

A sneaky satisfaction fills me. "Voila!"

Laila starts to clap. I cover her hands with my own to stop her. "Shh. They won't let us. At least my mom won't. Your mom would. You're lucky."

Confusion passes over Laila's face. "But we can't actually drink it."

"Don't you want more?" I prod.

"Hmm . . . we aren't supposed to."

Words that will guide the rest of my life. But I've done enough of what I'm supposed to do today. And it's still my birthday. "That's what makes it fun," I say.

Laila hesitates. Neither of us could be called delinquents. But if one of us were the instigator, it'd be me. The salt instead of sugar "we" poured in our mothers' coffee when we were eight, the heels "we" broke off my mom's pumps and glued to our own when we were twelve, the hunger strike "we" went on when they said we couldn't watch that vampire movie a couple of years ago, that was all me. And not because I'm a natural troublemaker. Because I bore easily, which explains the first two. The third is because I'm stubborn. And I hate to be told what I can and cannot do.

Each time, Laila stood by my side, always using the wrong pronoun and saying "we" when our mothers asked whose idea the mischief had been.

I pick up my glass and say the words I know will convince her. "To sixteen."

Laila snaps up her own glass, clinks it against mine, and repeats the toast. She takes the first sip. "Not bad." She licks her lips. "Hints of tobacco."

Wine shoots out of my nose. "Like you'd know that."

Laila runs her fingertip around the rim of her glass as a mischievous smile plays on her lips. "Maybe you're not the only one with a rebellious streak."

I could be blown over by fairy dust. "Well, well, well. Little Laila."

Embarrassment consumes her petite face. "It was only a couple of times."

"Of course," I say.

"See, there was this boy—"

"Of course."

The color springing to Laila's cheeks matches the wine.

"Tell me," I say.

And she does. By the time we finish the dishes, despite the supposedly higher tolerance of Jinn, Laila and I are tipsy. We share this first like so many others. And we talk like we haven't in months. Maybe years. The closer to sixteen I inched, the further from Laila I ran. Stubborn. And to what end? Though Laila's wearing those see-through pink harem pants and can't wait to be a genie, she's still the Laila I grew up with. My oldest friend. My only friend.

"Look at this," Lalla Nadia says as we take slow, measured steps into the living room.

Her long fingernail points to a plastic-encased photograph. "You two and my little Hana at Halloween. Too cute. Just like today. Well, except for Azra."

Of course except for Azra. Because I swore long ago that the matching genie costume my eleven-year-old self is wearing in that photo would be the first and last such outfit I'd ever step into. A vow not even the gold ensemble Hana brought for me tonight could break. The Afrit can make me be their beck-and-call girl but I'll be damned if I'm going to look like one. Still, the tug on my heart upon realizing Hana was including me means the costume now hangs in the back (the *way* back) of my closet.

While Laila peers over Nadia's shoulder, I scoop up an album of my mother's I've never seen before. The first picture of her and Sam sporting big hair and backpacks tells me it's from high school. I flip through until I arrive at prom night.

The abundance of photos of my mother, in a neon-orange dress only she could pull off, and Samara, who's spilling out of a tight, red, strapless dress, almost makes me miss the lone one of my mom and her date. Tall with hair the color of volcanic rock, the cute boy clings to her waist. She leans into him, the warmth in her gold eyes as strong as anything she's ever directed my way. I wiggle the picture out, wanting to ask my mother what happened to this boy she was so enamored of, when Hana calls from the garage, "Laila, Azra, where are you?"

Laila jumps up and grabs a shopping bag off the end table. I slide the picture of my mother and her prom date into my back pocket and follow her into the garage. I know something's up when I have to weave around a tall stack of cardboard boxes full of the books my mother and I packed away to make room for her growing collection of Moroccan tea cups.

Standing at the end of the makeshift wall is Farrah. She smacks her gum and holds out her palm. "IDs," she says.

Laila giggles and starts to move past Farrah.

"Back o' the line, blondie," Farrah says in a deep voice. "Unless you got an ID. Showing skin ain't everything."

Clearly Laila and I weren't the only ones who continued to drink.

The headband in Farrah's hair changes colors like a disco ball as she twirls the tassels dangling off the waistband of her teal harem pants. She then breaks into laughter. "They're here, Mina!" she yells over her shoulder.

Phone to her ear, Mina appears behind Farrah. She leans in and whispers, "Aiden," to which Farrah nods knowingly.

"That's right, babycakes," she says, curling a lock of her chestnut hair around her finger. "*Next* Saturday means the one at the end of *next* week. Oh, and be sure to wear those jeans I got for you." She hangs up and sighs. "Body of a Jinn, brain of a turkey. Anyway . . ." She digs her hand into her sapphire-blue bra top. "Here you go. Happy Birthday, Azra."

In my hand is a fake ID.

Farrah drops the bouncer act. "And I made one for you, Laila."

I wonder just how much Laila's been hanging out with them all lately because she seems as taken aback as I am.

"You guys made these?" she says. "With magic?"

I study mine. The fine lines of the background grid, the blue of the state seal, the glinting of the metallic stamp, everything looks perfect.

Downplaying her usual soda-pop effervescence, Mina taps her nail against her phone and shrugs. "It's just a side business."

"But why?" Laila asks. "It's not like we need to make money."

With a sly grin, Mina says, "Money's not the only thing humans will trade with."

"What else do you need?" Laila says.

"I haven't done homework since the day I turned sixteen," Mina says with pride. She nods to me. "I can teach you if you want."

Farrah taps Laila's ID. "She taught me."

Laila pokes me with her elbow, and I look at her license. It says she's five-foot-six and forty-two.

Behind Farrah's back, Mina holds her finger to her lips and shakes her head.

"A few more months," Farrah says, "and you'll be able to app, Laila. Then you can sneak out and meet us at a club. An over-twenty-one club. That's where the best bands are at." She starts ticking off her fingers. "Rat Tooth and Fungus and Bloody—"

"Weeks," Laila says. "My birthday is in weeks, not months."

"I know." Pink spreads across Farrah's cheeks. "Sure, of course, you'll be able to app right away. Unlike me. I bet Azra can already app."

I can, but does that speak more of my abilities or Farrah's?

"Are you going to let them in or not?" Hana calls.

Laughing, Mina and Farrah hook arms, spring past the wall of boxes, and cry, "Ta-da!"

Laila and I follow to find Hana sitting at a dark wood bar surrounded by five other backless stools with red-leather seats.

"Kickin', right?" Hana says.

Yasmin sidles up to the bar and, with a drawl that confirms her alcohol intake, says, "I don't know why you're bothering. She's never going clubbing with us." Her icy tone makes that sound more like a threat than a statement. "I mean, Azra's too stuck-up about being Jinn to even wear the outfit Hana made."

Made? I reach out and touch Laila's sheer scarf. The material's too rich to be dime-store quality. "Hana, you made these genie outfits? As in conjured?"

"As in sewed," Yasmin snipes. "By hand."

My stomach lurches.

"You know she's always had a thing for designing," Yasmin says. "No, wait, you probably don't."

Mina hides her head in her phone as she says slowly, "You haven't really been around much, Azra."

Hana's eyes dart to mine before fixating on a spot on the concrete floor.

Suddenly Farrah blurts out, "Neither have we." Everyone stares at her. She sets her hands on her hips. "Screw it, it's true."

With deliberate steps, Laila leaves my side and moves to the center of the room. "Well, we're all here now, so maybe the past can stay in the past?"

The hush that comes over the garage contrasts with the raucousness of our mothers that flows through the closed door.

Hana, Mina, and Farrah hover by the metal shelves against the far wall. With Yasmin on one side of the room, me on the other, and Laila in between, the dynamics of our Zar reveal themselves.

Yasmin breaks the silence by plunking a glass bottle on top of the bar. "Perhaps we need to take our cue from them." She begins to fill six shot glasses with a green liquor. "Absinthe." Her tone infuses the word with sex and danger. Surely she's been perfecting this. Nothing comes off sounding so velvety without practice.

"You conjured that?" Laila asks, eyes wide.

Yasmin wets her lips. Again, undoubtedly, a rehearsed move. "I could, but I didn't have to. Lalla Kalyssa had it."

Though she's used the respectful "Lalla," the way my mother's name spills from Yasmin's devil-red lips comes across as anything but respectful.

"Where?" I ask, my tone more accusatory than I meant. Not

that I didn't mean to accuse, I just didn't mean to *sound* like I was accusing. "My mom only drinks wine."

The edges of Yasmin's lips curl into a predatory smile. "Or so you think. I bet there's a lot you don't know. About your mother. About lots and lots and lots of stuff."

We've always rubbed each other the wrong way, but tonight there's something underlying Yasmin's posturing. She's the quint-essential silverback pounding her D-cup chest.

I should ignore her. But the impatient tapping of her foot makes me focus on the lineup of shot glasses. I'm preparing to send them and the green liquid inside flying as payback for slamming the door in Henry's face when I steal a glance at Laila, still standing be-tween us with hope in her eyes. I owe her. So instead of the first shot glass crashing to the ground, it soars across the room, thanks to my powers. I catch it with one hand.

"Nice, Azra," Farrah says. "Took me a week to get the hang of levitating."

"Thanks, it's no big deal," I say, though the glass shakes the tiniest bit in my hand.

With an exaggerated eye roll, Yasmin zooms the remaining shot glasses around the room. They stop with a jolt and bob in front of each of the other girls.

Laila raises her glass in the air. "To lifelong friends."

I focus on her as I repeat the words. I then feel the burn of my first, and last, shot of absinthe all the way to my toes. Laila's gri-mace as she sets her glass on the bar tells me she feels the same.

She loops the shopping bag around her arm and says, "Guess now's as good a time as any." With a wobble in her step, she returns to my side and pulls out a small blue box that she places in my hand. "Happy Birthday."

The burn in my gut turns to nausea as I lift the lid.

Connected to a silver chain lies a figure eight on its side. I touch the pendant that means "never ending" and am overwhelmed with guilt. The infinity symbol attached to this necklace matches the engraving on the gold locket that used to belong to Samara. The locket Samara gave Laila months ago. The locket Laila no longer has. The locket Laila knows is no longer in her possession but doesn't know is now in mine.

My "thank you" comes out in a whisper, causing Laila to bite her bottom lip. "Do you really like it? I wasn't sure since you've always worn your 'A.' But my mom thought maybe you'd be ready for a change."

Though I've worn my *A* necklace nearly every day of my life, I hesitate for only a moment before unhooking the clasp. I test the pendant's weight in my hand before dropping it in my pocket. It's lighter than I would have thought.

I bend my head forward, allowing Laila to secure the new necklace. She then unwinds the sheer scarf draped around her neck. Underneath, an identical figure eight sparkles against her rosy skin.

She envelops me in a hug. "I know it's not official yet, but you've always been my sister."

Behind Laila, Yasmin downs another shot, her eyes clouding over. My own are brimming with tears and so I close them, ignore Yasmin, and squeeze Laila right back, kissing the top of her blond head.

Laila then hurries over to the other girls and places a box in

each of their hands. "I know our Zar won't be legit until I turn sixteen, but since that's taking *for-ev-er,* I couldn't wait." Tears well in her eyes. "We'll all match, which is perfect because there isn't another group of Jinn I'd rather be bound to. Mina, Farrah, Hana, Yasmin, and Azra. My sisters."

Squealing, Mina and Farrah almost knock Laila over as they embrace her.

Hana pulls me next to her, and I'm wondering how to apologize for not changing into the genie costume when Mina comes around my other side. "Love your tunic, Azra," she says.

My thanks puts an enormous smile on her soft, round face, surprisingly not all that different from the one in the photograph despite the years and becoming Jinn in between.

Making human friends has always been a struggle. After Jenny was gone, these girls were all I had. But being friends with them meant I was like them—not just accepting of being a Jinn, but happy about being a Jinn.

Can I really dislike what I have to do without disliking them? I'm not sure, but I'll admit that as I touch the infinity symbol around my neck and eye the matching ones topping off everyone else's stripper-worthy ensembles, I find myself "oohing" a bit like Farrah. Okay, so only on the inside, but still.

Yasmin places her unopened box on the bar and instead reaches for the bottle of absinthe. Though I know better than to taunt a snake, my sudden urge to protect Laila causes me to echo Yasmin's earlier words. "You're going to just pour that? Like a human?"

Yasmin's head snaps up, and she freezes. My only warning is the slight narrowing of her eyes, but it's enough. When she hurls the bottle at the ground, my powers suspend it in midair. When she apps herself to the top step by the door to the kitchen, I immediately follow, knocking her to the bottom stair and into the wall of boxes as I reappear.

Fuming, Yasmin grabs Laila's hand and apps them both to the driveway. Using my powers, I raise the garage door and stroll outside. Hana, Mina, and Farrah trail close behind.

At either end of the driveway, neither of us makes a move. Though it's dark, any human who passed by could still see us. I may have a touch of an instigator inside me, but even I'm not going to do magic in plain sight on my first day. Yasmin, who's been at this for almost a year, apparently feels differently. She smirks and disappears.

Stunned, no one utters a word.

8

WHEN YASMIN RETURNS TO THE DRIVEWAY, IT'S WITH A PLUMP CAT IN her arms. And a red scratch on her cheek. She tentatively strokes the silver-and-black-striped fur, and I gasp. I recognize the cat. It's strictly an inside cat, specifically, the Carwyns' inside cat.

"Give it to me," I say, rushing toward her.

Burying her nose in the cat's fur, Yasmin turns away from me. "But he's so cute. Just like his owner."

The vicious hiss emanating from the animal causes Yasmin to jerk her head back.

Fear, astonishment, and anger mix with the alcohol to make my head spin. I turn to Laila. Somehow she puts the pieces together. "Did anyone see you? Did Henry see you?"

Hana, Mina, and Farrah each clasp a hand over their mouth at the same time.

"Too far," Hana says, shaking her head.

With her back still facing me, Yasmin shrugs. Or maybe that was a wince. "My mother always says we shouldn't have to hide who we are."

Laila marches over to Yasmin and plucks the cat out of her arms. "But we do. This isn't a game."

The front door to Henry's house bursts open. "Slinky? Here Slinky!" He races through the side yard, calling for the cat.

The six multicolored bangles Yasmin has stacked against her magical silver one clank against one another as she tries to hide the drop of blood springing from a fresh scratch on the back of her hand.

She pushes her shoulders back. "Oh, I don't know about that. Seems pretty fun to me."

Henry bolts across the front lawn to the other side of the house.

With a hiss for the cat and a wicked smile for me, Yasmin nabs Mina with one hand and Farrah with the other and heads for the garage.

Hana looks back and forth between me and Laila and the slowly closing garage door before rounding her shoulders. "You've . . . you've got this, right, Azra?"

Without waiting for an answer, she scurries behind the others and into the garage right before the door bangs shut.

The noise causes Henry to skid to a halt. He takes in Laila with Slinky in her arms and me standing awkwardly next to her.

"Slinky!" He runs barefoot across the street. "Man, do I owe you guys for finding her. Lisa's bawling. She won't go to sleep without this stupid cat by her side. One minute the thing was curled up on her pillow, and the next it was gone."

Laila swallows hard. "Did she . . . ? Did Lisa see anything?"

"No," Henry says. "She got up to use the bathroom and by the time she came back, the cat had made a break for it. How I have no idea. The central air's on, and my dad swears all the windows and doors were shut and locked."

"Crazy," I say just to have something to say. "Maybe . . . maybe . . ."

Laila tilts her head toward the Carwyns' garage door, bugging her eyes at me. Finally, I understand. I concentrate and watch the scuffed "A+J" rise as the door lifts a few inches off the ground.

I point across the street. "Maybe the garage?"

Henry turns around and studies his house. "Huh, how did I not notice that before?"

"Oh," Laila says, moving closer to Henry, "it's funny the things we miss that are often right in front of our noses." She gently lays the cat in his arms and retreats to the front door.

She doesn't look my way to see how my eyes are begging her not to leave this in my hands. What if Henry's still suspicious? What if they no longer keep the litter box in the garage? What if the door to the house is locked up tight? What if—

"Ouch." Henry sticks the finger Slinky just nipped into his mouth. "Stupid, demonic cat. I swear I don't know why Lisa's so attached. The mongrel hates me, and the feeling is mutual."

The giggle that leaves my mouth is so uncharacteristic that I blame the evil absinthe.

Henry smiles. "Find this funny, do you?" He shakes his head. "You wouldn't if you woke up to this mangy beast standing on your chest like it's contemplating whether or not to suffocate you with its fat belly."

I giggle again, enjoying the image of Slinky creeping toward Yasmin's pointy nose.

Wearing the same amused look from earlier, Henry says, "Well, I should get this thing back to Lisa before she has a complete meltdown, if she hasn't already."

I glance back at my house. For the first time in years, the idea of following Henry through his front door, even with all the memories of Jenny, is more attractive than walking through mine.

"I remember when you first got her," I say. "Jenny picked her out, didn't she?"

His smile turns bittersweet. "Yeah. I wanted a turtle. But Jenny said—"

"You can't cuddle a turtle." Tears pool in my eyes. Damn that absinthe. I start inching backward toward the garage. "I should go."

"Course, sorry, you're the guest of honor, and I'm making you miss your own party. Thanks again." He hurries across the street. When he reaches the sidewalk in front of his house, he turns around. "Oh, and I'm glad to see you went with that costume."

Looking down at my white pants and purple tunic, I say, "What costume?"

"You know, just a normal teenager. It suits you."

Music is playing, Jinn are dancing, and cameras are clicking as I walk through the door to my house. I hide out in the corner. The Christmas-tree-colored mix of red, white, and green alcohol combined with the rich tagine churns my stomach like a lifeboat on rough seas.

Eventually I'm dragged into the darkened dining room where

all sixteen candles glow on my perfectly iced chocolate cake. The shadows cast on the walls reflect the room full of Jinn, but the only thing I'm seeing is the shadow that should be here, blowing out sixteen candles of her own.

I puff, again and again, making the same wish I made when I was ten and Laila was standing before me, silver tinsel around her wrist, her brow creased, her tongue protruding from between her lips, concentrating so hard I thought she'd explode.

I wish I were normal. I wish I had a normal family. I wish becoming Jinn didn't mean losing everything else—Jenny, my father, me.

It is a wish I've made on every birthday, on every shooting star, on every eyelash since I can remember. It can never come true. I know it can't. *I know it can't.* Still . . . doesn't hurt to try. Just in case.

The forkful of chocolate cake hits my lips, and I know I'm going to be sick. I manage to app myself to my bathroom but land in the tub. I throw back the shower curtain and fall in front of the toilet. My mother's next to the bowl, having already lifted the lid. I'm grateful. I wouldn't have had enough time to open it myself.

In bed, tucked under the covers with Laila asleep next to me, her mouth hanging open, I hear my mother and Samara arguing.

"You've never hidden your contempt for this world," my mother says, "but that's my daughter. How could you let her? How could you start this?"

"Contempt is right," Samara replies, "because this would have never happened in our world. It's absurd, this making things taboo.

Of course all they want to do is defy us. But, whatever. We'll do things your way—again. But for the record, you're the one who agreed to let them have the wine with dinner."

I can practically hear the grinding of my mother's teeth.

"You were always so quick to take risks, Sam. You and Raina."

The harshness in my mother's voice surprises me.

"And you were always so willing to go along, Kalyssa. Always following the rules. Always so afraid to take a risk. And look how that's worked out. For them. For all of us."

"This isn't about that," my mother quips.

"The hell it isn't," Samara says. "Tell me, did you even get to see him today? Did his risk pay off? His risk *for you*?"

The heaviness of my eyelids pushes them down. I don't want them to close, but I can't help it. I hear the sound of crying from my mother, then from Samara. Forcing myself to stay awake, I strain until a few minutes later I hear the sounds of laughter, from Samara, then from my mother.

And then I'm asleep, silver bangle tight around my wrist.

"MY HEAD'S KILLING ME," LAILA SAYS. WITH A MOAN, SHE SHOVES her face under the pillow next to me.

I touch my forehead and wince. *Shh.* I don't think I manage to say it out loud. I roll onto my side and yank the comforter over my shoulder. Today, I will skip.

Again, my mother has other plans. She's perched at the foot of my bed. Samara stands next to her. They're both smiling. At least they're not fighting. Do I even know what it was they were fighting about?

"Since you two like trying new beverages so much," Samara says, "we thought we'd introduce you to coffee."

A tall, white mug appears on my nightstand next to Mr. Gemp. Steam swirls above it. A matching cup materializes next to Laila.

"Can't you just make it go away?" I ask, struggling to sit up. "I feel awful."

"Good," my mother says. "I want you to feel awful. Samara had to stop me from making you feel worse."

A long lecture about the dangers of drinking follows. We are too young, our Jinn bodies can't yet handle the effects, we have to follow the same rules as human teenagers no matter what our Jinn world might or might not allow, and on and on. My mother speaks while Samara tries not to smirk.

I sip the sugary coffee, and my head begins to clear. I nod from time to time—gently. It hurts to move too much. But I'm not really listening anymore. As the thumping in my head confirms, I'm not drinking alcohol again. I've found a much better replacement. Take that, Jinn blood. I tilt my coffee cup to suck down the last drops.

"Lalla Nadia's making pancakes. From scratch." My mother ignores Samara's huff. "I trust you two will be down shortly?"

My stomach turns at the idea of food, but I say, "Uh-huh." The heavy breathing next to me signals that Laila has fallen back to sleep, full coffee cup in hand. I smack her leg.

"Huh?" Laila jerks awake. Coffee sloshes over the side of her ceramic mug. "What cat? There was no cat."

I widen my eyes and shake my head.

"Oh, honey," Samara says, "if you're going to dream, dream big. Lion, panther, chupacabra, make it worth it."

Our mothers leave, and Laila offers me some of her coffee, pouring half her mug into mine. We sip in silence until something from last night comes back to me.

"How did you figure it out?" I ask.

Laila pries back her hand, which has been shielding her eyes from the sunlight. "Figure what out?"

"Last night, how did you know it was Henry's cat? Yasmin didn't say—"

"Cute." Laila covers her eyes again. "She said the cat was cute just like his owner."

I almost spit the last mouthful of coffee I'm savoring onto the bed. Cute. Henry? I'm about to ask Laila when the door opens and Yasmin prances into my room.

"Sooooo," she says, bouncing onto the end of the bed, "how are my sisters this fine summer's day?"

You've got to be kidding me. Jackhammers bore through my skull, and Yasmin sounds like a songbird. She tosses her mane of freshly coiffed hair around and smoothes out her flowered skirt. And looks like she ate a canary.

Laila throws back the comforter. "I need a shower. And I think I might be sick." She tumbles out of bed and heads for the bathroom.

"At least you can do both in the same place," Yasmin jokes.

Then she just sits there. Smiling. It's unnerving.

My fuzzy tongue rubs against the roof of my mouth. "I need a mint." The combination of coffee and stale alcohol has left me with a bad taste. Or maybe that's just Yasmin.

"Ooh, would you like me to conjure you one?" Yasmin's tone is sweeter than any candy.

"No. I've got some." I pull out the drawer to my nightstand and fumble for the mints. Yasmin's would probably be laced with arsenic.

My heart skips a *thump* when, along with the roll, out of my nightstand comes a gold chain. I manage to discreetly shove it to the back of the drawer before dropping a mint into Yasmin's flattened palm.

She pops it into her mouth, sucking loudly, before saying, "I'm glad we have a minute to ourselves. I want to explain about last night. Defend myself. I know it looks bad."

What Yasmin did last night seems unexplainable, indefensible, and doesn't only look bad, it *was* bad. My mother would forget about the alcohol in an instant if she knew about the real danger of last night.

"See," Yasmin says, "I think it's time for me to get some more high-profile candidates. All mine have been local nobodies."

Now that the art of granting wishes lies in covering our tracks as much as it does in fulfilling a human's desires, being well-versed in the customs and laws of each region and country helps us grant wishes in ways that won't draw questions from inquisitive humans. The first wishes we grant are usually close to home. As our magic grows and we prove ourselves, we start receiving higher-profile candidates all around the world. It's like the Jinn equivalent of being on the honor roll.

"My mother disagrees. She says I'm not ready." Yasmin snorts. "Not that she's concerned about my career path. It's the trash-talking from the other Zars. That's what she's all worked up about."

I sit up higher in bed. Yasmin hasn't confided in me since . . . well, ever.

Yasmin sighs. "I know I can do more, but it's just a lot of pressure."

I nod, slowly. This, at least, I can relate to.

"Anyway," she says, "you're lucky you're just starting out. Local wishes are super easy to grant. Well, for me."

I groan at her conceit. So much for being able to relate.

She pats my hand. "For you too definitely. But it'll get trickier."

Yasmin's eyes drift past me to Henry's sweet sixteen balloon. She reaches for the string, curling it around her finger. "I'm just under some stress. So last night when everyone was so impressed with your skill, I felt like I couldn't breathe, and I just kind of—"

"Lost it?" And we're back to relating.

She smiles weakly. "The alcohol might have had a tiny bit of influence."

I rub my temples. "You think?"

Her laughter hurts my head, but despite everything, I find myself joining her, softly, very softly.

"Oh." She lets the balloon go. "I have something for you." A lacy red bra and thong materialize in her lap. "I left them in the guest room until I was sure you'd be open to a peace offering." She hands me the delicate lace. "Happy Birthday."

My entire body flushes as I touch the bra. The push-up bra.

"Hope it's okay," she says. "I was working on it all morning. I wanted to make sure I got it just right. Not being in need of the push-up part myself, I had to do some research."

An insult and yet not an insult. That's always been Yasmin's specialty. I trace my fingertip along the lace front. But maybe this should be her new one. "You conjured this?"

Yasmin nods. "Hana's the only one crazy enough to use a needle and thread. If you like it, I can do more. Not that you can't. I'm sure you can."

How predictable. A world of things to conjure, and I started with a chisel.

Yasmin squeezes my forearm, and the signet ring that covers three knuckles on her right hand digs into my skin. I recognize it. "Isn't that your mom's?"

The light reflects off the gemstones as she draws back her hand. She nods hesitantly. "It's her talisman. I know it's a bit early for doing spells, but she's letting me work on a few. Please don't tell anyone. She doesn't want word to get out until I'm *perfect*." The gemstones sparkle again as she waves her hand dismissively. "You know my mother."

Actually, I'm realizing I don't know Lalla Raina all that well. My mother may want me to take this seriously, but she's not half the controlling stage mom Raina appears to be.

"Oh, for the love of Janna!" Laila's cry from the bathroom makes me jump.

"Huh." Yasmin's tongue pokes her cheek as she plays with the mint in her mouth. "Invoking the name of the Afrit's world is usually reserved for the throes of passion." She raises an eyebrow.

"Stop, don't even go there." I bite my mint in two and start gnawing off the sharp edges. Paradise . . . that may be what "Janna" means but something makes me think the Afrit's subterranean realm fails to live up to its name.

"Who used all the freakin' hot water?"

I forget about my head and laugh loudly. "Torture. Now that's more like it."

"A little help, please!"

Yasmin stands and pushes down her skirt. "Heating up her water is the least I can do."

"Azra, come on! I need your super-duper skills. Like. Right. Now!"

Yasmin stops halfway between my bed and the bathroom door. Her back arches as if she's taking a deep breath. Turning, she rolls her hand at me. "Your talent has been requested."

The abrupt end to our "relating" has nothing to do with me,

but that doesn't stop me from cringing inside. I hold up my hand. "I'm sure you'd be better. Faster. Go ahead."

"Azra!"

Yasmin's body stiffens. Spotting the pillow Hana embroidered with my and Jenny's initials, she clenches her jaw and the edge in her voice returns. "Just go before she hyperventilates."

Pushing back my comforter, I climb out of bed and slink past Yasmin, keeping my eyes on the floor as I hurry to prevent Laila from getting frostbite.

When I reenter my bedroom, Yasmin is gone. All that remains is a splash of red that pops like a bloodstain against my white comforter. I bury the bra and thong in my top dresser drawer, trying not to think about what I buried in my nightstand.

But not only do I think about it, I reach for it. My insides go as cold as Laila's shower as I pull out the worst thing I've ever done to the best soul—human or Jinn—I know. Attached to the gold chain I hid earlier is the antique locket with the infinity symbol etched on the front and the inscription to Samara on the back.

The locket I stole from Laila.

I sink into my bed and sit with my legs crossed and my back against a pillow. I swing the locket back and forth like a pendulum before prying it open and staring once again at the photograph inside. It is the first male Jinn I've ever seen. It is the first Jinn father I've ever seen. Laila's father. Gold eyes, but blond. An anomaly, just like her.

How could I steal from Laila? I've never stolen anything else in my life. And yet this, something so incredibly precious to Laila, somehow becomes the thing to make my fingers sticky? It was an impulse. A stupid impulse. When she brought me to her room six months ago at the end of the last Zar reunion, she had been so excited. She gushed with pride and honor and love. I really did want to share in her happiness.

Samara had kept the photograph hidden from Laila until then because such feelings go against the way our world functions. I don't know if it's so much forbidden as just impossible, seeing as how we live here and the male Jinn live in Janna.

The way my mother has always shrugged off my questions about my own father made me think she didn't care about him, doesn't miss him. Laila showing me the locket was like having my finger jammed in an electrical socket.

Some of our Jinn mothers and Jinn fathers might have actually loved one another? Might have wanted to live together as a family?

Some, but not my mother. My mother was the model Jinn, the most Afrit-abiding genie of her circle, maybe of her generation. She wouldn't think of wanting something the Afrit told her she couldn't have. And before I was born, the Afrit said she couldn't have my father.

Which meant neither could I.

I stroke the locket the same way I did that night when I snuck into Laila's room. In that moment, after an entire weekend of my Zar "sisters" making in-jokes and rehashing events I (admittedly, voluntarily) wasn't a part of, more than wanting to share in Laila's happiness, I wanted—needed—to *feel* her happiness.

Laila had been keeping the necklace wrapped in tissue paper in her nightstand, stealing a peek now and again to remind her that her father existed, somewhere.

In my nightstand, it did the same thing for me, even though the father in the picture was not my own.

Laila's frantic call when she discovered the locket missing should have prompted me to return it on the spot. Instead, I allowed her conspiracy theories that the Afrit had somehow found out and taken it away to continue. I may have even encouraged her, once or twice, just a little.

I meant to return it. I was . . . I am going to return it.

"Azra," Laila calls from the bathroom. "Think there's still cake?"

I clutch the locket in my hand as Laila, whose blond hair appears two shades darker when wet, enters my room. She's wearing my robe. The white, waffle-knit fabric drips from her arms, concealing her small hands. She rolls the sleeves and bunches the material in front so she won't trip as she moves to my closet.

"Mind if I borrow a top?" She slides hangers aside. "Geez, an old black-and-white movie has more color than your wardrobe. That's it. I'm taking you shopping. No arguments. You'll pick something out for your birthday present. Subject to my approval, that is."

Remorse makes my insides roil. "But you already gave me a present."

Still facing the closet, Laila says, "It's a milestone birthday. Certainly you deserve more than one."

I'm about to open my palm when I realize something. Now that I can app, I can slip into her bedroom and stow the necklace under her bed or in the pocket of an old coat. She'll have it back. That's what's important. Not how she gets it back.

Coward.

The bond between Zar sisters is revered above all else. We share everything, from learning to grant wishes to raising daughters to leaving the human world. We swear to be friends—sisters—for life. We promise to help one another. Not to hurt one another. So why tell her and hurt her for no reason?

Nope. Sorry. Still a coward.

By the time Laila faces me, holding up a sleeveless tank that's been too small for me for two years and yet still lands at her hips, the locket is no longer in my hand.

"Mint?" I ask, holding out a piece of candy instead.

Sometimes the lie is better than the truth. If being Jinn in a world of humans has taught me anything, hasn't it taught me that?

By the time Laila and I make it downstairs, our Zar sisters are almost finished returning the garage to its normal state.

"Your mom was *pi-i-i-ssed*," Farrah says, as she runs a broom over the floor using her magic. The bristles hover an inch above the ground but the dirt still collects into a small pile.

Thanks to Mina. She catches my eye and winks.

Hana caps her yellow highlighter and closes it inside the Coco Chanel biography she's reading. "Think you'll be grounded?"

I haven't done anything to get me grounded in years. Mostly because I haven't *done* anything in years.

"Because," Hana says, "if not, we're all going to hear some band—"

The broom clatters to the ground. "Some band?" Farrah turns the rhinestones in her headband scarlet. "The bass player was wooed from Drunken Toad. *Drunken Toad,* I mean, come on."

Mina throws a hand in the air. "Plus, they're hot."

Hana says, "We'll text you, then?"

It's likely the brief pause before my "sure," that elicits the snort from Yasmin. She then drops the bottle of absinthe into her bag. "We're done here. Time to go, my little Jinnies." A perfect imitation of the Wicked Witch of the West.

With promises of being in touch soon, a flurry of arms encircle me and Laila before Hana, Mina, and Farrah disappear.

Yasmin stays behind. "I forgot my coat."

Laila looks back and forth between us. "I'll get it?" she half says, half asks.

Once Laila slips into the house, Yasmin opens the garage door with her powers and gestures across the street. "That's always been easier for you, hasn't it? Being friends with the humans?"

All that happened last night, all that's happened this morning, I'm at a loss for words. Thankfully, I'm pretty sure this is a rhetorical question.

"But you should know," Yasmin says, "my Zar is open to you. You just have to be open to it."

My Zar?

"But we come first." She plays with her mother's ring. "I realize now that's the lesson my mother was trying to teach me all this time. She wouldn't let me be friends with humans." She drills her beautiful gold eyes into mine. "And yours shouldn't have either."

My heart twists, and I'm not sixteen, I'm not a full Jinn with all the powers that come with it. I'm ten, back in my room, listening to Yasmin mock my pain over losing Jenny.

After everyone is gone, the effects of the shredder my heart's just been rammed through must show on my face, because my mother agrees to let us have the birthday cake we didn't get to eat last night for breakfast. The slice with the "16" goes to Laila. Not surprisingly, it's always been her favorite number. My mom gets the "Az," and Samara gets the "ra."

I stare at the exclamation point on top of my piece. Maybe eating such excitement will help me feel it.

Samara pushes herself back from the table. "Let's go, Laila, before we leave the birthday girl with only crumbs for leftovers." As she hugs me good-bye, she touches the infinity pendant around my neck. "What a nice idea Laila had."

I'm going to be sick. Again.

"What's with the long face, doll?" Samara says. "Was this all really so traumatic?"

Yes, and no. Laila and I made a pact to keep Yasmin's cat burglary a secret from our mothers. Laila thought we should tell, but the look on Yasmin's face when Laila called for my magical help made me push for giving her a pass. A pass I now regret.

"No, it was great," I force myself to say. I try to draw on that exclamation point in my belly but can tell from the look on my mother's face it's not working.

Laila places her arm around my shoulder. "Come on, Az, the Zar sisterhood is tradition. We have to stick together."

"Indeed." Samara grabs my mother's hand and twirls her around. "Look at us. Don't doubt what the Zar bond can give you. After all, we're all we've got."

That's not true. The locket proves it.

"*Here,*" I say. "We're all we've got *here.*"

Silence. Complete silence. We don't talk about this. We don't talk about how, for the past fifteen years, the Afrit have forbid all but us mothers and daughters from living among humans. We don't mention how it feels to be separated from the rest of our families and every other Jinn who isn't integral to granting wishes. We don't waste a single breath discussing what this means for my generation of Jinn, the first to never know our fathers, our grandfathers, our grandmothers, to live under the harshest reforms, to be subject to the whims of the Afrit.

For centuries, granting wishes has formed the core of our society and taken precedence above all else.

But retired female Jinn still have their powers. So do male Jinn, though they haven't granted wishes in decades. When the order came, why did they all just go? Why did we let them all just go? Why is travel between the two worlds prohibited? Why do we let the Afrit—a council of but twelve Jinn—dictate so much about our lives? Aren't they an *elected* council?

The ballot competition must be beyond pitiful if these Jinn keep winning.

All of this runs through my head, but none of it spills from my lips. It already has. Many times. And the answer is always the same: "to protect us from being exposed." My mother has refused to give another answer. Samara has refused to give another answer. But there must *be* another answer.

Today's times may be different from my mother's, but not different enough to require such drastic changes to our world. I nudge Laila's shoulder. Clearly destined to be the model Jinn of our circle, she intervenes, but only to make peace.

She swings her purse in front of her stomach, pulls out a piece of ribbon, and pushes it into my hand. "Here. For luck. And rest up. Tomorrow's a big day. I'm so jealous!" Laila waves good-bye as Samara hooks an arm around her daughter's waist and makes them both disappear.

Luck? Tomorrow? She must think that's when my job starts, but my first day behind the snack bar at the beach isn't for a couple more days.

Though most kids in school have had jobs for years, my mother wouldn't let me work until this summer. Apparently sixteen is quite the loaded age, bringing with it enough maturity to dole out hot dogs and wishes.

I fall into the couch and hug a sequined throw pillow to my chest. "I didn't know Laila wanted a summer job." Between the residual alcohol and the residual Yasmin, it's a good thing I don't have to start work yet. I turn to my mother. "How long do Jinn hangovers last, exactly?"

The double entendre doesn't register until the words have left my lips.

My mother gives an empathetic smile. "How about I make you feel better?"

She lays one palm on my forehead and the other on my stomach. With her eyes closed, she whispers an incantation I recognize as a healing one. The instant she removes her hands, my lingering headache and nausea are gone.

"Better?" she asks.

I nod, tentatively, wary of what made her change her mind about healing me.

She gathers her hair into a bun, using a long strand to keep it in place. I've tried, but can't do it with my own. Guess I'm sticking with the elastic and the ponytail.

"Good. Because today . . ." She takes both of my hands and swings my arms. "Today, we get to practice. Your first wish-granting ritual is tomorrow! Fun, right?"

Wrong.

My mother continues, "Your powers are so advanced that the Afrit think you're ready for your first candidate."

Damn, has this stupid bangle actually ratted me out? Or was it my mother?

"This is a good thing. Your talent is being recognized. You're being rewarded."

"Whoopee." My queasiness makes a comeback. Rewarded for all my misbehavior. Is that really the lesson I should be learning?

I open my clenched palm. The silver glistening in my hand isn't a ribbon. It's a piece of Christmas tree tinsel. Surely it's *the* piece of Christmas tree tinsel. The one Laila fashioned our pretend bangles out of when we were ten.

Maybe it's too late. Maybe being rewarded for my misbehavior is a lesson I've already learned.

10

My mother has chosen for me. This is the first thing I'm annoyed about. She has chosen Mrs. Pucher. This is the second thing I'm annoyed about.

What does Mrs. Pucher need? She's probably just going to wish for another yappy Pomeranian. If I didn't live next door to the mutt, I'd never believe something so little could be so loud.

At least she didn't choose the crazy old lady on the other side of us. And I mean literally crazy. As sorry as I feel for Mrs. Seyfreth, the way she silently paces her backyard decked out in high heels, a full-length lace dress, and a camel-colored fur coat creeps me out. I'm certain my powers aren't advanced enough to rewire whatever's wrong with her brain.

I don't want to waste a choice on either one of our next-door neighbors because I only get three. All any Jinn gets is three. While we have few restrictions on using our powers for our own personal magic, we are forbidden from granting wishes for humans unless they are officially assigned to us by the Afrit. The only exception are those humans chosen to serve as guinea pigs. Like in a teaching hospital, newbie Jinn learn by doing. In an effort to make it easier for us to get the hang of this wish-granting thing, we are permitted to choose our first three candidates.

Or in my case, my mother is permitted to choose.

Whoever my great-great grandmother times a hundred was had it way easier. Unlike when humans believed in spirits, magic, and the unknown, today, changing someone's life overnight risks exposure. We need to research and learn all we can about our candidates in order to grant their wishes in a way that won't attract attention, that won't reveal our magic. My unlucky generation of Jinn is granting wishes in an age when every human with a cell phone, which is essentially every human, holds the ability to out us in the palm of their hand.

This, my mother claims, is why she chose Mrs. Pucher. Since I've lived next door to her my entire life, I should know her well. She even babysat for me a few times when I was little. My mother rationalizes that this connection means I'll be more relaxed, more at ease, and more able to focus solely on my magic.

"That may have been true," I said yesterday when we were role-playing as seventy-five-year-old Mrs. Pucher, the easy wishee, and newly sixteen-year-old Azra, the frustrated genie, "if I wasn't still ticked off that her new dog was yapping away, ruining my birthday plans to go back to sleep."

My mother hesitated. "New dog? I'm pretty sure she only has Pom-Pom. Are you positive you heard something? You didn't actually see anything, did you?"

"No, but I heard barking. And it didn't sound like Pom-Pom."

"Well, that's good," my mother said with relief.

I wrinkled my nose at her.

"I mean," she said, "good that if there's another dog, it's probably not right next door."

If that new dog doesn't belong to Mrs. Pucher, then picking her was a mistake. She doesn't love anything more than her Pom-Pom. My bet's on her using the one wish she gets to clone him.

After practicing late into the night, my mother let me sleep in this morning. I'm supposed to be using my remaining time to read through the cantamen and further prepare myself for granting my first wish.

For centuries, the cantamen's main goal has been to guide and inspire new Jinn as they hone their magic. Part rulebook, part spell book, part history book, part memoir, part diary, the pages and pages of entries are a hodgepodge of information. Each family maintains its own cantamen, building on and adding to it as rules are enacted, as practices change, as new members are born, as someone invents a self-proclaimed unparalleled recipe for fudge they feel the need to share.

Passed down from generation to generation, each Jinn in my family has recorded the wishes they've been asked and how they went about granting them. In detail—minute detail.

Reading that entire tome before I grant Mrs. Pucher's wish is a feat I cannot accomplish. What I can accomplish is altering my concession-stand uniform.

When I was hired last week, the manager gave me two beige polo shirts with the beach conservation's logo stitched on the left pocket. Like all my tops, the tees now skim my belly button. I concentrate the same way I did when my mother was teaching me to light my first fire. The beige fabric extends. I slip it over my head to test it. The hem has moved the perfect amount. And it's even all the way around. Who needs to study the cantamen?

The only requirement for the bottom half of my uniform is the color. I can wear pants, shorts, even a skirt, so long as they're khaki or white. I pull on the white jeans I bought for my first day. They are now cropped pants. About to lengthen them, I channel my inner Hana and fashion them into shorts.

So what if I'm a bit chilly on the cooler days? Even I can admit my long legs look killer in these. Maybe even murderous enough that a cute lifeguard will notice.

Right, Azra. "A" cute lifeguard? Not "the" cute lifeguard? The one doing timed sprints up and down the beach while you were lying to Ranger Teddy about your knowledge of deep fryers?

I spin around in front of the mirror, more excited for drizzling cheese sauce on nachos than any normal teenager would be.

"Azra, it's time," my mother calls from downstairs.

My excitement fizzles out. Moving as slowly as I can, I change out of my uniform. I'm hit by the tiniest pang of regret at not flipping through the cantamen. Who knows? Maybe I could have found a loophole.

Mrs. Pucher disappears into her kitchen to make a third pot of tea. My mother stares at me from the flowered armchair next to the grandfather clock—the clock that has ticked for a full hour. I haven't been able to muster the courage to begin the wish-granting ritual.

Though my mother walked me through this at least ten times

yesterday and once more before leaving the house, my palms are sweating so much I'm afraid I might short out the bangle.

"Can't I just do the stupid dog?" I whisper to my mother.

She picks a wad of white fur off her denim skirt. "You can do this, Azra." Checking to make sure Mrs. Pucher's back is turned, she dumps the contents of her teacup in the fern. "No pressure, really, but do you think you might do it soon? I can't stomach much more of this stuff."

I could say it serves her right for choosing Mrs. Pucher, but I know how hard it is to swallow the old lady's bitter, barely sweetened Earl Grey. I bowed out after half a cup, claiming too much caffeine might give me a migraine.

Mrs. Pucher returns to her seat on her yellow tufted couch. "Thank you, dear, for the tomatoes," she says to my mother, who brought a basket of our homegrown tomatoes as an excuse for our uncharacteristic stopping by. "I've always been jealous of your green thumb. I mean, my tomato plants barely have flowers, and yet you've managed to coax yours into giving you plump, red fruit!"

My mother squirms, clearly not having considered that it's only June, far from the height of tomato season in New England.

"Yes," my mother says, "well, it's a special variety. Maybe I can plant it for you next year."

Mrs. Pucher clasps her hands in her lap. "Oh, that would be lovely. Maybe the young man from across the street can help. He was here just yesterday mowing the lawn. Wouldn't take a penny, if you can believe that in this day and age. He was kind enough to take a gander at the sorry state of my vegetable garden. Even offered to bring me some fertilizer. Such a sweet boy . . ."

Enough.

I need to tune everything out: Mrs. Pucher's questions about tilling the soil, Pom-Pom's low growl, the clatter of doubts ricocheting in my head. I need to concentrate because I'm supposed to be able to read Mrs. Pucher's mind.

If only I could read my mother's mind, maybe I'd get a clue as to *how* I'm supposed to read Mrs. Pucher's mind. But we can't read fellow Jinn's minds. Even reading human minds only kicks in during wish-granting rituals.

Which is why, when we arrived at Mrs. Pucher's under my breath I muttered the first of the incantations I spent yesterday memorizing. And ever since I've been waiting to find myself plopped inside her head.

On and on, Mrs. Pucher's peppering my mother with questions about bottom rot and calcium, and even though my pupils are drilling a hole into her white-haired head, I'm getting zip. Supposedly the longer I do this and the more I practice, the earlier in the ritual I'll be able to read my wishee's mind. But that doesn't help me today.

Today, I'll have to rely solely on the circulus incantation, which, bizarre as it sounds even to me, will allow me to connect with Mrs. Pucher's psyche. It is there that I'll find her truest wish. Being able to read her mind first is like seeing the trailer to a movie. It preps me for what she might want, what and who in her life might be an obstacle to this, and what elements I need to be conscious of when crafting the wish.

The psyche is all heart. All emotion. Without the mind-reading, without the head and the logistics, I'm working with a genie handicap.

My mother's I-just-ate-a-lemon face as she sips a cup from

the new pot of tea means it's go time. I give up on mind-reading and nod to my mother, who moves to the edge of her peony-covered chair. I'm looking Mrs. Pucher in the eye, starting to utter the words that will set things in motion when my mother interrupts me.

"Azra! Your . . . your cloak!"

Mrs. Pucher cocks her head. "Cloak? Why it must be seventy-five degrees today." She turns to me. "Dear, are you ill? Is it that migraine? Heavens, if it was my tea, I'll never forgive myself."

I assure Mrs. Pucher it wasn't her tea, smoothly transitioning into a lie about getting over an early summer cold.

My cloak. Pretty clever of my mother, really, but I can't believe she had to remind me. I almost forgot the cloaking enchantment. The incantation that blocks this memory from forming. I was about to grant Mrs. Pucher a wish without ensuring she wouldn't remember the event. That's basic stuff. I know better, and even if I didn't, my mother's lessons should have made sure I did.

Angry at myself, I whip through the rest of the required incantations and have Mrs. Pucher where I need her to be within seconds. I ball my hands into such tight fists that I'm cutting off the circulation to my fingers.

One moment I'm planning how I'll get around conjuring her another puppy since we can't actually conjure living creatures, and the next I'm wondering if I'll die before my sister forgives me.

What? I don't have a sister.

Phyllis, what I wouldn't give for us to bury the hatchet.

I don't know a Phyllis. I have never used the word "hatchet."

I am in Mrs. Pucher's head. I am reading her mind. *I am doing this.*

I spy my mother out of the corner of my eye. The worry lines creasing her face cause me to turn away from her. I can't lose my focus. Especially as I'm flooded with such intense emotions that tears spill down my cheeks. My stomach hurts, my hands shake. I push through and go deeper.

The intimate details of Mrs. Pucher's life fly at me. Mrs. Pucher—Eva. Her sister, Phyllis. Phyllis's husband, Frank. Eva and Frank. Kissing. More than kissing. Phyllis walking in. The anger, the fight, the tears, the relationship, broken. Sisters no more.

The wrongness of invading Mrs. Pucher's privacy makes me want to stop, but I can't. Because underneath the aching sadness lies her wish: to reconcile with her sister before it's too late.

Was there any amount of research that would have led me here? To this?

My mother thought this would be easy for me because I've known Mrs. Pucher my entire life. This proves how much I don't know Mrs. Pucher. How little I've tried to know her. She used to change my diapers, but this is the first time my mother or I have sat down with her for tea. That's why we had no idea she had such an aversion to sugar. This is the problem with being Jinn. We can't open ourselves up to the humans we should know best.

I'm determined to grant her this wish, but I don't know how. We are all in limbo for several more ticks of the grandfather clock when I finally have an idea.

"Mrs. Pucher, call your sister," I instruct. "Call Phyllis."

My mother widens her eyes, but I raise a finger to indicate I'm in control. Mrs. Pucher is already at the phone, dialing.

When Phyllis answers, I know she's about to hang up. I know because I can read Phyllis's thoughts too. I burrow into her mind via the receiver both Mrs. Pucher and I are listening through. Underneath the painful betrayal is Phyllis's yearning to reconcile with her sister—with Mrs. Pucher.

In Phyllis's mind, I find the words Mrs. Pucher must say in order to earn her sister's forgiveness. I prompt Mrs. Pucher to recite them, but I don't have to make her believe them. She already does. And once I get her going, she adds more of her own.

"It was just the one time, Phyllis. I promise you that. I loved him. I did. But I loved you more. I still do. Oh, how I've regretted that moment. Every day of my life, I've regretted that moment of weakness that made me lose you. Made me lose us. I'll never forgive myself, Phyllis. But I pray that you can."

Once the two women are laughing instead of crying, I relax the cloaking enchantment, easing Mrs. Pucher back into a place where she can remember this part. She'll want to remember this part.

Weakened and a bit dizzy, I allow my mother to guide me to the couch. We listen as Mrs. Pucher talks with a voice full of lightness and joy.

My mother stares at me, tense lines still drawn on her face.

"What?" I ask, gulping down air. "I know I almost messed up with the cloaking enchantment, but the rest of it was good, wasn't it?"

My mother rests her hand on my trembling knee. "Tell me exactly what happened."

When I explain about hearing Phyllis's thoughts, my mother's hand shoots up to cover her mouth.

I groan. "Was that not allowed?" If I'm going to have to actually read that entire cantamen, it's going to be a really long summer.

"No, no, it's fine. It's just—"

"Just what?"

My mother looks at Mrs. Pucher and then back at me. "It's just... unusual to be able to read the mind of someone whose physical presence you're not in."

Whew. I didn't violate some cardinal Jinn rule. "But Phyllis was on the phone. Same thing, right?"

Though her expression is strange, my mother nods slowly. "It must be. Because the ability to read human minds outside the wish-granting ritual is rare. If it even exists at all. Most think it's extinct, simply gone from our species."

Seriously, sometimes it feels like I'll never be able to please her. How can I be expected to compete with her reputation as the model Jinn?

"But I *was* in the middle of the ritual. I was granting a wish."

She shakes the worry lines from her face. "You were, weren't you?" She claps her hands together. "You did, didn't you? Granted a wish. My little baby Jinn."

"*Mom.*" I'm desperate for sugar. "Can we go home now? There's still chocolate cake, isn't there?"

My mother pecks the top of my head. While she makes our good-byes to an elated if somewhat disoriented Mrs. Pucher, I go outside for some fresh air, feeling my legs wobble underneath me as I fight back the torrent of emotions still swirling my insides.

I circle to the back of the house and find Mrs. Pucher's vegetable garden. Sorry doesn't describe it. I steady myself against the weathered trellis a potato vine is unsuccessfully trying to climb. Full of weeds, squirrel-dug holes, and spindly tomato plants, it looks far beyond anything fertilizer can help. I move closer and concentrate on the dandelion field strangling the rosemary and chives. In an instant, my powers clear it.

My energy slowly returns as I use my magic to fix up the garden, even turning most of the tiny yellow flowers on the tomato plants into green orbs of fruit. It's more fun than I would have thought. Besides, Mrs. Pucher used to babysit for me. She wiped my bottom—without the help of magic. Even granting her greatest wish isn't enough to make up for having to do that.

Her greatest wish.

I grab hold of a bamboo tomato stake and take a deep breath. I granted someone's wish. And not just any wish. A wish for family.

Maybe this won't be as bad as I thought.

When my mother comes up behind me, slipping her arm around my waist to guide me across the lawn and back to our house, I lean into her, grateful for the support.

"It really was okay, then?" I ask tentatively.

She smiles a kid-on-Christmas-morning smile. "More than okay. Next time, though, if you open yourself up a bit more, your magic will demand less energy."

I nod, happy this is her only real criticism. I may not be my mother, but perhaps I'm just talented enough to coast my way through this, to fake it straight through to retirement. Whenever that is. We work until the Afrit tell us not to.

My mother and I are at our front door when Henry crosses to our side of the street. He lifts his chin instead of waving because his hands are full of gardening supplies.

Did Mrs. Pucher say Henry checked out the garden just yesterday?

"Come inside, Azra," my mother says. "You need to rest."

I should tell my mother about my magical green thumb. But that will erase all the goodwill I just built up by successfully granting Mrs. Pucher's wish. She might even make me quit my job at the beach before it begins so I'll spend time studying the stupid cantamen.

Mrs. Pucher was probably exaggerating. How closely could Henry have studied her garden anyway? Surely teenage boys have way more important things on their mind than bottom rot.

11

A damp, gray mist clung to the shoreline for my entire first week behind the snack bar. Yesterday's flip of the calendar ushered in July and, with it, the sun. Just in time. As my white shorts make painfully clear, my legs need a tan.

I leave myself ample time to bike to the beach and arrive early. The weathered wood shack that serves as the concession stand creaks as I prop my new bicycle against it. The overly complicated twenty-four-speed contraption is a birthday present from my mother's Zar sisters. The irony of giving me an external method of transport now that I have my own internal one isn't lost on me.

With time before my shift begins, I follow the arched wooden path over the dunes. I sweep my fingertips along the tall grass that rustles on either side, feeling the air crisp with each step. When I arrive at the last plank, I kick off my sneakers. It's low tide. The beach spreads out before me, empty, quiet, calm. This is my favorite time of day in my favorite place.

If it were up to me, we'd open our front door to this. But the location of our home, like so much else, is not up to me. My mother says a flashy house at the beach would raise more questions than it's worth. Draw too much attention—the worst thing for a Jinn. Funny, I gather the attention my mother garners by being drop-dead gorgeous has yet to cause a problem.

I walk the wide expanse of open beach down to the water. The frigid Massachusetts waves reach for my toes.

I can't resist. I inch forward and let the icy ripples surround my feet.

Standing at the edge of the ocean, everything seems possible. The endlessness of the sea makes me believe in beginnings.

Mere seconds pass before I cry out, unable to withstand the torture any longer. My toes sting as I race toward a patch of sun and bury my feet. The cool sand lurking underneath does little to alleviate my chill, but still . . . it was worth it.

Returning down the same wooden path, I run into the clique of beautiful bods—the lifeguards. A morning beach run is a requirement of their job. Of the three female lifeguards, only Chelsea does the run in a two-piece bathing suit. Emblazoned with "guard" across the chest in capital letters, the red, sporty bikini is even more intimidating than her orange-and-black cheerleading uniform. And that has a tiger paw plastered across the front.

A couple of the guys nod slightly as they pass me. Though we all recognize one another, the rules in play in the halls of the high school extend to the dunes of the beach. If you wave to me during homeroom, you wave to me here. If you nod to me during the change of classes, you nod to me here. If you ignore me during gym, like Chelsea does, you ignore me here.

If you make me unable to speak in the cafeteria, you make me unable to speak here. Like Nate. Nathan Reese, *the* cute lifeguard, star lacrosse player, soon-to-be senior. He's heading straight for the path I'm hurrying down. I reach the end and duck through the side door of the concession shack.

I shouldn't really worry about running into him and being rendered mute. So far, "hi," "here you go," and "thanks" form the core of our conversations. Nate does his part to save the world by bringing his own reusable water bottle to work, and I've spent the past week being his water girl, refilling the stainless steel bottle from the sink in my little shack two, sometimes three, times a day. Yesterday, when he tilted the bottle toward me and winked before returning to his perch on the lifeguard stand, I was especially grateful the transactions don't require much verbalization.

I jump as Zoe, my coworker, swings open the door and lets it clank shut behind her. Her short, dark brown hair, secured by a dingy white scrunchie, juts out from the back of her head like a stunted tail.

She stomps over to the counter, plops her bag on top, and grunts a hello. "It's your turn to refill the ketchup bottles."

She's been in a bad mood all week. It took me two days to realize when she was complaining about not being good enough to be a point guard, she was talking about basketball and not some branch of the military.

The only way out of a Zoe mood is to allow a Zoe rant. "Tough day again yesterday?" I ask, tentatively.

"He thinks I'm hopeless. He actually said that. My own brother. What does he know, right?"

A lot, as she's explained to me. Zoe's older brother is a superstar basketball player at Providence College. He's home for a couple of weeks before heading to some training camp, and

Zoe's desperate for him to turn her into a female version of himself before he leaves.

"If only I were taller," Zoe says. "That's his expert advice."

She opens a pack of gum and shoves three pieces into her mouth. She holds the pack out to me, but I shake my head. On the list of annoying Zoe traits, her gum popping comes in a close second to her incessant talk about dribbling.

She smacks her gum as her eyes travel up and down my body. "How tall are you, anyway?"

I shrug before bending over and hiding among the condiment containers.

Zoe's in the bathroom and I'm still playing with ketchup bottles when I hear a voice.

"Anyone know whose bike this is?"

Not *a* voice. Nate's voice.

I peek above the sun-bleached wood counter. Nate is standing in front of the snack bar, his lifeguard shirt slung across one shoulder and his hands on the handlebar of my flashy bike.

Sometimes I wonder if he hasn't been granted a wish. Those are not the abs of a normal seventeen-year-old boy.

I smooth the sides of my hair, ensuring all the ends are tucked inside my ponytail, before fully surfacing. I chicken out. Instead of answering with words, I wave.

"Azra, you really shouldn't leave . . ."

I know he's talking, but I have no idea what he's saying because I'm stuck on the "Azra." *Nate knows my name?*

He's staring at me, and I know I'm supposed to reply. I just don't know *what* I'm supposed to reply. I brace myself against the counter and mumble, "Uh-huh."

"Do you have a minute now?" he asks. "I can show you where to lock it, but we have to do it fast. You have a lock at least, right?"

I don't, but I can get one. I hold up one finger and sink down, concentrating as hard as I can. When I return to an upright position, it is with a conjured bike lock in hand.

"Great," he says, "I'm late for the run."

He can close the gap. He's faster than all of them—something my mild stalking has permitted me to notice.

"You'll catch them easily," I say before I realize my mouth has opened.

Imperceptible to anyone not ogling him as I am, his muscled shoulders fall the slightest bit as he curves them in. "You've . . . you've seen me run?"

"No, well, yes. Maybe just a couple of times. When I was picking up garbage on the beach." *Garbage,* how romantic.

Walking behind Nate to the bike rack I had no idea existed, I resist the urge to touch the top of his head to see if his close-cropped black hair feels as soft as it looks.

"Here," he says. "Lock it next to mine."

"You bike to work?" The water bottle is one thing, but everything else about him screams red convertible.

He maneuvers my bike into the rack and takes the lock from my hand. His fingers brush my palm, and a tingle spreads through my body. I try to pay attention to his words instead of his abs as he talks about the cost of fuel and the danger of emissions and the increase in global warming.

He snaps the lock shut. "What's with the old-school lock for the killer bike?"

I compare the lock on my bike to the one on his. Mine is literally a silver chain and black lock with a center keyhole, a keyhole for which I don't even have the key. His is a sophisticated, black-and-yellow, U-shaped crossbar that I couldn't figure out how to open—even using magic—if I tried.

I'm forcing back my nerves to ask him where I can buy one when Chelsea shows up. Standing next to the petite Chelsea makes me feel like an Amazonian warrior.

"Nate, we were waiting for you," she says with a pout on her shiny red lips.

Who wears lip gloss at the beach? I chew on my lower lip, tasting only lip balm. With SPF.

"Oh," she says to me, "I think you have something in your hair."

My fingers pat my ponytail and come away with ketchup. Chelsea tucks a length of flat-ironed hair behind her ear. Despite how I may now look, I'll never act like a cheerleader.

I return Nate's good-bye wave and watch him run off, Chelsea at his side.

I don't care. I've never wanted to be a cheerleader, having to worry about being popular and boys and calories and leg waxing.

Being popular is all about pretending to be something you're not.

I pause mid-step. Seems I've been training to be popular my entire life and didn't even know it.

The day is insane. The combination of sun and Saturday draws a full crowd. PB&Js, BLTs, BBQ wraps, I serve more sandwiches with acronyms than I would have thought existed.

Thankfully, we close at four o'clock. My plan is to find an unpopulated corner of the beach and soak up the sun.

Zoe skipped out early to go practice. I'm wiping the counter when Henry and his family, hot and sweaty from their trudge off the beach, drop their gear in front of the soda machines. When Henry sees me, he picks up three Carwyn beach chairs and approaches the snack bar.

"That's quite the green thumb you have," he says.

What? Do not panic. Do not panic. My brain struggles to come up with a way to explain Mrs. Pucher's suddenly perky garden as I twist the rag in my hands. I look down. And laugh, feeling my jaw relax at the sight of green relish smeared all over my thumb.

"You seem to do that a lot around me," he says.

"What?"

"Laugh. I might start to get a complex. You are laughing *with* not *at*, right?"

I laugh again. He's wearing the T-shirt of a band whose songs I just downloaded, giving me the perfect way to steer clear of Mrs. Pucher's miraculous tomatoes. "Did you see them in concert?"

"I wish," he says, which causes me to laugh once again, though Henry has no idea why. We debate the best track until his little sister tackles his legs.

"You know the stray we can't get out of the house, right, Azra?" Henry scoops up Lisa. "For six years, this one's been hanging around."

Fighting the pangs in my chest, I look Lisa directly in the eye and smile. To my surprise, her giggle, which naturally reminds me of Jenny's, dulls the ache. I better understand how Henry can be around her.

"Ooh, tough," I say. "We had one of those once. I think I may have something around here that helps get rid of the little critters."

Surveying the shelves and back counter, I realize we are sold out of everything but limp salad. Dipping so far down that my stomach almost rests flat against the floor, I conjure a carton of french fries and then plop them on the snack bar. "Fries, lots and lots of fries."

"I l-l-love fr-fr-fries," Lisa says.

Henry shoots me a worried look. Though I haven't spent much time around Lisa, I don't blink. I simply pass her a freshly topped-off ketchup bottle. "Hmm, guess I was misinformed. Fries seem to be having the opposite effect. I think you may be stuck with this one, Henry."

Lisa giggles and pops three fries in her mouth at once. I breathe a sigh of relief when she chews and swallows without spitting them out. At least my skills are good enough for a six-year-old's palate.

Henry sets Lisa down and hands her the container. "Easy, don't choke."

He mouths a thanks, which I dismiss. It's sweet that he's so protective of her. Just like an older brother should be, or so I imagine, never having had one myself.

"Funny," Henry says, "earlier, the other girl said you were wiped out. Not a single greasy potato was to be found."

Uh-oh. I make a face. "Oh, Zoe's clueless. All she cares about is b-ball and bank shots."

I'm hoping Henry's quizzical look is because he's as ignorant about sports as me, not because of the fries.

"Basketball," I say.

He grins. "Oh, I know. It just sounds funny coming out of your mouth."

"Yeah, well, it feels even funnier."

His grin widens as he searches his pockets. "Well, anyway, what do I owe you?"

I wave my hand. "It's on me."

Henry tenses. "You don't have to do that. I've got money."

His tone is gruff. I've offended him. I don't know why. It's just some fries. When I fib that they were leftovers and would only be tossed, he relaxes and offers an apologetic thanks.

As I lay down a few napkins, my silver bangle hits the counter, causing Henry to say, "I saw that the other night."

Now, I tense.

"It's cool," he says. "New? Birthday gift?"

I nod, though that's not exactly the truth.

"Your necklace is cool too."

I touch the pendant from Laila.

"Someone must really like you," he says.

I nod again, though that wouldn't exactly be the truth if Laila knew what I did.

Henry's eyes linger on me. I pat the counter, feeling for my sunglasses. As I hide behind them, he says, "That spa change your hair? Looks nice. Different, but nice."

I tighten my ponytail elastic. "Highlights. Laila made me."

Like on my birthday, guilt piggybacks my lies. I quickly lean over the counter and call hello to his parents, a distraction tactic

I regret when I hear the pain in their voices as they wish me a happy belated birthday. They politely ask about my mother before heading for the parking lot. Lisa stays behind. She's waiting for Henry.

"See you tomorrow?" Henry asks.

"I'm off tomorrow."

"Oh." Brief disappointment passes over his face. "Well, in that case, the pool's open if you want to stop by. You know, if you're hot." He raises an eyebrow before crossing his arms in front of his chest. "Come on? Nothing? You're supposed to say, 'I'm always hot.' "

I bite my lip. "But I'm not. Actually I tend to be on the chilly side."

Henry throws back his head, laughing, and I finally get his joke. My cheeks burn, contradicting my statement.

Taking Lisa's hand, Henry says, "Try to stay cool, then, Azra."

"Oh, it's not that I like to be cold, it's just . . ."

Henry closes his eyes and shakes his head. I wait for my body to shrink in embarrassment. But it doesn't.

It must be wrong to be this jealous of a six-year-old. Henry's playful teasing lets me know what it'd be like to have a brother. What I missed out on. Yes, because of the Afrit's rules. But also because of mine. Because over the years, each time Henry came knocking, I refused to answer, literally and figuratively.

Which is why, when I'm walking to the bike rack later on, trying to conjure the key to go with the lock, and hear Chelsea's voice, my fists clench.

In the center of her little clique, she's dropping fake bits of bread on the ground. "Here, b-b-b-birdies." Chelsea cracks herself up.

Right, *that's* what's different.

He throws one leg over his bike frame and pauses, studying me again. "Nope, sorry, but I still miss the old one. Then again, I don't handle change particularly well."

That makes two of us. Nate missing any part of the old me, even if, consciously at least, it's just a necklace, binds us more than he'll ever know and unties my tongue.

We bike home, side by side, and he tries to convince me to read *Zeitoun,* which is on my summer reading list and was on his last year, about a guy saving lives after Hurricane Katrina. I counter by suggesting he read *Into the Wild,* which is on his reading list but I've already read, about a guy ditching his life and disappearing into Alaska, unfortunately quite literally in the end.

When we hit the street where I need to turn left and he needs to turn right, we brake, pop off of our seats, and rest our feet on the ground. The pain from the bump of my ponytail makes me remove my bike helmet. I take off my sunglasses and stick them in my backpack.

"It's getting late," Nate says. "Maybe I should make sure you get home okay."

With my powers, it's actually the other way around.

"Thanks, but I'll be fine," I say, never knowing what may be waiting (or floating or materializing out of thin air) at home.

"Would you . . . ?" Nate gnaws his bottom lip. "How about you text me when you get there?"

Text him? That would require him giving me his phone number. I'd have *Nathan Reese*'s phone number? "S-s-ure." I fumble in my bag for my phone, almost dropping it as I hand it to him. I clear my throat. "I mean, yeah, no problem, if you want."

He enters his number into my phone and asks if it's okay if he puts mine in his. Is it okay? Is he serious? Is he . . . ? Is it possible Nate's shy? That *he's* uncomfortable around *me*? I lean against my bike to hide the quiver in my knees, but I lean too hard, and the bike clatters to the ground.

Immediately Nate bends to pick it up. As we right the bicycle together, we brush shoulders. We are the same height. He looks me in my un-sunglassed eyes. I hesitate before lowering my gaze to the bike, making a show of dusting it off.

"It's funny," he says, circling in front of my handlebars. "I didn't realize how tall you were."

Deflect, Azra, deflect.

The best I can come up with is so girly I'm not sure he'll buy it. "That's what happens when you wear heels one day, flats the next." I kick my sneaker against the bike frame. "Sneaks with loads of cushioning." To further sell it, I pull out my ponytail holder and give my hair an awkward flip. "We girls have tons of tricks that make it more challenging."

Nate almost misses the seat as he slides back on. He says in a voice barely above a whisper, "You should think about wearing your hair down more often." He then rises from his seat, feet on the pedals, ready to cycle hard and fast. In his normal tone he says, "Put that helmet back on though. Better to be safe than sorry. Never know when you might hit something and be thrown for a loop."

I pull the helmet on and snap the buckle under my chin. Apparently I should have been wearing this thing all day.

12

"What do you do if someone wishes to have never been born?"

My teeth sink into the lamb kebab right as my mother springs the first question of one of her pop quizzes on me.

I chew and chew and chew because I have no idea. I swallow slowly, reach for my glass of water, and drink the entire thing, tiny sip, by tiny sip. My stalling doesn't fool her and doesn't help me find the answer.

"Because you know you can't kill anyone, don't you?" she says. "Well, it's not that you can't, but it's highly frowned upon. It can result in severe punishment unless it's absolutely necessary. There's almost always a way around it."

I'm not sure what shocks me more, the realization that I have the power to kill someone or that my mother thought me doing so was a possibility.

My appetite takes a hike. I push back my dinner plate and think for a moment. "Maybe I could give him a new identity?"

"Perhaps, but he'd almost certainly be missed." My mother pauses. "You're on the right track, but you have to dig deeper.

Find out what's making him feel that way and what you can do to fix it."

So maybe mine's only a C answer, but considering the difficulty of that hypothetical, we really should be grading on a curve. Just like my mom to kick things off with a zinger.

She's deep in thought, pondering her next question, when a pulsating *buzz buzz* in my thigh makes me sit up straighter. It took me fifteen minutes to come up with the uninspired *"Home"* and a smiley face that I sent to Nate before dinner.

I ease my phone out of my front pocket, convinced the text won't be from him. But it is.

Alone? ;)

My head snaps up to my mother, who's cutting the fat off a piece of lamb. The *thunk, thunk* of my heart, the nearness of my mother, the very idea that *Nate*'s texting me ends with me nervously dashing off a terse:

No.

Warmth from embarrassment and . . . something else floods my entire body as I read Nate's reply:

Too bad.

My trembling fingertips hover over the keyboard as I contemplate my response.

"Azra!" My mother snatches my phone. "Is it too much to ask you to pay attention to me for five minutes?"

I shake my head, extending my hand for the phone. She can't read it. *She can't. She can't.*

My racing heart slows to a trot as she rests the phone at the far end of the table and resumes her questions, which despite my now even more unfocused mind, I answer pretty well, definitely in the B+ or higher range. This likely makes her believe I've actually been studying, and I don't indicate otherwise. If I can fake it this good, why hit that stupid old book?

"Well," my mother says, "I think maybe you're ready for your second candidate."

That's what I get for being so good at bluffing.

Her forehead crinkles. "Again, it should probably be someone we know . . ."

Henry's kindness to me and Chelsea's meanness to him rush back to me.

The algorithm the Afrit use to select candidates is a mystery. Supposedly, when they see evidence that an individual may be able to do important things for society, they give that person a little prodding by selecting them to receive a wish. There's a Jinn to thank for everything from the first light bulb to the first supercomputer.

They'll choose my candidates for the rest of my life.

My mother chose my first candidate.

This time, I want to choose.

Before the creases on my mother's brow flatten out, I say, "What about Henry?"

Her olive skin doesn't turn pink, despite how tickled she looks. "Huh, I didn't realize you two were a thing. Sure, I mean, the balloon and all on your birthday was a clue, but I thought the crush was a bit more him on you."

My skin, on the other hand, must match the color of the tomatoes left on my plate. "What? Crush? I don't have a crush.

Neither does he. We're just . . . just friends. He's nice, and I think it'd be nice to do something nice for him."

Nice, very, very nice.

"Whatever you say." My mother smiles. "Still, I'm not sure that's the best idea. Considering the history you two share, I think you might be too . . . invested. Predisposed to grant the wish *you* want to grant, which may or may not be what he wants. Restraint can be difficult when it's someone you like—"

"I don't *like* him."

"Or hate, I was going to say. Remember how you felt with Mrs. Pucher?"

I do. The tsunami of emotions surging through me while granting Mrs. Pucher's wish didn't just disappear when I was done. A sense of melancholy hung with me all day.

My mother scoops up her last spoonful of cardamom-scented rice. "Now think about how long the human's residual anima may stay with you if it's someone you have a connection with. The circulus holds great power over us."

Reciting the circulus incantation is what allows us to grant a human's purest wish. It links our spirits, a magical mumbo jumbo I always scoffed at. I still want to, but I can't. Not anymore. The circulus incantation is what made me feel Mrs. Pucher's pain. It gave her soul a temporary home in mine. This is how I was able to delve into her inner psyche, into her unconscious "anima," and understand her needs, her wants, her desires. In that moment, we were one.

I imagine feeling that with Henry. Henry, who has Jenny's eyes. Suddenly the idea of granting Henry a wish seems like a very bad one indeed.

"It really is . . . intimate, isn't it?" I say.

My mother lays her fork and knife across her plate. "It lessens over time." She relaxes back into her chair. "The stronger you become, the more control you have over the depth of the connection. Still, the process takes a lot out of us."

And takes a lot of energy, so much so that if we ever invoked the circulus for a candidate not assigned to us, the Afrit would be able to recognize such a spike in magic instantly.

"And their anima," I say, the word still feeling foreign to me, "their souls, do they really stay with us?"

"A piece."

"But I don't feel any different." Except being more than a little weirded out.

"You may not. Not yet, but it builds. Eventually it weighs us down. Not that there isn't as much lightness as there is darkness. But they're always there, the effects of linking with a human's soul." My mother runs a finger along the rim of her wineglass. "And then, one day, you'll recite the circulus incantation and find you can't link anymore. You can't enter the human's psyche. Your wish-granting days are over."

The Afrit retire some Jinn before their circulus powers are bled dry, but my mother, predictably, was one of the ones kept in rotation until she was the equivalent of the Sahara. She granted her last wish when I was five. Sometimes I wonder if the hairline creases around her eyes don't just come from me.

Her eyes glisten. "Maybe you can't yet accept it, but making someone's wish come true is special. It's what we are meant to do. It completes us as much as them. You see that now, at least a little?"

I shift in my seat. Did helping Mrs. Pucher make me feel good? Of course. How could it not? Did it complete me? Fill all the Swiss cheese holes the Afrit have punched in my life? Of course not. How could it?

My mother sighs as she wraps her hand around the gold bangle that replaced her silver one when she retired. Though she lost her ability to grant wishes, she gained the powers of healing (which is why I never suffered so much as a nose bleed) and tracking (why I never got far when I packed my pillowcase, hobo style, and bolted).

She slowly gets up from the table. "It's nice that you'd think of Henry, but trust me, you don't want to make this more complicated." As she clears our plates, she adds, "Unless you want to be stuck trailing some human for the rest of your life. Remember Farrah? She was tied to that old man for a week."

We both laugh. We can't help it. But it must have been awful for Farrah. Scary too.

Without the circulus link, we can't grant a human's wish, but *with* the circulus link, we can't *not* grant a human's wish. Once we recite the incantation, we are magically commanded to grant whatever wish the human makes first. There are no do-overs, for them or for us. We have twenty-four hours to show signs of beginning the wish-granting process, after which the circulus curse kicks in.

Like it did with Farrah. It was her second official candidate. He wished for a "room," but the old man's lack of teeth made her think he wanted a "womb." Her mind-reading skills weren't, and still aren't, great so she relied on what she heard with her ears, neglecting to fully enter his psyche. The grace period came and went, and a baffled Farrah became tied to the old man. Magic physically compelled her body to shadow him. She couldn't be more than a hundred and fifty feet away from him until she completed his wish.

The lore of a genie being tied to a master likely has its roots in the circulus curse. A thousand years ago, a smitten female Jinn probably refused to grant some hot dude's wish and was forever compelled to remain by his side. Insta-myth.

I think of the flubbed fake ID Farrah made for Laila as I pack the leftover kebabs in foil. "A womb. Can you imagine if Farrah had tried? Now that would have taken one killer genie trick."

As I place the silver packet in the fridge, my cell phone starts ringing. It's Ranger Teddy. I answer and immediately head for the couch. I've only worked at the beach for a week, but that's plenty of time to have learned that I don't want to be standing for the duration of this call. He tells me a story that starts with taking his dog to the vet and ends with him eating what he hopes wasn't a bad mussel at the Pearl, but it's the middle that concerns me.

"Yeah, see you Monday," I say before hanging up.

My mother, who poked her head in several times during the fifteen minutes I was on the phone, says, "I thought you were off until Tuesday."

"So did I. The other girl in the rotation can't come in. Something about a crab. I zoned out, so I'm not sure if it bit her toe or she bit its toe, but either way, she's in no shape to work."

So much for having two Zoe-free days. If only I could grant myself a wish and put an end to her constant griping.

That's it. I pop up to a sitting position.

My research on Zoe is already done. I've spent five days with her, which is four days and seven hours longer than I needed to ferret out what she'd wish for. Granting her wish to be a basketball phenom should easily grant mine too.

"Hey, Mom." My voice drips with sugary innocence. "How about Zoe? I've gotten to know her pretty well this week, but not well enough to be *invested*." Well, I *am* invested, but not in a way that's going to be a problem.

"Hmm." She's studying three containers of ice cream, contemplating which to open. Why, I don't know. She's going to open all of them by the end of the night. "Why Zoe?"

"Why not? Don't you always say it's not fair that young people don't get chosen by the Afrit very often?"

"So you *do* listen to me." She leans against the counter. "What's in it for you?"

I widen my eyes and point to my chest.

"Drop the act." She sets aside the pint of Tahitian vanilla.

I slide to the edge of the cushion. "She's not happy. I want to help her."

"Why?" She nixes the caramel gelato.

"Because . . . because it'll *complete* me."

"I meant why is she not happy."

"Oh."

She locks eyes with me. "But now my 'why' is for you. Spill."

"Fine." I give up. "She's driving me crazy. She's obsessed, bouncing that stupid basketball our entire shift. She wants to be as good as her brother. I can help her, right? And is it really so bad if granting her wish also grants one of mine?"

She tears the cellophane off the third container, the mint chocolate chip, our mutual favorite. "Well, it's not going to cure cancer, is it?"

"Who knows?" I move to the kitchen. "Maybe she'll get a college scholarship and major in biology."

Her cherry-red fingernail taps against the container. "Oh, all right. Just tell me what time on Monday."

What? I don't need . . . *anyone* (Nate) seeing my mother babysitting me at work.

"Can't I do this one myself? I know what Zoe wants." I conjure my mother a spoon. "How hard can it be?"

She purses her lips. "You really want to do this alone? Because it's normal to be afraid."

"I'm not afraid," I say brusquely, though what I mean is, I'm not going to tell her I'm afraid.

She takes the spoon out of my hand. "I'll agree—"

"Great." I head for the doorway.

She plunges the spoon into the ice cream. "I'm not finished."

My hand braces against the doorjamb.

"I'll agree, *if* you promise to study the cantamen."

I relax. "Okay."

"And—"

I tense.

"*If* you promise to call me the second something bad happens."

"Bad?" I whirl around. "Why would something bad happen?"

"Sorry, *if* something bad happens."

Why do I feel like she just jinxed me? "I promise."

She sucks the ice cream off the spoon. "And one more thing."

I swallow my groan. At this point she may as well come.

"Bring one of your sisters with you."

Should have seen that one coming. "It doesn't have to be Yasmin, does it?"

Her eyes smile, though she refuses to let her lips follow. "No, it doesn't have to be Yasmin."

I conjure a second spoon and dig in. "Deal."

Upstairs, I plop onto my bed, feeling satisfied. When negotiating with my mother, getting one's second choice is still a major win. Plus, if Zoe were toned down, I wouldn't mind working every shift. Every shift? Or every shift Nate and his abs are also working?

I grab my phone and flip to Nate's text: *"Too bad."*

Now this is what I need magic to figure out. Is he joking? Is he . . . flirting? Does he want to throw a kegger here? Powers, useless powers. My neutral *"Why?"* zooms off, and I yank the covers over my head. An eternity passes before my phone dings:

Oh, just glad U R home safe.

That's it? Home safe? Nate the lifeguard. Nate the protector. That's all he's doing. I'm an idiot if I thought it was something else. I stare at my phone but it doesn't make a *buzz*, a *ding*, or a *beep*. Probably for the best. Despite my bravado in front of my mother, I probably should study some before granting Zoe's wish.

Hanging upside down, I stretch to reach the worn, leather-bound cantamen I shoved underneath the box spring more than a week ago. My hand fumbles under the dust ruffle and lands on an old shoe box. I slide it out, knowing exactly what's inside. I blow the dust bunnies off the box and lift the lid.

Amid the stickers, candy necklaces, and two tiaras sits the framed photograph of me, Jenny, and Laila. Buried for too long. I wipe it clean with the end of my bedsheet and set it on my night-stand next to Mr. Gemp.

More photos of Jenny and me—Henry too—line the bottom

of the box. I flip through, feeling selfish and guilty about not fighting more to grant Henry a wish. Or Lisa. I should have asked about Lisa. But as soon as my mind zeroed in on Zoe, all other thoughts disappeared.

I lie on my back and toss the contents of the box in the air. Before everything floats to the ground, I use my powers of levitation to create a memorabilia mobile.

I stare at the revolving photos and Hello Kitty playing cards until I fall asleep.

My arms have a rash. A red, blue, yellow, and white rash. One lick identifies it as candy necklace.

Crushed pastel mounds of the multicolored sugar dot my bed. I must have rolled over the brittle necklaces in my sleep. And the photographs. Fortunately, most of those survived unscathed. I flatten out the ones my body creased and return everything to the shoe box.

As I wipe the sleep—and sugar crystals—from my eyes, I check my phone. No new texts. Did I really expect there would be?

Downstairs, I fix myself a bowl of cereal. Eating while carrying the bowl into the living room, I almost choke on a pink heart marshmallow when I see my mother through the open front door.

What is she doing?

She's on the sidewalk in front of our house alongside Henry's mother. With Jenny gone, my mother's need to socialize with Mrs. Carwyn dwindled. Socialize with, not be friends with. Though being friends with humans isn't explicitly forbidden, there are reports of the Afrit punishing Jinn who become too entwined with a human, fearing we'll slip up and let down our guard. Which is why my mother adheres to the caution against becoming too attached.

So what's changed? The little hairs on the back of my neck stand up. The nonexistent crush, that's what's changed.

Watching (spying) through the front window, I make a mental note to search the cantamen for a spell to amplify one's hearing. When the two of them start hugging, I dive into the couch and slurp the last of my cereal.

My mother strolls through the door, the contents of our mailbox in her hand. Upon seeing me, she hurries over and kisses the top of my head.

"Azra, you should have told me. Not that it would have changed my mind, but I'm so proud of you for wanting to help Henry and his family. I had no idea Mr. Carwyn's been out of work so long."

Out of work? Me neither.

She drops a pile of catalogs on the end table on her way into the kitchen. "Six months? That's a long time. Poor Elyse." My mother's voice lowers to a whisper. "Apparently Mr. and Mrs. Carwyn have been fighting a lot. On the verge of separating, it sounds like. It's affecting all of them, Henry and little Lisa too."

The sugary milk churns in my stomach. The fries. That's why Henry was so weird about the free fries. He thought I was pitying him.

Popping up from the couch, I'm ready to go to battle over Henry being my next practice candidate. We're a lot alike, at least we used to be, which is why I don't need research to know what Henry would wish for. He'd use his one wish to find a job for his father because his family is hurting, and because it might make them whole again, and because . . . because it's the wish I'd make.

Oh . . . *invested.*

My mother pours coffee into two mugs and adds a cavity-inducing amount of sugar to each. She returns to the living room and gives one to me.

As I blow on the hot liquid, I debate asking my mother if I can switch to Mr. Carwyn. She'll probably still say I'm too invested. But why can't I just help Mr. Carwyn without invoking the circulus, without risking granting the wish *I* want to make, not the one *he* wants to make. If what I give him just happens to be what he or Henry would wish for, lucky coincidence, right?

I take a sip. "So, how can we help? Can't be that hard to get Mr. Carwyn a job."

Before she can respond, a feather tickles the back of my neck and Samara and Laila materialize on the staircase landing. And I burn my tongue on my coffee.

My mother didn't tell me they were coming over. If past behavior is a predictor of future behavior, I guess I understand why.

"Perfect timing," my mother says to Samara. "I could use your help. Azra's confused, despite *all* her studying."

That emphasis on all is definitely going to come back and bite me in the—

Ooh, cake . . . ice cream cake. My eyes follow the familiar white box my mother takes from Laila, whose past behavior is always an accurate predictor. She and Samara never show up without my favorite dessert from their local shop.

Closing the freezer door, my mother says, "Azra's asking about the kitten clause."

Laila drops her polka-dot tote bag on the couch. "What's the kitten clause?"

I'm relieved that not even she knows what this is.

Samara hugs me from behind and purrs softly in my ear. "The tugging of the newbie's heartstrings. In other words, the desire to use your freshly liberated magic to help humans. No surprise you'd feel it, Azra. Not all Jinn do." She coughs, and under her breath so only I can hear, she says, "Raina, Yasmin." She resumes in a normal tone, "You will too, Laila, dear, so listen up."

Laila scrunches her delicate face. "But why even consider it? If we grant wishes for humans not assigned to us, can't the Afrit tell?"

Samara tilts her head back and laughs. "Sometimes I think our little Jinn were switched at birth, Kal." She tousles Laila's hair as she moves next to my mother. "We're not talking about granting wishes, babe. Because Janna forbid we choose our own wish candidates. The mighty Afrit are the only ones who could *possibly* know who deserves to benefit from our powers."

"*Sam,*" my mother says.

Samara bows. "Apologies." She turns to me. "I assume we're talking about other things, Azra?"

I refill my coffee cup using my powers. "Yup, like this. Or like helping Henry's dad get a job."

She raises an eyebrow. "Henry? Your birthday suitor?"

"Stop. We're *friends,* Lalla Sam."

"Uh-huh," Samara and my mother say at the same time. The way they giggle with each other gives me an instant picture of them at my age.

"Anyway," I say, looking at Laila. "His dad needs a job. Why can't I do something to help?"

Samara waves her hand. "Technically, you can. There's nothing to prevent it."

"Except," my mother says, snatching Samara's hand and lowering it, "it's risky. Sure, you can conjure Henry a shirt or light a candle while he's out of the room, but how are you going to conjure him a car and explain it away? The greater feats of magic you do for humans, the more chances you have of someone getting suspicious, catching you in the act, and spilling the beans to some reporter—"

"Blogger," Laila says.

"YouTube," I say.

A deep sigh precedes my mother's "Whatever. The point is, there's too much unknown to feel safe. If you recite the wish-granting ritual incantations, the Afrit will catch you, but if you don't, the human might, because you won't be able to read his mind. You'll be working blind. The human could be fishing, even trying to trap you and you'd never know. If a human figures out what you can do, you put all Jinn in jeopardy. Think humans are going to discover magic exists and just let us stand behind them in line and order a mocha latte?" She pauses, but it's clear she doesn't really want an answer. "Even if you escape the human's notice, what about the Afrit?"

Laila sucks in a breath. "Tortura cavea," she whispers. "If they find out you exposed our magic to humans, it's an immediate life sentence."

Locking us up in tortura cavea, the equivalent of jail in the underground world of Janna, is the Afrit's punishment for most infractions. But from what our mothers have described, there really is no equivalent for the human version of jail in Janna. Think less metal bars and more fire-breathing dragons. Or snakes. Or ghosts. Or clowns. Or in Laila's bizarre case, squirrels. Whatever your fear, the Afrit tap into it and make it your cellmate. In the most extreme cases, for life. Jinn aren't exactly a "trial by a jury of our peers" kind of species.

"*If*," I say. Part of me has always believed tortura cavea is nothing more than my mother's way of ensuring I behave.

My mother stares at me.

"*If* they find out. And I'm not even talking about conjuring a car in the Carwyns' driveway, I'm talking about floating his dad's résumé to the top of the stack. The Afrit can't track everything we do, right? Just the circulus incantation. So if we're careful—"

My mother seizes my arm and draws me to her. "The circulus is the only thing we know they monitor." Her eyes bore into mine. "Don't push the boundaries, Azra." She swivels her head to the side. "Laila?"

Like she's surrounded by squirrels holding tiny pitchforks, Laila can't even nod she's so scared stiff.

Samara circles in front of us. "I know I like to tease, but your mom's right. You girls do need to be careful. So conjure your paramour an argyle sweater but wrap it in a box from the mall." She winks. "Just don't screw up, and you'll be fine."

We'll be fine. Henry, his dad, his family, less fine. Guess serving the "greater good" all depends on one's perspective.

Laila finally takes a breath. And what she says may be even worse than what my mother's said. "Speaking of malls, wait until you see the swimsuit Mom and I got for you, Azra."

Samara hooks her arm through my mother's, and the two step in unison into the kitchen. The start of their discussion signals the end of ours.

"Come on." Laila grabs her bag and slips her arm around my waist. "App us to your room."

With a loud sigh I hope reaches my mother's ears, I app upstairs.

We're in my bedroom and Samara's shouting "show-off!" from downstairs before I realize this was my first time co-apping. I should be proud, but right now I'm feeling anything but proud to be a Jinn.

I CAN'T BELIEVE I'M WEARING THIS. A TWO-PIECE BIKINI THAT WOULD make Chelsea's look like a muumuu. Even in the privacy of our fenced-in backyard, I want to conjure a blanket.

Fidgeting in the lounge chair next to Laila—the definition of confidence in her pink, strapless bikini—I tug on the sides of my halter top.

Laila drops her magazine on her stomach and lowers her gold aviator sunglasses. "Enough! I mean, it's not exactly a challenge to ensure you're fully covered up there."

I use my powers to playfully whip the glossy magazine off her lap.

Jumping up to catch it before the wind does, Laila says, "So not fair!"

"You know what's not fair? The way my mother licks the Afrit's boots." I pick up my iced coffee. "Look at everything she can do. If she wanted to help Henry's family, she could figure it out."

Sitting back down on the side of her chair, Laila shakes her head. "It's a slip and slide, Azra."

"A what?"

"A slip and slide. You know. One thing leads to another."

"You mean 'slippery slope.' "

She cocks her head. "Really?"

"Positive."

"Strange . . . slide seems more dangerous than a slope."

"They're both dangerous if you get pushed down them."

"This." She swats my forearm with the rolled-up magazine. "This right here is the attitude that worries me." She flattens the pages against her thighs. "Because . . . because maybe you do one thing and get away with it, so then you do another. And another. But eventually they catch you. And you get taken. It happens, Azra. Tortura cavea is real. There are stories in my cantamen."

I forget that Laila, the model Jinn of our Zar, has had her cantamen memorized since she was twelve.

"I know you feel bad about Henry," she says, tying back her blond curls. "But if you really want to help, I have a way."

"You do? What?"

The edges of her lips curl. "Let him see you in that." She winks and is the spitting image of her mother. "Now, are we going swimming or not?"

I flop back into my lounger. Henry's backyard has been my private sanctuary. I'm not sure I want to enter in broad daylight. And I'm positive I don't want to enter while wearing this.

She touches her infinity necklace. "If so, we should take these off so they don't get tarnished."

I'm still wearing my matching necklace. And I still haven't returned Laila's locket. I fiddle with my bikini top again.

Laila leans over and tightens the knot in the strings of my

halter. Her fingertips trace the circular scar at the nape of my neck. "Yours is so tiny." She turns around and points to her scar. "Mine's like a dime."

Her inhibitor scar makes mine look like a pinprick. Before we are even a week old, the Afrit apport into our human world to inject us with a compound that blocks our magic until we are old enough (apparently sixteen) to handle our powers. The bangles cancel out the injection and release our magic. In reality, today, it's not so much magic that runs through our Jinn blood but the obstruction of magic. Makes sense, I guess. Can't have baby-fat-legged toddler Jinn waddling around conjuring stuffed animals on the playground.

At least a human playground. I finger my scar. "Think the males are injected too?"

Laila nods. "My mom said they are. But she could have been lying to make me feel better about having to wait. Seems silly to block their magic in Janna."

The Afrit's theory that keeping our numbers among the humans low reduces the risk of exposure means all nonessential genie personnel live in Janna. Since males don't grant wishes, this includes the boys. All the boys. Including Lalla Nadia's son.

I sit up straighter. "Does Hana ever talk about it?"

Laila mutters a "what?" but her eyes are closed. Purposely? I can't tell.

Lalla Nadia gave birth to a boy before she had Hana. She's the only Jinn in my mother's Zar with another child. Something else we don't talk about. Along with how my generation of Jinn is the last to be conceived naturally. And how there won't be any photographs of my little Jinn's father in any lockets in my house because I won't even know who my little Jinn's father is.

The Afrit's mix of science, nature, and magic has revolutionized Jinn procreation, allowing them to keep male and female Jinn apart and still propagate the species. When the Afrit decide it's time, whether I'm ready or not, my DNA will be merged with that of a male Jinn of the Afrit's choosing. Following the Afrit's "one in, one out" rule, after I give birth to a girl, my mother will transition into Janna, where she'll live with the rest of the Jinn who no longer grant wishes. Where she'll live with my father. If she wants to, that is.

"Three to one," I say.

"Hmm," Laila moans, settling deeper into her lounge chair.

"Three girls for every one boy." Since they now control the process, the Afrit ensure we pop out more females than males. "That's the ratio, right?"

Laila mutters an "uh-huh."

"Doesn't it bother you?"

Flipping her palms to expose the underside of her arms to the sun, Laila says, "What?"

I swing my feet to the ground. "That the odds are at least some of us will have a boy." A boy who will be taken away.

Though her eyes narrow the tiniest bit, Laila responds as a model Jinn should. "But they'll be raised with their families in Janna. And we'll see them one day."

One day? She can't really believe that's good enough.

"Is that how you feel about—" I bite my lip, stopping myself from saying, "meeting our fathers," knowing we don't talk about this. But *why* don't we talk about this? Or is it just my mother and I who don't talk about this?

The way my throat threatens to close makes me change the end of my sentence. "About having a boyfriend for the first time too? I mean, we'll be older than our mothers."

Laila laughs. "Oh, you can have boyfriends here. Human ones. Multiple human ones if you're like Mina. Just so long as you don't get too—"

"Attached." I sigh.

"And you pretend not to know how to be a Jinn."

I skim the bottom of my foot against the perfectly manicured blades of grass and, for the millionth time, check my phone for texts from . . . from . . . anyone. *Right, Azra.*

"How can you be so Zen about it, Laila?"

She shifts in her seat and fiddles with her sunglasses.

"*Laila . . .*"

She whips off the shades. "What do you want me to say, Azra? Focusing on what we can't have takes away from what we can have. What we *do* have. Like our Zar sisters? If you just tried a bit more, you wouldn't have to be asking me what Hana does or doesn't talk about. I know you've always been jealous of humans, but it goes both ways. If they knew, most of them would give up what we give up and more to have our powers."

Maybe. At least at first. But considering how many human wishes revolve around love, loss, and family, I'm not sure that's true in the long run. Laila must know that. If she didn't, then the locket with her father's picture wouldn't have been so important to her. The idea of her parents being in love wouldn't be so special.

"Besides," she says, replacing her giant aviators. "We have so much to do until then, we won't even have time to think about it."

Laila picking up her magazine shuts down the conversation, proving she's as skilled in pretending as the rest of us.

As I reach for my copy of *Zeitoun,* I wonder just how long she's been waiting for an opening to talk to me like this. I'm about to settle back into my chair when I see movement across from us. "Don't get spooked, but she's back."

Laila jerks upright. "That squirrel? The one as big as Henry's cat?" She whirls her head around.

I roll my eyes. "How would I know if a squirrel's a she?"

With my chin, I gesture to the house next door, where Mrs. Seyfreth is perched on top of the crumbling stone bench in her backyard peering over the fence. Fur coat and all. This time, she's added a sun hat.

Laila hides behind the spread on *Thong Your Thing? Find Your Perfect Fit.* "She's still doing that?"

"Unfortunately. And it still creeps me out."

"Um, yeah, I can see why." Laila nudges her chair closer to mine. "Do something."

"Something? Like what?"

"I don't know, make the fence taller."

"Because that won't attract attention." I snort. "Or be the first slip down your slide."

She squirms. "This is different. It's for us, not her."

"Uh-huh." I stare back at Mrs. Seyfreth, trying to creep her out instead, but it doesn't work. Her lifeless eyes continue to be aimed our way. Forcing myself out of my lounge chair, I close the distance between us.

The gap between the lilac bushes along the fence lines up perfectly with the location of Mrs. Seyfreth's stone bench. If only that bush on the right shifted closer to the one on the left, it'd obscure her view.

I wave my hand in front of Mrs. Seyfreth's face. Nothing registers in her glassy eyes. I jump up and down. Still nothing. I wave my hand and jump up and down. Not even a blink.

Oh, why not?

Swiveling my head to ensure we're otherwise alone, I hold my book in front of her face and focus my mind on the lilac bush. I dig my toes into the grass, imagine the system of roots underneath, feel the air gently caressing my mostly naked body, and command the lilac bush to move. It does. Purple flowers rest where Mrs. Seyfreth's face used to be.

My pangs of guilt don't get the chance to deepen because a distant male voice saying, "Hey, Azra," replaces every little twinge of remorse with debilitating stabs of panic.

"Azra?"

Henry's voice. Louder now. Popping up on tiptoes to get a better view over our tall fence, I see Henry in our front yard. How long has he been in our front yard?

As he approaches the fence, he runs his hand through his hair and his eyes bug out.

He's seen me! He must have seen me.

Clutching my book to my bare stomach, I leap forward so my line of sight matches Henry's. Not until I confirm he couldn't have seen the magically moving bush from here do I breathe again.

Now directly across from me, Henry's gaze travels the length of my body. Oh, he's seen me, all right. I curse myself for not conjuring that blanket.

14

"It's too cold!" Laila cries, skimming just a single toe along the surface of the Carwyns' pool.

Henry's inside getting us more sugar for our iced teas.

"You're the one who wanted to come over here so badly. *'Oh, Henry, I've been dying to take a dip!'* Well, dip away, Sister."

Serves her right for forcing us to come over here. If my mother's remotely right about Henry having a crush, I don't want to encourage him. He's Jenny's brother. The idea of him having a crush makes me more uncomfortable than Mrs. Seyfreth's blank stare.

Before we followed Henry into his backyard, I conjured myself a long black T-shirt, which I'm now wearing over my skimpy bikini.

"But it's like ice!" Laila scoops up pool water and sprinkles it on my toes.

"Stop that!" I jerk my foot back, but Laila catches me by my ankle and points at my toenails.

"Why haven't you painted them? I'm sure you're way better than the salon we went to last week."

"We?"

"Oh, not our Zar." Laila cringes slightly. "Just some girls from school."

Laila's always been less insular than the rest of our Zar sisters. Still, it hadn't occurred to me before now that everyone else getting their powers might be making her feel left out.

"I should have called you," she says.

I cannot let Laila feel bad about this. "We both know I would've turned you down."

"But maybe not next time?"

"But maybe not next time," I say, not expecting to mean it. But I do, or at least I want to.

"Maybe you can do both of ours later?"

I exaggerate an eye roll. "Fine, but no foot massage."

Her pleased look morphs into a pout as she attempts to submerge her entire foot. "Azra, come on. For me."

She's back to that. The pool, which she wants me to heat up. Standing at the shallow end, I wonder why inground pools have to be so big.

Laila sighs. "Shall I call Yasmin to help?"

My head springs back. Such a little instigator. First Mrs. Seyfreth and now the Carwyns' pool? Laila's becoming a bad influence. A bad influence who has just proved how well she knows me.

Through gritted teeth, I say, "I'll do it," and brush past her. I barrel down the top two steps and immediately flail and grasp for the handrail. I have to bite my tongue so I don't cry out. Before I know what's happening, little bubbles simmer at the surface of the water the entire length of the pool, from shallow to deep end.

Instantly, Laila slides the rest of the way in, even plunging her head under the water. "Ooh, it's like a hot tub." She plays with the bubbles, purring like a kitten. "Admit it. This is better."

"Well, sure it's better." I plant myself on the top step. "Seriously, how do humans swim in anything below ninety degrees?"

Oh crap. Humans. Like Henry, who's opening the screen door. I meant to warm the pool just enough that Laila and I wouldn't get frostbite but not so much that he'd notice.

"Laila," I say, but she's on her back, floating into the deep end. I need her to distract Henry from coming into the pool while I try to lower the temperature to something that isn't suitable for boiling lobsters.

Raising my voice, I say again, "Laila."

She flips over. "Something wrong?"

I splash the water and nod toward Henry. "I need time. A little help?"

It takes her a second before she understands, but then she says, "I'm on it," and begins to breaststroke over to the ladder in the deep end.

I'm working as hard as I can, but it's not fast enough. The pool temperature hovers below hot tub but above something believable for this early in the summer in Massachusetts.

Henry sees us in the pool and deposits the sugar bowl and his eyeglasses on the patio table. "Get your scorecards ready, ladies." With expert form, he dives into the pool.

Apparently, fear stokes my powers. The water temperature plummets, but not before Henry's head bursts above the surface. "Holy smokes, it's like bathwater!"

Already at the ladder, Laila jumps out. "Oh, no, it's freezing."

She crosses her arms in front of her chest and chatters her teeth as she runs to get a towel.

By the time Henry swims to me, the water has cooled to a believably tepid level.

"Not bathwater," I say, showing him my very real goose bumps. "At least not my bathwater. I guess you like yours lukewarm?"

Again, like on my birthday, Henry gives me a look I can't quite make out. This time, it's not amused, it's not even the expected confused. It's . . . intrigued?

As if distancing myself from the evidence would help, I hop out of the pool and wrap a Wookie-emblazoned beach towel around me, another relic from the days when Jenny and I would spend hours floating on inflatable rafts, fleeing from Henry, who was determined to dunk us.

I settle myself on the lounger farthest from the pool, sinking as the saggy bottom gives underneath me.

"That's the oldest one," Henry says, following me. He points to a chaise across the yard next to Laila, right by the pool. "Those are better."

I wring the water out of my T-shirt. "I'm good."

Tousling his hair and inadvertently, I think, flinging droplets over my legs, Henry pulls up a chair next to me. "You really didn't think the water was warm?"

I shrug.

Henry studies the pool. "It's funny, I was in earlier, and it was really cold. It's just . . . weird, I guess."

Tilting my head back, I squint. "Sun's out now."

"Yeah, still . . ." Henry clasps his hands together and lowers his eyes. He taps his foot against the splintering wood decking.

"I . . . I left my phone up on the porch." He pauses, still not looking me in the eye. "Too bad, I wanted to show you something I have on it. An app."

My body tenses at the word before I understand what he means.

"I wonder . . ." He sneaks a glance at Laila before continuing. "Think you could get it for me?"

I twist my head around. He wants me to get up? "Uh, I guess, but I'm pretty wet too."

He swallows, meets my eye for only a split second, and in a low voice, says, "Then don't get up."

My cheeks scrunch up, bumping against my eyelashes. "But then how—"

He clears his throat and leans forward. "Well, see, I was watching this documentary the other day. On ESP and telekinesis . . ."

Confusion jumbles my thoughts, fear quickens my pulse, but my instincts are in control, and they tell me to get out of the chair. I push my hands against the arms of the lounger, which somehow causes the worn fabric to suck me in even deeper.

Henry's staring at me, expectedly. *Knowingly.* But he can't know. Maybe he thinks he saw something earlier with the lilacs. Maybe he thinks something's off about the pool. And, fine, maybe he's even thinking back to the great Slinky escape. But two plus two plus two does not equal anything close to Jinn.

He leans in even more. The surprise that consumed my face before I managed to hide it must be what bolsters his confidence. "Well, it's too bad." He steals another glance at Laila, presumably to ensure she's still out of listening range. "Because the app's pretty cool. It lets you use the phone like binoculars. Pretty good ones, too. Last night, I could, well, I could see all the way across the street. Your mom . . . she sure loves ice cream, huh?"

This time, I vault out of the chair. "You spied on my mom?"

The real question is if he spied on me. If he saw me levitating the contents of my shoe box. The app can't be that good. Can it?

Indignation seems like the best way out of this. "We could call the police, you know. Being a Peeping Tom isn't just creepy, it's against the law." I turn around and raise my voice. "Laila, it's time to go."

Even though she's wearing those ridiculous aviators, I can tell she's giving me a disappointed look. "Already? I was going to go for another swim."

"Nuh-uh. It's *way* too cold for that. Besides, my mom's expecting us. Yours too."

Though she cocks her head, she mutters, "fine," and starts gathering her things.

It's not until Laila appears next to me in her crocheted cover-up that I face Henry again.

"Thanks for the swim," I say, to which Henry simply nods. Confidence gone, he seems as disappointed and confused as Laila.

Laila slings her tote bag over her shoulder. "What were you two talking about anyway?"

"Nothing," I say quickly, cringing inside that she had to ask. *Cool, Azra, stay cool.* Henry has no idea. He couldn't have any idea. I nonchalantly toss my wet ponytail off my shoulder.

"Well, not exactly nothing." Henry stands. Like me, he towers above Laila. "Just this documentary I was watching on . . . well, on . . . telekinesis."

Laila's hand flies to her mouth. Her eyes flicker to mine before she taps her fingers against her lips, pretending to yawn. Then, with a nervous laugh, she says, "You can't actually believe in that stuff."

Henry shrugs. "I . . . I don't know. Maybe. I mean, why not?"

As Henry stares at his feet, I realize he's embarrassed. *Way to be paranoid, Azra.* Looks like my mother was right not to let me grant his wish. Here I am reading into Henry's small talk because of what I know, not because of what he knows. *Invested.*

Grabbing Laila's arm, I try to further diffuse the situation by making a joke. "Maybe you're right. Pretty sure I did see the Loch Ness Monster lurking in the deep end. See you around, Henry."

Dragging Laila toward the gate, I stop cold when he says with renewed confidence, "Don't have to see the future to count on that, Azra."

One, two, three, I flop dollar bills onto the snack bar, beginning my third count of the morning.

I'm supposed to confirm the total in the register before my shift begins, but I'm too busy replaying yesterday's encounter with Henry to concentrate.

Five, or is it six? I scoop the bills off the counter and start counting for the fourth time.

Telekinesis? ESP? *Pfft.*

My mom's right. We are not sideshow freaks.

Eleven, or is it twelve? Or ten?

"Not again." I slam down the bills and push them to the side. Zoe can do it. I've already made sure the ice is full and the fridge is stocked and the ketchup bottles are topped off.

When Zoe returns, it's with the napkins we needed in one hand and her basketball in the other. She dumps the napkins on the counter in front of me, sits on the metal stool in the corner, and dribbles.

Tap, tap, tap, tap.

My fists clench. *Breathe, just breathe.* She can't possibly do that when service starts.

Tap, tap, tap, tap.

"Look, Azra." Zoe fills a soda cup with one hand and bounces the basketball with the other. "I can work and practice at the same time. This is really going to help my training."

Tap, tap, tap, tap.

That's it. I'm not spending my summer listening to the slapping of fake leather instead of the ocean. Spinning around, I open the shack door, snatch the ball out of her hand, and hurl it all the way to the dunes.

Zoe's mouth hangs open. "Hey! How am I supposed to practice?"

I check to make sure the shack's front shutters are all the way down before moving in front of her. "Do you really need to practice so much?" I take both her hands and push her back onto the stool. "I think you're already the best player on the team."

"But my brother says—"

I take a deep breath. "Your brother doesn't know everything."

The incantations spill from my lips. It's like I've done this a million times, not just once. Zoe's head is far easier to get inside of than Mrs. Pucher's. And connecting with her anima barely elicits a blip on my emotional radar. The one thing she wants, the thing her brother said was the only thing standing in her way of being a rock-star basketball player, is to be tall.

I exhale slowly in relief. That I can do. I already have—sort of. I stand back, and just like Mrs. Pucher's tomato plants and potato vines, Zoe sprouts. Once she's at least two inches taller than I am, I try to halt her growth, but she creeps up another half inch. I shake out my arms and roll my neck. It's too stuffy in here.

I turn to crack open the door, but that's as far as I get. All at once it's like my body's being entombed in concrete. Starting with my feet, rising past my knees, strangling my lungs, seizing my heart, shrouding my lips. I can't move. I can't speak. But I can see. And I can think. I can think the most frightening thoughts that before this moment I'm not sure I even believed.

Because the door to the shack's already open. Because standing in the door to the shack that's already open is Henry.

His movement makes up for my immobilization. His feet move forward, then back. He approaches, then pivots as if to flee. He spins around again. One hand rubs his eyes, the other flattens against his chest. His eyes bug out, showing white, white, and more white. His jaw drops. His lips quiver. The only thing we have in common is that neither one of us can make a sound.

Finally, Henry raises a finger, pointing behind me. I hear it before I see it.

Thunk!

I mentally shatter the concrete holding me hostage and whirl around to see Zoe's head bump against the wood ceiling.

Air in, air out. One breath at a time. One disaster at a time.

Using my powers, I swing the door shut and fasten the lock. I slide the stool over with my hands and point to Henry. "Sit."

Without a word, he does, leaving me free to work on containing my Zoe disaster before her head cracks through the roof. So much energy courses through me that once I push all other thoughts from my mind, I'm able to harness it to curb her growth spurt. I ease her back down to an inch or so above her original height. Doing what I should have done originally, I engage with her body and tap into her growth hormones, magically commanding them to increase their output slowly—not all at once like I just did—over the course of the next several months. By basketball season, she'll be the tallest one on the team.

Holding Zoe's hand, I lead her outside. Behind the concession shack, I ensure no one is watching as I bring her out of her trance-like state and complete the wish-granting ritual.

She blinks as the sun hits her eyes. "What . . . ? How are we . . . ? Weren't we just inside?"

With a sympathetic look, I rub her upper arms. "You weren't feeling well. Don't you remember? You thought you were going to be sick."

"I did? I . . . Was I?"

I wince and rest my hand against the closed door. "Yeah, I wouldn't go in there if I were you. It's not pretty. Probably make you sick again if you're still queasy. Are you?"

Zoe wraps her arms around her stomach. "Actually, I am. A little."

Probably a side effect of the infusion of hormones. "Why don't you go home and rest. I'll talk to Ranger Teddy. I can handle it myself today. It's a Monday. How busy can it be?"

Zoe hesitates. "If you're sure . . ."

"I am."

"But, what about . . . ?" Zoe gestures to the snack bar. "I can't let you clean that up yourself. I mean, gross."

Placing my hand on the small of her back, I guide Zoe toward the parking lot. "I've got a strong stomach. Seriously, don't worry about it. But you might want to pass along the warning for everyone else to steer clear for a bit."

After thanking me repeatedly, Zoe heads for the women's restrooms and I prepare to face my next—and a Jinn's worst—disaster.

With a deep inhale, I reenter the scene of my crime. Henry hasn't moved from the stool. The only part of him in motion are his fingertips, which furiously tap the screen of his smartphone. The Jinn who helped create these damn things should have her bangle stripped. They really will be the downfall of us all.

Without thinking, I use my powers to wrest the phone from his hand. A small huff escapes my lips as I focus on the screen. "Top 10 Ways to Identify a Witch." A witch? Really? That's so *pedestrian.*

He leans forward and his hands clutch the bottom of the seat like he's forcing himself not to . . . not to what? Not to make a run for it?

"Whoa," Henry says. "That's awesome."

No, forcing himself not to bounce. With excitement.

His barely contained fidgeting causes his glasses to slide down his nose. "At first I thought it was just moving things with your mind. Telekinesis, levitation, maybe some ESP. Your basic psychic stuff." He pushes his glasses back. "But the pool . . . I mean, there's no way telekinesis explains that. And Mrs. Pucher's garden? She swore she didn't plant anything new overnight, and I wanted to believe her. I did believe her. But if she didn't, then . . . And now, here, Zoe . . ." He raises his arm above his head, reaching toward the ceiling, and his glasses skate down his nose. "Too awesome. A real live witch."

My hands tremble as the reality of what's transpiring sets in. Henry's conclusion may be the wrong one, but his evidence can't be explained away. Gut-wrenching panic drop-kicks my fleeting moment of offense.

"Why do you live here and not in Salem? Oh, to be more incognito? Do you have a coven? Does your mom know? Is your mom a witch too? Can you—"

Henry's questions continue to fly at me. Between my sweaty palms, thumping heart, and shaky legs, I cannot focus. I wipe my moist hands against my shirt and hold up a finger to Henry.

No matter how much I understand him having, like, a million questions, I can't answer any of them until I figure out what to do next. I need to think. I've violated the biggest rule of the Jinn world by exposing my magic to a human and apparently not once but many times.

Feeling every carved inch of my silver bangle, I search for a hidden camera or a microphone. My mother said the circulus is the only thing we *know* they monitor. Was she trying to scare me or is it possible the Afrit could be tracking more? But how could they be tracking more?

Time. Give it some time. The Afrit acted fast when the clock struck on my sixteenth birthday, doling out the bangle for my mother to slap on my wrist while I was still asleep. If I'm to be sent to the tower, surely the Afrit won't procrastinate.

Six steps forward, six steps back, I pace the claustrophobic shack and wonder why I didn't wait for Hana. The surprise in her voice when I called last night was only outdone by her appreciation at being asked.

When five full minutes, which feel like hours, pass without any Afrit hands bursting through the floor to yank me down into Janna, I figure—*and hope*—that, like in the human world, punishment for breaking the Afrit's rules comes down to being caught. Or being ratted out.

But my potential rat, Henry, has been waiting, more or less patiently. Facing him, I make a feeble attempt at mind control, trying to force him to forget what just happened. Two strikes against this tactic are that I have no idea what I'm doing and I'm ninety-nine percent sure mind control isn't an inherent Jinn power.

Unsurprisingly, it doesn't work. Henry still demands answers. This requires a level of damage control that's far out of my league.

I raise my finger in the air again to silence Henry. "I need . . . give me . . . just another few minutes. Is that okay?" Instantly, Henry stops talking and looks at me with the excitement of a little kid finally tall enough to go on the adult rides at Disney World.

"Can you stay here?" I ask. "I have to do something really important."

Henry's vigorous nod again sends his glasses down his nose. Half joking (I think), he says, "Like official coven business?"

I sigh. "Something like that." My heart thuds in my chest. I don't want to hog-tie Henry to the stool. "You won't . . . what I mean is, you can't . . . if anyone—"

"Azra, it's me." Henry takes off his uncooperative glasses and folds them in his lap. "You can trust me."

Looking into his eyes, Jenny's eyes, I know I can.

I hesitate. "You weren't . . . you're not, like, scared or anything?"

"Azra, it's you." He smiles, and dimples I forgot he had appear in his cheeks. "I know I can trust you."

The drumbeat of panic my heart's been beating to fades into a slower rhythm.

"If anyone comes, tell them we're still working on cleaning up Zoe's mess." I'm not stupid enough to take chances, though, and on my way to the door, I slide his smartphone into my pocket. "I'll be back."

Henry grabs an apple-cinnamon muffin. "I'll be waiting."

I know I can trust him. At least for a little while. Still, after closing the door behind me, I magically barricade the outside so he can't get out. Better than slapping a piece of duct tape over his mouth.

15

My intention was to apport to my mother. Apparently my subconscious thought better of it because when I materialize I find myself not in my own living room but in Samara's.

I'm preparing to app home when my brain begins to side with my subconscious. Laila is a walking cantamen. Maybe she can help. And maybe then, my mother will never have to know.

Music drifts down from upstairs. I creep to the second floor rather than app. If Samara is home, she may have failed to sense my arrival once, but twice? I can't risk it. Sam knowing equals my mother knowing.

At the top of the stairs, I'm about to open Laila's bedroom door when the knob turns from the inside. Immediately I duck into the nearest bathroom. Which I only realize is a poor choice when a human teenage girl rushes in, forcing me to hide in the tub with my fingers stuck in my ears.

When the brunette with the impressive bladder capacity returns to Laila's bedroom, she leaves both the bathroom and the bedroom doors open. I slink into the hall and flatten myself against the wall.

"I'm next!"

"Dibs on the coral polish!"

"But I brought it!"

"Wow, Laila, where did you have your toes done? They're perfect!"

The *ooh*ing and *aah*ing I can make out belong to at least four voices, one of which is Laila's.

Even if I backtrack to the front door and ring the bell, I have no obvious mode of transport. If I make it past that hurdle, then I'd have to extract Laila from her friends without being sucked in—

"My cuz Azra did them." Laila's voice floats into the hall. "Here, this is from her birthday. Isn't she gorgeous?"

Well, there goes that. My cover is blown. Surely they'd try to enlist me to—

"Oh, I wish she was here to do my toes!"

Yup, exactly. I'm taking too long as it is. By the time I get Laila alone, by the time I explain it all, by the time I convince her not to tell our mothers . . . it's time I don't have.

Peeling myself off the wall, I'm about to app home when Laila says, "So do I. My wish has always been having Azra close." Her voice lowers as she says, "And, lately, it seems like it's coming true."

My lungs lose air at the same rate as my eyes fill with water. An image of the gold locket with the infinity symbol etched on the front is all I can see as I apport home. It's all I can see as I race through what turns out to be my empty house, calling for my mother. It's all I can see as I wrestle the cantamen out from under my bed and frantically flip pages, searching for a clue, a spell, a way out of this mess.

Tears dot the pages of the cantamen, and I slam it shut. *How could I be so selfish?* I was ready to ask Laila to risk herself—to put herself in danger—to help me. And she would have. Because she trusts me. But trust has to be earned. Which, unlike her, I haven't done.

As I reach for a tissue from the box on my dresser, something clatters to the floor. Crouching down, I see the silver key to the Carwyns' fence. I pick it up and wrap my hand around it, knowing I have the solution to this whole thing in the palm of my hand. Because as far as who I can trust goes, aside from Laila, of course, the answer is Henry. Henry, who kept my past secrets. Henry, who, if for no reason other than honoring Jenny's memory, will, I feel more surely than anything else I've ever felt, keep this secret.

By the time I return to the beach, Nate's pounding on the concession shack door and Henry's shouting in response, "You'll lose your breakfast, I'm telling you."

Nate rests his knuckles against the splintering wood. "But I don't understand. Why would she leave you in there alone? You don't even work here."

I hide behind the other side of the snack bar to conjure a bucket of water.

"Wrong place, wrong time," Henry says. "Happened to pass just as Zoe hurled, and Azra asked me to make sure no one saw the mess, so she . . . and by she, I mean, Zoe, of course . . . so Zoe, then, wouldn't get in trouble for . . . for . . . for ducking out of work."

"That doesn't make any sense," Nate says. "Even Ranger Teddy wouldn't make someone work who's sick. Especially around food.

And if that's really true, why do you sound so nervous?" Panic floods Nate's voice. "Where's Azra? Is she really not in there with you?" He pummels the door again. "Azra? Azra, are you okay?"

Great, he thinks Henry's hiding something. Something dangerous. Then again, he is. Just not what Nate thinks.

Henry yells over the banging. "She's fine! She . . . she wants me here."

"Oh," Nate says in a quiet voice, bringing his intimidating fists to his sides. His brain must be churning. What it zeroes in on causes him to sound both embarrassed and flustered as he says, "Oh! She's . . . you two are . . ."

Oh, so not what Nate thinks!

"I'm back!" I shout as I hurry over, conjured bucket of water in hand.

Relief washes over Nate's flushed face as he sees me. "Azra! You're not . . . you and he aren't . . ."

"About to get sick ourselves? We're getting close. It's nasty in there."

Nate shakes his head. "I thought . . . I'm just—"

"Just keeping an eye on things, right?" I try to suppress my hope that it was more than that. I struggle for a poker face as I raise the bucket in the air. "I better get started."

Nate steps back, extending his hand as if to clear my path. "Well, I'll leave you to work your magic then."

Henry's muffled laugh escapes through the door.

The way Nate cocks his head prompts me to move next to him and whisper, "Must be the fumes in there. Getting to him." I open the door and am about to step inside when I feel compelled to turn back to Nate. "Thanks for . . . just, thanks."

Nate's flush spreads to his ears. "Anytime, Azra."

He smiles, and I almost drop the bucket. Of all the times for Nate to come check up on me. Check up? Or visit?

Focus, Azra, focus.

Tightening my grip on the bucket handle, I steel my nerves and walk into the shack.

"So," Henry says, a grin spreading across his face, "broomsticks all squared away?"

Now I purposely drop the bucket to the floor. Water sloshes over the side as I rush forward, pushing Henry to the back wall.

"Let's get three things straight." I jab my finger against his chest. "First, if I tell you this, you have to swear on your life that you'll never whisper a word to anyone. Ever. And I mean *ever,* Henry. This is serious. I could get in trouble. Real trouble. It'd hurt me and my mom and—"

"I swear." Henry looks me in the eye and presses his hand on top of mine, flattening my palm against his heart. "I swear on Lisa's life."

I swallow hard past the lump in my throat and nod slowly. "Okay, then." I place my hands on my hips, trying to stop their trembling, and reinstate my authoritative voice. "Second, you do as I say and don't challenge me. Don't do anything that could get me into trouble."

More trouble.

Henry crosses his heart. "And third?"

Third . . . there's only one thing left.

Am I really going to do this? Yes, I have to. There's no denying what he saw. But he thinks I'm a witch. Would it be less dangerous to leave him thinking that?

Maybe, and maybe not. That's a risk I can't calculate. What I can calculate is how much lighter the idea of him knowing already makes me feel. Not to mention that this might be my one and only chance to stick it to the Afrit.

With a sly smile, I say, "Third, you don't ever—and I mean *ever*—call me a cheesy witch again."

"But I—"

"Because I'm no witch, Henry." The words I'm about to say I have never before said in the presence of a human. I'm not sure I've ever said them out loud at all. Why would I? Somehow, it feels time. "I'm a Jinn."

Henry's enthusiastic nod follows his widening eyes. He knows what being a Jinn means. Henry knows I'm a genie.

16

I've kept Henry with me all morning. I don't know what else to do with him. Together, we serve orange juice and doughnuts, and alone, I give myself whiplash with the way I keep twisting my neck around, half expecting the Afrit police to come for me and trade in my silver bangle for stainless steel handcuffs.

But they don't. At least they haven't yet.

"Stop that," I say, ducking the apple Henry beams at my head.

The apple thuds against the floorboards and rolls to the back corner where it joins the four other bruised Granny Smiths he's lobbed at me. He's trying to get me to use my powers again.

Two things I didn't count on when I made the decision not to leave Ranger Teddy in a bind and to stick it out for the rest of my shift with Henry glued to my side: one, his insatiable curiosity, and two, his weakness for Azra au laits (a quarter coffee, three-quarters milk, and a scoop of vanilla ice cream). He's had four since we've been cooped up in here. Four.

"That's it." Henry darts to the corner of the shack. "There better not be a hole in your conjured bucket, dear Azra."

So I admitted I can conjure things. After what Henry saw with Zoe, that revelation seemed minor. Besides, he tricked me. He definitely has a future as a lawyer.

His hand seizes his zipper.

"No!" I cry.

"Unless you're going to conjure me a toilet . . ."

A lawyer or a blackmailer. "Fine. Go. But straight there and back." I nod to the wooden bathhouse directly across from us. "And don't talk to anyone."

"Your wish is my command." Dimples carve into Henry's cheeks as he bolts for the door.

That's it. I can't stifle my smile anymore. It's not my fault. His excitement is infectious, and I'm a Jinn. I absorb energy.

I groan. *What's wrong with me?* Forget about the Afrit, my model Jinn mother is going to disown me. I flop my stomach across the metal stool and hang upside down, feeling the weight of the blood rushing to my head.

Like dueling consciences, Henry's gate key purrs in one pocket and my cell phone nags in the other. I know what I'm supposed to do. What I said I'd do. What I promised my mother I'd do if something bad happened. (And for the record, her little if-when gaffe totally jinxed me.)

Slumping farther over the stool, every last drop of blood seems to pool in my head. But no matter how heavy it gets, it doesn't outweigh the lightness I feel everywhere else.

The Afrit haven't come for me. Which I have to assume means they don't know. If Henry stays quiet, if I stay quiet, they might never know.

No, Azra. This is dangerous. You know this is dangerous. I shake my head.

I should . . . I will . . . I am . . . I am going to confess to my mother. I have until the end of my shift to work up the nerve.

If only my powers included the ability to manipulate time.

"Green tea soy latte." A hand slaps the wood counter. "And make it snappy."

I pop up and smack my head against the shelf behind me. "Sorry, we don't have—" My dizzy eyes focus on the customer in front of me.

Yasmin.

What is she *doing here?*

She raps her talisman-wearing knuckles against the counter. "I'm waiting. Or do I have to make one myself?"

A mother and daughter get in line behind Yasmin. She turns and tips her black, cowboy-style beach hat at them. "This may take a while."

Then she starts whistling. A theme song. The theme song to that silly old TV show that just happens to have a version of the word "genie" in the title. Has Yasmin always been this brazen or has something changed in the past year she's been a Jinn?

Her whistling gets louder. I don't need this today. I send her daggers with my eyes before yanking a cup from the stack. I've never had green tea or soy milk. But I've had green beans and tofu.

I conjure a steaming cup of the disgusting concoction and place it on the counter in front of her. "Here you go, Miss."

The smell makes everyone step back. The mother takes her daughter's hand and whispers, "Let's just get something from the vending machine."

Yasmin's glaring at me, but my eyes search for Henry. Him returning now is a complication I'm desperate to avoid. But when I find him, he's already hanging back, watching Hana bound down the ramp of the women's bathhouse. I haven't told him the true identity of my "cousins," but from the way he nods slightly, I'm guessing he's figured it out.

Hand over her mouth, Hana zigzags through the picnic tables and stops directly across from me. The wide brim of her sun hat flops up and down as she addresses Yasmin. "I told you I'd meet you on the beach."

Yasmin flicks her wrist in my direction. "But it would've been rude not to say hello to Azra."

With a wince, Hana faces me. "I didn't ask if she wanted to come help with the you-know-what. I . . . I just figured why not make a beach day out of the trip here? Since you'd be working and she was over when you called . . ."

Yasmin waves both hands and a different set of colored bangles clanks against one another. "*She's* still right here."

"It's fine," I say to Hana brusquely, even though it's so not. But the sooner they leave, the sooner I can get Henry back here. "Besides, I'm already done."

"Oh, am I that late? I knew—"

"No. Zoe wasn't feeling well. She was leaving early so I just went for it."

Hana lays a hand on my forearm. "It went well, then?"

The warmth of her voice pulls me to forgive her for bringing Yasmin. The same way the feel of her skin against mine makes me consider asking for her help with Henry. But she's only been doing this a couple of months longer than I have.

My peripheral vision catches a yawn from a bored-looking Yasmin, who's been granting wishes for a year but who also slammed the door in Henry's face and stole Lisa's cat. No, I refuse to ask for Yasmin's help. But maybe if I can get Hana alone . . .

At the edge of the facilities area, Mina and Farrah emerge from the dune-lined path. The physical linking of their arms as they stroll toward us speaks to how close they are. That they're here too with Hana and Yasmin speaks to how close *all* of them are. Much more than I realized.

That weight from my head settles smack in the middle of my chest. My birthday party may have brought us closer, but that doesn't change the fact that if we were in school together, they would all be on Chelsea's cheerleading squad and I wouldn't even know there was a game.

There's no way Hana would keep this a secret from our Zar sisters. She's too loyal to them. Unlike Henry, who's patiently waiting, hands folded in front of his stomach, mouth shut tight, knowing without me having to tell him that he should keep his distance.

With a hop in her final step, Farrah lands in front of me. "You look super cute in your uniform, Azra."

Mina slides her cat-eyed sunglasses to the top of her head. Today's eyeliner is a subtler blue, a perfect match for the ocean. As she picks a leaf out of Farrah's long bangs, she says, "Woods. Good for concealing our arrival—"

"But swarming with mosquitos," Farrah finishes, scratching her ankles. She then gets a whiff of my mock green tea soy latte. "What's this?" She brings it to her lips.

"Don't!" I say, but she's already licking green goo off the corner of her mouth.

"Oh, soup. Not bad." She passes it to Mina, who wrinkles her nose and pushes it away.

Farrah shrugs and is about to take another sip when Yasmin plucks it out of her hand and sets it on the far end of the counter. "I assume we're all set up on the beach?"

The sun glints off of the crystal headband in Farrah's hair as she nods. "Should be by now. I promised this albino boy he could rub suntan lotion on Mina's back if he carried our stuff to a less busy spot."

Rolling her eyes, Mina says, "What she thought was an albino boy. I had to point out four more just like him to convince her it's just that your Massachusetts boys are a pale lot."

"Like porcelain dolls," Farrah says. "Ooh, like that cute one over there." She points to Henry.

"Mmm," Mina says, "but not like that tanned Adonis over there." She points to Nate.

Hana lifts the brim of her hat. "Wait, that's your boyfriend, isn't it, Azra?"

My head feels like the ball in a tennis match. "No. Which? No, no, neither."

Just when I think nothing can fluster me more, Yasmin's face looks weird. It's not until I hear what, if coming out of anyone else's lips, I'd call sincerity that I realize it's just her face without its coating of smug.

"Be careful, Azra," she says. "Don't forget they're humans. Don't forget what that means." She then conjures a small piece of paper and places it on the counter. "My new number." She morphs back into herself. "You know, when, I mean if, you ever need tips."

Great. Another jinx.

Yasmin then claps her hands together. "Come on, Sisters, let's get on the beach before the sand erodes. Azra doesn't need us."

Like on my birthday, this hovers between a threat and a statement.

"Wait," Farrah says, pulling something out of her beach bag. She places a homemade CD on the counter with the words "Drunken Toad" written in her rounded, swirly handwriting. "This way you can learn the lyrics before tonight."

"Tonight?" I ask.

Hana's high cheekbones flush. "I didn't get a chance to ask yet." She side eyes Yasmin. "I . . . I got distracted." Her red hair spills out around her freckled shoulders as she removes her hat and meets my eye. "But we'd love for you to come with us tonight."

Mina nods with her usual enthusiasm. "Yeah, for sure. It's a last-minute surprise show thing. I'm making us VIP passes."

I hold the CD in one hand. Were they really planning to invite me?

Doesn't matter, because I can't go. Tonight . . . I have other plans.

"I can't tonight," I say, looking past them.

Yasmin follows my line of sight that ends at Henry. She shoves her black-tinted sunglasses on her narrow nose and nabs Farrah, whose energetic good-bye wave I can't help but return.

"Another time," Hana says, to which Mina adds, "We'll check our calendar and be in touch."

Our calendar. As if they move as one.

And they do.

My four Zar sisters parade down the path to the beach like it's a catwalk. What I thought were individual mismatched bikinis actually add up to a whole. Hana's polka-dot top matches Farrah's dotted behind. Mina's red hipster matches Farrah's top. Yasmin's overflowing yellow halter matches Hana's toned bottom. Mina's black strapless matches Yasmin's black boy shorts. And underneath my beige shirt and white shorts I'm wearing a one-piece.

"You okay, Azra?"

The concern in Henry's eyes as he quietly slips back through the door makes me cling to the devil in my pocket. The gate key.

Suddenly what I should do is no match for what I want to do.

17

I'm alone with Henry in his backyard.

"One more?" he says.

"Just one." I drag my toe along the surface of the water in the Carwyns' pool. I've resisted the urge to heat it.

"And it's really just the one wish?" He runs his hand through his hair. "Not three?"

In response to my nod, Henry takes off his glasses and rubs his eyes. It is at this moment that I wonder if the weight that lifted from my shoulders upon sharing my secret with Henry found a home on his.

He slides his glasses back on. "Even so. That's what I want."

And that is how I wind up using my third and final practice ritual to grant Lisa's wish to be rid of her stutter. In this case, being invested wasn't a problem. Because his wish was also hers.

I should . . . I will . . . I am . . . I am going to confess to my mother.

But not today.

When Mr. Carwyn came outside to ask Henry to babysit Lisa and saw the two of us together, tears snuck into his eyes. The same way they filled mine when Henry and I heard Lisa speak without a hint of a stutter for the first time.

After their father left, Henry was reading to Lisa. He prompted her to try a page. Lip trembling, she looked at me and hesitated.

"Remember what your therapist taught you and go slowly," Henry said.

The mix of astonishment and pride on Lisa's face when she read the page out loud made my heart stop.

"It worked, Henry! Just like Ms. Denise said!"

Barely holding back his own tears, Henry hugged Lisa and immediately began to cover for me. "Well, we've been working hard this summer, haven't we? Doing all Ms. Denise told us to do. Now, don't forget, she said it might take time. So don't worry if it comes back, okay? We'll just work even harder."

Lisa vigorously shook her head. "It's gone. I believed. Just like with Tinker Bell."

Tinker Bell or a genie. In that moment, I was okay with being either, but proud, and maybe even the tiniest bit grateful, to be the latter.

And that is why today has simply been for floating on a raft in the Carwyns' pool, for getting to know Lisa, and for opening the door and finally letting Henry in.

From my yellow-and-blue inflatable boat, I watch Henry finish wrapping a waterlogged Lisa in a towel. She curls up on the lounger, clutches her book, and begins to read aloud to herself.

Henry dives back into the pool, rocking my plastic boat as he swims underneath me.

He pokes his head above the water and, with a Cheshire cat grin, says, "Leprechauns?"

"Nope." I inch away from the water dripping off his unruly mop as he rests his forearms on the side of my raft.

"Mermaids?"

"Please."

He groans. "Don't tell me vampires exist."

"Not as far as I know. But what's wrong with vampires?"

Henry squints and issues a decent brooding stare. "They're leeches. I'll never understand what you girls see in them." He widens his eyes. "Wait, you are a girl, aren't you?"

"A Jinn girl."

"Which means?"

"Same but not. Different species."

"Really?" He shakes his head and chlorinated water flies at my nose. "Like snakes or baboons? Wild."

Laughing, I shove him off my boat with so much force I end up capsizing myself.

Henry's string of questions is so long, I'm convinced he spent all morning preparing them. No one could have this many questions about magical creatures off the top of their head. He thinks being Jinn means I'm plugged into some supernatural hot line.

As I flutter kick my way to the stairs, I realize the high I'm riding must be at least partially due to the effects of invoking the circulus with Lisa. I didn't recognize it at first because I didn't feel much (aside from panic) after granting Zoe's wish. But the pureness of Lisa's spirit has made me all giggly. Me and giggly are usually more oil and water than chocolate and peanut butter.

Enveloping myself in a beach towel, I place another one over Lisa, who's fallen asleep, tired out from us double-teaming Henry all afternoon. Not wanting to wake her, I sit in a chair at the opposite end of the pool. The jig is up about my birthday night makeover so I go ahead and pull out my ponytail holder and use my dark purple nails to untangle the knots in my long hair.

Leaving his own trail of wet footprints on the decking next to mine, Henry plops down across from me. "I knew there was something different about you that night."

Just like a boy to focus on a girl's looks.

"You exuded this . . . this confidence," he says.

Just like Henry to not be a normal boy. He's so honest it scares me a little—and not because I think he'd out me. Because my entire life has been one of deception. Being open feels wrong. How's that for a warped lesson to have learned?

"I should probably go," I say even though it's the last thing I want to do. Going home, thinking about what I have to do at home, erases the joy of Lisa's residual anima.

I've told Henry enough to satisfy him for now. Though he probably won't get the chance to find out more. I have no idea if my mother can fix this, but if she can and does, I'm pretty sure that'll mean I'll lose another Carwyn because of being Jinn.

"Wait, not yet." Henry gestures toward his sleeping sister. "Should I be worried about her? I know you said most genie lore is pure myth, but she's not going to wake up without her vocal cords or something, is she?"

I cock my head. "I'm not following."

"You know, like in the movies. One of those genie tricks. Like a girl gets her wish to be stick thin but the cost is puking her guts out every morning."

I'd laugh but Henry's too worried. "No, she'll be fine." To reassure him, I add, "I promise, no tricks with this one, even though a lot of the myths do seem to have a kernel of truth in them. Like my mom thinks the whole idea of wishes coming with strings attached is because our magic has its limits. A lazy or an untalented or even a mischievous Jinn might go the literal route. Way back when, people knew they had a wish granted. We didn't have to make them forget like we do now. If they spilled the beans, the wish was reversed."

Henry relaxes back into his chair. "So if someone's wish wasn't granted the way they wanted, it probably seemed like the wish came with a cost."

I nod. "That's not an issue anymore since wishees don't remember the experience. The hardest part now is covering our tracks and making sure the wish is believable to them and to everyone else. Like with Zoe. She wanted to be tall, but if I left her bumping the ceiling, she'd—"

"Totally go viral."

"Be dissected by your human doctors."

"Military."

This time, I do laugh. A little. "Either way, it'd raise suspicion."

"Viral." Henry slaps his leg. "Damn. Can you imagine if we could put this on the Internet? Make a documentary? Real-life paranormal? We'd be rich."

My heart leaps to my throat. "You can't. What I said about the Afrit wasn't an exaggeration." Though I kept the specifics vague, I had to tell Henry the consequences of him not keeping my secret. "If you hint to anyone, even your mom or dad—"

Henry grabs both of my hands and looks at me with such intensity, I break out in goose bumps.

"It was only a stupid joke, I swear, Azra. I swear on—"

"It's okay." I don't want him swearing on anyone's life again. "It's only jail." Granted, if my mom isn't exaggerating, it's a perverse, living nightmare kind of jail, but Henry doesn't need to know that.

He squeezes his eyes shut as he shakes his head. "No, it's not okay. You're trusting me with all this. With . . . with your life."

But only for today. A rush of sadness and guilt overwhelms me. Henry must mistake this for fear because he clenches my hands so hard, my bones feel as though they might break.

"And if they found out, you'd be taken away. From . . . all of us. For good." He gently touches my silver bangle. "I'd never let that happen, Azra."

Henry's honesty is never more on display than in his light green eyes. One look, and I'm positive nothing has ever been more true.

"Thank you, Henry," I say. "For today. It's been a long time since . . . well, since I've had a day like today."

A cloud comes over his eyes. "Did you tell her? Did you ever tell Jenny?"

It's all I can do to shake my head no.

Our awkward silence is interrupted by Lisa, who barrels into me and hugs my legs. I'm momentarily panicked, thinking the cloaking enchantment didn't work. But it did. To Lisa, I'm just the girl from across the street who gave her french fries.

The gratitude in Henry's smile guts me. To him, I'm the girl from across the street, the best friend to the sister he lost, and the genie who helped the sister he clings to and puts before everything, including himself.

I should . . . I will . . . I am going to confess to my mother.

But not today.

18

DEEPER. I SHOULD HAVE DUG DEEPER. THAT'S WHAT MY MOTHER HAS to say in response to my (abridged) report on how I (more or less) successfully granted Zoe's wish.

She paces the living room in front of our bookshelf as I fidget on the couch. "Did you feel her emotions? Like you did with Mrs. Pucher?"

"No, not with Zoe," I admit. I then force myself to add, "But I did with Lisa. A little, I think."

She freezes. "What?"

Words tumble out of my mouth. "It just happened, Mom, I swear. I didn't plan it. I know it was wrong. One minute Lisa was stuttering and . . . have you heard her stutter?"

She places her hand on her chest and nods slowly. "Elyse mentioned it too. And that this past school year was particularly difficult for her. Though she had been making some strides since she started seeing a speech therapist."

"Then it's a good thing, right?" I pause to take a breath. "Wait until you hear her. Even Henry said—"

Her jaw drops. "Henry was there?"

Perfect opening. I should tell her. Now.

"Yes." Her face is a beet with eyes. "I mean, not *there* there."

I will tell her. Tomorrow.

"He ran to the store and asked if I'd watch her. Anyway, the point is, I'm pretty sure I did better with Lisa." It's only as I say this that I realize I did actually do much better with Lisa. I smile. "Guess third time's the charm and all is true."

Unlike this convoluted story.

I am going to confess. I just need to prepare Henry first.

"And don't worry. I was able to do the ritual quickly, way before he got back."

She crosses her arms in front of her chest. "Well, I should hope you could do it quickly. Lisa's only six. I'm sure it couldn't have been difficult to get into her psyche."

Ouch.

"You know you should have asked me first?"

I nod and apologize again.

She sighs. "Well, if the worst thing is that Elyse gets a wonderful surprise and the speech therapist gets a big bonus, then no harm done." She starts pacing again. "As for Zoe, I'm worried you didn't fully connect with her. Maybe because you didn't try hard enough. Are you still blocking yourself, Azra? You can't do that once you receive your assignments. Did Hana explain . . ."

Her silk slippers barely make a sound as she paces back and forth in front of me, but each silent footfall still judges me. She's talking and pivoting and talking and pivoting and finally I succumb to everything that's happened today. Tears creep into my eyes. I look away, but not fast enough.

"Oh, honey." My mother's feet stop, and her body is instantly at my side. "I'm . . . I'm being too hard on you. I'm sorry, kiddo. I'm just worried. But the purpose of all this is so you can learn. So I can teach you. I was expecting . . ."

I know what she was expecting. She was expecting me to be her.

"Nothing, absolutely nothing." She strokes my upper arm. "It was sweet. What you did for Lisa. Jenny would have been so proud."

That's it. The levee holding back my tears breaks.

My mother wipes my damp cheeks with the edge of her thumb. "All I'm trying to do is to help you to realize there was probably a reason why Zoe wanted to be tall."

"There was." I suck back the moisture clogging my nostrils. "She wanted to be a better basketball player."

My mother nods gently. "Sure, but why?"

"Because her brother is."

"Warm." She smiles and rolls her hand. "And so . . ."

"It'd make him happy."

"Warmer. But what else?"

"It'd make her happy."

My mother wraps her arms around herself and exaggerates a shiver.

Her trying to make this easier for me is only making it—all of it—harder. Eyes down, I pick lint off the couch. "I don't know what you want me to say."

"Here," she says, patiently, "think about it this way. Zoe wanted to be tall to be a better basketball player, but I'll bet you the last piece of ice cream cake that it goes deeper than that. Maybe she only wants to be a star basketball player because she feels insecure, especially compared to her brother. Maybe she thinks she doesn't live up to his or even her parents' expectations."

Something I happen to know a little bit about.

Moving closer, she sweeps my hair off my face. "That's what you should have strived to uncover. If she was insecure or had low self-esteem, you could have helped. The changes you might have made would go way beyond basketball. It's not enough to simply recite the circulus. All that does is provide the link; you're the one who controls how deep you go. And you have to go all the way, no matter how hard it may be. That's what you'll be expected to do when you have official candidates." She forces me to meet her eyes. "Humans are rarely attuned to the things they really want. And most of the time, what they want isn't actually what they need. It's your job to figure that out."

"But why? Why do we bother helping them?"

"Because we can. And because we have to. You know the deal. Our powers only continue so long as we use at least a portion of them for the greater good."

"So we stop granting wishes, stop helping the humans, and our magic disappears? What's so bad about that?"

And how fast can that happen, anyway? Can I bribe someone so it's fast enough that no one ever has to know about Henry?

"What's so bad about that is eventually we disappear too. The Jinn will cease to exist."

I snort. "A little dramatic, Mom."

"If only it were." She raises her eyebrows. "You know we can't have children with humans?" Without waiting for an answer, she continues, "Well, nature also made sure our powers are entwined with our ability to bear children with Jinn. Once we stop using our powers to grant wishes, our magic will fade, and eventually that'll be it. We'll be gone."

"Nice blackmail."

"More like insurance."

This really is some messed up species. "But with Zoe? How can you be so sure that wasn't her real wish? Frankly, I'm not sure she goes all that deep."

"Experience." She pushes herself off the couch. "Which you'll learn. But only if you open yourself up to all this. Otherwise, you'll never do this to the full extent of your abilities." She starts walking backward toward the kitchen. "Now about that bet. Since we'll never truly know which one of us is right about Zoe . . ."

As soon as her hand hits the freezer door, I app right next to her. And so we sit at the kitchen table with two spoons and the last piece of cake still in its box. I'm a living cliché, having my cake and eating it too. Because Henry knows, my mother doesn't, and I'm not in a subterranean jail cell. I just wish I could pass on the topping of guilt.

Letting the ice cream on my spoon melt, I say, "How can you be so sure my abilities have a fuller extent?"

"You're my daughter, for one." She winks. "And because I saw what you were able to do with Mrs. Pucher. That's what you're going for, Azra. It means you're accessing your strongest powers. The more closed off you are, the less magic you can access. The more open, the more content, the more—"

"Angry?" Like when I heated up the water in Henry's pool. "Afraid?" Like when I cooled down the water in Henry's pool.

My mother plunges her spoon into the icing-rich back of the cake. "Yes, those emotions work too. But once you fully embrace all this, there's an inner peace that will allow you to fully connect with the human's anima, accomplish the highest levels of magic, perform the most complex spells—"

I steal my own icing-loaded spoonful. "Be the Afrit's poster Jinn?" Or another model Jinn like my mom? "No thanks."

Suddenly, the last bite of cake that was on my spoon is now on my mother's.

"There are other advantages," she says. "Especially when it comes to spells. Magic is for the tangible. But spells are for the intangible. The uses are endless."

She smirks and my mind goes back to the group of teenage boys jabbering away in the movie theater who came down with laryngitis at the same time . . . to the police officer who, despite all the scribbling on his pad after pulling my mother over for speeding, handed her a ticket with nothing but a smiley face on it . . . to the newlywed at the beach who lost her wedding ring, which my mother, who had never seen it and couldn't have conjured it, inexplicably found.

Suddenly I'm both in awe and very scared of my mother.

"Come on."

I've barely crossed the threshold, and Henry's tugging my arm, dragging me into his living room. Tufts of hair flop over his forehead. Even with the glasses, if only his haircut didn't resemble something done by his mother, I can see how he might be called cute.

As he pulls me toward the kitchen, the muscles in my neck throb.

"Wait, Henry." I yank my aching arm free. "We need to talk."

Because I cannot endure another night like last night. My guilt meant I let my mother program our evening. Which means we did yoga. Not the yoga humans have been doing for centuries. My mother has to be trendy. Have conjured hammock, will suspend body from ceiling. For two hours. I hurt in parts of my body I didn't even know had muscles.

"I know, I know," Henry says. "I have so many more questions. I could barely sleep last night."

Me neither. But that's because the second stop on our mother-daughter bonding tour was terrifying. Literally.

Henry stops in front of the door to the basement. "Down here."

I step back. "No way."

My mother loves scary movies. I despise scary movies. Especially ones with stone-faced, creepy kids. Especially ones with Prince of Darkness themes. So what did she make me watch? The trifecta. *Rosemary's Baby, The Omen,* and *The Exorcist.*

I'll be lucky if I sleep again by the time school starts.

Henry glances at my white shorts. "Right, sorry, the dirt." He starts down the stairs. "Listen, no one's home, so why don't you go on up to my room?"

"But Henry, about yesterday—"

"This is about yesterday." His eyes plead with me. "Trust me."

The power in those two words, that's real magic.

Even though it's been more than six years, my feet proceed on autopilot to the second floor of the Carwyns' home. The pile on the carpet treads may be flatter, the paint on the railing may have more chips, but the second-to-last step at the top still creaks in the center. I force myself past Jenny's—now Lisa's—door and enter Henry's room.

Remnants of the Henry I remember, the black-and-white space shuttle poster, the Red Sox bobbleheads, the model AT-AT he painstakingly put together one Christmas, mix with the Henry I'm just getting to know, the guitar in the corner, the map of the world on the wall, the pile of keyboards, monitors, and wires on his desk.

Surveying the room, I try to figure out where I should sit. On his blue-striped comforter? The clothing-strewn floor? The red locker at the end of the bed? Where do I tell Henry I'm going to confess the truth to my mother? Where do I tell him that I have no idea what will happen after that?

Hearing that second-to-last step groan, I head for his desk chair. Stacks of books surround his computer. Software manuals, biology textbooks, and . . . *really*?

"Is this a romance novel?" I wiggle the bare-chested blond hunk tearing at the dark-haired maiden's lace bodice at Henry as he walks through the door.

Not even a tiny bit of pink rushes to his cheeks. "I like to be well-rounded. I read a lot."

I set the paperback down next to a thick book on ancient spirits, which must be how he knew what a Jinn was, and one on . . . witchcraft. "*Seriously, Henry?* A witch?"

"What was I supposed to think? *Seriously, Azra?* A genie?"

I toss the witch book at him, which he catches in one hand despite the box he's carrying in the other.

"What's that?" I ask.

"This is what's going to stop you from saying what you came here to say."

"And how do you know what I came here to say?"

"Because I know you, Azra. I'm more of a rebel than you, and that's saying something. If telling a human about your world is the worst thing a Jinn can do, then my guess is you've been taking a whip to yourself all night. I bet yesterday was like my stay of execution."

"Don't say execution."

His weak smile doesn't mask how anxious he is. "You feel guilty. You're going to tell your mother, that's what you came here to say."

"I have to, Henry. It's—"

"Okay."

"Wait, what?"

"Go ahead and tell her. Just not today."

Standing next to his bed, Henry flips over the dusty box and out falls . . . Jenny. A flower-covered scrapbook, a flutter of photographs, the seal stuffed animal she loved, the Big Bird with the broken neck I used to drag around, and a diary with a yellow lock. A broken yellow lock.

Henry spreads everything out across his mattress. "My mother wanted to throw all this away. She wanted to move, did you know that? After. My dad refused. Still does. That's why things are so . . . messed up right now."

I sit on the end of the bed and run my fingers along Jenny's things. "Because your dad lost his job?" To Henry's surprised look, I add, "Your mom kinda told my mom the other day."

"They did always get along, didn't they?" He pushes his glasses up his nose. "The truth is, he only lost his job because he wouldn't relocate to New York. My dad . . . he couldn't leave this place. My mother's furious with him. Not just because now he can't find another job, but because it was her way out. Out of here. This house, this town . . . I guess sometimes there can be too many memories for one person and not enough for another."

Henry's describing his mother and father but a weight in my chest makes me think he could be talking about my mother and me. About my father, my mother, and me.

"Here," he says. "Read this, and if you still want to tell your mom, I understand."

The diary's cracked open to a page at the end. The entry's dated a few months before Jenny died.

Mrs. Nadira got our favorite ice cream again today. This time, I dug the bag out of the trash before she emptied the can. I was right. It does say Paris. I wrote down the street name: "rue Saint-Louis-en-I'lle." It's not in Missouri. I looked it up. It's actually in Paris. There's something special about Mrs. Nadira. Azra too. One day, when she's ready, she'll tell me. She's my best friend. And best friends share secrets.

I don't read anymore. I can't. I can't see through my tears.

"This doesn't change anything, Henry."

"But it should. All of this should." He lowers his eyes. "Listen, Azra, we all have secrets. We all have inside and outside selves." He kneels next to the bed and sorts through the photographs. "But eventually we need to let someone in. I know you wish it could be Jenny."

He places a photo in my hand. Jenny and me. Linked arm in arm, just like Mina and Farrah. Like Samara and my mother. Probably like Laila and the brunette with the killer bladder.

"You and Jenny would have had so much fun with this," Henry says. "Tell your mother. Just not today."

IT'S BEEN TWO WEEKS SINCE THE ZOE INCIDENT. TWO WEEKS OF HANGING out with my first non-Jinn friend since elementary school. Because that's what Henry is.

Thankfully, my mother was wrong about the crush. Henry and I are friends, normal friends, without jealousy, romance, or being Jinn getting in the way.

I add a blue-glass hurricane lamp to the collection of lanterns on the coffee table. Unlike my birthday party, official Zar gatherings are lit exclusively by candlelight. It's quite beautiful actually. The upcoming reunion, which we're hosting, is as official as they get. Laila will have finally turned sixteen, and my Zar will have its full-fledged initiation.

Even though we have plenty of time, I'm filling all the lanterns we own with oil now, per my mother's request. I've been a very diligent daughter and Jinn lately. It's a wonder my mother doesn't realize something's up.

The key to my new plan for telling her about Henry is time. The longer he knows and she doesn't, the better his track record will be. Keeping our secret for a day? A week? Maybe she can brush that off. But if Henry goes a month, two, six? She won't be able to deny his loyalty.

And I won't risk him being taken from me. So I'll confess, just not today. Call it my Scarlett O'Hara plan. Because, after all, tomorrow is another day.

I top off the final lantern and slip my phone out of my back pocket, scrolling to find the last text from Nate. After he assaulted the concession shack door, he texted to apologize. We've had a few, mostly banal, exchanges since then. His last message is from a day ago.

Greenheads vicious today. Hope gone when U back.

Me too. Luckily my two scheduled days off coincided with the worst of the biting greenhead fly season. Merciless little suckers.

I reply, *"What's the buzz today?"* Then, wondering if that makes any sense, I add, *"Flies?"*

And with that, our texting remains on a second-grade level.

Returning a black, latticework-style lantern to its hook by the front door, I notice Mr. Carwyn leaning against the railing on his front steps, watching Lisa play in the front yard. The suit and tie he's wearing is a good sign—another job interview. But not my doing. To my secret relief, Henry won't let me risk getting into trouble to help.

In private, though, Henry can't get enough of seeing me use my powers. I spent yesterday magically stitching up the holes in his pockets, sprucing up a pair of his weathered loafers, and flattening out the gathered fabric surrounding the crotch on the ugliest pair of khakis I've ever seen. Even I know teenage boys shouldn't wear pleats.

Still, aside from his wardrobe, a perpetually warm pool, and a fire in the old pit in his backyard, the extent of our magical mischief has been so tame it doesn't deserve to be called mischief.

When a minivan pulls up to the house, Mr. Carwyn buckles Lisa inside next to another little girl, sending her off on what must be a playdate. He straightens his tie, climbs into his own small SUV, and backs out of the driveway. Mrs. Carwyn's at work, but I know Henry's home. And this means, now he's home alone. It's time to turn the genie volume up to eleven.

I know just how to start. I'm going to scare the pants off him.

Before I change my mind, I app to Henry's bedroom. Hearing his clomping footsteps, I slink into his closet.

I'm about to launch out from behind his hanging oxfords when Henry appears in a towel. Though he's at the beach almost as often as I am, his fair skin tends to burn. He usually wears one of those long-sleeved rashguard surfer shirts, so I had no idea his upper body was so . . . so . . . *toned.* Without his glasses and with his usually unkempt hair wet and plastered against his skull, he doesn't look anything like my friend Henry.

Droplets of water run off the ends of his hair, sprinkling his shoulders. His hand reaches for the tucked-in corner of the towel, freeing it from his waist.

I should look away.

I don't.

He's drying off his back, and I'm staring at his rounded butt cheeks. This is *Henry,* my *friend* Henry.

Mortified, I try to app home but lack the necessary concentration and only succeed in hopping two steps forward, crashing right into the skis propped in the corner of Henry's closet. He turns, and I squeeze my eyes shut. This is why, when I open them back in the safety of my own bedroom closet, I have no idea if Henry saw me or not. My pulse thumps in my temples as I force the picture of Henry's taut derrière out of my head.

So much for *scaring* the pants off him. As if I'm the one who's been caught naked, I wrestle a pair of jeans off its hanger and pull them on right over my shorts. The pile of sweaters on the shelf tumbles to the floor as I extract a gray cardigan from the center of the stack. I'm nervously braiding my stupidly long hair when I hear Henry's voice.

"Azra? Are you home?"

He's been in my room a zillion times, but suddenly I don't want him to come in here. I give up on the braid, rake my fingers through my hair, and rush out of my room.

Henry's at the bottom of the stairs. I stroll down, trying to act casual. But I can't look him in the eye. As I pass by, I tell him my mom's not here so he knows he can speak freely. I lead him into the living room where I begin putting lanterns back on the bookshelf.

Henry helps, setting a brass lamp on the top shelf. His finger glides across the Russian nesting dolls, floats over the Italian mortar and pestle, and stops at the hand-carved Indian chess set.

"Imports, right?" Henry gives no indication that he caught me spying on him. "That's what your mother supposedly does? How you explain all this cool stuff?"

I utter an affirmative "uh-huh" but keep my back to him as I return another lantern to its original position.

Importing goods from around the world is my mother's cover story. Like most Jinn, she's never actually had a human job. Aside from money not being an issue for Jinn, human jobs, like human friends, risk us becoming too ingrained in this world. They grease up Laila's slip and slide. Most Jinn abstain from both. No surprise I'm one of the few, not one of the many.

Henry sits on the couch across from me. "You'll be able to travel anywhere. Everywhere." He snaps his fingers. "Just like that. You're so lucky."

Henry's right. My mother's ability to apport allowed her to plop us on a beach in Hawaii for the afternoon as the snow piled up at home and whisk me off to that shop on the Île Saint-Louis, the little island in the center of Paris, just to have a cone of the best ice cream (or so she assures me) in the world.

But Henry's also wrong. I think I was twelve when I fully understood that the ability to wake up in my bedroom in Massachusetts and be eating a fresh-from-the-oven pizza in Naples for lunch came with a price tag that wasn't paid in dollars or euros. My mother's souvenirs were a constant reminder that the day I turned sixteen, my desires and choices would be irrelevant. I would be irrelevant. A necessary cog in a wheel whose inner workings I didn't—and still don't—quite understand. That day, I shattered my mother's favorite Chinese vase, swearing I'd never amass such a collection of junk.

Maybe one day I can app to China and find a replacement. If only I could take Henry with me.

He lifts another lantern. It's Mr. Gemp, the kitschy, tarnished-gold, Aladdin-style lamp with the long spout and curved handle that Hana gave me on my birthday.

"Cheeky and bold," he says, "hiding in plain sight. I like it. Better than sneaking around and hiding in closets."

Immediately my face burns. Henry's innocent look doesn't fool me. He caught me spying on him. Even I can't bluff my way out of this one.

"You're being careful with him, right?" my mother asks after Henry leaves.

Suppressing my gasp makes the sound that comes out of my mouth closer to a gargle. Has she discovered our secret?

"I know you two are growing close . . ." she says.

Oh no, it's worse than her finding out about Henry. This is going to be *that* kind of talk.

". . . but you can't slip up and let him catch you using your powers."

Whew. Instantly my relief gives way to guilt.

She tips her head toward the bookshelf. "Thanks for doing the lanterns. Mind if I ask one more favor?"

To ease my conscience, I'd agree to just about anything.

"You'll stay in this refreshingly pleasant mood for dinner? Nadia, Samara, and the girls are coming for dinner."

"Great," I say.

My mother raises an eyebrow. "I invited Mina and Farrah too."

"But not Yasmin?"

"Raina said she had plans."

"Then yes, great."

Skepticism lurks in my mother's smile but she wants to believe.

So do I. Pretty sure we have Henry to thank for that. He was with me when my phone buzzed like a swarm of bees as texts came in from my Zar sisters. They'd added me to a running chain joking about how Farrah could have tried to give that old guy a womb. Henry insisted this was proof that they really did want me to go with them to see Drunken Toad, which turns out to be a pretty decent band. I think he just wants the chance to see them next time—them meaning both the band and my smokin' hot "cousins."

A couple of individual texts with Mina (asking about "the Adonis") and Farrah (asking about my favorite Drunken Toad track) followed, and Hana and I have been e-mailing (mostly about her flash-card strategies but also about my apparently not-short-enough shorts).

My phone dings, and I sneak a peek. Nate: *"Flies not bad. Perfect now for hanging."*

I squeeze the phone in my hand. *Perfect now.* Is that an invitation? Do I have time to accept if it is?

"When's dinner?" I casually ask my mother.

"They'll be here at seven-thirty."

Butterflies kick into gear as I realize the answer to my second question is yes. If only I knew the answer to the first.

Taking the stairs two at a time, I debate texting him back to ask. If it's not an invitation, and I act like it was, my bug-eyed sunglasses won't be enough to hide how mortified I'll be for the rest of the summer. But if it is and I don't reply . . .

I'll just show up. That's it. That way I don't have to ask. If Nate still happens to be there, if I happen to run into him, I'll let him talk first. Life is compromise, right?

I open my sparsely filled jewelry box and let my fingers graze over my *A* pendant. Have I really not worn it since my birthday? Before then, I could count on one hand the number of times it left my neck. Worse than feeling naked without it, I felt like I was missing a limb. I remove my infinity necklace and hook my *A* back around my neck. It no longer calms me the way it used to. In fact, since Nate mentioned it, it seems to have the opposite effect.

After brushing out my hair and putting on some lipstick, I pry open my dresser drawer and eye the red lace thong. I'm feeling bolder than usual, but not bold enough for that.

Leaving the thong where it is, I pull out the bra and finger the delicate lace. I have to admit, Yasmin has excellent conjuring skills. And good taste. I peel off my cardigan and T-shirt, slip on the bra, and top it with a light cotton V-necked sweater. The mirror on the back of my bedroom door shows a curvy version of myself thanks to the push-up bra that I don't want to like but do. It also shows the bright red lace through the thin, white sweater. In an instant, I change the sweater to a deep jade green. Sure, I could have changed the bra to white but then it would no longer match the thong.

Nice try, Azra.

I'm in the hall when Samara's voice spills through my mother's closed bedroom door. "I know I'm early. But Laila's at the mall with some girls from school, and I'm bored."

Sounds about right, boredom being another Jinn trait and all.

"Just in time," my mother says, "I'm trying to finish writing this spell. Want to help?"

"*Pfft,*" Samara says. "Me? What's with the lack of confidence, Kalyssa? That's certainly not the girl I remember. The one who spelled that nice policeman to forget the massive after-prom party that set the house on fire?"

My hand seizes the railing. There's a spell to make someone forget? A spell my mother could use on Henry? A spell I *should* use on Henry? *No, Azra, remember: Scarlett O'Hara plan.* Think about that tomorrow. Which, right now, is easy to do since I'm actually less shocked by the idea that there's a spell to make someone forget than that my mother threw a party. A party that set the house on fire. Is Samara speaking metaphorically?

"Led to my first time conjuring water," Samara says, answering my question. "Ah, one of my top five nights ever."

"That was a long time ago," my mother says. "Powers fade."

"Powers don't fade unless you make them, Kal."

"Not now, Sam."

"What?"

"I'm not in the mood for one of your lectures on how I'm not living up to my duties. If that's why you came early—"

"*I* wasn't going to say anything of the sort," Samara says, feigning innocence. "But since *you've* brought it up . . . just what do you think you're doing with Azra?"

I release my grip on the handrail and inch closer to my mother's door.

"How much have you told her?" Samara asks. "Maybe the rest of the girls aren't ready, but they will be soon. I'm already dropping bread crumbs for Laila. We know Raina told Yasmin long ago. As for Azra, even I can admit she's smarter than the rest of them, mine included, which means she's more likely to get herself into trouble. She needs to know everything."

So I'm not the only Nadira keeping secrets. Maybe hiding Henry isn't my fault. Maybe it's hereditary.

My mother inhales and exhales loudly. "You're right. I

know. She's always been more like you than me. Skeptical, questioning—"

"That used to be you too, Kalyssa."

"Precisely why I want her to have this time. You know how moody and withdrawn she's been the past couple of years. I was hoping, just maybe, she'd have some fun, enjoy it, appreciate the good before learning the bad."

"It doesn't have to be bad," Samara says. "It wasn't for our parents or their parents. It can be that way again."

"I thought we were talking about Azra."

"We are. We're talking about Azra and Laila and all of them. And us. I don't know what it's going to take for you to realize that."

"You think I don't miss the way things used to be as much as the rest of you? But I can't, Sam. I can't lose anything more."

Samara's voice lowers, and even with my ear pressed against the wood, I can't hear what they're saying. Maybe if I crack open the door, just a smidge . . . my hand reaches for the doorknob when all of a sudden a gust of wind rustles my hair.

"Oh my Janna!" Mina's voice calls from behind me. "Is this . . . it is!"

I squeeze my eyes shut and drop my hand to my side. *Opportunity missed.* I turn around to see Mina in a gold sequin crop top and skintight white jeans wiggling my phone.

"The Adonis," she says, one hand slapping her jutted hip. "Azra, you little vixen!"

"Shh," I say, pushing her farther into my bedroom and pulling the door shut behind me.

"What?" asks Farrah, who's wearing a matching silver sequin crop top and black jeggings.

Should have known Farrah would be here too. These two make my mom and Samara look like strangers.

Mina holds up the blurry photo of Nate I snapped while he was on a morning run. She must have backed out of the text message to my contacts.

"The dark-haired boy," she says to Farrah. "He just asked Azra out on a date at the beach." Mina faces me. "The question is, why are you still here?"

Farrah grabs the phone. "Let me see that." She returns to the text. "That's not an invite."

"Sure it is." Mina reclaims the phone. "And I should know."

"Maybe." Farrah snatches it again. "But maybe not."

Before they give me whiplash, I hold up my palm. "Wait." I hesitate. Am I really about to ask them for dating advice? There is no part of that thought that feels possible to me. I take a breath. "So, what do I do?"

"You go," Mina says. "But let him find you."

Farrah fluffs my hair. "And if he's with another girl, find one of those alabaster boys and kiss him on his milky-white lips!"

Another girl? Nate could be *hanging* with another girl? With a group of girls? With his lifeguard buddies? "I-I-I don't know. Maybe I shouldn't—"

"Farrah?" Mina reaches for my elbow.

"Just say when." Farrah latches on to my other wrist.

I back up, which only pulls them forward. "What are you—"

"When," Mina says.

Farrah's long bangs falling across her winking eye is the last thing I see.

Ptah! I lift my head and spit out sand. Tiny grains trickle down my V-neck.

Mina and Farrah apped me to the beach.

I'm lying on my stomach at the unpopulated end, facing the ocean. In front of me, the two of them twiddle their fingers.

"Oh," Mina says, "we came by to say a quick 'hi.' So you knew we weren't lying about wanting to come to dinner."

Farrah gasps, but I laugh. "At least not this time, I say."

"Touché, Sister." Mina gives me a wry smile. "But we do have to decline your mom's invite."

Farrah changes her black headband to silver. "That anemic boy asked us out."

Us?

Mina dabs gloss first on her own, then on Farrah's lips. "And Azra?" she says, puckering. "Zar sisters always kiss and tell. Text us your details and we'll text you ours."

Ours? Really?

They disappear and I make a mental note to delete all incoming texts from Mina.

I prop myself up onto my elbows and wipe my face. My heart's pounding from apping but also from a feeling in my gut that, for once, Farrah was right. Nate wasn't inviting me. I was simply too *invested* to think clearly.

Flopping back down, I lie with my cheek on the sand and listen to the gentle break of the waves. Hypnotized by the sounds of the surf, at first I think Nate crouching down next to me is a mirage.

"Azra?"

But mirages don't speak. Right?

"I was waiting for a text that you were coming," he says. "We must have missed each other at the entrance somehow."

So Nate's text was an invitation. I should have known better than to doubt Mina's well-honed expertise.

I scramble to sit up and discreetly brush grains of sand off my new cleavage, but Nate's too close for me or my new cleavage to be anywhere near discreet.

Looking into his dark caramel eyes, I call on the confidence of my red bra. "Yeah, strange. Must have slipped right by you." I push my hair behind my ears. "Anyway, sorry about not responding. I wasn't sure until the last minute. I've got a family thing tonight."

"Oh, I didn't mean to pull you away."

"You didn't. My family thing is why I'm here and not there."

He laughs. Nate actually laughs at my joke.

"It's getting dark." I realize I have no idea how long I've been here. Mina and Farrah neglected to app my phone along with me, and I never wear a watch.

Nate looks at the darkening sky. "I know people come here for the sun and all, but I love it at night."

And with that, my fleeting worry that I'm late for dinner goes out with the tide because I couldn't agree more. The deserted beach at night, lit only by the moon and the stars . . . magic couldn't do any better.

"Me too." I tilt my head at the rolling surf. "It's like a private screening. All this, just for me."

Nate starts to stand. "And here I am interrupting. Sorry, do you want me to go?"

"No," I say too loudly. "I mean, I think there's maybe one more seat at this showing." I am the definition of looks being deceiving. No matter how sexy the bra and being Jinn may make me, my brain cannot keep up.

Maybe Nate's a fan of corny, because he sits on the sand so close to me that our shoulders touch. He then fills me in on the beach gossip I've missed. Ranger Teddy busted a group of football players from our school who weren't even trying to disguise the beers in their hands. Chelsea, desperate to deepen her tan, refused to put on sunscreen and her body is now as red as her lipstick. A stopped-up toilet overflowed, and the bathroom attendant quit rather than clean it up.

"Oh, and the best part," Nate says as he lays his hand on my knee. Even through the thick denim, his warmth penetrates, flushing my body with a heat ten times stronger than apping.

He arches his back. "I saved someone."

"You . . . you what?" Though not even this can make me forget about his hand on my knee.

"Rescued from the clutches of death," Nate says dramatically. "Okay, well, not exactly, but this guy was swimming really far out and got a wicked cramp." His grin is both self-deprecating and proud. "I reached him before anyone else."

I'm not surprised, which I say before I think maybe I shouldn't. He already knows I've watched him running. I need to be careful not to cross into stalker territory. But Nate's genuinely taken aback. He seems touched by my compliment.

It's gotten late, and though I don't want to, somehow the decision is made to head back.

I sweep the sand off my jeans and bend to pick up my shoes. In a single smooth motion, Nate plucks my sandals off the ground with one hand, rights himself, and slides his other hand into mine.

My body tenses from pinky toe to earlobe. Nate must feel it because he starts to release my hand, but I tighten my grip, interlacing my fingers with his. I savor the lightning bolt jolt that comes as he guides me through the dark, down the long empty beach, and over the dunes.

Before this, the last hand I held was Lisa's. It was wet and sticky. I was desperate to let go. Not the case with Nate. Our fingers are still intertwined when we reach the ranger's office. The first-aid kits are lined up on the table in the center of the room.

Nate stacks the plastic boxes in the metal cabinet. "I was making sure everything was stocked up. No one thinks to replace what they take."

I hand him the last one. "You're into this, aren't you?"

Nate's smile is slight, almost shy. "I'm a medical-show junkie. Always have been."

"You're okay with blood, then?" My mother has healed me so fast my entire life, I'm not even all that comfortable with a blister.

Nate bobs his head. "I think so. If I'm helping somebody, it'd be okay."

"I assume one day I'll be calling you Dr. Nate?"

He laughs softly. "Nah. Sports trainer. Maybe a paramedic. Not a doctor."

"Why not?"

"That's a lot of school. I . . . I don't think people see me that way."

"What way?"

"You know, smart. My guidance counselor talks to me about lacrosse scholarships, not academic ones."

It surprises me that Nate sounds so unsure of himself. Based solely on outside appearances, it would be Henry, not Nate, one would expect to be lacking in the confidence department. But Henry exudes confidence while Nate seems almost insecure.

I hesitate before saying, "I think if you're lucky enough to have control of your destiny, you should take it."

Nate nods, slowly. "You're nothing like I imagined, Azra."

Nate's imagined something about me?

"Yeah, well, I guess Chelsea's not my biggest fan."

"She's just jealous. Practically half the guys in school want to ask you out, but they're too afraid."

Afraid? Want to ask me out? Suddenly I fear Nate's a mirage after all.

"Right, I've got so many dates, I need two calendars," I say sarcastically.

"You really don't know? Your whole aloof thing isn't intentional? Guys have been watching you all year, too scared to approach because of your . . . your vibe. Me, I figured if I kept bugging you to refill my water bottle, maybe eventually I'd break through."

I laugh and shake my head.

"I'm serious." He places a hand on his stomach. "I have never peed so much in my life as I have this summer."

From the "aloof" comment to the image of Nate's bursting bladder, there's so much here I can't wrap my head around. "But I'm not . . . I've never been popular. With the 'in' crowd."

"That's because you don't want to be. But considering how good the summer's been to you, next year, you may not have a choice." Nate touches the ends of my hair, which fall past my shoulders. "I really do like it this way. Especially with your old necklace."

As he touches my *A* his fingertips graze my throat, and again my skin prickles. Who needs to feel calm when the alternative is this?

Nate closes the cabinet and locks the office door. We walk to the bike rack together. And this is where the inevitable lies to Nate begin.

"Oh, I walked," I say.

"But your house must be as far as mine."

I look away so I don't have to lie to his face. "More time away from my family thing. I needed a break."

Though I should app to save time, Nate's adamant that it's too dark for me to walk home alone. I climb onto his handlebars, which naturally he thinks is too dangerous. It's only when I say my mother's expecting me that he secures his helmet on my head and starts pedaling.

The ends of my long hair whipping around my face, Nate's warm breath on my neck, the single beam of the bike's front light revealing only a few feet of the path ahead, I forget anyone might be waiting for me at home.

But no one at home has forgotten me. When Nate and I roll up to the curb in front of my house, two doors open, one across the street from the other.

On one side, out comes my mother, Samara, Nadia, Laila, and Hana. On the other, out comes Henry.

Taking in the five beautiful Jinn heading down the front sidewalk, Nate's jaw drops.

I take off the helmet and hand it to him. "Aunts. And cousins."

"I see the resemblance," Nate says.

Henry stays on his front steps. Nate waves to him.

"Well, there she is," Henry says loudly, looking at my mother. "She's not lost, then."

Oh, but I am. Totally lost.

21

Not even the rain pelting my mother's windshield bothers me. Working at the beach in gloomy weather translates into a long, cold, boring day. But the idea of seeing Nate again supersedes anything Mother Nature could hurl at me. Hurricane, cyclone, tsunami, bring it on.

Illusion or delusion, being with Nate makes me feel less like a Jinn. When this drive ends, I'll get to spend the day shivering in the concession stand, waiting for beachgoers who will not show, pretending I'm nothing but the hot-dog girl.

We arrive at the beach. I pop the door latch, ready to escape the car that traps me as a Jinn, when my mother says, "You and I need to talk."

"Mom," I groan, "I'll be late."

The rain beats against the glass.

"Probably not going to be a rush for fries today," she jokes. She then shifts in her seat to face me. "Listen, I know the transition hasn't been easy, but I need to make sure you're being careful around the humans. Henry, and now Nate—"

"I thought you wanted me to have friends? To go out and do things?"

"I did." She shuts off the car. "I do. But you know how important it is that you bond with your Zar sisters, and since you seem to be getting along better with them, I just thought maybe . . ."

No, no, no. I've done everything she's asked lately. Please don't let her ask this of me.

"Mom," I say softly. I owe her the truth. "You don't have to worry." Part, not whole, but still the truth.

Past her head, a dripping-wet Nate stops his bicycle next to her side of the car.

He taps the glass, and she looks at him, her lips curling. "Oh, but I think I do. Those arms. I swear it's like that boy's been granted a wish."

"Mom!" My cheeks burn, but at least this ends our conversation.

"Ms. Nadira," Nate says, as she lowers the window, "I wanted to apologize for last night. If Azra was gone for too long, it's my fault. I hope her aunts and cousins forgive me." He issues a shy grin. "Azra's just so easy to talk to."

My mother covers her snort with a fake cough. "That's my Azra. Little chatterbox, isn't that right, honey?"

I grit my teeth. "Thanks for the ride, Mom."

As I walk beside Nate to the bike rack, a cold raindrop finds the opening at the back of my sweatshirt and rolls down my spine. I don't even mind.

"Watch that," Nate says, gently pulling my elbow.

I narrowly avoid sloshing through a huge puddle.

"It's going to be messy today," he says.

Those are the words in my head when Henry shows up a few hours later.

Clouds linger, but the rain has stopped. Mothers stuck inside all day with rambunctious toddlers pour onto the beach, desperate to run off their children's energy.

Having come without their parents, Henry and Lisa arrive via the town shuttle.

I slip Lisa an ice pop, and Henry and I quietly watch it drip down her hands. He uses the napkins I give him to clean her off.

"Thanks," he says, finally.

"Sure," I reply.

Awkward.

Feeling like I need to apologize for coming home with Nate, I begin, "About last night—"

"Forget it," he says, not letting me finish.

Flashing through my head is the thought that he doesn't want me to finish.

"I'm just glad you're okay," he says. "Your mom figured you were at my house and when you weren't . . . well, guess she got worried."

Popping into my mind are the words "so did I," but he doesn't actually say them.

My Nate guilt gnaws at me as I flag Zoe to pantomime that I'm taking a break. She's watching another basketball training video on her phone with, thanks to my repeated insistence, her earbuds in.

Henry and I sit on opposite sides of a picnic table in front of the snack bar. I clear my throat and gesture toward Zoe. "Last week, she beat her brother in a one-for-one game."

Henry shakes his head. "One-*on*-one."

I knew that. "Right, anyway, she's convinced she willed herself to be taller. She has me marking her height against the wall three times a week."

Henry laughs. "And is she going to be called a miracle?"

"Thankfully no. The changes are too small for me to measure. And even if they weren't, I'd pretend."

Now running through my mind are the words "something you excel at," but, again, he doesn't actually say them. Still, it must be the way he won't look me in the eye that convinces me he's thinking them. And this is why I feel like I owe him an apology.

Lisa interrupts before I figure out whether or not to give him one. "I'm bored," she says. The children she had been playing with at the edge of the dunes were corralled down to the beach by their mother. "Let's swim."

Without the warmth from the sun, the usually nippy ocean may very well trigger frostbite. Of course Henry still says, "Sure."

As I walk them to the wooden path, I brush my shoulder against Henry's. I need him to know how important his friendship is to me. "If I had a brother, I'd want him to be just like you."

He stiffens and then relaxes so fast I almost think I imagine the sad look in his eyes. Almost.

"We Carwyns aim to please." He twirls his hand and bows. "My lady, if there is anything else you desire—"

Following his lead, I curtsy. "Thank you, kind Sir."

This momentarily distracts Lisa from her desire to swim, but after she mimics me with a few dips to the sand of her own, she tugs Henry's hand and says, "Let's go!"

They're only two steps down the path when Henry turns back

around. He then lets me know that, whatever may or may not have been running through his mind earlier, we're okay. "S'mores at the fire pit after work?"

On my way back to the concession stand, I notice Chelsea off to the side. I hope she's been watching—and listening. I hope she heard Lisa talk without any trace of a stutter. I wave so obviously that Chelsea's forced to acknowledge me.

After my shift ends, I go down to the beach to find Henry and Lisa. Since my mom's picking me up, they can hitch a ride.

Despite the crowds, I have no trouble finding them. Because they're with Chelsea, who's perched on top of the white lifeguard chair like a queen on a throne. By her side is Lisa, cupping her hand and offering a royal wave to the entire beach.

I run to the chair. Henry's at the bottom, laughing.

"She's not supposed to be up there," I say, out of breath.

Henry frowns. "It's just for a minute. And since when are you such a stickler for the rules?"

His reference to me breaking the Afrit's rules doesn't deter me. "But it's not just Chelsea who will get in trouble."

"Wild guess," Henry says. "The mighty Nate's the head honcho who will also get a slap on the wrist?"

Not exactly the head honcho. Nate's the lead lifeguard. But I don't think Henry really cares about the distinction, so I simply nod.

"Azra, I'm a princess!" Lisa shouts, drawing even more attention to herself.

My eyes plead with Henry. He rolls his own in response, but he gets her down. "Come on, Lisa. Azra wants you to practice your curtsying again."

While I chase Lisa up and down the beach, Henry stays behind. With Chelsea. Chelsea, who leans her tiny, bikini-clad body against the bottom of the lifeguard chair and swings the red rope of her whistle as if she were posing for the cover of a swimsuit issue. When Henry laughs, I can't fathom what Chelsea could have possibly said to elicit such a reaction. That a half-naked girl doesn't have to say much to cause a teenage boy to be enraptured crosses my mind. But Henry's too smart to be taken in simply by Chelsea's assets.

I check my watch and am more relieved than I have a right to be when I see it's five minutes past my mom's pickup time. Lisa sprints ahead of me toward Henry.

As I follow her, Nate sidles up next to me. "Turned out not to be so bad of a day after all."

This, like so much else in my life at the moment, I have conflicting feelings about.

The four of us stand at the lifeguard chair. Chelsea who's looking at me who's looking at Henry who's looking at Nate who's looking at me.

"My mom's probably here if you want a ride," I say, desperate to break up the awkward gathering.

As we leave the beach, Henry and I trail behind Lisa. He then turns, waving to Chelsea.

Seriously?

Before we cross over the dunes I steal a last glance at Chelsea. Her back is arched and she's laughing. I'm convinced she knows I'm watching when she lands a teasing slap on Nate's stomach.

In my head, the satisfaction of telling Henry how Chelsea

mocked Lisa battles against the fear that it would hurt him too much. But it's not even a fair fight. If I've learned anything from what I did to Laila it is this: from this moment on, not hurting my family will always come first. And without a doubt, Henry is now my family.

22

It is happening. My first assignment arrives, sealed inside a gold envelope with my name embossed in an ornate script across the front.

Azra Nadira.

It doesn't fall from the sky or anything, just from my mother's hand.

My bowl of chocolaty cereal no longer holds my interest. The soggy mess and I stare at each other for so long, my mother gets fed up.

"Oh, come on, Azra. Just open the damn thing."

The lightness of the envelope belies what's inside. I wedge my nail in the small gap at the corner. Sliding my finger across, I jerk my hand back. Paper cut. Apropos. I stick my finger in my mouth, sucking the blood. Who cares what Henry thinks? Vampires would be a cool supernatural being. Grass is always greener, right?

I nudge the textured linen note card out of the envelope and read the gold lettering. Anne Wood. My first candidate is a woman.

The only other information this paper gives me is her address. As expected, she lives right here in town.

I dump my soggy cereal in the trash. "So, want to come along for the ride?" I'm only half joking.

"You know I can't. No one can. You're supposed to be fully trained and able to do this yourself." My mother's model Jinn answer is accompanied by a glint of worry in her eyes. Especially as she adds, "Which, you are." She takes the paper out of my hand and her body relaxes. "Or you will be by the time you need to do this. You have a week."

She lays the card facedown. On the back, in between two squiggly lines is a 7.

"That's how long you have before you need to grant Ms. Wood's wish."

As my mother pours me a new bowl of cereal, she launches into her Jinn lecture of the day: research.

In this, I'm lucky. The Internet affords Jinn of my generation a huge technological jump on how our ancestors performed this least glamorous part of the wish-granting ritual. Even during my mother's genie days, recon had all the hallmarks of some cheesy movie. Jinn would shadow their candidates like a detective trailing some rich woman's cheating husband, camera hidden inside a trench coat, binoculars at the ready.

I now understand how proficiency in mind-reading might be a desired skill. The more a Jinn can read their victim's—*er*, candidate's—mind, the less external prep work required.

Learning about the wishee through a combination of research and mind-reading helps us craft the right wish the right way, most importantly, the way it won't wind up on the evening news.

Whatever genie was responsible for the building of the Great Sphinx of Giza or the Roman Colosseum certainly didn't have to worry about paparazzi, twenty-four-hour news cycles, and conspiracy bloggers.

I go through the day feeling like I have an itch on my insides that I have no possible way of scratching. I even texted Hana, Mina, and Farrah to ask their advice. Well, I *wrote* texts to Hana, Mina, and Farrah. Knowing my butterflies would get back to Yasmin, the only text I actually sent was to Henry.

Which turned out to be a huge mistake.

"World peace?" My phone dings with another message from him.

He's been quizzing me all day on potential wishes. Thinks he's hilarious.

I slide my laptop onto the bed, taking a break from my barely started cyberstalking of Ms. Wood to reply,

Trick. Make her feel the current state of the world is perfectly peaceful as it is.

Cheater. Sure I can't come? Love to see you do real magic.

Real magic? As opposed to . . .

How those spiffy loafers working for ya?

That's baby stuff.

You try it.

*I **wish**.*

LOL.

When's big day?

One week.

'K. Grams giving me evil eye. H out.

He's out to dinner with his visiting grandparents and still he's texting me? I delete all the incriminating messages and toss the phone on my bed. Baby stuff. Hardly. Then again, world peace? What the hell *would* I do with that? I rub my hands to warm them. What if he's right? What if everything up until now *has* been baby stuff?

I close my laptop. Maybe I'd better flip through the cantamen instead. I search my room, but the book's nowhere to be found.

Right. My mother said she was working on a spell. I cross the hall and enter her bedroom where I easily find the codex on her nightstand. When I pick it up, a stack of travel magazines falls to the floor. Along with something else. Staring up at me from in between the pages of an issue on desert oases is a small, red leather book with one word written across the front.

DIARY.

Five block letters centered on the cover saying so little and yet so much. Instinctually, my eyes flicker across the room. My mother's downstairs "reading," which means she's probably fast asleep. Using my powers, I shut and lock her bedroom door.

Clutching the diary to my chest, I pace in front of the bed. A simple snap keeps the journal closed. No lock needs picking for me to invade my mother's privacy.

My hand rests on top, as if I could absorb her thoughts by osmosis. I can't. I tell myself I don't have to open it—to which my self replies, *What if she wrote about your father?*

A gentle pop and the snap closure releases. The spine cracks so that I'm somewhere in the middle of the diary, but the page is blank. I thumb forward a few pages. Blank. I move a few pages back. Blank. I go to the very first page. Blank. Flipping through the entire diary, I can't find a single written word.

I slam the book shut. Total rip-off.

Wait, of course. Magic must be concealing the writing. I sit on the end of the bed, open to the beginning, and concentrate. Still blank. I really have no idea what I'm doing, though. If my mother's thoughts are hidden by magic, she probably used a spell. I know nothing about using spells.

I fling the book toward the headboard, and a page falls out. *Great.* Now I damaged the stupid thing. But I didn't. It's not a blank sheet of diary paper. It's a photograph. My mother, younger and just as beautiful, planting a kiss on some guy's cheek. Even though her eyes are closed, she exudes a happiness I've never seen. The dude in the photo, though? Him I think I've seen. In fact, I know it.

In her closet, I find the white linen pants I wore on my birthday. I slide my fingers into the back pocket. It's still there: the picture of my mother and her prom date that I pulled from her old photo album. Holding the two photographs side by side, I confirm the guy whose cheeks are attached to my mother's pursed lips and the guy whose arm is wrapped around my mother's tiny waist are one and the same.

Both my mother and her beau look slightly older in this new photo. I turn it over, searching for a date or a name or any clue as to who he is or why my mother would have a picture of him stashed in a blank diary.

In the corner, surrounded by a tiny heart, are the letters "K+X." That's it. "K" for "Kalyssa," my mother, and "X" for, appropriately enough, "mystery man."

As far back as I can remember, my mother's never gone on a date. She's not a hermit. Though most of her socializing hours have been spent with either Samara or her Zar, she has gone to parties, to the movies, to the occasional dinner with human friends. But not with a man. If a man was involved, he was always part of a larger group.

Though Samara's dated lots of men, it never occurred to me before now that my mother's nonexistent love life was peculiar. Can't blame me, really. No one wants to see their mom making out with some random stranger. I still don't, but knowing how I feel when I'm around Nate, who's not even my boyfriend (cue mixed feelings), it's a bit sad to think my mother hasn't felt that, at least not in my lifetime.

Her soft footsteps don't make much noise as she walks toward the stairs, but sixteen years of listening assures I'm attuned to even her lightest tread. I place the diary and the magazines back on my mother's nightstand, unlock her door, and app across the hall with the cantamen. I leap onto my bed and slip the two photographs inside my pillowcase.

"Come in," I say over my drumming heartbeat in response to her gentle knock.

She sits at the foot of my bed. "Feeling okay, kiddo?"

I nod. I don't know why I lie any more than I know why I don't ask her about the guy in the photographs.

"Well," she says, smoothing out my comforter, "I just wanted to say if you were playing host to a swarm of butterflies, they will eventually find themselves a new home. It gets easier."

So weak is her smile that I doubt she expects me to believe this. I mirror the forced grin right back, and we stay that way, each pretending we aren't aware the other is full not just of butterflies but of bull—

"Night then." She eyes the laptop. "Don't stay up too late doing research. I imagine Ms. Wood will be pretty straightforward."

But she wasn't, at least not in my dreams. All those random potential wish texts from Henry gave me nightmares. Another reason I should have texted my Zar sisters instead of him. Is that karma or hindsight? Probably both.

On the kitchen table is a note from my mother. "*At the beach with Samara.*" She hasn't been all summer. Funny that she waits until my day off to go. Aren't I the one who's supposed to be embarrassed to be seen around her?

I traipse around the house, trying to send the butterflies that are ricocheting off my intestines back into their cocoons. Iced coffee, the latest mermaid book, texting with Laila, binge-watching TV shows with pithy HITs, nothing slows down the flapping wings.

The only thing that will is granting Ms. Anne Wood's wish.

Which is why I grab the note card with her address and settle into the couch with my laptop. Having not really used my mind-reading skills with Zoe or Lisa, I have no idea if they're good enough to rely on. No matter how silly it feels, I need to do some research.

As I flip the paper over to double-check the address, my eye is drawn to the 7.

The 7 that's not a 7.

The 7 that's a 1.

How can it be a 1*?* I could have sworn it was a 7. My mother even said I had a week. But I don't have a week. I have a day.

I check the time on my computer. Scratch that. I don't have a day. If 1 means twenty-four hours, I have exactly forty-five minutes.

I have no time to do external research. *Mind-reading, it's all on you.*

The panic I feel inside oozes out of my fingertips, which are slimy and shaking as I pound out a text to my mother, a text that resounds from across the room. She forgot her phone. Again. And Samara doesn't believe in those "smart thingys."

I could app to the beach and find them, but what are they going to do? They can't come with me. They'll see how nervous I am, and all I'll end up doing is ratting myself out. My mom will realize how little studying I've been doing all summer. Gone will be days off ogling Nate at the beach. No more evenings around Henry's fire pit. And I can hang up my beige work polos for good.

I grab my mother's phone and erase my message. Pausing, I then pick up my own and text Henry: *"I have to do it today."*

He's spending the day with his grandparents before they return to New Hampshire.

"But you haven't done much research," he replies.

Why do I tell him so much? *"It has to be enough,"* I text back. Though I add, *"I'm ready"* so he won't worry, I can't help but feel mildly betrayed when he simply replies, *"Good luck."*

My first, second, and third attempts at apporting fail. I'm so rattled, the only thing I can do is hop on my fancy bike and pedal until my thighs burn.

I've granted three wishes. I've granted three wishes. Like a mantra this plays on a loop in my mind as I ride. By the time I turn down Ms. Wood's street, my head is clearer. I circle the block, again and again, letting the sun and the wind calm my nerves.

The Afrit wouldn't give me an assignment—an assignment to do in *one* day—if they didn't think I could. And the clincher, if her wish proves to be more complicated, is that I have twenty-four hours before the circulus curse kicks in. I'll be ready by then.

One last lap around the block and I stash my bike behind Ms. Wood's hydrangeas. I stride up to the door, hoping to exude much more confidence than I feel as I rap my knuckles against the door.

A muffled sneeze makes me flinch. But the door hasn't opened yet. I'm peering through the front window when a second, louder sneeze comes from . . . from the arborvitae at the front corner of the house. The arborvitae at the front corner of the house wearing shiny loafers.

He didn't. Please tell me he didn't.

I slowly swing my head.

He did.

HENRY. CAMOUFLAGED BEHIND THE GROUP OF TREES BORDERING Ms. Anne Wood's house. He must have followed me.

He pokes his head past the arborvitae, and I glare at his dimpled, sheepish smile.

My knock takes so long to elicit a response, I'm cruelly teased by the initial relief that washes over me when I think Ms. Anne Wood is not home.

But she is. Too pale, a messy bundle of dark hair piled atop her head, bags under her vacant eyes, Ms. Wood cracks open the door and stares at me.

"Is anyone else home?" I ask.

Despite me being a complete stranger, the frazzled Ms. Wood shakes her head.

Perfect. Needing as much time as possible to read Ms. Wood's thoughts, I launch right into the wish-granting ritual.

The arborvitae to my right sneezes a third time, but I remain focused. Either my mind-reading skills have progressed or Ms. Wood's a particularly open human.

I'm so tired I can't see straight. What I wouldn't give to sit on a beach for two weeks with nothing but a bag of books and an endless supply of piña coladas. I'm not even working. Would be the perfect time to go to a tropical paradise—

That's her wish? Easy enough. I'll arrange for her to win a bogus contest, get her plane tickets to Hawaii and a paid-in-full hotel room, and she'll be all set. Might take me a few days, but that's expected—that's the responsible way to grant wishes.

I won a contest? I won a contest!

What? Ms. Wood hasn't uttered a word since her frazzled "Yes?" upon answering the door. I check Henry's position, but he hasn't moved—or spoken.

I'll be in a hotel room. On the beach. All expenses paid. Ahh . . .

I'm still in her head. In her thoughts. But wait, aren't those my thoughts? Am I actually giving her my thoughts? *No way.* The mind control I sought to erase Henry's knowledge of me being a genie does exist? And I can do it? Only during wish-granting rituals or all the time? *Please, please, let it be all the time.*

Ms. Wood remains in front of me in her trance-like state. Why not test this new power now? She mentioned not working. I check her ring finger. Bare. Good, not married. If she has a boyfriend, she can call him from her tropical paradise and tell him to come join her.

Going further into her thoughts, I discover she's been so busy lately, her friends and family have barely heard from her in weeks. A sudden vacation wouldn't seem so sudden to them. So, really, there's no reason not to send her today. Who needs the paraphernalia of a bogus contest for cover when I can simply implant the idea in her head and park her on a beach this afternoon? I have yet to apport a human, but it's supposed to be the same as apporting a Jinn.

My mind instructs Ms. Wood to pack a bag, and she's up the stairs before I know it.

It's working.

Henry peeks out from behind the tree, but I shoo him away. I can't have my concentration broken.

When Ms. Wood returns, I inspect her suitcase. She's a neat, efficient packer. Clothes, toiletries, books, cell phone, even some snacks in little plastic baggies. Excellent. I grab her arm, and we're gone.

By the time I return from Hawaii, Henry's lying on Ms. Wood's couch, watching TV and drinking a beer.

I swipe the bottle from his hand. "What are you doing?"

"Relax, it's only my first. And they were so far back in the fridge, I'm pretty sure she'll never miss them. Guest beers, most likely. I figured you could replace them."

"I wasn't talking about the beer. I was talking about following me. Though you shouldn't have done either one."

"Like your text wasn't a thinly veiled invite."

A what? "No it wasn't!" *Was it?* "Even if it was, *which it wasn't,* why are you inside the house? What if someone came home?"

Henry scoffs. "Please, like I didn't do recon?" He points to a stack of self-help dating books on the side table. "Between those and the one car in the garage, pretty sure she's single." He nods to a pile of tiny clothes half folded in a laundry basket and tosses in the plastic doll sitting next to him. "And considering the amount of clothes she's got for this creepy thing, she'll stay that way. Besides, you were gone a really long time. What was I supposed to do?"

Henry swings his legs to the floor, making room for me to sit. He holds out his arms, which are red and splotchy. "And I'm pretty sure I'm allergic to those shrubs."

"Arborvitaes."

Eyebrows raised, fear in his voice, Henry says, "Is that dangerous?"

I roll my eyes. "The trees, you doofus."

Making sure I can conjure replicas first, I let Henry open one more beer and agree we can stay long enough for him to finish it. He's apparently "stressed," which makes me laugh. I just granted my first official wish and he's the one stressed? He passes me the bottle, but one sip is enough for me to discover that beer is not to my liking.

He turns on the stereo, and I can't help cringing as he pops his hips up and down. I may be a shy dancer, but I'm better than Henry. Not that he cares. He's almost two beers in and grooving like he's got something to prove. What and to who, I'm not sure.

"Not too loud," I say, regretting my decision to let him open that second bottle. At least I stopped him from eating the box of Goldfish crackers he found in the kitchen. "And less dancing, or whatever that is you're doing, and more chugging. Finish up so we can get out of here."

He taps his foot nowhere close to in time with the music and takes a swig as I tell him first about the mistaken 7 and then how I granted Ms. Wood's wish.

"You apped all the way to Hawaii?" Henry says after I finish. "Nice work, Azra."

Huh, I guess it was. That's the farthest I've apped, though it was probably so easy because I've been there already.

"That's not even the best part." My adrenaline soars as I describe the mind control.

Once his shock wears off, Henry plunks his empty beer bottle on the coffee table. "Now that's the kind of magic I was talking about."

As he begins to plot all the ways we can take advantage of this in the upcoming school year, I rein him in. "Don't get your hopes up. I couldn't get it to work on the woman at the hotel." I then relay what took me so long.

It wasn't until I'd apped Ms. Wood to her tropical paradise that I realized there were more details to iron out than just convincing her she'd won a contest, spent fifteen hours on a plane, and could now enjoy her vacation.

Having not thought things through, I had to use my mom's credit card to secure her a room, book her a return flight, and leave her with enough spending money. I had to bribe the woman at the front desk to add a note in the reservation system: All employees dealing with Ms. Wood must go along with any comments she may make about having won this all-expenses-paid trip. I pretended I was her niece and my mom was treating her but wanted to remain anonymous. It was not an easy sell. I stayed long enough to tie up all the loose ends and then watch the exhausted Ms. Wood curl up on a lounge chair at the side of the pool and fall asleep.

Sitting in Ms. Wood's living room now, my rush from testing out the mind control fading, I know I shouldn't have let my excitement usher me into granting her wish so quickly.

Henry turns up the music. "I love this song."

He's bobbing his head, and I'm running through things, making sure I've covered all my bases. Can't hurt to do some after-the-fact research. My snooping starts in the hall closet. I'm pushing coats aside when I hear a faint noise I can't identify. I shut the music off from across the room, causing Henry to whine. Like a baby. *Please.*

As I fumble for the light switch, my hand lands on the vacuum handle. More crying. Wailing, actually. What's wrong with him? I turn toward Henry. His mouth hangs open, but he's not making a sound. The crying isn't coming from him. It's coming from upstairs. And that handle I'm grasping? It doesn't belong to a vacuum. It belongs to a stroller.

"Oh, shi—" Henry starts, but I'm already taking the stairs two at a time.

I come to such an abrupt halt on the landing that Henry barrels right into me. Through the open door directly across from where we stand lies the source of the crying—lying, literally, in a white wooden crib.

No, no, no, no, no, noooooooo!

Ms. Wood didn't have a single thought about a baby.

The truth nags at me: I didn't let Ms. Wood have a single thought about a baby.

But Ms. Wood wished to go to a tropical paradise.

Nag, nag, nag: Ms. Wood never actually used the word "wish," which she's supposed to do.

But Ms. Wood didn't give any indication of living with someone else.

Nag, nag, nag: the Goldfish crackers, the "doll" clothes, the snacks packed in little baggies, the bags under Ms. Wood's eyes, the messy hair, the being too pale, the frazzled hello.

"Um, Az, what now?" Henry says from behind me.

My feet won't budge. The baby's shrieking prevents me from being able to think. All I want to do is app myself home and forget this ever happened. All of it. Everything. This is why I've dreaded this moment my entire life. Because this, this howling child, is the perfect symbol of what being Jinn is really like. It's not heating up swimming pools, it's not making backyard fires, it's not fun with mind control. It's being responsible for people's lives. It's making colossal mistakes that *ruin* people's lives.

Gently but firmly pushing me aside, Henry enters the room. "Shh, it's okay, little one," he says to the baby in a soft, comforting voice. Lifting it—her, as the PJs with pink flowers on them reveal—from the crib, he rocks her tenderly and, despite his two beers, carefully. "Everything's going to be just fine. Isn't it, Azra? Azra?"

My instinct was to app us away. Henry's instinct was to console the little girl. Maybe it's a good thing my life as a Jinn won't afford me a normal family and friends. Clearly, I am anything but normal.

"Now," Henry says, his voice still dripping with warmth, "if Auntie Azra can move her tush and go retrieve your mommy from her probably much-needed but poorly timed getaway, all will be right with the world."

Duh. Henry's not a Jinn, his brain's muddled by alcohol, and still he's more rational than I am. Because he's less afraid. Samara was right about me being more likely to get myself into trouble than the others.

"Anytime now," Henry says.

Though the baby has quieted down, I ask with a trembling voice, "You'll be okay here, alone?"

"This is not my first rodeo. Lisa was a screamer. Me, I'm a light sleeper, unlike my parents."

Henry's love and protectiveness of his sister goes back to when she was this little. Lucky kid.

"Now, *go*," he instructs.

"Right." I desperately want Henry to come with me, to calm me like he's calming the little girl. What if my mind control was a fluke? How do I stop Ms. Wood from freaking out? Calling the police?

Stop it, Azra. You have to do this. Yourself.

Or not.

Before I can depart the nursery, my mother appears, hair dripping, beach cover-up sticking to her wet bathing suit, feet caked with sand.

"Mom!" I cry, way too distracted to have had a shot at sensing her imminent arrival.

Her already furrowed brow and tense lips chisel deeper grooves into her face when she sees Henry. "Oh, Azra, how could—"

"I can explain. Henry's just . . . But how did you . . . ? Why are you . . . ?"

My mother violently shakes her head. "We don't have time." She expertly extracts the baby from Henry's arms, whispers to the little girl, and settles her into the crib without waking her. In a controlled but insistent voice, she says, "Now, Henry, I trust you can get home yourself?"

Tentatively nodding, Henry's even more shocked and speechless when Samara, wearing a string bikini top and a full-length sarong around her waist, materializes in the doorway.

"Oh, Azra, how could—" Samara says when she sees Henry.

"No time, Sam." My mother cuts her off. "Henry's leaving. *Now.*"

"But he's helping me, Mom. I've . . . I've got this under control."

The sleeping baby must be the only thing keeping my mother's voice at a reasonable volume. "Control, Azra, really? You have no idea how out of control this is about to become." She glares at Henry. "And you're not moving, why?"

Cheeks flushed, Henry mumbles a "Sorry" and squeezes past Samara, whose serious face is so out of character, it's almost what scares me the most.

With Henry gone, my mother ushers Samara and I into the hall, pulling the nursery door halfway closed behind her. She turns to Samara. "How long?"

"Minutes, a half hour at most," Samara says.

After a deep breath, my mother takes charge. "Azra, tell me exactly what you did and how you did it. As abridged as you can make it."

Swallowing my million questions as to how she knew I was doing this, why we have so little time, and what happens if we run out, I offer the abbreviated version of how I screwed up granting Ms. Anne Wood's wish. "I'd never have taken her there if I knew about the baby."

"But you didn't know because you didn't do any research, did you?" If she were a snake, she'd be spitting venom. "No mother's anima would have allowed her to leave her child. Did you even bother to enter her psyche?" My mother briefly closes her eyes. "Later. Let's move on. What I don't understand is how you got her to Hawaii without her questioning it. Oh, please, no, don't tell me you're now just announcing to the world that you're a genie?"

"No, no, of course, not. Henry was a mistake. I—"

"Not now," she interrupts. "Oddly enough, that's the least of our concerns at the moment. Tell me about the candidate."

"Well, I was going to do it the right way, I was going to fake a contest and everything, but when the mind control started working, I just kind of went with it."

Samara backs up and leans against the wall. "Mind control? Azra, you mean reading her mind?"

"No," I say, "well, yes, I was reading her mind, and then, all of a sudden, she was thinking what I was thinking. I figured it was a way to get her to accept the contest without having to actually make up a contest. Why didn't you guys ever tell me about being able to do that? It's so much easier. I don't get why we wouldn't always grant wishes that way."

My mother's clearly ticked off. "Since when have you been studying spells?"

"Spells? I haven't. Not a one."

My mother's and Samara's moods shift into such an alarmed state, I expect the baby to feel the tension and begin wailing again. Fear consumes their eyes as the two evaluate each other.

Gently, my mother says, "But Jinn can't control people's thoughts, Azra, not without spells. How . . . how did you do it?"

I shrug. "It just kinda happened. But I'll fix it. I was about to go get her back when you guys showed up."

Silent for longer than I think is a good idea if the Afrit's hit-man or whoever is about to make an appearance, my mother finally speaks. "Mind control requires more power than Jinn are capable of. Even using spells, it's not something most Jinn can do."

Samara nods. "The Afrit can do it. It's coveted by Jinn but—"

"But feared," my mother quickly finishes. "Mind control is not something to be used casually. Azra, it's not something you should use at all. Ever. It's dark. It's dangerous. The risks . . . the consequences . . . I can't stress enough how you mustn't tell anyone about this. Not Laila. Not anyone."

I stare at my feet. "But Henry knows. Though maybe the two beers will make his memory foggy."

"The what? The beers? The *two* beers?" My mother breathes long and hard through her nose. She rubs her temples. "Another item for the long list of things we need to discuss. But for now, just promise me you won't tell him anything more and you won't try it again. *Please, Azra.*"

I'm nodding so hard I'm dizzy. Her tone, her face . . . she's scaring me. A lot. I've lost my desire to use mind control ever again. But . . . wait . . . don't I have to do it again?

"What about Ms. Wood?"

"I'll do it." My mother enters the baby's room and returns to the hall with the little girl in her arms. "Tell me where your candidate is, and I'll bring her home, hopefully before they find her."

"Who?" I ask, frustrated. "Before who finds her? What's going on?"

"Samara, take Azra home. Stay with her. Make sure . . . just stay with her."

Samara wraps her arm around my waist. "Of course."

"But," I say, "don't you need me to get into Ms. Wood's head?"

"Kalyssa's got this," Samara says hesitantly, directing her statement to my mother.

"Yes, yes." My mother's large, emerald signet ring gets snagged in her hair as she gathers it into a bun. She extracts the jeweled ring along with several hairs from her head.

"Don't worry, Kalyssa," Samara says. "You can do this."

My mother kisses my cheek. "I know. I have to. Now, go."

The tight squeeze on my hand convinces me I have to stay and help, but before my mouth opens, she's gone. And then so are we.

24

My butt cheeks are numb from the amount of time I've been sitting in the wooden chair at the kitchen table waiting for my mother to return. When we first got back, there was a note addressed to "Kalyssa" affixed to the refrigerator door. Samara snatched it, read it, and tucked it into the pocket of the shirt she conjured for herself. She won't tell me what it says or who it's from. Her feet do the running her mouth usually does as she paces the kitchen.

Her nerves beget my nerves. Unable to stand it, I ask for the third time why we had to leave so quickly. As before, she refuses to look me in the eye let alone answer.

"At least tell me what you were both so afraid of," I say.

This stops her, right in front of the stove, where she attempts to cover her reaction by filling a teapot with water and lighting the burner.

My mother, still in her swimsuit cover-up, pops into the doorway. "Not what," she says, answering me, "who."

Samara rushes to embrace her. Whispers too low for me to hear are exchanged, followed by a soft moan from Samara. She pecks my mother's cheek, her hands holding the sides of my mother's head almost as if she's the only thing keeping her upright.

Finally, my mother settles into the chair next to me and says, "The Afrit."

Clasping my hand around my silver bangle, I whisper, "Did they . . . ? Were they somehow watching me?"

The baby girl, Anne Wood, the mind control, my mother having to fix my mistake, her and Samara finding out about my mistake, about Henry, so many claws dig into my heart at once, but the sharpest one is the thought that something might happen to Henry, that the Afrit might make something happen to Henry.

My mother grabs the leg of my chair and twists the whole thing so I'm facing her. "Henry? That's what you're most concerned about?"

Feeling like it shouldn't be but unable to help it, tears spring to my eyes.

She leans forward and pulls me into her chest. "He's going to be fine."

My body slackens in her arms. "And the baby? Ms. Wood?"

She strokes my hair. "Safe, home, together."

In this moment, I feel nothing but gratitude that my mother is a model Jinn.

When the smell of mint wafts over us, she lets me go. Samara places three mugs of tea on the table.

Enveloping the warm cup with my hands, I take a sip. "Ooh, sweet."

Samara kisses the top of my head. "Is there any other way?"

My mother thanks Samara but doesn't reach for her mug.

Instead, from the side pocket on her cover-up, she extracts a bronze bangle—thicker, shinier, and more deeply carved than either my silver version or her gold one.

Apologizing in a voice weak with sadness, my mother asks for my wrist. She opens the bronze bangle, gently tugs my arm forward, and lowers my hand.

Fascination mingles with fear as the bangle clamps around my wrist and instantly seals any evidence of a hinge, clasp, or seam. The moment the bronze bangle secures itself, the silver one breaks in two and vanishes before either half gets the chance to land in my lap.

My mother slides her mug in front of her. "The answer to your earlier question is 'no.' The Afrit can't watch you the way you're thinking. But they do follow up on every candidate."

Samara sits across from me. "Every assigned candidate. We do the practice ones."

Afraid to move my wrist I ask, "What does follow up mean, exactly?"

"They check in on the human," my mother says. "To make sure a wish was successfully granted and that no undue attention was garnered."

Samara adds, "They can trace the energy of invoking the circulus to your bangle so they know when you grant the wish."

And so they do act fast. Which means, I'm damn lucky that the Zoe Incident occurred with a practice candidate.

My mother glosses over exactly who alerted her to the mess I'd created (and how), simply saying it was someone doing her a favor, someone with both our best interests at heart.

Though it was too late to hide what I'd done, my mother's goal of intervening was to fix my screwup before the Afrit had to step in and do so themselves. She figured this might lessen my punishment. Maybe it did and maybe it didn't. All she knows is that by the time she successfully returned Ms. Wood to her home, using a spell to leave my wish candidate thinking she'd spent the afternoon having a vivid and bizarre dream, the bronze bangle was waiting for her, well, waiting for her to bring to me. She found it in the baby's crib. A perverse teething toy.

"This," my mother says, laying her hand on my forearm, "will prevent you from using your powers."

"I . . . I can't do magic anymore?" Faced with what I've hoped for my entire life, my urge to celebrate is tamped down by what I know of the Afrit. And surprisingly, by a twinge of disappointment.

My mother answers, "Yes and no. This will block your magic, except—"

"Except when I'm granting a wish." I tentatively touch the bronze bangle. "They'll let me access my powers for that?" I wedge my hands under my thighs to stop their trembling. "Seriously, I still have to grant wishes after what I did today? Is that . . . wise?"

Samara reaches across the table and gestures for me to do the same. She cocoons the clammy hand I extend with both of her warm ones. "Don't you start doubting your abilities, Azra. Certainly, you can never again do what you did today. It was impulsive. It was wrong. But it was also a mistake, an unintentional mistake. Believe me, when I was your age, I knowingly did worse things that should have earned me one of those."

"But times have changed," my mother says in a strained voice.

"Yes." Samara sighs. "Indeed, they have."

My mother explains that the bronze bangle will release my magic when I utter the words that begin a wish-granting ritual. When I close the ritual, it will send my powers back into hibernation. If it's not a wish I can grant in that moment, then each time I need to draw on my magic to accomplish a portion of the wish, I'm supposed to ask permission by saying *"izza sambat."* We Jinn who prove to be less skilled, who require additional training, who violate the rules forfeit our silver bangles for this amped-up Big Brother bronze number.

Not fair.

Having my magic restricted should mean not granting wishes at all. Like failing a class and being kicked off the football team. Leave it to the Afrit to make it more like every pass, every catch, every tackle is being watched by an elite team of MVPs ready to pounce on the slightest misstep. I'm already perspiring at the thought of performing under such pressure.

Given all that I've done, all that I've lied about, I'm lacking the moral high ground to chastise my mother for not fully explaining what would happen if I botched a wish.

Still my lips flatten into a thin line. "You should have told me."

My mother's eyes widen. "Told you what, Azra?"

I spin the bronze bangle. "About this. About what this would mean."

The last thing I expect is the end-of-the-world look on her face to morph into a smug, I-told-you-so grin.

She leans over and pats me on the head. "Thanks, kiddo." She then holds her empty palm out to Samara. "Pay up."

Samara frowns. "That's not confirmation."

"Fine," my mother replies to Samara. To me, she says, "So you didn't reach that part of the cantamen yet?"

That part? All my bluffing through my mother's random pop quizzes is about to be for naught. "I guess not. I'm . . . I'm taking it kind of slow. Making sure I absorb fully before moving on."

Samara exhales a huge sigh. "Thanks a lot, Azra."

My mother laughs. "Do I know my daughter, or do I know my daughter?" She points at me. "Take that look on her face, right now. Confused, anxious, knowing she's been caught in a lie but not knowing exactly how or which one. Isn't that so, honey?"

"I . . . I don't know," I stammer.

Samara pushes her chair back. "Oh, give it up, Azra. You're cooked. And now I owe your mother the finest bottle of wine in my cellar. A 1906 Bordeaux. Even she can't conjure something that good. All my flirting with that twerp at the fancy rare wines store in Boston for nothing. He was going to put it up for auction. *For auction.* Can you imagine? Some rich blowhard would bid an obscene amount of money and put the damn thing under glass, displaying it like some fossil. Wine like that deserves to be enjoyed."

"Oh, it will be," my mother says.

Samara, trying to prove to my mother that I was taking all this Jinn stuff seriously, claimed that the only way I could be so talented so quickly was by having already read and internalized everything in the cantamen, spells included. My mother assured her I hadn't even cracked the book open.

My own mother bet against me.

Apparently, the explanation of the bronze bangle as the first penalty for not properly granting a wish is on page two. All this time, through every stupid quiz, my mother knew I hadn't been doing squat. And yet she sent me out there to do a wish, on a real candidate, by myself. This is all her fault.

"How could you let me go?" My anger flares. "How could you let me do an assignment if you knew I hadn't prepared? If you knew my success with Mrs. Pucher was just a fluke?"

The screech of her chair against the floor precedes my mother standing over me. "How could *I* let you go? *I,* who had no idea you were embarking on this today? *I,* who would have never let you go if I did? *I,* who saw your very real finesse with Mrs. Pucher but still stressed the importance of research. Of fully linking with the human's psyche? Both of which *you* ignored?"

"But I didn't have time for research." I pull the folded note card out of my pocket and toss it on the table. I flatten it with my hand. When I lift my palm, staring up at me is a 7.

A 7?

My mother taps the paper. "You had six more days. What you mean is you didn't have time for research because you couldn't wait to show Henry your powers in action, isn't that right?"

"No, I . . ." My voice trembles. Did my nerves make me see things that weren't there? No, no, no. It was a 1. I know it was. I could try to explain, but she's never going to believe me. I whack my bangle against the table. "This . . . this . . . sucks." The anger gone from my voice, all that remains is the fear.

"Yes, it does, for all of us. This doesn't just affect you." My mother bends so that her arms fall around my neck and her cheek rests next to mine. She whispers in my ear, "Scared?"

I nod as tears obscure my vision. I'm mourning the loss of my powers but also of my ability to be in denial. This bronze bangle makes the Afrit and their punishments, including tortura cavea, more than a tale my mother told me to make me behave. The Afrit are real. My need to stop behaving like a selfish jerk is real.

"Good," she says. "Because if this were them finding out about Henry rather than a mishandled wish, you'd be gone. No probation. No second chance." She swallows. "So don't forget how this feels—ever." She kisses my wet cheek. "And if it seems like you are, I'll remind you because no matter how hard I may want to, I'll never be able to forget."

She stays that way, her body protectively wrapped around mine, until my shaking subsides.

Samara conjures a tissue and hands it to me. "Don't worry, Azra. They don't know about Henry, so you're still a blunder or two away from your date with the guillotine."

I blow my nose, laugh, and wince all at the same time.

With a wink, Samara says, "Too soon?"

"Way too soon," my mother says despite her weak smile. She rubs her tired eyes. "Tell me, Azra, you haven't let anyone else in on our little secret, have you?"

I assure her I haven't.

After she and Samara study each other, my mother asks Sam, "You're positive they don't know?"

Samara lifts the note that was on our refrigerator out of the pocket of her conjured shirt.

My mother reads it, and her eyes flutter shut. She holds it against her heart. She then locks eyes with Samara. "We could try to make him forget."

Panic sets my heart racing. *She's going to take Henry from me.* She's going to use her spell to make him forget. Or . . . no, she's going to make *me* make him forget.

I roughly shake my head. "I won't do it. I won't use mind control on him."

At my mention of mind control, both my mother and Samara unconsciously touch their foreheads. My mother then says, "No, no, of course not. I told you not to do it again, I'd never ask you to. Not that you can now, anyway."

Right. I forgot. Funny how second nature using magic has become to me.

Leaning over the table, Samara evaluates me. Her lips curl up slightly. "You could though, right? If you weren't wearing that thing? You could do mind control?"

"*Sam*, maybe it's time for you to go. Azra and I still have a lot to talk about."

Samara frowns at my mother. "Hold on, Kalyssa. Making Azra's candidate forget an afternoon is one thing. But we both know using a spell to make a human forget something this big won't be easy. It's not designed for that. Isn't that why Isa never tried it with Larry?"

Larry? A memory comes back to me. A pair of fur-covered hands pinching my cheeks, a gravely voice singing "*Azra-cadabra!*"

"Hairy Larry?" I ask. "Lalla Isa's old boyfriend?"

The fling Farrah's mom had with Hairy Larry lasted longer than any other relationship I know of between one of my mother's Zar sisters and a human. From when I was probably seven until just a couple of years ago.

My mother starts to speak, but Samara cuts her off. "Lalla Isa's old human boyfriend who knew about her." She places her hands on her voluptuous hips. "And us."

The ball of fear in the pit of my stomach begins to unravel.

Relief mixes with a sense of betrayal for what's been drilled into me my entire life. "But what about the whole 'telling a human being is the worst thing a Jinn can do' thing?"

"It is," they both say.

"If the Afrit find out, that's it, Azra," my mother says.

"It really is a life sentence," Samara adds, the two of them playing off each other like a perfectly timed duet.

"It's reckless," my mother says. "It puts us all in jeopardy. Which is why the punishment is so severe."

"And why it's a risk few take," Samara says. As she stands and faces my mother, the dynamics of the conversation seem to shift. Less between them and me and more between the two of them. "Still, Jinn slip, purposely and not. It's happened before, and it's bound to happen again."

My mother purses her lips as she leans against the counter behind her. "Sam's right about the spell. Making someone forget requires a delicate touch."

Samara keeps her eyes focused on my mother. "And it's dangerous. It doesn't even appear in the majority of cantamens. Of the Jinn who do have the spell, most won't ever use it."

"Shouldn't," my mother says.

"Isa wouldn't," Samara says. "She refused. Rightfully so."

So I'm guessing erasing memories of a house-blazing after-prom party is on par with wiping away one afternoon? Were they joking then? Or are they just trying to scare me now so I don't use the spell to, oh, I don't know, make Henry forget he ever met Chelsea?

"But they broke up," I say, deciding not to ask about the party. If I ask, they'll know I eavesdropped, which will make it harder to do again. "How did Lalla Isa know he wouldn't tell?"

Samara's deep laugh reverberates off the cabinets. "The three cars and the mansion in South Beach. Plus, if he opened his mouth she's got that fake video of him with a hooker." Samara looks at me. "He's a state senator. The hooker is your Lalla Jada in disguise but the ruse never went far enough for him to figure that out."

"Blackmail," I say. "Would have thought that'd work the other way around."

My mother shakes her head. "Security, perhaps, not blackmail. Because Sam knows full well the real reason he keeps Isa's secret is because he loved her. He still does."

Samara loops around to my side of the table and lifts me out of the chair. "How long has your little loverboy known?"

"He's not my—" I stop, thinking maybe this, combined with my Scarlett O'Hara plan, will actually help my cause. "Weeks."

"Weeks?" my mother repeats.

Samara nudges my chin upward. "You trust him?"

"As much as I trust you, Lalla Sam." Looking at my mother, I add, "He swore on Lisa's life, Mom."

She tears up as I say this. Samara goes to her, gently wrapping her arm around my mother's shoulder. "Let her have him, Kal. Who knows? Maybe things won't always be this way."

A chill runs through me as Samara hugs me good-bye. I cling to her, waiting for the comfort her apricot-scented embraces always provide to come. But it doesn't. All that's there is the fruity smell.

Apparently, my magic isn't the only thing this bronze contraption can take away.

25

The noxious odor causes my eyes to water. I'm mopping up sewage from an overflowed toilet, humming this new song I just heard on the radio. Even the putrid smell doesn't make me want to return to the stale air of my bedroom that I've been stuck breathing in for the past week.

My mother grounded me, forbidding me from leaving the house for all purposes, including work. Today's my first day back, thanks to Nate. Somehow he made sure I had a job to return to. That they gave my snack bar shifts to the new girl and saddled me with bathroom attendant duties doesn't even matter.

Wringing out the mop, I force back bile. Okay, so it matters a little.

Still, I'm here. Nate's working. Henry said he'd stop by. Even seeing Chelsea can't bother me today.

Back at the desk at the front of the women's restrooms, I strip off my two pairs of gloves and kick off the work boots I borrowed from Ranger Teddy's office. I agreed to clean up the mess, but there was no way I was wading through that cesspool in flip-flops. I text

Henry my locale and stare out the tiny holes in the screen door, waiting for him to arrive.

My mother allowed him a single, brief visit during my imprisonment. She kicked things off by securing his eternal promise to never reveal our secret. Something in the way she muttered under her breath and kneaded her hands when Henry repeated the exact sentence she demanded ("I shall never utter, write, or think a word about the Jinn world in anyone's presence other than a member of the Nadira family.") makes me wonder if she wasn't sealing his vow with some sort of spell.

Even though her decision not to erase Henry's memory came less out of the goodness of her heart and more out of her fear that Sam was right about the spell not being powerful enough, I was grateful. I not only endured but agreed with her lecture on how irresponsible my behavior has been, how the infringement on my freedom is a result of me not taking things seriously, and how I need to be conscious of the fact that my actions have a ripple effect on others.

The last part stung. Seeing that baby all alone, knowing I was the one responsible, confirmed every fear I've ever had about being Jinn. Granting wishes in real life is nothing like in the movies or on TV. These are real people who want real things that I have no real idea how to give them—at least without hurting them, someone else, or, apparently, myself.

Henry's convinced if he hadn't followed me, none of this would've happened. While I have my doubts about that, I'm pretty sure the fact that he blames himself played a role in my mother's decision. As did my renewed dedication to the cantamen.

The codex and I spent the week of my grounding together. We

may not know all of each other's secrets, but we are certainly on a first-name basis.

And, it turns out, a description of the bronze bangle does indeed lie on the second page, but it offers no details beyond what my mother told me. How to get the probation lifted? What kinds of mistakes might ramp me up to the next level of punishment? What that next level might be? Nothing. Despite flipping through the book every day of my grounding, I couldn't find another reference. Figures that my Jinn ancestors would think it was cute not to include an index. There's not even a table of contents. *Isn't that funny?* Um, no. Not at all.

The haphazard way the cantamen is organized means there's no sense in trying to read it as a straight narrative, starting on page one and following sequentially to page whatever (apparently my ancestors also believed page numbers were superfluous). Over the years, newer generations of my Jinn family magically inserted their own pages ahead of those of previous generations, sometimes smack in the middle of a spell or a Jinn's personal history. There's even an entire section in the middle left entirely blank. The thing is less user-friendly than a software manual.

If I didn't think tapping Henry to upgrade the relic to the digital age would send my mother's blood pressure skyrocketing, I'd have asked him. Because studying the cantamen appears to be as worthwhile as my mother said it would be. The nuts and bolts of wishes my family has granted are documented in such detail that if only I didn't have to slog through recipes for sugar cookies and reviews of the best beaches in Mexico, I just might be on my way to becoming a model Jinn (minus the whole exposing us to humans thing).

Nature laughs at the thought, sending a stream of sun through the open restroom window that reflects off my bronze bangle and blinds me. I cover the shiny metal with my hand. If I still had my powers I could have used them to clean up this disgusting mess. That's what I get for being so cocky, so flippant, so superior to all of this. Poetic justice indeed.

I'm more scared than I've admitted to my mother that the Afrit will be evaluating my magic so closely. Before my probation, I'm not sure I believed tortura cavea was real. Now, well, the Afrit not only have my attention but my full benefit of the doubt. The question is, how many chances do I get before they take me away from everyone I care about? My mother. Henry. Lisa. Laila. Samara. My Zar sisters (most of my Zar sisters). And Nate. Don't forget Nate.

Maybe the Afrit should rethink their rules about keeping Jinn separated from our families and discouraging attachments to humans, because the more I gain the more I have to lose.

Afrit, I am humbled. Can you give me my life back? Who would have thought I'd actually be asking for my trusty silver bangle? Or that it would equate to me having a life?

Cheap toilet paper scratches my chin as I retrieve a tall stack from the supply closet and carry it to the long line of stalls. A knock on the screen door makes me pivot, and the rolls tumble to the ground. At least the floor's clean, having been freshly mopped by me.

I'm expecting to see Henry, but it's Nate. Nate with a fresh haircut, a deeper tan, and a sexy smile aimed squarely at me. Score one for absence and fondness.

Weaving my way through the toilet-paper obstacle course, I approach the entrance. I draw upon my learned skill of pretending to disguise the fact that my heart's about to bust through my rib cage. I lean my arm against the doorjamb and stretch out my leg, keeping the screen door open with my courtesy-of-being-Jinn, pre-probationary, perfectly pedicured toes.

"Is your mom okay?" Nate asks.

This is not the reaction I expected. "Um, yeah, I guess."

"Because your aunt seemed pretty freaked out last week. I was coming to say hi when she nearly tackled me, asking me to gather up their beach gear, saying they had no time. That your mom wasn't feeling well. Seemed 911 emergency worthy."

It was. But the sirens were for me, not her. "Oh, that. My aunt has a flair for the dramatic. My mom gets migraines." From me. "Lal—, I mean, Aunt Sam just overreacted. But she's fine. Thanks for asking. And for getting their stuff."

"I dropped it off a few days ago. I was hoping to see you, but your mom said you were grounded. Do anything really good?"

His raised eyebrow and mischievous grin make me glad for the support of the doorway.

"I mean good in a bad way," he adds nervously. "I know you wouldn't get grounded for being good, of course."

Books and covers and judging, Nate's the poster boy for that warning. Outside he's all underwear model but inside he's just as much a self-conscious dork as the rest of us.

"Maybe you could tell me about it over lunch?" Nate's rock-hard forearm that rests against the door frame and his smooth palm that envelops my hand compensate well for his inner geek. "Unless you've got other plans."

"Yes," I say, adrenaline soaring so high I expect to see a syringe sticking out of my chest. "I mean, no, no other plans. I mean . . . lunch sounds nice." I do not cover my inner dork nearly as well.

"Cool. I'll meet you on the beach near my usual chair?"

"Okay. I can grab something from the snack bar for us, if you want."

He squeezes my hand. "Azra, don't you know I'm a gentleman? The guy always picks up the tab on the first date."

Date. First date. As in an expectation of a second.

He smiles. His teeth gleam toothpaste-commercial white.

"I've got it covered. Trust me on this."

On this. On that. On anything.

The vomit on the ramp up to the restrooms is not my problem. I'm on lunch break. I shove the mop in my fill-in's hand as I skip down the planks.

The beach is jam-packed. Being sequestered in my bedroom all week and the restrooms all day, I've got a touch of stranger anxiety.

Knowing Nate likes my hair down, I've taken it out of its usual ponytail and the wind blows the long strands across my face. I tuck as much as I can behind my ears as I scan the area around Nate's lifeguard chair. I see him a bit past it, waving both arms above his head. I kick off my flip-flops and jog toward him. Too eager. I downshift to a casual stroll. Too uninterested. My jerky-paced trot ends at a red blanket and a spread worthy of ten people.

He said "date." I know he did. Was he joking? Is this actually a group thing? I should have known.

"Are we expecting company?" I try not to sound disappointed.

Nate rounds his shoulders. "Guess it is a lot, huh?"

He's blushing. At me.

"I just wasn't sure what you liked," he says.

"Wow," is all I can think to say.

There's a plate of cheese and crackers, rolled cold cuts and sliced bread, a heaping Tupperware of potato salad, a matching one with a green salad, even a container of sushi. Not to mention the pile of chocolate chip cookies and the tower of fudge brownies, which in truth is all he needed for me.

We don't sell any of this at the concession stand. "You brought all this from home?"

Nate kneels on the blanket, pulling plates made from recycled plastic out of his backpack. His sheepish smile forces me to sit rather than risk my knees actually buckling.

"Well," he says, "I knew you were coming back today, and I . . . I wanted to do something special."

That's it, Azra, he likes you, accept it, I hear Samara saying in my head. *Now work it, honey.*

I stretch out my legs and reach for a cookie. "But why?" I ask Nate.

Samara groans at me.

"Because . . ." Nate runs his hand over his newly cropped hair. "Geesh, Azra, this is that vibe I was talking about. You are not easy to read."

I like you, don't you know that? What's it going to take for you to know that?

The cookie gets caught in my throat. These words are not Samara's. They are not mine. They are Nate's.

I choke, unable to swallow. My coughing results in crumbs spewing from my mouth.

Instantly at my side, Nate's ready to do the Heimlich. "Azra, are you okay?"

I hold up a finger and clutch my throat. Nate might not be able to read me, but I can read him. I can read his thoughts. I accept the water bottle he offers me and drink slowly.

How is this happening? Panic overwhelms me. The Afrit. They'll think I'm doing this on purpose. But I'm not, I swear I'm not. I'm not using my powers. How can I? I'm not granting him a wish. How can I be reading his mind?

All this for nothing. Makes sense. She's so super smart. And funny. Of course, she doesn't like me. I was wrong.

"No!" I cry in response to Nate's thoughts before I can stop myself. I clamp my hand over my mouth. How could he not be sure if I liked him? How could he question such a thing? Does he not know how sweet he is? Does his house have no mirrors?

I cover by wiping crumbs off my mouth with the back of my hand. "I mean, no, please, don't do that choking maneuver on me or anything. I'm okay. Just took too big of a bite." I pick up the cookie, nibble the edge, and force myself to swallow. "It's good, really good. Thanks."

"You're welcome." Nate moves hesitantly in front of me. "But take another sip of water, okay?"

Nate lays his hand on my leg. He pats my kneecap and then rubs my lower thigh, gently, reassuringly, like a caring doctor. But I'm not a patient. And his hand *is on my thigh.* We look at each other, and sparks may as well fly.

I feel it. And he feels it. I know because I can still read his mind. "The ability to read human minds outside the wish-granting ritual is rare," my mother had said. How rare is it to be able to read minds when one's powers are blocked? Is my mind-reading not actually tied to my Jinn blood? Am I like a psychic now too or something? The surprises keep on coming. Why do I think this is going to prove to be a problem?

Hot, she is so hot.

When Nate's thoughts travel further than his hand, I close my eyes, not wanting to follow. At least not right now. My face burns so strongly, I expect it to actually shoot out flames. As inexplicably as I entered his mind, I'm out again.

Nate's making me an assorted buffet plate. My pulse races and my hands shake from both the astounding realizations I've just had: *Nate likes me. I can read minds.* The two battle for supremacy.

Henry's at the water's edge. Oh man, wait until he hears about me actually having ESP. My bronze bangle clanks against the green plate Nate's handing me.

On second thought, maybe I shouldn't tell Henry. With me on Jinn probation, it'll only make him worry. Still, it would feel strange not to say anything. He's experienced everything else with me. It's almost like it's not real until he knows.

Then again, my desire to share the second bulletin about Nate is less intense.

Chelsea sprints down the beach, stops behind Henry, and places her hands over his eyes. Making a show of it, Henry fumbles behind him, trying to catch Chelsea's petite body, which wiggles and keeps itself just out of reach. She inches forward, playfully testing him, and Henry nabs her. His long arm sheathes her small waist. His hand slides to her bikini-clad bottom. And cups it.

Henry! That's not my Henry!

Giggling, Chelsea leans into his palm. Henry spins around, picks her up, and dashes into the ocean. He toys with her, pretending to drop her. She shrieks and slaps his chest.

Nate sees me staring at them. "They've been spending a lot of time together this week."

"Uh-huh," I say.

"You guys are neighbors, right?"

"Friends."

"Friends," Nate repeats in a tone that suggests a dozen question marks would follow its written form.

I nod, still watching the couple who appear to be reenacting a cheesy romantic comedy.

"She's not so bad," Nate says. "Chelsea. I know she can come off as a b—"

"Bitch."

"Bit strong, is what I was going to say. But, yeah, I guess 'bitch' isn't that far off. But not to everyone. If she likes you, that is."

The way she hangs on Henry's arm as they walk up the beach seems to indicate Henry is getting a big thumbs-up.

Nate raises his hand and waves to them.

"What are you doing?" I ask.

"We have so much food. And Henry's your friend."

I notice he doesn't say, "And Chelsea's mine."

Henry's smile fades as he gets closer. It's almost like he doesn't want to see me.

"Hello," "Hi," "Hey," and "What's up?" make the rounds before Nate invites Henry and Chelsea to share our lunch. The only good part of them saying yes is that Chelsea adds she can't stay long. Her break's almost over.

The blanket has shrunk with the four of us crowded onto it, likely closer than most of us want to be to one another.

I can't help myself. "I texted you earlier," I say to Henry.

"I know," Henry replies, "I was looking for you."

"Yeah, I can tell."

Chelsea scooches closer to Henry. The look on her face surprises me, more anxious than anything else. Our subsequent painful, banal small talk is mercifully interrupted by two ten-year-old boys who begin to use the empty lifeguard chair as a jungle gym. Chelsea swallows her last piece of sushi. Her third, I think. The only thing she's touched since sitting down. Meanwhile, I've had a turkey sandwich, potato salad, and two brownies.

"Damn," Chelsea says, "I better go deal with that." She checks her watch. "I'm back on the clock anyway."

Nate's on his feet. "I'll help. I've already yelled at those two twice today."

Chelsea looks directly at me. "It was nice to see you, Azra."

I don't think she's ever said my name. I'm waiting for the catch, but all Chelsea does is smile. It's so genuine, I know it's fake.

"Talk to you later, Henry?" she says.

He flirtatiously replies, "Absolutely, my lady."

My lady? Wasn't long ago that Henry referred to me that way. How quickly ladies can be dethroned.

"So," I say when Nate and Chelsea are out of earshot, "what's that all about?"

"I could ask you the same thing," Henry says gruffly.

Holy attitude. Henry can't actually like Chelsea, can he? He can't actually think she's for real? Every brain cell screams for me to warn him against trusting her, but his tone makes me strangle each tiny voice into silence.

"Did I . . . do something?" Chelsea or no Chelsea, I can't risk losing Henry.

Henry's face softens. "No, course not. I'm happy to see you."

"Doesn't seem like it." I don't want to be pouting, but I'm pretty sure I am.

"Oh, Azra, I'm sorry."

"What's wrong?"

"Nothing," he says too quickly.

My skin still crawls from Chelsea's phoniness. I need to know that Henry's not being duped.

"Well, *I'm* worried something might go wrong. Horribly wrong." I gesture to Chelsea. "Are you guys seriously . . . friends?" I don't want to ask if they are more than that.

"She's not so bad," Henry says defensively.

I don't want to (okay, so maybe I do), but now I feel I have no choice but to tell him how Chelsea was making fun of Lisa's stutter. I'm being careful, not indicating how truly awful she was, when Henry cuts me off.

He waves his hand. "Don't bother. She told me."

She what? That seems completely and totally out of character. Unless she's playing him.

Henry continues, "See, she's not as bad as you think. She told me the other day. Lisa wanted to go up on the lifeguard chair again, but I said she couldn't. Chelsea helped avoid a meltdown by giving Lisa her whistle and pretending it was a princess pendant or something. She's into music, did you know that? She's going to be choreographing the cheerleading routines this year. Anyway, after we talked, the next day, Chelsea came right up and apologized."

I'm dumbfounded. I would have bet I'd get my silver bangle back before Chelsea would apologize to anyone. "So you like her, then?"

Henry shifts, sliding next to me so he no longer has to look me in the eye. "I don't know. She's okay."

"But what could you possibly have in common? She's so . . . so . . ."

"Fun? She's fun, Azra. Easy. Uncomplicated."

The opposite of me.

"Oh, okay," I say, trying not to sound hurt.

"Hey, Az, it's just that a lot's going on right now."

I touch my bangle. "I know this makes things different, but we can still hang out. It wasn't just my powers we had in common, you know."

"I know, but it's harder. There's more at stake. I don't want to make you mess up again."

I thought Henry knowing I was a Jinn would make things easier. Maybe there really is something to TMI. Because now he feels solely responsible. And afraid. Afraid I'll get hurt because of him. I know because I am apparently in his head. In his head *again*. That day at the picnic table, the day after he saw me come home with Nate, when I thought I was just being intuitive, I must have been reading his mind. And Mrs. Pucher's sister? It wasn't being in the middle of the ritual that allowed me to hear her thoughts, was it?

"It's not just stuff with you either," Henry says. "My parents. Lisa. A lot's happened since we last talked."

"Like what?"

He shrugs.

"Tell me." I put my hand on his forearm, and he tenses.

No. Because you'll want to try to fix it. And you can't.

"Henry, forget my magic. Just talk to me like you don't know I'm the great, all-powerful Oz. Because I'm not. At least not right now."

Mind-reading aside, of course.

Henry creases his forehead, eyeing me like he knows something's not quite right. My words hit too close to his thoughts. Still, he off-loads everything that's been going on while I've been under house arrest. And before that. Why didn't he tell me sooner? Or had he been trying to? By following me, by saying he was stressed, by having that second beer?

Did me, my magic, and I push his problems to the back burner? Or did he use us as an excuse to push his problems to the back burner?

His voice lowers to a hair above a whisper as he explains his parents have been fighting more than usual lately. Lisa's been upset, acting out.

"She's peeing her bed," Henry says. "She hasn't done that in years."

Of course Henry's the one changing her sheets.

In one long breath, Henry then says, "My mom's sick of having to work two jobs and says my father's exhausted all possibilities for work around here so she wants us to move in with her folks in New Hampshire and rent our house so they can make their mortgage payments again and my father's furious with her, saying he'll never leave and never let strangers sleep in his house."

My heart beats so fast it makes me dizzy. "So you're not going?"

Henry picks at a cuticle. "I don't know. My mom says she's still leaving. She's going to take Lisa and just go without my dad."

"And you?" Henry can't move to New Hampshire. He just can't.

"She says it's my choice. I can stay with my dad or go with her and Lisa."

Breathe, Azra, breathe. "So what are you going to do?"

"I don't know." Henry drops his head into his hands. He rubs his face roughly. When he reemerges, his cheeks and eyes are red. "Because there's only one reason to go and only one reason to stay."

He doesn't have to say it. Even if I couldn't read his thoughts I'd know what both those reasons are. The only reason to go is to be with Lisa. And the only reason to stay is to be with me.

"Stop the moping," Henry says. "It's not a done deal or anything."

It's my day off, and Henry and I are walking to the far end of the beach. We stroll down the path over the dunes and wind our way through the overpopulated swathe of beach dominated by families. Loaded down with toddlers, toys, and tents, moms and dads plop themselves on minuscule patches of sandy real estate rather than haul themselves any farther down the beach.

Amid this first wave of beachgoers sit the lifeguards. Including Nate.

In the week since Henry first told me about New Hampshire, my feelings about my probation have vacillated between love and hate. And that line is not just fine, it's dotted, it zigzags, and it occasionally stabs me square in the chest.

I wave to Nate and my bangle shimmies down my wrist. On the love side of the line is how freeing it is to be relieved of the temptation and the pressure of using magic. My probation has turned being Jinn into a job. I'll clock in, grant a wish, and clock out. Strangely, my bronze bangle has made me feel more like a normal HIT than ever before.

Henry hops over two boys buried up to their necks in the sand. "Don't make a big thing out of it yet. My dad's track record is far from encouraging."

Mr. Carwyn has two job interviews within easy driving distance of Henry's grandparents' house, so his mom, dad, and Lisa are staying in New Hampshire for a few days. The only reason Henry was allowed to stay behind is so he can let in the real-estate agent who needs to assess the property and determine a fair price for renters and for . . . for buyers. And that's what makes me scurry on over to the hate side of my probation line.

Because if I had my powers, maybe I could help his family and Henry wouldn't have to leave. Though, in truth, from the way things sound, what's been going on inside the walls of Henry's house may take more than magic to solve.

At the very least though, if Henry does have to ditch civilization to go live free or die in the woods of New Hampshire, having my magic back would mean I could app there to visit him.

"It's not fair," I say as we transition into the stretch of beach home to the second category of beachgoers: couples and surreptitiously day-drinking teens whose respective intolerance for screaming children and desire for privacy outweigh the ten-minute trek to the restrooms.

"You know what's not fair?" Henry says. "You being a total tease."

My neck spins like I'm possessed. With the amount of time Henry's been spending with Chelsea, I figured we were past whatever may or may not have been going on between us because of boy-girl, Nate-Chelsea drama.

"I mean," he says, smirking, "you can't even shape-shift."

That book. That stupid encyclopedia of spirits book. He checked the monstrous tome, half the size of my cantamen, out of the library again and keeps taunting me with supposed Jinn facts. Many cultures, especially in the Middle East and Africa, believe in spirits called *djinn* who, like angels, are supposedly part of a community of intermediary spirits who run the world, each having a specific function and dominion.

"Isn't granting wishes enough?" I say. "I need to be able to turn into a rabbit or something?"

"Dog. Or snake, mostly, according to the book."

"And the book is always right."

Henry peers over his sunglasses at me. "Do I need to remind you it was spot-on with how to summon the djinn? Entice them with their favorite gifts of sweets and alcohol and you can get them to do everything from guard your house to chase away your bad luck. Then again, I've been feeding you wine-soaked marshmallows in those s'mores, but so far my luck hasn't changed."

"Hilarious." I bump into a thick, tattooed arm carrying a guitar. "Now do I need to remind you what it said about us hating crowds?" I grasp onto the rash guard shirt he's wearing, which happens to be the last item I conjured before my probation, and let him lead us through the bustling boat town.

This third and final group of beachgoers sees beer-bellied dads anchoring their floating vessels and spending the afternoon offloading and then reloading what appears to be the entire contents of a small house (standing grills, full-height tables and chairs, coolers the size of a five-year-old).

Henry guides me around a nearly invisible fishing line. "Hating crowds and the cold, a given. But that thing about feeding you salt provoking you? That I had to learn the hard way."

I forgot about the salt thing. Grains of truth actually do seem to lurk in most of what Henry read in that book. Who influenced who will forever be a mystery.

Approaching the estuary where the ocean meets the river, we arrive at the empty span of beach home to a cornucopia of large black rocks. During high tide, they disappear. It being low tide, I weave through until I reach the widest one.

I climb up and sprawl out. "Earlier you could walk right by and never know these were here." Seaweed and unidentifiable slime creep through the cracks and dampen the backs of my arms and legs. "If something can't be seen by the naked eye, does that mean it ceases to exist?"

My powers, my father, my Henry.

Henry groans.

Eyes closed, I'm waiting for him to join me when all of a sudden a wave of frigid water washes over my legs. My body jerks upright. Not a wave. A Henry. Having dove under the water, he now stands above me, his feet planted on either side of my torso. My cries only fuel his torment. He balls up the fabric of his long-sleeved tee and wrings it out, dripping ice-cold saltwater onto my stomach.

I slap at his ankles and scoot back. He takes off his wet shirt and drops it on my head. "The all-powerful Jinn's afraid of a little water?"

"I can't help it if my species is more advanced than your primitive one. Our roots are in the desert. We know better than to risk frostbite by frolicking in glacial waters."

Henry shakes water from his hair as he sits down next to me. "The desert? Thought you said the rest of the Jinn make their home underground. Like worms."

I punch his bare shoulder. I'm wearing a tankini top and boy shorts over my bathing suit bottoms. In all the time we've been hanging out, this is as close as we've ever been with this little clothing on—aside from the time I apped myself into Henry's closet to find him wearing only a towel, and then, not even that.

Whatever Henry's been doing with Chelsea and whatever I've been doing with Nate has remained undefined. Or at least Nate and I have yet to label ourselves. It's possible Henry and Chelsea have slapped a name tag on their relationship and neglected to mention it.

Henry's finally started wearing the contacts I conjured for him while I still had my silver bangle. And he's gotten a haircut since the last time I saw him. Maybe this new attention to personal grooming is a sign of his budding relationship. The next time I see Henry and Chelsea together, I might very well find a white rectangular sticker on their collective forehead saying, "Hi, my name is Dating."

Chelsea's niceness toward me continues. Since I've been hanging out with Nate so much, I know I should be happy that Henry has someone to be with too. I tell myself I would be happy if only that someone was someone other than Chelsea. I tell myself, but I'm no stranger to lies, white or otherwise.

Henry leans back on his elbows. "Janna's really underground?"

"Sounds bizarre, I know." I remember how I felt hearing this for the first time. "When my mom told me, I didn't believe her. I thought it was like when parents tell their kid that the dog went to go live on a farm. Like a metaphor or something. But now, well, I understand that a little dirt and rock are no match for magic. If you're an Afrit or on their good side, it's a game of name your paradise." I jut my chin toward the water's edge. "Crystal clear ocean and pure white sand? Check. Tropical jungle with secluded tree house? You got it. Opulent castle wallpapered in gold? No problem."

"Have to admit, sounds cool."

"Except if you're on their bad side," I say before it registers that I didn't want him to know this part. Ever since I received the bronze bangle, he's been treating me like something breakable. If I tell him more, he's going to seal me in a bubble. Not to mention, I'm pretty sure keeping Henry's sense of wonder at me being Jinn intact has been helping to keep my resentment at bay.

He sits up. "What do you mean?"

"Nothing."

"Doesn't sound like nothing."

I concentrate on picking fluorescent green goo off the back of my calves. I'm starting to better understand my mother not telling me things. Because sharing secrets can be as much of a burden as keeping them.

"Azra." Henry nudges my chin to force me to meet his now, predictably, worried eyes.

"It's not a big deal, really. It's just that the jail I was telling you about? If I . . . if a Jinn messes up? Supposedly it's less tiny cells and orange jumpsuits and more pitch-black caves and dungeons full of rats."

He cocks his head.

"They take your greatest fear and make you live it."

Before his jaw falls into his lap, I add, "Don't worry, mine will just be a pantry stocked with nothing but salt-cured meat and fish."

Henry flips his sunglasses to the top of his head. "It's not a joke, Azra."

"Well, it was, just maybe not a good one."

He stands up and crosses his arms over his chest. "I thought you were taking this more seriously."

I rise to my feet to look him in the eye. "I am." I spin my bronze bangle. "This makes sure I am." My lip chooses this moment to quiver, and I bite down. Hard.

"It's okay to be afraid, Az."

As I turn to watch the incoming tide, I'm overwhelmed with a sinking feeling. A flash of someone saying the same words in this exact same place skips through my head so quickly I can't grab hold. It's followed by an image of my mother, younger, tanned, and smiling, kneeling on the sand, facing the water. Facing me in the water. Her look so loving, so intensely happy, I can't place it.

Instinctively, I jump off the rock. My feet move toward the ocean, and my body goes farther, deeper in, hoping my mind will follow and let me reclaim this memory, this figment of my imagination, whatever it is. Without me realizing it, my feet no longer reach the sandy bottom and my body is so numb, I start to descend. But Henry's there to pull me back up.

He wraps his arm around my waist and propels me out of the water so fast it feels like apporting. But it's just plain, old, normal brawn that sets me back down on the toasty black rock baked by the sun.

My teeth clank against one another. "N-n-n-need to w-w-w-arm u-p-p-p."

He reaches for his shirt, which is still drenched. Dropping it, he crouches in front of me and places a hand on each of my upper arms. He rubs until the friction stops my teeth from chattering.

"What was that?" he asks, freaked out.

"Not really sure."

He points to my foot. "You're bleeding. You must have hit a rock or a shell."

Surprised, I look down and wipe the trail of blood off my ankle. "It's okay. My mom can heal me later."

Henry falls back. "What?" His hands rummage through his wet hair as if looking for something he lost. "Your mom . . . she can heal?"

Jenny, he's thinking of Jenny.

My stomach drops. "Only fellow Jinn. Not humans. Not . . . Jenny."

Moisture pools in Henry's eyes. His lids shut tight, and he presses a finger on each to keep his contacts in place.

I reach for his hand. "I begged her to try, Henry. She just couldn't. She doesn't have that power. Magic . . . it can't fix everything. I swear if there was any way, even a chance, she'd—"

He slides back. "I know. I know she would've." His hands clutch the back of his neck as he hangs his head. "Same as I know it's not her fault. I know because it's mine."

"Yours?" I stare at him. "You weren't even there."

"Which is why it's my fault. I was supposed to be there." His shoulders roll in, and his body starts to tremble. "My mom asked me to keep an eye on her. I was supposed to be at your house.

I was supposed to be watching her. But I was building this stupid model airplane, and I had to hold this piece in place for ten minutes so it'd dry. I chose a model airplane over my sister. My *sister,* Azra."

I move toward him, but he holds up one hand and wipes his eyes with the other.

"My mom's always blamed me. She's never actually said it, but it's obvious. Do you know how hard my dad had to fight so she'd let me watch Lisa? Sometimes I-I-I still think she doesn't trust me with her."

It's like a lasso is strangling my vocal cords. Even if I could make a sound, I have no idea what to say, so I simply throw my arms around him. At first, his body is hard, resisting, but soon he crumbles.

"I understand how my dad felt now," he says quietly. "If we move away I feel like I'll lose her. That's why . . . why I always wanted . . . why I'm so glad I've got you back. It's like having a piece of her."

My heart pummels my chest. Henry and I don't talk about Jenny. We don't need to. We both understand how absence can define one's presence.

I always thought my mother was the lucky one for having memories of my father, of my grandparents, of what life was like before. Maybe she was right not to call them up, not to share them, because, is it possible my memories of Jenny, Henry's memories of Jenny, make it worse? Harder for us to move on?

All this time, Henry's been blaming himself. I've been blaming magic. He latched on to Lisa, tried to latch on to me. I pushed him away, pushed Laila, my Zar sisters, my mother, pushed them all away. I thought being Jinn was holding me back from friends, from love, from family. But it wasn't being Jinn. It was me. Just me.

Together on our rocky perch, our arms encircle not just each other but secrets—shared secrets, and shared burdens. They will always be between us. For better and for worse.

27

"Want to see the tent?" I ask Henry as he pulls his mom's car into his driveway.

Our ride home from the beach was silent, save for the sounds of Drunken Toad. We said enough and yet not nearly enough on our black rock.

Circling around to the side of my house, I stretch to peek over the top of the fence, which has no gate as a way of discouraging outsiders from finding their way in. Taking over the backyard is the conjured tent my mother and I worked on all morning for tonight's Zar gathering.

"Wait," I say as Henry comes up behind me. The front corner of the tent glows a soft orange. Inside, a lit candle casts a shadow against the canvas wall. "Someone's inside."

"Your mom?"

"Probably. Still, she'd freak if I showed you now."

"Okay, then."

He turns to leave, and my hand rises, wanting to reach for him, to make him stay, to tell him how sorry I am that my mom couldn't heal Jenny, that he has to stop blaming himself, that I kick myself every day for pushing him away, that I need him at the same time as I need Nate, and how sorry that makes me, but instead, I lower my arm to my side, say, "Okay," and, with a weight in my chest, watch him cross the street.

I lean against the fence, taking a moment to clear my head. I expected tonight, my Zar initiation, to be the hardest part of today. Life sure likes its curveballs.

The lack of a gate and my inability to apport means I need to travel through the house to reach the backyard. As I near the tent, I begin to worry that curveballs, like bad things, aren't satisfied with just one. Because the shadow on the wall is curled into a tight ball. And rocking back and forth.

I lift the entry flap. "Mom, what's—" But it's not my mother. It's Yasmin.

She's hunched on one of the couches my mother conjured this morning with her feet on the cushion, her arms around her legs, and her chin tucked to her knees. Her normally smooth black curls lay in twisted, matted clumps. No makeup, eyes puffy, she barely acknowledges me as I sit next to her.

Before I can ask the obligatory and yet pointless question, "Is everything all right?" she speaks.

"I saw you today." Her eyes remain focused on the ivory taper candle on the table in front of her. "At the beach. I came early."

"Why didn't you—"

"Saw you with that boy, your neighbor," she says over me. "He's your friend's brother, isn't he? The girl who died."

"Jenny." My teeth clench. "You know her name is Jenny."

"*Was.*"

Blood pounds in my ears and it's like I'm under water again.

She spins to face me, grabbing both of my wrists and drawing me close. "I didn't mean it the way it sounded. It's just . . . she's gone, Azra. You do realize that, don't you?" Balled-up tissues poke out of the ends of her sleeves. "But we're here. We've always been here. Waiting."

She releases her hold on my wrists and wipes her nose. "But we can't wait anymore. The initiation's tonight. Either you're with us or with them."

"Them?"

"The humans. I told you to be careful. Looks like you didn't take my advice."

Does she know? Does she know Henry knows?

"Henry and I are just friends," I say.

"Oh no. You're more than that."

"We're not together, if that's what you think. I'm kind of . . . interested in someone else."

"The lifeguard." Her eyes search mine, and the softness in her voice turns to stone. "And there's my answer. Closer to them than you are to us." She turns away. "Like I said, don't ever forget they're humans, Azra."

My anger burns like the flame of a struck match but dies out just as fast. Because we don't have to inherit everything from our mothers. Their fights don't have to become ours.

Without hurt or spite or bitterness, I say, "Why does it have to be us or them? Why do you hate them so much?"

Yasmin whirls around, knocking into the candle and almost setting the black pashmina that drips off her shoulders on fire. "Is that what you think? That I hate the humans?"

"Don't you?"

"No. I hate the way they make us live."

"Then your anger's misplaced. The Afrit are responsible, not the humans."

"But you can't win a fight against the Afrit." She tosses the end of her wrap over her shoulder. "And you know what they say if you can't beat 'em."

With a *zap* that shoots through to my fingertips, she disappears.

I will never understand her. Tonight we'll officially be sisters, but Yasmin and I couldn't be further apart.

More than two hundred candles simultaneously ignite, illuminating the tent like a full moon. The flickering light dances across the canvas flaps, which may be the only white in the room. Between the maroon fabric on the lush sofas, the gold tablecloth draped over the long, communal table, and the kaleidoscope of colors on the skirts, tunics, and dresses of the assorted Jinn under the big top, not a single hue remains unaccounted for. It's like a three-dimensional color wheel.

I'm doing my part in my short, jersey dress. No one else would be representing black. In the heels Laila insisted I wear, I look and feel nine feet tall. Maybe it'll give me the edge I fear I need tonight with Yasmin. I haven't seen her since our earlier conversation—a conversation I can't help but feel I lacked sufficient information to fully participate in.

Ignoring the knots in my stomach, I pat Laila on the head. "Think you'll be as tall as me?"

Her sixteenth birthday isn't until tomorrow. Per tradition, the initiation is being held on the eve of the last member's final night without powers. Since Zar gatherings usually last for days, we'll all be together when Laila turns.

She stuffs her hands in the pockets of her white linen shift dress and frowns. "I hope not."

Before I can ask why, Hana joins us. The open back and plunging neckline of her champagne-colored halter dress seem to defy the laws of gravity. She holds out a tray of cheese-filled dates and says, "Did you hear? Lalla Raina's not coming."

Another knot ties off in my gut. "What? Why?"

Hana levitates the tray, freeing her hands to snag a date. "Everyone's tight-lipped."

In mid-reach for one of her own, Laila stops and pulls back her hand. "I can't believe they're fighting. Today. So much for our Zar following their example."

It's Laila's disappointment that prompts the lightness in my voice that I surely don't feel. "Whatever it is, it'll blow over. They've always had squabbles. They've always made up."

"Just like us," Hana says. She then conjures a gold belt that she cinches around my waist and a rose that she tucks into Laila's blond curls. In the process, she forgets about levitating the plate and it crashes to the ground.

From across the room, Farrah shouts, "It wasn't me!"

Laughing, Mina tackles her, and together they app to our side of the tent. When they appear, I realize they're wearing matching saffron-yellow kaftans, gold headbands, and cobalt-blue eyeliner.

As Hana tells them about Lalla Raina, Yasmin slinks into the room, significantly better groomed than earlier in tight black jeans and a red silk camisole, but instead of coming to us, she stakes out a position next to the bar and pours rum into a Coke can.

Farrah picks a date up off the floor, blows on it, and takes a huge bite. Mouth full, she mumbles, "I'd be PO'd too if my mom wasn't here."

Mina whacks the dirty date out of Farrah's hand. "Sure, but that upset?"

Yasmin's eyes meet mine and my usual desire to escape to Henry's backyard makes a resurgence. But I can't. I can't do that to Laila . . . I can't do that to any of them.

We transition into the feast, narrated by proud speeches from each of our mothers, which only highlight Raina's absence. Once the dishes are magically cleared, Samara moves to the center of the tent. She begins the initiation ceremony by instructing us six daughters to form a circle.

I slip in between Laila and Yasmin. As tightly as Laila clutches my hand is as loosely as Yasmin does. Across from me, Mina mouths, "How's the Adonis?" and Farrah winks.

Lalla Nadia places a lei made from white henna flowers around each of our necks. My mother lights the sticks of incense spread throughout the tent, infusing the air with the strong aroma of tea roses.

Samara interlaces her fingers. "Nothing, not the silver . . ." Her eyes flicker in my direction. "Or bronze . . . Not the silver or bronze bangles you wear today nor the gold ones you will wear in the future, will ever be as tight a circle as the one you form now. As important a role as we, your mothers, have played in your past, even we cannot compete with the role your Zar will play in your future."

I glance at Laila. She squeezes my hand, and I find myself squeezing back even harder.

"You lovely Jinn will have some human acquaintances," Samara says. "Women to lunch with, women to shop with, women to have your daughter's playdates with. Men too. Give your powers a break, and on occasion, let a male friend tinker with your plumbing—oh, and fix your sink too."

"*Sam,*" my mother admonishes, to which the other mothers howl and the daughters giggle—the daughters except Yasmin.

"But," Samara continues without a pause, "the role your human friends will have in your life will pale in comparison to that of your sisters. For with this ritual, you six will be forever linked. And the increase in power you experience when drawing upon nature is no match for the surge that comes when accessing the collective strength of your Zar."

Linked? Our magic is linked? That my wide eyes and open mouth are mirrored on the faces of my Zar sisters confirms this is news to all of us.

"When attempting the most difficult feats of magic, you can rely on the spirit of your sisters to ensure your success. Tap into this connection and learn to sense each other's joy and sadness. You will hopefully laugh more than you cry, but if and when you do both, let it be in the arms of those to whom you are now bound for life.

"In one united voice, daughters, repeat after me: *'Akul wahid, wal wahid lalkul.'* One is all, all is one."

Laila starts, and we all join in. As our voices merge into one, a golden orb of light appears in front of each linked set of hands. On the final syllable, a trail of light zooms through each glowing sphere, connecting all six.

Samara smiles. "Welcome, daughters, to your Zar."

The circle of light collapses into a straight, thin line and shoots upward, evaporating into the air above our heads.

Applause fills the tent, my sisters embrace one another, and Yasmin drops my hand. She barely gets out her "I'm going inside" before she disappears.

The rest of us continue to hug and receive the congratulations from our mothers, but after, we huddle to one side, sharing first our shock at the meaning of our initiation and then our confusion about Yasmin's behavior.

Farrah says, "Let's just hope she's not going to abduct another neighborhood pet."

Mina smirks. "Or neighbor."

"Maybe we better go find her." Hana reaches for Laila and me. "Come on, apporting-challenged sisters. I'll app you both to Azra's room."

"It's okay," Laila says, "you three go. Azra and I will walk. We don't want to overwhelm her."

While Laila might mean this, something tells me she's more interested in us having the chance to talk alone. This is a lot for me to take in, and I can do magic. I glance at my bronze bangle—with permission, of course. We slowly make our way across the backyard and into the house.

"Do you feel any different?" Laila asks.

"The whole linked thing?" I say, to which Laila nods. "No. Did you know?"

Laila shakes her head. "But now it makes sense. How close they are. Our mothers. Do you think tapping into one another's emotions is a choice?"

"I hope so. Forget Yasmin, can you imagine knowing every little goofy thing Farrah feels?"

Even sweet Laila laughs at this. Pausing as we enter the kitchen, she points to my bronze bangle. "How are you doing with that thing anyway?"

She says "thing" like I've got the plague, which I guess, in her mind, I do. I can't expect Laila, who has yet to grant a wish, to understand there are perks to not doing magic.

But as we move to the couch, talking and catching each other up on our summers, I realize she actually might. Her lack of enthusiasm for potentially shooting up six inches tomorrow stems from the fear that she'll have to change schools. That because of her magical makeover, she'll have to say good-bye to her friends, something she won't even be able to do in person. Whether the downsides to becoming Jinn are something Laila has just started to realize or just started to admit, I can't tell. But it binds us more than any ceremony could.

I wouldn't trade having Henry in my life for anything, but it's not the same as this. It's not the same as sharing being Jinn with Laila. As much as I want to hate it that my mother's right about what a Zar can give me, I don't. Not at all.

We're at the top of the stairs when Laila says, "Don't you think it's a bit odd that the Afrit zeroed in on your candidate so fast?

My mom says if they'd waited even five minutes you'd have had everything back to normal and it's likely no one would have ever known."

I'm about to tease Laila for her conspiracy theories when I realize she's probably right. It is strange. Do they always check up on wish-granting rituals so quickly? The gnawing in my gut says no. But that makes me seem conceited, like I'm worthy of some super special Afrit attention.

I shrug, voicing the most likely conclusion, "It's just bad luck I guess."

Laila looks unconvinced. "Hmm, just be careful, okay?"

Her tone gives me goose bumps. Before I push open my bedroom door, I ask, "So you really don't know where Raina is?"

"Nope. All I know is she's away. That's what my mom said when she told me Yasmin would be staying with us."

"She's staying with you? For how long?"

"Beats me." Laila lowers her voice. "But I hope not long. She's been weird."

"She's always been weird."

"This is different. She's . . . sad."

As we enter my room, that changes to "drunk."

Yasmin's levitating an empty shot glass, laughing, and dancing. No music is playing. At least none outside of her head.

Hana rushes over to us. "She's about to conjure a third round. She's acting crazy. And not normal Yasmin crazy."

Mina wiggles her shoulder under Yasmin's left arm. "Let's take her to the guest room and try to get her to lie down."

Farrah scoots in under Yasmin's right. "Come on, Yas."

The way Yasmin's gyrating her hips makes me think getting her to lie down won't be easy.

"She needs coffee," Hana says. "Homemade, not conjured. That way we can make sure it's good and strong."

"In the cabinet next to the sink," I say to Hana who then apps downstairs.

Mina and Farrah drag Yasmin to the door, and the shot glass falls to the floor. As they're about to cross the threshold, Yasmin frees herself from the other girls and takes one hand of Laila's, hesitates, and takes one of mine.

"You two," she says with a slur in her voice. "Don't let them risk it."

She crushes our fingers, and Mina and Farrah have to force her to let go before they can guide her out into the hallway.

Linked or not, I will never understand Yasmin.

"What was that all about?" I say.

Laila flops onto my bed. "Told you she's been weird."

I bend to pick up the shot glass, which, having landed on the rug, thankfully didn't break. From my crouched position, I see Laila sit up, smile at the framed picture of her, me, and Jenny, and then reach for the drawer of my nightstand.

"Whatever Lalla Isa brought was full of garlic," she says. "Gross. You still have those mints?"

My stomach lurches the instant Laila's hand hits the knob. I can't get up fast enough to stop that third curveball I should have never doubted was coming. All I can do is suck in my breath as Laila sees, for the first time in months, her gold locket with the infinity symbol engraved on the front.

"But how—" Laila looks at me. "You . . . you found it?"

It's like my heart is being torn in two. I swear I'm trying to speak, but I can't find my voice any more than I can find my words.

Laila's lip trembles. "Azra? Where? When? And why . . . why didn't you tell me?"

Forcing myself to say something, anything, I squeak out, "I didn't exactly find it." I back up and lean against my dresser. "You see . . . I . . . what I mean is . . ." I can't defend myself. Because there is no defense for what I did.

Laila's small forehead creases. "But I don't understand. You had it all this time?"

I'm desperate to turn away from the betrayal in Laila's eyes, but she deserves to see me squirm. And I do.

My cowardice takes over, and I lower my gaze to the floor. "Yes, but I can explain. See, when you showed it to me, I was . . . not in a good place. I was mad at my mother, mad at everyone, and the locket, well, I thought, if only my mom cared about my dad as much as yours, then, maybe, this would be different. Maybe—"

Holding on to my dresser, I inhale and exhale, trying to compose myself before attempting another explanation, equally as flawed, but Laila's not really listening. Her fingertips caress the locket over and over again, as if she can't believe it's real.

The piece of silver tinsel she gave me on my birthday, which I'd placed in the drawer, must have been stuck to the chain, for it floats to the floor as she wraps her hand around the locket and brings it to her chest.

She lifts herself off the bed, steps on the tinsel, unintentionally, I think, before moving in front of me and forcing me to look at her. "That's why you took mine? Because you don't have one?"

Choked up, I nod slowly. "But . . . but I was going to return it, Laila. And then—"

I swivel my head around the room, desperate for someone, something, to blame. But there's no one.

"And then, I didn't."

No one but me.

Laila slips the gold chain over her head. "I was the only one there for you, Azra. The. Only. One." She closes her eyes but still loses the fight against the tears she's been holding back since the moment she opened the drawer.

In a harsh voice I've never heard before, Laila says, "I put up with all your . . . your . . ." She presses one hand against her stomach. When she speaks again, her tone is strong but calm. "With all of your *attitude* because I know this has always been harder for you than for the rest of us."

I turn my face to stone. Seeing me cry would only diminish Laila's hurt. She's the victim. Not me. Seeing my tears . . . that's not what Laila needs. My voice barely above a whisper, I say, "Only because I make it that way."

It isn't until Laila's eyes focus on my rock-hard jawline as she brushes past me that I realize my tears are exactly what Laila needs.

28

I HAVE TO GO AFTER HER. I HAVE TO EXPLAIN. BUT I CAN'T. NOT NOW. Not tonight. Not while our whole Zar and my mother's whole Zar is here. A Jinn here, a Jinn there, everywhere a Jinn. I can't breathe. I need my escape hatch.

I open my jewelry box and snatch the silver key Henry gave me on my birthday. I fly down the stairs, swing open the front door, and land on Henry's front steps. My knock on the door elicits no response. Neither does my text. His whole family is still in New Hampshire. But lights are on all over the place. Henry must be somewhere.

The fence that surrounds the backyard is too tall to see over. When I open the locked gate to let myself in, it's like the pillow that's being held over my face, preventing me from breathing, is crammed down my throat.

If one could successfully untangle the mass of arms and legs squeezed onto the lounge chair at the shallow end of the pool, they'd find one pale set belonging to Henry and one deeply tanned set belonging to Chelsea.

I don't have to read either of their minds to know what's happening here. I'm backing away, desperate to escape unnoticed, when my phone begins belting out the first few bars of my favorite song. My favorite song from my favorite band. The band Henry and I bonded over that first day at the beach. He downloaded the track for my ringtone weeks ago.

The caller ID displays Nate's name along with his photo.

Henry jumps up, nearly knocking Chelsea to the ground. His shirt's off, as is hers.

"Sorry!" I shout. "I should have called."

I don't know why I say that since I did call, well, text, basically the same thing, but someone has to say something, and neither of them are talking. Guess their lips are too sore.

Waving awkwardly, stupidly, I hightail it out of there, retracing my steps through the gate. I'm in the middle of the street when Henry catches up.

"Hey." He clasps a hand on my shoulder.

I spin around, and he gasps, taking in my dress, heels, and general nine-foot-tall edge.

We hold each other's gaze, neither of us speaking. What is there to say? It's not like Henry's doing anything wrong. His parents are away. Most guys would be having some huge rager. All he's doing is making out with some girl.

Not some girl. Chelsea.

Does it really matter that it's Chelsea? Would this feeling of . . . of . . . oh, let's just say it, *betrayal* be any different if it were some other girl? *Betrayal? Really? Nate's smiling face is in the palm of your hand. What nerve, Azra. Oh, and why don't you ask Laila if her feelings of betrayal would be any different if it were some other Jinn?*

Smack in the middle of the street, halfway between my house and Henry's, I suddenly have nowhere to escape to.

"Azra," Henry says, "I'm sorry."

He truly has nothing to be sorry about. That's what I should say. He deserves . . . deserves whatever this is . . . especially after what he told me today about Jenny, about moving . . . but somehow Laila's wounded eyes and Chelsea's naked stomach lead to me simply shrugging. "If you want to be another one of Chelsea's lovesick puppies, that's your choice. Go ahead and strap on a collar. Just make sure it's a flea-and-tick one."

It is then that I hear Henry's thoughts: *Some best friend.*

My heart crumples like a piece of paper.

He kicks the ground and tosses his hands in the air. "You're impossible!"

Wearing down the asphalt, Henry paces between me and the sidewalk in front of his house before finally stopping and facing me. He shoves his fists into his front pockets. "I don't know what more you want from me."

More. As if I've asked so much, I've drained him. I probably have. While he's made my life easier, I've made his harder. It is only now that I realize the pressure he must feel to always be on guard. To not slip up. To not reveal who I really am. Maybe it's time for me to let him go. Let him out of all of this. All this lying. All this Jinn stuff. All this me.

"Nothing. I want nothing more from you." Though I mean this in the most altruistic way, in that "if you love something, set it free" way, the nuance is lost on him.

"Damn it, Az, you're too much. Maybe everyone's right."

Everyone?

"I heard the way the guys at school would talk." The muscles in Henry's face tense. "Half afraid to talk to you because you're so freaking pretty, they knew they didn't have a shot, and the other half choosing not to talk to you because you're so freaking pretty, they figured you must be a total bitch."

At the start of the summer, Nate had mentioned gossip about my "vibe," but I couldn't imagine being a topic of conversation for anyone at our school. This being true stuns me almost as much as the *bitch* part stings me.

I say softly, "Which camp were you in?"

Henry sighs. "Neither. Because I . . . I figured you were lonely. No one ever visited except Laila. Course, that was before I knew why."

I rest my trembling hands on my hips. "And now?"

I'm still waiting for a response when a fully clothed Chelsea appears on the front lawn. At the sound of her tentative, "Henry?" he turns and replies, "I'll be right there, promise."

I snort at his sugary tone before I can stop myself.

His nostrils actually flare. "Now," he says in a tone lacking even one molecule of sucrose, "now, I'm squarely in both camps."

He walks away from me, wraps an arm around Chelsea's waist, and tucks a finger (which is all that will fit) into the waistband of her cutoffs.

I'm standing in the same spot watching them disappear through the fence gate when the full weight of Henry's answer hits me. He thinks I'm a bitch. He also thinks I'm so pretty, he didn't have a shot with me.

Didn't or doesn't?

Didn't. It has to be. Because if he still wanted a shot with me, how could Henry be groping Chelsea?

Then again, if it's Nate's legs I want to be intertwined with mine, why am I this rattled to discover Henry groping Chelsea?

Clichés exist for a reason. Somewhere inside lurks a hidden truth. Turns out one of the truths behind the cliché that romance ruins a friendship is that it can apply even when the friends remain platonic.

A trick without any magic involved.

When I hit my front yard, I wrest the heels from my aching feet. The cool grass tickles my toes as I walk in circles. I move slowly, trying to absorb what just happened with Henry. That was our first fight. But friends fight, don't they? And we're friends, aren't we? We are. We always have been. But maybe we're more. Maybe we always have been more.

Just like with me and Laila. My heart pounds as I struggle to find the words to say to her to make her understand. To make her forgive. She will, right? I mean, if Mrs. Pucher's sister could forgive her, Laila has to forgive me for this. Then again, it took Mrs. Pucher's sister thirty years and a genie to get there.

As I approach the fence to our backyard, I see Mrs. Seyfreth out of the corner of my eye. The lilac bush still blocks most of her view. She doesn't brush a single leaf aside. She just stands there in her little world, peering into ours. But there's nothing to see here. Not even the tent. I force my dirt-smudged feet back into the high heels to get a better view over the top of the fence. All I see is our normal backyard.

A Zar reunion has never before ended on the same night it began. Laila must have told. My heart aches with the thought of Samara finding out what I did.

I inch open the front door. The living room is empty. I tiptoe upstairs, desperate to make it to my room without being noticed.

"Poor Yasmin," my mother says through her open bedroom door.

Samara replies, "Hana and the other girls got her settled in at Nadia's. Laila seemed so upset by it all that I thought it was better if Yasmin spent the night elsewhere."

"It's understandable," my mother says, "but sad. I just wish it didn't have to ruin the girls' night. Yasmin needed it more than any of them."

"It didn't ruin it. They had their initiation. That's what's important."

There's an edge to my mother's voice. "Is it really though? The Zar sisterhood. Sticking together. Raina would likely have something to say about that."

"When didn't Raina have something to say?"

My mother responds with a soft laugh. "Especially to me."

Samara sighs. "So much history. So much to remember. So much that's hard to let ourselves remember."

Yasmin and Laila and Henry and Chelsea. All of their wounded faces, at least half of which I am responsible for, float before me. I round the corner and plant myself in the doorway.

"Like what?" I demand. Being Jinn is so full of secrets and lies, I need a playbook to keep track.

My mother snaps her head in my direction. "Azra! Where have you been?"

I drop her high heels to the floor. "I want to know what's so hard for you both to remember." My mind returns to Henry and me on the black rock. Maybe having memories does make it hard to move on, but not having any makes it impossible.

My eyes dart from my mother to Sam. "But it's not what, is it? It's who. My father. Laila's father. Is that why we don't talk about them? Because it's hard?"

Their shocked faces but thin-lipped silence fuel me. Lots of things in life are hard. And as I've just discovered, avoiding them doesn't make it any easier.

"Did it ever occur to you both that it may be hard *for us* because you don't . . . because you won't talk about them? Don't you want to, Sam? I know you cared for him. I know you loved Laila's father."

Samara lifts herself off of my mother's bed. "Azra, I'm not sure what's gotten into you—"

"Stop. I know about the locket." My guilt lashes out in the form of anger at my mother. I narrow my eyes at her. "How do you think it felt to know Lalla Sam actually *loved* Laila's father? That she knew it'd be important for Laila to be able to see him one day?" I push past the lump in my throat. "You . . . you just gave him up, didn't you? You didn't care about him at all. Is it the same with Raina? What happened? Did she chip your tagine so you banished her from the house? Did you just give her up too?"

Samara takes my mother's hand. The two of them have always had each other. Guess they didn't really need anyone else.

In my hand, my phone buzzes. A text. I close my eyes, selfish enough to want it to be from Laila, naïve enough to hope it's from Henry, but in my heart, knowing who it's from. I look down. Nate. I'm both disappointed and not disappointed.

My mother releases Samara's hand. "This doesn't concern you, Azra." She crosses her arms in front of her chest and says stiffly, "I get that you're upset, but whatever's happened, it's no excuse to talk to me, to either of us, like this. Maybe you should go to your room before you say something you'll regret."

A harsh laugh rumbles through my nostrils. "Sorry, Mom. I'm what you wanted me to be my entire life. A Jinn. Which means, I'm an adult. You can't ground me."

Without a backward glance, I march across the hall into my bedroom. I realize I'm effectively grounding myself but I have nowhere else to go.

I turn the lock and slide down my door, sitting on the floor with my back against the frame. Like that could stop my mother if she wanted to get inside.

Which she does.

A soft knock precedes her, "Azra?" The scolding gone from her voice, it now cracks as she says, "I'm . . . I'm sorry."

No, no, no. This is worse. I can't handle her hurting. Not on top of everyone else's. Not on top of my own.

"Honey," Samara says, "it can't be that bad."

Oh, but it is, Lalla Sam. I can't face her . . . because I know I'll see in her eyes the same hurt, betrayed look I saw in Laila's.

"Please." I don't bother to disguise the quiver in my voice. "Not now."

Whispers on the other side of the door.

My mother then says, "Okay, kiddo, but I'm always right here."

"*We're* always right here," Samara says, and I hear her hand tap the door.

The light their bodies were blocking shines under my door as they retreat. It surrounds my hunched, shaking frame, highlighting me, here, alone.

My hand still clings to my phone, the message from Nate on the screen. Followed by another one, asking if everything's okay. Right now, he's the only one in my life separate from all of this. Looks like I've found a new escape hatch.

I wait until I hear my mother's bedroom door close before unlocking my phone. I flip through pictures of Henry, Laila, and Nate before opening my messages. I answer Nate's text, he answers mine, and I go again. With each zoom, I distance myself from today, from everything Jinn, and slowly, my guilt at texting Nate, at letting myself enjoy texting Nate, diminishes.

Nate not knowing I'm a Jinn means I have to lie to him, but as I'm discovering, it also means I *get* to lie to him. I lose my Jinn self and for now am just a girl learning how to flirt with a boy.

We text for so long, my back spasms from lying on the wood floor. Finally, as we're saying good-bye, I get the feeling Nate sends the text he's been working up the nerve to type all night.

Staff bonfire tomorrow night. Would you like to be my mate? . . . Date.

face palm
Either one works for me.

Despite everything, or maybe because of everything, Nate officially proving that the "first" in front of his "date" from the other day was a necessary adjective makes my heavy heart do cartwheels.

A second date with Nate, a second date with Nate. I bounce my head from side to side as I sing the rhyme in my head.

My lack of response other than bouncing brings a follow-up text:

Work thing, I know. Promise to make it up w/ third.

Third, oh really? I prove I've gotten the hang of this flirting thing as I tease:

Presumptuous much?

Know what they say about assuming . . .

That it brings u and mi together? ;)

So maybe Nate the underwear model doesn't quite hide his inner dork as well as I thought. Nothing could make me happier.

The late hour combined with the lack of feeling in my thumbs signals it's time to go to bed. We sign off, and my joints crack as I change into my pajamas. Passing by my window before climbing into bed, I catch sight of Henry and Chelsea fused together, illuminated by the light on the Carwyns' front steps.

My mix of jealousy, anger, and guilt is an entirely normal response. My wish has finally come true. And this weight in my chest confirms that wishes do indeed come with a price.

Too small for my wrist, the silver tinsel stayed wrapped around my ring finger while I worked my morning shift at the beach. Chelsea, the only one from last night I've seen today, seemed both embarrassed and a little frightened when we crossed paths at work, neither of which made me as happy as I would have expected.

I now twist the tinsel in my hand as I sit on my bed, preparing to apologize to Laila. While I also owe Henry an apology, Laila comes first. Especially because today is her sixteenth birthday. The day she's been waiting for her entire life.

Since my bronze bangle prevents me from apporting, I steel my nerves and dial her cell. She doesn't answer. I call the house phone. No answer. I open my laptop and try her that way. Nothing. I probably wouldn't answer either.

I load my e-mail and type my rehearsed apology. It takes me almost an hour. I read it over. Twice. And then delete the whole thing. Because it sounds rehearsed.

As much as I want to forget all things Jinn, as much as I don't want anything to ruin my date with Nate, what I should do is skip the bonfire and ask my mother to app me to her house. I should, but rust is beginning to eat away at my steel nerves. My guilt on the other hand is all spit shined and gleaming. Because I'm more relieved than disappointed that Laila didn't answer any of my calls.

Coward that I am, I type an e-mail that simply says, *"I'm sorry. Happy Birthday, Sister."* I send it along with a photo I take of the silver tinsel wrapped around Mr. Gemp—the genie lantern Hana gave me on my birthday that I should be passing to Laila today.

This is when the tears I should have shed last night come.

30

Nostalgia for a past whose simplicity eluded me at the time makes me choose the purple linen tunic my mother gave me for my birthday. I'm wearing it over the lace bra and thong conjured by Yasmin. She really does have impeccable craftsmanship. The thong doesn't itch like I thought it would.

At the bathroom mirror, I keep one eye on the YouTube instructional video that plays on my laptop while I attempt to apply more than my usual lip gloss. The angled brush draws a line of deep pink on my cheeks, and I force my guilt to take a time out, just for tonight. A sparkling green camouflages my lower lid, and I bury the image of Laila's sad, knowing eyes. Mascara thickens my long lashes, and I replace the image of Laila's blue—now, gold—eyes with Nate's blissfully unaware chocolaty ones. With each brushstroke I cover the part of me that is Jinn. I become a normal teenage girl going on her first real date.

I put down the tube of cinnamon-colored lipstick and assess my work. Paired with the copper accents in my long, dark hair, the end result causes me to do a double take, not out of conceit but out of astonishment for how much I resemble my mother when she was my age. I could stand in for her in any picture in her high school album and I'm not sure anyone could tell the difference.

Tonight calls for something better than jeans. Fortunately, the benefit of being my mother's doppelgänger means I have effectively doubled my wardrobe. In her bedroom, I try on three different skirts before settling on a white denim mini I can't ever remember her wearing.

Before leaving, I sift through her jewelry box. This may be the first time I've ever thought about accessorizing. I feel a twinge in my chest when I think how proud both Hana and Laila would be.

Checking out the stockpile of jewels in the bottom drawer, I spy a thick, African-style wooden bracelet that looks like it'd pair well with my bronze bangle and slip it over my hand.

I rummage through, holding up black pearls from China and glass beads from Italy, but decide the necklace I'm already wearing works best. I start to close the drawer. That's when I notice what the large wooden bracelet was hiding.

Tucked into the furthest reaches is my silver pendant with the cursive *A* engraved on the front. But it can't be. Because that pendant's currently around my neck. I pick up the duplicate *A*, which feels much heavier than the one I'm wearing. It's the weight I remember it being before I turned sixteen.

It seems no matter how hard I try to prevent anything from ruining my date with Nate, the universe has other plans. Because the large piece of jewelry was hiding something else: the two pictures of my mother and her beau that I last stashed in my pillowcase. That was weeks ago. Of course, my mother's changed my sheets since then. Why didn't she say anything? The Jinn secrets' playbook keeps getting bigger.

I return the pictures and the heavier clone of my *A* pendant to her jewelry box. I'm reinstating my Scarlett O'Hara plan and giving myself tonight off. I have a lifetime to decipher this Jinn playbook. I'm not going to let anything ruin my night.

A melted bowl of mint chocolate chip ice cream sits on the coffee table in front of my mother. Neither one of us can eat ice cream slow enough that it melts. If that isn't enough of a clue that something's amiss, I catch the look on my mother's face as she slides something between the sofa cushions.

"Beautiful," she says in a voice two pitches higher than usual.

We made peace (sort of, more like we passed the sugar bowl and ignored what happened last night) before I left for work this morning. So her current twitchiness must have another cause. Why should I expect anything else?

She clears her throat. "You look great, honey."

"What's wrong?"

"Wrong? Nothing." Her eyes scan my body. "Hey, is that my skirt? And my . . . my bracelet?"

"Don't change the subject."

She must wonder if I found what the bracelet was hiding, but my instincts tell me whatever she's trying to cover up here is even more important.

"What subject?" she says. "This conversation's barely started."

I point to the small rectangular chips floating in the sea of creamy white. "Something made you stop eating that. The thing is, I can't imagine anything in this world that would cause that to happen."

My unwavering stare compels my mother to talk.

"They sent an assignment."

So it turns out it's not something in this world after all.

The smile that follows my mother's statement is so forced it makes me wince even more than the idea of granting another wish. Another wish. Already.

Breathe, Azra. Air in, air out.

It's just a job, right?

In through the nose, out through the mouth.

Just like slathering mayo on a BLT. Just like disinfecting a toilet.

"It's okay," I say. Knowing how much we look alike, my fake smile must be a perfect match for hers. "I'm ready this time."

My mother still hesitates.

"I am," I say, trying to convince her as much as myself. "I've actually been studying. I've even been reading about spells. *Azra-cadabra, I'm ready!*"

I'm standing there waving jazz hands and still nothing. Not even the slightest upturn of her lips in response to my joke. *Work with me here, Mom.*

"You're kind of freaking me out," I say.

Her plastered smile returns. "Azra, honey, it can wait. Tonight, just be a normal girl, okay?"

Normal girl? She's never once told me to be a normal girl. Not even when I begged her to. Something's very very wrong.

I hold out my palm. "Let me see."

Worry lines draw a gloomy mural on her face. But she gives in, compressing the side of the cushion she's sitting on. I slide my hand down the crack and yank out the gold envelope with my name perfectly embossed on the front.

The seal's broken. She's already opened it. I untuck the flap and pull out the single slip of paper.

No, it can't be.

My hands drop the whole thing as if it were on fire. The sheet lands face up and stares at me from its spot on the floor.

They're pushing things too far. They're pushing *me* too far.

I back up, slowly, until I hit the front door.

It feels almost intentional. Purposeful.

Clasping my hands behind my back, I press my body against the door as if I could push myself through it and away from here.

It's not fair. One night. One normal night. That's all I wanted.

My mother, still calmly seated on the sofa, picks up the envelope and the sheet of paper and lays them on the coffee table. Like last time, the letter contains the name and address of my wish candidate. But this time, I don't need the address. Though I've never been there, I know exactly where he lives.

Dizzy, I lean against the front door until I'm able to regulate my breathing. I ease my way across the room and lift up the paper as if it were a live grenade.

Nathan Reese.

Nate. My Nate. Nate is my next assignment.

I make it to the hall bathroom just in time.

Between the cold cloth my mother presses against my forehead and the streaks lining my face from the tears I couldn't hold back, my careful makeup application has just become collateral damage.

Staring at the unmistakable 3 on the back of the note card, I say, "This can't be a coincidence."

"Sure it can," my mother says, but something in her voice suggests otherwise.

"I like Nate. A lot. And you said it yourself. Being invested makes granting wishes messy."

"Oh, that." She balls up the damp washcloth. "I was being melodramatic."

"No you weren't. You were right."

She waves her hand to dry the fabric but instead soaks it. Water pools on the table and cascades over the edge onto the floor.

"You're nervous. You think I'm going to screw up again."

She grabs a dish towel to mop up the water. Her cleaning without magic confirms she's worried.

Her hand shakes as she sets the towel on the table. "You said you've been studying, right?" Her question sounds more like a plea. "We'll make sure you're ready. You'll be fine." She starts nodding her head. "Yes, we'll make sure you'll be fine."

I'm worried too, but right now, I'm less concerned about what might happen to me and more afraid of what could happen to Nate. "What if I hurt him?"

"You won't hurt him. How could you hurt him?"

I suck back the mucus clogging my nose and throat. "Maybe . . . like what if he wishes to be a Tiger, meaning on the varsity team, and I turn him into an actual tiger?"

Her tension releases in a laugh. She smiles and squeezes my shoulder. "Let's not go totally off the deep end, kiddo."

I shrug off her hand. "Okay, so what if I don't hurt him but he wishes for something that makes me lose him? Like being with Chelsea or some other rah-rah cheerleader?" Or me. What if he wishes for me? And what if granting that wish makes me lose Henry?

"He likes you," my mother says. "Let's also try not to invent problems, okay?"

I'm all out of reasons, but still I don't want to grant Nate a wish because . . . because I just don't. My pulse quickens, and I struggle to take my next breath. That's not true. That's not why. All of a sudden, my brain seizes on what my heart knew instantly.

My mother may be worried about my safety, but for me, the overarching reason why this sucks as much as it does is because it means my two worlds are colliding. The two worlds I was starting to think I could keep separate will become one. The part of me that could be normal Azra with Nate will vanish the moment I begin the wish-granting ritual. He won't know it. But I will.

I'll always know his deepest desire. And I'll have to make it come true. Once I link with his anima, a part of him will always be with me. I'll know him in a way he'll never know me. But I'll have to pretend I don't.

I was wrong. Getting to lie to Nate isn't better. I was delusional. Human attachments are indeed too hard. I will be exactly like my mother and Samara and every other Jinn.

So much for the liberation I thought the bronze bangle gave me. I've become a Jinn. A Jinn I will always be.

31

But do I have to be the Jinn that grants Nate a wish? Why not let me swap out Nate for another candidate?

When I ask my mother if she thinks this is possible, her olive-toned face goes pale.

"We don't question the Afrit," she says, setting down two cups of hot chocolate.

"Baa. Right. Because we are sheep. Drones. Worker bees. Mindless—"

"Please, Azra, don't," my mother says softly. "There are things you don't know. The Afrit . . . they can do things."

I tap my bronze bangle.

"Yes," she says, "they can restrict your magic. And if you defy them, they can extract you from this life and force you to live months, years, a lifetime, alone. And not just alone, but terrifyingly alone."

This I know. Which makes me scared of what I don't know. "There's a but, isn't there?" My mother nods. "And I don't want to hear it, do I?"

Another nod as my mother lifts her mug to her lips. "But you have to. Because what you don't know is there are a few steps in between. Having to remove young Jinn from the human world is not in the Afrit's best interest. They need you. They need you here to grant wishes. Extracting you is a last resort."

"Oh, really?" My grin is automatic. "So I *can* push the envelope before they'll slap real handcuffs on me?"

Her pained smile and the sadness in her gold eyes cause a tightness in my chest.

"You can." She shifts her gaze away from me. "But there are consequences."

"Like what? More years of granting wishes? More time on probation?" I flex my arm muscles. "I can take it." I'm desperate to make light because of the darkness I feel coming.

"Sometimes, but they've found that's not as effective as other methods of keeping Jinn in line."

I blow on my hot chocolate. "What kinds of methods?"

"They . . . they use us against one another." My mother pushes back her own mug. "If you were to continue to defy them, they won't take you away from this world." She now looks me in the eye. "They'll take me. They'll take me from you. From everyone."

Stunned into silence, I struggle to absorb her words.

She squeezes my hand reassuringly, but her voice shakes as she says, "I'm the one they'd send to their little torture chamber. I'd never see you again, Azra. I'd never see Samara or Nadia or any of my other Zar sisters again." Her eyes full of longing, she continues, "One day I'm supposed to be rewarded for following their rules—reunited with my loved ones who have been kept away from me, from us. But the truth is, before they'd do anything else to you, they'd make me pay for your crimes."

I'm light-headed, and my throat is so tight, I'm having trouble swallowing. If I screw up, my mother will be punished, and I will never see her again. *Never see her again.* As many times as I've angrily hoped for such a thing since hitting puberty, I cannot wrap my head around the idea.

"But why?" I finally ask.

She wrings her hands, and her tone shifts to one of anger. "They'll say it's because I didn't teach you properly. But it's simply a way of controlling us. Forbidding contact between loved ones serves as a pretty damn good deterrent for acting out against the Afrit. They use fear to get what they want. Fear and the hope that our love for each other is stronger than our hatred of them."

I lean forward in my chair. "But if they did that, if they . . . *took* you, it wouldn't be. I'd despise them."

"Well, I'm relieved to hear it, kiddo." She smiles weakly. "Unfortunately, they've thought of that. So it doesn't end with me. Once I'm gone, they'll place you with one of my Zar sisters for retraining."

My stomach drops. Yasmin's staying with Samara. Does that mean . . . ? No, Yasmin would have gotten a bronze bangle first, wouldn't she?

My mother continues, "If you act out, that sister will be taken away, and you and her daughter—your own Zar sister—will move on to the next, and the next, and the next, until you've exhausted everyone. And as each sister is ripped away and thrown in tortura cavea, we all feel it. Our Zar connection means one sister's living hell is felt by all."

My body grows so cold, it's like my blood has been replaced with ice. "Then I'd be taken?"

My mother shakes her head. "Not quite. There's one more thing they can use against us."

"Humans," I say, piecing it together. "That's why Jinn don't form attachments to humans."

My mother exhales slowly. "Underneath it all, the Afrit do want us to serve the human world. We need to if we want to keep our powers. But they'll go after humans if they have to. It's rare. Most Jinn don't let it get that far. But the Afrit have done it, if only to show that they can and will."

Henry. I pick up my hot chocolate, hoping whatever warmth is left will stop me from trembling, but I can't stomach a sip. "What . . . what do they do?"

"They ruin their lives. Even for the Afrit, mind control is tricky. Whether it's inserting thoughts or erasing memories, it's risky. Dangerous. The Afrit's goal is to wipe the human's memory of the Jinn they know, leaving the Jinn without their trusted friend, lover, what have you. But in far too many cases, they've left humans as amnesiacs or damaged their brains so much that the person winds up in a mental institution. They've even killed a few humans in the most dire cases."

My mug falls from my hand. My mother's powers catch it before it drops to the floor where it would have shattered into a million pieces, the same way my heart seems to be doing.

"Are you sure?" I say. "I mean, have you actually seen it?"

"A human being killed? No." My mother bites her lip. Though she forces back the tears I can just see forming, she can't stop her voice from trembling. "But the other part . . . the damage . . . I'm sure it's true because I've done it."

My pulse thumps in my ears. "I thought you couldn't do mind control?"

She stands abruptly, moves to the back door, and stares out the window. "I can't. Not like you did. Not unassisted. I've never known a Jinn who could do what you can do. But with a spell, like the one I used on Ms. Wood, I can come pretty close. It's probably the hardest spell to pull off. Most Jinn can't."

"But of course you can, being the model Jinn and all."

My mother turns to me, sadness darkening her eyes. "It's not something to be proud of." She beckons me over. "Come here. I need you to see this."

Dread makes me hesitate before pushing back my chair.

She steps to the side and taps the glass with the tip of her fingernail. "That's how I know the dangers of mind control are real."

Crazy old Mrs. Seyfreth from next door, wearing her usual fur coat, is staring over the fence into our backyard.

She's farther down, no longer blocked by the lilac bush I moved. She must have found something else to stand on. I say tentatively, "Why does she do that?"

My mother speaks slowly. "She can't help it. It's not her fault. It's . . . it's mine."

Mrs. Seyfreth's vacant eyes float in our direction.

"Your fault?" I fall back against the counter. "But how?" I know the answer. She just told me the answer. I don't want to hear it. But I have to hear it.

My mother pulls the shade over the window and returns to her chair.

"But why didn't you tell me? I'm sure it was a mistake."

"Mistake after mistake after mistake." Her eyes fixate on her lap. "I was careless, and she saw something she shouldn't have. It was all so horrible, but I was desperate. And arrogant. I thought I could fix it. I'd never used a spell to make someone forget something so huge, but I thought I could do it."

This is why she didn't want to try the spell on Henry. *Thank Janna she didn't try the spell on Henry.* "So . . . so you're the reason she's . . . the way she is?"

She raises her eyes to meet mine. "Yes, and no. She'd already been showing signs. Her senility or whatever poor thing she's suffering from was already there. What I did just accelerated it. The worst part is, I could tell. When I was doing the spell, I could tell I'd erased her memory, but I went a little further, just to be sure."

I place my hand on hers. "You were protecting yourself. And me. I'm sorry about Mrs. Seyfreth, but if the alternative was the Afrit taking you—"

"Don't say that, Azra. We can't use our powers to hurt people, no matter the cost."

Though she says this, I can tell from the way she's looking at me, she'd do whatever she had to in order to protect me. "Why isn't all this in the cantamen?"

"It is and it isn't."

"The blank pages," I say, remembering the section I found in the middle that was completely empty.

"Hidden by a spell. The spell's in the cantamen. I may as well reverse it now so you can learn the whole sordid history of how this came to be our Jinn world. I'm sorry. I know I should have told you. I was just trying to protect you. I wanted you to be able to be a Jinn without all this—"

"Hatred?"

"Fear, was what I was going to say." My mother forces a smile. "You know, if you didn't look so much like me, sometimes I'd swear you were Samara's daughter."

"But I don't understand. Why do we let them get away with it? Why don't we—"

"Fight? You and Sam really are peas in a pod." My mother waves her hand. "Look around, who's here to fight?"

"That's why the male Jinn have to live with them?"

"And your grandmothers and everyone else who's not a practicing Jinn, a retired mother raising a daughter, or the daughter being raised. Keeping our community separate, preventing us from living in clusters, ensuring our numbers here remain on the low side, it's all a way of preventing an uprising."

"But we're here. Us mothers and daughters. We have powers. We could take them on."

"No. The Afrit have powers beyond ours. And Janna is so well-shielded now that we can't get in without them apporting us in. The same way every Jinn there can't get out. We wouldn't stand a chance."

"But some want to try, like Samara?" The harsh words exchanged between my mother and Samara on the night of my birthday about taking risks now make sense.

My mother sighs. "Yes, like Samara. Like Raina."

My head jerks back. "And the Afrit found out? So they took

her?" I was right. What happened to Raina isn't Yasmin's fault. "She's . . . gone? *Gone,* gone?"

Tears fall down my mother's cheeks. "See, Azra, talk is one thing, but the consequences are real. Even Sam knows that. We've all lost so much. We can't risk losing what we have left. I know I won't. I won't put you at risk."

And neither will I.

I surround my mother's cold hand with both of mine. I won't risk losing her. I won't risk having Henry's brain fried. Or worse.

So that's it. I'll be granting Nate his wish. I'll be granting every assigned candidate their wish—and I'll be granting them perfectly. I'll follow in my mother's footsteps and be a model Jinn. I . . . I won't form attachments with humans. I won't form *any more* attachments with humans. And maybe, probably, I should, I will, I might undo the ones I have. Because the alternative . . . because there is no alternative.

Exactly as the Afrit planned.

I'm in my room trying to reapply my makeup, but my hands are shaking too much. My mother is insisting, despite everything she's just told me, or maybe because of everything she's just told me, that I go on my date.

Can I still call it a date if it's also research for my new assignment? Can a Jinn mix business with pleasure? Not if she can't draw a straight line under her eyelashes, she can't.

Setting down the eye pencil, I attempt to apply a thin layer of blush to my pale cheeks. Stress has drained all the blood from my face.

Not that I'm normally a fan of being kept in the dark, but the way my insides are knotted up, I understand my mother keeping the truth about the Afrit a secret. I'm afraid to breathe wearing this bronze bangle, I can't imagine using magic.

But not only do I have to use magic, I have to use magic to grant Nate a wish. One wrong move in doing so, and that's it. I'll lose what, I haven't realized until now, I love and need most in this world: my mother. What's worse is if I grant Nate his wish and botch it, I also risk losing what, I haven't realized until now, I'm beginning to love and need almost as much: Laila and Samara and Hana and all the rest . . . even Yasmin? Yes, even Yasmin. And maybe even Nate.

And, of course, Henry. Because of what I've done, Henry will always be in jeopardy. Henry, who defies categorization. It's as if we've become so intertwined, I cease to exist without him. How can I ever summon enough courage to break my attachment to him?

I've spent so much time concentrating on the family I didn't have because of being Jinn, I never suspected the family I do have could be taken away. My mother, Samara, Laila, Nate, Henry, I can't put any of them at risk. I have to be the perfect Jinn.

Well, hello pressure, nice to meet you.

I smudge the eyeliner under my lashes, hoping to make my imperfect application look purposeful. This second round of makeup will certainly benefit from the shadowy light of a fire. After sweeping my cosmetics into the drawer, I move to my desk where my cantamen sits, calling to me. As tempted as I am to flip through and find a way out of granting Nate a wish, I know it's no use.

Funny, despite everything, I still hate being told what to do. Maybe it's a Jinn trait, like craving sweets and warmth, because certainly control's the only thing the Afrit seem to care about.

Every mandate put in place by the Afrit serves one goal: to keep them in power. To keep them in power, they must be feared. To be feared, there must be consequences for rebelling against them and their rules. The way they use our love for one another as a weapon to keep us in line and maintain control sickens me. But I'll admit they've got a good thing going. It works.

In response to the gentle knock on my bedroom door, I say, "*Entrez.*" Henry would be proud of my French pronunciation.

My mother bears the gift of sugar in her hand. "Figured you could use a little pick-me-up."

I pop one then two nonpareils into my mouth. As she conjures me two more, I think maybe I can go through with this date after all. And I should. Who knows? If I do manage to cut my ties with humans, it might very well be my last one.

"Nervous?" my mother asks.

My quivering voice is at odds with my sarcastic reply. "Not really. What with the fate of everyone I know hanging in the balance, worrying about whether Nate will kiss me is no longer on my radar. Unexpected bonus, right?"

My mother smiles. "I see your flair for the dramatic is intact. But, really, nothing's changed."

I cock my head. "*Everything's* changed."

She gently touches my bronze bangle before taking my hand. "I know. Which is why I didn't want to tell you all this. I wanted to protect you. And maybe let you enjoy it, or try to anyway. But of course, Samara was right. You're not like the others. Hana, Mina, Farrah, they don't need to know what the Afrit are capable of. They'll never question anything. But you, you my dear, control is in your blood."

"Maybe that's a good thing," I say. "Because now that I know, I can be in control. Total control." Suddenly I pull her into an embrace. "I promise, I'll be careful. I won't . . . I won't let them hurt you."

She tightens her grip, and surely we are both thinking of Yasmin and Lalla Raina.

The sound of a car idling draws me to my window. I'm expecting to see Nate, who, since it's a date, conceded to use petrol instead of pedal power, but instead I see Henry. He's closing his front door and walking toward a car I don't recognize. The back door opens, and Chelsea's head pops out.

"Don't worry," my mother says, "Nate seems like your average boy. What do teenage boys want? Cars? Bigger biceps?"

Henry disappears into the backseat.

"Girls," I say. "Teenage boys want teenage girls."

The question is, where does that leave teenage Jinn?

At the moment, it leaves this teenage Jinn with a clammy hand wrapped around a warm beer can. I take a tiny sip and wince as the liquid hits my tongue. Though my taste for beer has yet to be acquired since the last time I tried it with Henry, the beverage selection at the bonfire is sorely lacking. But with Nate on one side of me and Henry and Chelsea across from me, I'm desperate to blend in. So this aluminum-flavored skunk urine will have to do.

A small group of us have distanced ourselves from the rest of the staff, specifically from the rest of the staff who would not condone underage drinking. Our own mini bonfire burns inside a ring of rocks Nate and his two lifeguard buddies dragged from down the beach.

Though I'm supposed to be paying close attention to Nate considering he's, one, my date, and two, the candidate I need to be doing due diligence on, I can't help but watch Henry.

The sheer number of in-jokes proves this is not the first time

Henry's hung out with the members of our little offshoot here. Between his relaxed posture, his untucked oxford with the rolled-up sleeves, his contact lenses, and his spiffy hair—*Is that gel?*—he's not the tousle-haired Henry who gave me a balloon at the start of the summer. He's not the boy whose family is on the verge of bankruptcy. He's not the boy defined by losing his little sister.

Transitioning into this new crowd, he can be whoever he wants to be. His secrets are safe with me. As mine are with him.

Our eyes meet.

I'm sorry, Azra.

This is running through Henry's head, and even though I suddenly hear it in my own, I don't need to. Even in the dim light of the fire, his face says it all. Since he can't read my mind, I hope the same can be said of the look on my own face. We're going to be just fine.

I love you, Azra.

Oh, no. Oh, damn. This thought of Henry's I don't want to hear. And it too is written all over his face. I'm now panicked by what's scrawled across my own.

Henry's eyes shift away from mine and land on Chelsea, who shimmies closer to the fire to warm her hands over the flames. I lean into Nate just as Henry puts an arm around Chelsea's shoulder.

Chelsea's eyes are shut tight. Her thoughts fly at me.

How did I get so lucky? The nice guys never want me.

"That's it," I say too loudly, not wanting to dive deeper into Chelsea's inner world. I don't want to find out she's actually the saint Henry's making her out to be. I can't. I've learned enough for one night.

I'm not sure how I'm reading everyone's minds, but I need to stop. I step back from the fire and fan myself. "Whew. Fire. Hot."

Apparently I'm now a caveman.

"I mean, it's a bit warm, isn't it?" I say, happy to have managed a full sentence. "I think I could use a break."

Henry's eyes dart in my direction. He knows me well enough to know I'm lying. He just doesn't know why.

"Excellent idea," Nate says. He picks up the backpack he set on the ground earlier and knocks off the sand before slinging it over one shoulder.

I hear Henry's mind contemplate coming with us, and I hear Chelsea's mind wanting Henry to walk somewhere alone with her, and I break into an uncharacteristic run. Henry must really know something's up.

Since running is very much in character for Nate, he catches up to me quickly.

"I know the private jokes can be a bit much," Nate says, "but those guys are okay once you get to know them. Henry can tell you that. We should hang out with them all more. You'll see."

"Yeah," I say, "I'd like that."

And I would like it. I just don't think it's a very good idea to extend my circle of human friends. It's as bad an idea as not ending my friendships—relationships, whatever "ships" I have—with Nate and Henry. I know I should. But I just can't. At least not yet. I will if I have to. But not yet. Fortunately and unfortunately, I've got many, many horrific stages to get through before I'd get there.

We walk in step with one another, doing a lateral dance with the incoming tide to keep our feet out of the water.

"Not that I'm complaining," Nate says. "I've been wishing we could be alone together since we got here."

Nate is unaware of how careful he needs to be using the "w" word. Still, if he's going to be wishing for anything, I don't mind it having something to do with me. Here we are, on a date, with me doing research without even having to try.

Nate takes my hand, and it's like I've touched a live wire. An electric charge shoots through my body. Is it the same for Nate?

Wow. Oh, wow.

Apparently it is. But I've got to get a handle on this mind-reading stuff. It's not right to be privy to everyone's innermost—

She has to know how much I like her. How much I'm dying to kiss her.

Okay, maybe I could stick around for one or two more thoughts. Really, I mean, this is something I should be practicing since it'll help me grant wishes. Being able to read minds like this is rare. It's a gift, right?

But does she want to kiss me?

How could he possibly be asking that? He has to know I like him as much as he likes me. Probably more. How could he not know? Am I still giving off that stupid vibe?

Because I see the way Henry looks at her. And she him. Maybe I should back off.

Is that the vibe I've been giving off? I didn't mean to. Or did I? No, Henry's my best friend. I need Henry to be my best friend. And I need a best friend, now more than ever.

Nate's hand begins to slip from mine. I hang on to it, interlacing my fingers with his. I'm not sure what Nate is right now, but I need him too.

I don't know how to verbalize all this. Part of me thinks it'd be easier if Nate could read my mind. Not necessarily less complicated, but easier.

I've spent the evening convincing myself that I am in control. That I'm smart enough to grant Nate a wish without hurting him or exposing myself or bringing the wrath of the Afrit down on everyone I care about. If that's true then this, being my teenage self with a boy, should be a snap.

Moonlight shining down on us, whoosh of the ocean serenading us, Nate smiling at me, it is easy, but not necessarily uncomplicated.

"I'm a little worried about you," Nate says, pulling a flashlight out of his backpack.

He guides us through the marshy area at the far end of the beach, scanning the ground ahead of us until the beam of light settles on a sandy patch partially concealed by the dunes.

"That book you told me to read? About the guy who goes to live in Alaska and eats the poisoned apple?"

"*Into the Wild*?" I say. "It was seeds, I think."

Nate grins. "I was trying to be cute."

Oh, right. Flirting, which I thought I was getting better at.

"You don't have to try," I say.

Okay, not bad.

Nate winks at me as he slips off his backpack. He takes out a red blanket and shakes it to unfurl it. After spreading it out on the sand, he kneels down and adds to the ambience with a few battery-operated votive candles, two canned cappuccinos, and a bag of almonds—sugar-coated, not salted. Presumptuous to some, but the realization that Nate was thinking about me enough to plan all this has me approaching giddiness. I don't approach giddiness lightly. I may have never before been in sniffing distance of giddiness. I may have never before used the word "giddiness."

My miniskirt hikes even farther up my thigh as I sit next to him. Any more and Yasmin's carefully crafted thong will threaten to make an appearance. I tug the hem of my skirt with one hand and accept the cappuccino Nate offers me with the other.

Our cans don't make much of a clinking sound as we tap them, but that's okay. Nothing could detract from this moment. It feels like a real date.

"It's just that the dude in the book . . ." Nate shakes his head. "He up and left his entire family. Didn't keep in touch. I couldn't do that. The way he acted . . . I just couldn't relate to it, to him. He's out there alone doing his thing while his parents and sister are worried sick."

"I never thought of it that way before." I hadn't, but I do now.

Nate stretches out, resting his head in one hand. "Guess it was over my head, maybe. The whole soul-searching thing. It's just, personally, I don't need to go anywhere to know what I want."

As Nate takes my hand, it's clear that, unlike me, he has mastered the art of flirtation.

I lie on my side, facing him. I have to, right? I mean, Nate's about to tell me what he *wants*—code word for what he *desires,* what he *wishes.* It's my *job* to encourage him. If only my heart would slow down and stop echoing in my ears, I might be able to concentrate on what he's saying. If only my mind wasn't so jumbled with my own thoughts, I might be able to focus on reading his.

But I don't need to do either. What Nate wants is written all over his suntanned face. It boils down to three little words: "me," "kiss," "you."

The sand shifts underneath us as he presses the length of his body against mine. His hand rests on the rivets of my denim skirt, gently cupping my hip as I fall flat against the blanket. Careful not to rest down his full weight, he uses his swimmer's arms to suspend himself above me. He positions his head in line with mine and lowers himself toward me. I hesitate before dismissing my fleeting thought to start the wish-granting ritual right now. Granting his wish to kiss me seems like cheating. Not to mention what would happen if he wished for more. If he wished to do more, to be with me, to *really* be with me, would I grant it? Would I have to grant it? Would I want to grant it? Would it make me a Jinn prostitute if I granted it?

Our lips touch, and all thoughts of his wishes leave my mind. For once, I'm granting my own wish. And that wish is to be right here, kissing Nate.

Turns out I really am one talented Jinn. My wish comes true for so long that when I open my eyes, I'm surprised the sun isn't rising.

Though my thong has remained unseen, the same cannot be said of the matching lace bra. I'm lying on Nate's bare chest as he runs his finger along my collarbone.

"Goose bumps," he says. "You're freezing."

For the first time in my life, the cold isn't bothering me.

Nate removes his shirt from behind our heads and lays it across my torso. We stay that way, just talking. He asks about my aunts and cousins, and I start to tell him about everyone who's been in my life since the day I was born. But thinking about

Yasmin ignites a stabbing in my chest and I have to stop before tears escape my eyes.

I didn't want anything to ruin my date with Nate, but the Afrit and what they are capable of will loom over everything I do for the rest of my life, worming their way into even the most unexpected of circumstances.

I make Nate tell me about his family instead. I'm envious when he mentions his dad has been teaching him to sail.

"I'd love to go out on the ocean like that," I say.

"I'll take you," Nate says. "I'm getting pretty good. Though my sister, Megan, she's awesome. She's only twelve, but she's a natural."

"You two get along?"

Nate nods. "Oh yeah. I think it helps that we're further apart in age. Always felt like I wanted to watch out for her. Like Henry does for his little sister."

"Lisa," I say softly. I pat the blanket until I find my shirt and pull it over my head. Being half naked with Nate and picturing Henry makes me uncomfortable in ways I don't want to think about right now. Fortunately, a faint *wop-wop-wop* quickly builds to the point where it drowns out everything.

Nate points to the sky. "Helicopter."

"It's really close," I shout. "Like it's going to land right on top of us."

Nate stands up. I reluctantly hand him his shirt and he puts it on, his eyes still following the helicopter.

"Looks like a medical copter," he says. "It's setting down on the main road, I think."

Before I know it, Nate's pecking me on the cheek, asking if I'll be okay waiting here alone for him, and sprinting down the beach in the dark. He leaves me with the only flashlight. Naturally he's going to see if anyone's hurt, if anyone needs help. He's done so much extra first-aid training than is required for a lifeguard, he's probably halfway toward being a paramedic.

I know from firsthand experience he's very good at mouth-to-mouth. Here I am, all alone in the dark on a deserted patch of beach, and I'm blushing.

I finish the almonds and wash them down with the sweet cappuccino. I've had enough coffee to know it's not the caffeine that's filling me with this tingling feeling. But the longer I sit waiting for Nate to return, the more the feeling fades and the faster the cold coming off the late summer ocean seeps in.

I'm now a Jinn burrito, wrapped in the blanket, standing and shining the flashlight down the beach. I check my cell phone, but I'm not getting a signal this far down the beach. I wonder where Nate could be? He should be back by now.

Between the cold, the dark, and the rustling of something in the tall dune grass, I'm done. I pack up Nate's backpack and slip my arms through the straps. I start walking, using the flashlight to keep me on the sand and out of the water, but it's a long walk all alone without Nate. The moon seemed much brighter on the way here.

Pointing the beam of light in midair, searching for Nate, I miss any advance warning of the huge rock in my path and fall flat on my stomach. I stand and spit grains of sand out of my mouth. Oh, sure, I had to go on and on about how much I love the beach at night. Perfect place for a date. It is, provided the date doesn't abandon you. I just want to be back with everyone else, warming up by the fire. I'd even settle for being inside the splintering wood walls of the drafty concession stand.

Thunder rolls through my empty stomach as I picture the vanilla-glazed doughnuts and chocolate chip muffins. I close my eyes. I can smell the cinnamon buns. I breathe in. The air floating up my nostrils warms my lungs. It lacks both the chill and the brine of my previous inhale.

This would be strange if I were still on the beach.

But I'm not.

I open my eyes to find the dark walls of the concession stand surrounding me.

The flashlight falls from my hand. I jump at the thud it makes against the wood planks before diving to the floor to turn the damn thing off before the light penetrates the cracks in the walls and someone comes to find me inside a building locked from the outside.

Crawling into the corner, I position my back to the door and rest the flashlight against my stomach. I press the ON button and direct the shaft of light toward my wrist. The bangle is still bronze as I knew it would be. Ridiculous, maybe, but I had to make sure the Afrit hadn't replaced it with my silver one while I was otherwise occupied with Nate. But, no, I'm still on probation. I'm still wearing the bronze bangle. I'm still unable to do magic. I'm *supposed* to still be unable to do magic.

But I just apported. The flashlight slides in my sweaty palms. How could I have apported? Panic rises in my chest. Do the Afrit know I apported? My pulse quickens. No, no, they can't know. They only track the energy we use to do the circulus, right? Isn't that what my mother said? I'm light-headed from the short breaths I'm struggling to take. What if she's wrong? Will I be punished? Will she be punished?

Numb, I wait in my corner for the Afrit to come. But they don't. No one does. I'm alone so long my heart rate slows and my stomach remembers it's hungry. The dizziness I feel when I rise to my feet makes me grab a stale doughnut. I take small bites and lean against the counter, letting the truth of what just happened sink in.

The bronze bangle didn't block my magic. How is that possible? I lick icing from my thumb. Was this a one-time thing?

A stack of napkins sits at the far end of the counter. I concentrate. Now the napkins are in front of me. *No freakin' way.*

I swallow the last bite of doughnut. Needing something to wash the dryness down, I picture a tall glass of milk. The tingle down my spine lets me know it's there before I open my eyes. So I'm not a psychic after all. I could mind-read because I still had my powers.

Maybe this bangle's a dud. Maybe however it's supposed to restrict my magic is on the fritz. Maybe whatever turns it on when I begin a wish-granting ritual is jammed in the "go" position. Or . . . maybe, despite the scar on the back of my neck, I don't need a bangle to release my powers. Maybe I can do magic without one.

Preposterous . . . and yet my gut says otherwise. Impossible . . . isn't it? Wouldn't I have done *something* magical before? Even inadvertently, at some point during the first fifteen years of my life, wouldn't I have used my powers?

Jenny. Of course. Best friends since before we could walk, my mother said. So much so that I wandered across the street and plopped myself on the Carwyns' doorstep. How gullible was I? I'm sure I landed on their doorstep but not because I scooted across the street on all fours. As a toddler, I must have wanted to see my best friend so badly that I apported myself to her.

Is it really possible I've always been able to do magic? If so, my mother must know. And if she knows, why did she keep it a secret? And why haven't I done more?

"I'm flying, Azra!"

Poor Jenny. I head for the side door of the concession shack, undo the latch, and peek out, still thinking of Jenny. As much as I wish it wasn't, the memory of that day on the swings is seared into my brain.

"Higher, Azra!"

A memory, which until now, I didn't fully understand.

"Higher, Azra! Make me go higher!"

I slam the door shut without thinking of the noise. I clutch my *A* pendant and fall back against the wall, sliding to the floor. Bringing my knees to my chest, I tuck myself into a ball. As I rock back and forth, tears gush like water from an open fire hydrant. Me always having the ability to do magic adds a horrifying subtext to the events of that day.

Jenny and I were on the swings in my backyard, alone. We had each just finished a three-scoop ice cream cone. Chocolate had dripped down my chin and onto my neck and chest. My mother had gone inside for a washcloth, taking my *A* necklace with her to clean. She had told us not to go on the swings until she returned. Like we were babies. I wasn't going to be told what to do.

"Come on, Jenny," I said.

She followed, and we sat on the swings, kicking at the ground with our feet.

"I wish I had a push," Jenny said.

"I'll grant your wish," I said to Jenny, teasing. Though I wanted to, I knew I wasn't allowed to tell her I was a genie.

But then all of a sudden our legs managed to propel us into the air. Up and up, we went, swinging faster and faster, higher and higher.

"I'm flying, Azra! Higher, Azra!"

It was all my fault.

I must have used magic to push us on the swings, to push us higher and higher in the air, to push us so high, we could touch the clouds.

The force of my trembling threatens to knock the rickety concession shack down. I was a kid. I didn't know what I was doing. I didn't mean for anything bad to happen. I'm sure I only wanted to make Jenny happy. I couldn't have known. I *know* I couldn't have known. But that doesn't matter.

When you're responsible for the death of your best friend, nothing else matters.

My hand goes numb from its tight squeeze on my *A* pendant as I remember something else. That day, Mrs. Seyfreth was going to the ballet. I remember Jenny and I begging her to bring us back the program. She was at the back fence, peering over, booklet in hand, when Jenny fell. That must be what she saw. My mother using magic to try to save Jenny. Mrs. Seyfreth going crazy isn't my mother's fault at all. It's mine.

Forcing myself to breathe, I release my hold on my *A* and flex my fingers, trying to stimulate the feeling to return. My mother gave me this necklace when I was so young I don't remember it. I never took it off, feeling a compulsion to always have the pendant against my skin. That is, until the day I turned sixteen. It's not that I didn't like it anymore, but the insistent *need* to wear it was gone. Because . . . because that pendant was gone.

I once again test the weight of the *A* around my neck. I knew it was too light—unlike the one tucked in the far corner of my mother's jewelry box. The one she must have spelled to block my powers. The one she must have spelled so I'd never remove it.

If that's true, then my mother really does know I don't need a bangle to release my magic. She knows I'm unlike every other Jinn. But she didn't want me to know. Because she's protecting me or because she's afraid? Considering what I now know about the Afrit, the two go hand in hand.

My world suddenly unstable, I'm as shaky as a three-legged table, but I can't just apport home. Me disappearing would surely draw unwanted attention. And as my mother taught me, I can't have that.

I check to make sure no one's watching before sneaking out the door. Nate must be looking for me. Scratch that, Nate must have organized a search-and-rescue mission for me. I enter into a chaotic mess of people, police cars, and ambulances. There's even a news van.

I wander through the throng of bodies, but Nate's nowhere to be found. Wait, there's Chelsea. Is she crying? The rest of the beautiful bods are slumped over a picnic table. I'm heading toward them when Henry comes up behind me.

"Where have you been?" His voice is full of worry.

I never lie to him, but there's so much to tell, I don't know where to begin. My chest tightens and tears again creep into my eyes.

Jenny. All this time Henry's been blaming himself. For what I did. He deserves to know the truth. But he can never know the truth.

"What took you so long to get back here?" he says. "I've been looking for you." He touches my cheek. "You've been crying. So you do know? I'm so sorry, Azra."

Henry puts one hand on each of my upper arms, rubbing gently. He's scaring me.

"Know what? What's happened?" I swivel my head. "Where's Nate?"

Henry bites his lower lip. His eyes won't meet mine. I grab his chin and force him to look at me.

"What is it, Henry?"

His Adam's apple bulges as he swallows. "The helicopter. His parents. They were stopping by on their way back from dinner. There was a car accident on the road to the beach. Some of the kids at the bonfire. They . . . they drank too much. It's bad, Azra, really bad."

Henry looks like he's about to cry, which makes the tears I'm fighting all the more difficult to control. But this time, I do. I ask him where they're taking Nate's parents. I ask him if he thinks Nate's already there.

Once I have my answer, I'm off, running back to the concession stand. All I care about is getting to Nate and his parents. The only wish Nate could possibly make is to save them. And it's a wish I'll be able to grant. I don't know exactly how or what I'll do, but I know I'll be able to figure it out. I'll be able to grant Nate's wish and keep his family together.

After this afternoon, I was convinced the whole Afrit notion of "greater good" was a bunch of bull. But I was wrong.

No, I WAS RIGHT.

I'm in the ER surrounded by noise. I apped myself to the woods behind the hospital parking lot and sprinted through the sedans, SUVs, and minivans. Having barreled through the sliding glass doors into the waiting room, the blaring TV, crying babies, and chattering nurses momentarily overwhelm me.

I struggle to catch my breath while scanning the crowded room for Nate. Finally, I see him, huddled in the far corner with a young girl who must be his sister and two older adults who are most likely his grandparents.

My rush of adrenaline plummets. My feet won't budge. The effects of the caffeine long gone, the leftover acid gnaws at my stomach lining. I shut my eyes and breathe, steadying my rapid pulse. When I open my eyes, a man in green scrubs is crossing the room, approaching Nate and his family.

The din of the ER fades into the background. The doctor gets farther from me but closer to Nate. I'm no good at judging distances but I have to be at least twenty feet back. That far away and still I can read his mind.

My throat tightens, my knees buckle. I'm dizzy. *It can't be. It just can't be.* My feeble attempt at mind control doesn't stop the doctor from saying what he's about to say.

I plunge deeper into the doctor's mind: internal bleeding, ruptured lung, trauma to the head, gone before he arrived. Gone. *Gone.* Nothing we could do. Nothing anyone could do.

Anyone, not even me? Was there nothing I could do to save Nate's father?

Gone before I even got here. Before I had a chance to do anything. How can that be? Did I waste time lying on a blanket, snacking on sugary almonds when I was supposed to be here? Did I waste time feeling sorry for myself, eating stale doughnuts in the concession stand? Is this all my fault? Did I miss out on being able to grant Nate the most important wish of his life? Was this not the wish I was supposed to grant? Was this not why Nate was chosen as a candidate? What could make him more deserving of a wish than this?

I can't look at Nate's face as the doctor tells him the news. I can't hear his thoughts. I can't bear the pain of hearing his thoughts. Selfishly, I shut him out. I shut everyone out. My heart is breaking. Nausea churns my insides. My breathing is rapid, irregular. I want to app away from here, far away. It's too much. Everything that's happened tonight, and now, this too, it's just too much.

I back up until I hit the wall behind me. I lean against it and steal a glance at Nate. His eyes are welded shut, and he's clutching his sister so tightly I'm afraid he might crush her. If I think it'd be painful to hear Nate's thoughts, what must it be like to *be* Nate, to be the one thinking those thoughts?

I think of Jenny, and I know. I think of the Afrit taking my mother, and I know. I think of the Afrit erasing Henry's mind, and I know.

I also know, I'm not going anywhere. I'll be right here, whether he needs me or not, I won't leave him. If he has to take this, so do I.

I tune back in to the doctor who's telling them about Nate's mother. Facial lacerations, broken ribs, significant blood loss. The older woman, who my mind-reading confirms is their grandmother and Mrs. Reese's mother, holds her breath through it all. But when the doctor says "investigating possible spinal cord damage," she releases a moan, too soft for me to hear externally, but the strength of the one inside her head almost knocks me off my feet.

Nate and his grandmother follow the doctor to see his mother. In her grandfather's arms, Megan folds in on herself, hands tight against her chest, head hanging down, knees bent—the equivalent of a standing fetal position. I take the nearest seat and try not to lose it.

My head between my knees, I feel a hand rubbing my back. I look up. *Henry.* I fly out of the chair and throw myself against his chest with such force that we almost fall to the ground. Like Nate, he has long, strong swimmer's arms. They envelop me, and that's it. I lose control.

Now that Henry's here, I give in to my fear, my guilt, my worry, my . . . pain. I'm dragging out a memory from the furthest reaches of my brain, but the details are just beyond my grasp. But the feeling, the feeling comes. A hurt so raw and deep, it surpasses even this. I'm small and being held by some other boy's arms. Some other boy's arms that have the same ability as Henry to ground me, to make me feel like the world is not ending. The memory retreats, scurrying back to the dusty corners of my mind, but the feeling remains.

"Breathe, Azra, just breathe," Henry says.

Chelsea comes up next to us and rests her hand on Henry's shoulder. Tears fall down her cheeks . . . her freckled cheeks. Weird that this is the first time I've noticed the smattering of cute little dots. I stare at them, mentally drawing lines between them. Somehow, it is these tiny speckles that soften her to me, and then soften me toward her.

She lays a hand on my forearm. "They're not . . . Nate's parents . . . they're not . . ." Chelsea is unable to say the words.

I don't make her. I look into her sympathetic eyes and whisper, "Just his father." *Just.*

Finally, I push myself back from Henry. I take the tissue offered by Chelsea and blow my nose. She hands me another one and I blow again, still leaning one shoulder against Henry.

"Az." Henry lifts his chin, gesturing to the other side of the room.

Nate and his grandmother are returning to his sister, grandfather, and a few other family members and friends who have arrived. The entire group shares the same tortured expression.

Nate's bloodshot eyes float around the room, and he sees me. He kisses the top of his sister's head before rushing to me. I meet him halfway, holding him, I hope, at least half as well as Henry held me.

My condolences don't need to be verbalized. I'm reading

Nate's mind, and without me having to say anything, he knows how sorry I am, how much I'm hurting for him, how much everyone in this room is hurting for him. And that's becoming a problem.

They all mean well, but I can't face them. Not yet. I need . . .

Ending our embrace, I take Nate's hand. "Want to go outside? Get some fresh air? Just for a minute?"

Nate glances at his grandmother, tilts his head toward the exit, and raises a shaky finger in the air. Once she nods to him, Nate allows me to guide him through the well-meaning but rubbernecking friends and strangers. Though he's beginning to cut off the circulation in my hand, I let him squeeze as hard as he wants, as hard as he needs to, until we pass through the front doors of the ER.

"Is there anything I can do?" I ask the question to which there is no answer because I have to say something.

That was . . . seeing her . . . seeing my mom . . . and Grandma . . . she went to see him *. . . I . . . I couldn't . . . I—*

Even Nate's mind can't finish this nightmarish thought. He wipes his tear-dampened cheeks with his free hand. "Just . . . just walk with me."

And so we travel through the parking lot, hand in hand, up and down the rows of cars. Unlike the beach, the moonlight barely shines here, drowned out by all the harsh lights.

"You'd think this would make me feel better," Nate says, running a finger along the back window of a hatchback, leaving a clean, straight line in the dust. "That most of these cars probably belong to someone who's hurting. Someone whose loved one is in the middle of surgery or being treated for cancer or just . . . just . . . I can't even say it."

He stops and rests against the end of a pickup truck. "What now, Azra? What will we do now, without . . . without . . . my dad. And my mom . . . all those machines and wires." He bends, placing his hands on his thighs, staring at the concrete. "This can't be happening. This can't be happening."

But it is. And I can't do anything about it. Because there are some things even our magic can't do.

We can't heal humans.

We can't bring people back from the dead.

We can't grant a wish for a candidate not assigned to us by the Afrit.

But Nate was assigned. To me.

"He was going to help me get a scholarship," Nate says. "He and Megan already signed up for that sailing competition. He and my mom were going to go to Italy, move back to Boston once Megan graduated, become grandparents. And now, now, I just wish . . . I wish . . ."

I'm momentarily paralyzed. There's so much Nate might wish for that I can't give him. Doing the ritual now is risky. The last thing I want to do is have to employ a genie trick.

No, that's not right. The last thing I want to do is nothing—to stand here and do nothing when I have a chance to help Nate.

I move in front of him. "What, Nate? What do you wish for? Is there something, anything, that would make this even a little bit easier?"

Nate nods as tears return and spill down his cheeks. I grab his hand and pull him farther down the row until we are camouflaged between the pickup and the SUV next to it.

I focus on the bronze bangle but nothing in or on it changes as I begin the wish-granting ritual. After clearly enunciating all the incantations, I fix my gaze on Nate. The hurt in his eyes locks my heart in a vise. I force myself to continue, to fully connect with Nate's anima, to give his soul a home in mine.

The weight and the lightness of nature somehow course through my veins at the same time. It's . . . calming . . . peaceful. I am right where I'm supposed to be. Doing exactly what I'm supposed to be doing. It is the first time since becoming Jinn I have felt this way.

"I am now ready to grant you one wish." I say the line that is required before adding more of my own. I need to do this right, for myself, for my mother, but mostly, for Nate. "Think before you answer. Search your heart and your mind for your deepest desire, the one thing you wish beyond all else, the one thing you need above all else to make your life better. Now, Nathan Reese, what is your one wish?"

The answer in the depths of his soul I feel in my own. He doesn't need to verbalize it but he does. In the trance-like state I've put him in, he says slowly, "I wish to be able to take care of Megan."

Nate the protector. Of course this is his wish. He wants his father back. He wants his mother to get better. But he can't live without knowing his sister will be okay. And he needs to be the one to make that happen. Which means, I need to be the one to make that happen.

I'm about to begin the concluding incantations when Nate continues to speak.

"And I wish Azra will always be with me. She makes the hurt less."

He's already made his one wish. So this second wish I cannot use magic to grant. Fortunately, this second wish I do not need to use magic to grant.

Thinking the day could not get any more surreal, I find myself sandwiched between Chelsea and Henry in the backseat being driven home from the hospital by one of Nate's lifeguard buddies. Nate's residual anima has me numb, figuratively and literally. I'm grateful for the warm bodies on either side of me.

The car stops in front of my house. Solemn nods are exchanged between those in the front seats and those in the back. Henry leans across me, smiles weakly at Chelsea, and steps out onto the curb.

I slide across the seat and reach for Henry's extended hand. Chelsea catches me by the elbow and breaks the silence that clung to the darkened interior for the duration of the ride.

"We should do something," she says.

My confusion must show on my face, because she elaborates.

"Help out," she says. "Do you cook? We could make something together. Something they could freeze. We, my mom and I, we did that when my uncle passed away last year. I can get some recipes from her. You could come over, or I could come back here, or—"

I pat Chelsea's knee. "Sure, that sounds . . . nice."

"Yeah?" Chelsea's eyes widen.

"Yeah," I say. "This is all new to me."

Chelsea nods. "I'll get your number from Henry."

I manage a slight smile and place my hand in Henry's. The car leaves us standing on the sidewalk. If the Afrit took my mother away, is that what I'd be left with? A freezer of baked ziti, banana bread, and enchiladas?

Using my keys, Henry unlocks the front door of my house. The noise draws my mother's attention. From upstairs, she calls down in a frantic voice, "I was about to use my locator spell to find you."

She pauses on the landing. "Oh, Henry, I didn't know you were here. It's just . . . it's only you two, right?"

Henry nods. "Just us."

Relieved, my mother continues down the stairs while I work my way up. We meet halfway, and I hug her, hard. She must feel me trembling because she says, "Azra, honey, what's wrong? What happened? Where's Nate? Did he take you both home?"

My eyes are so full of tears that I miss the next step. "I can't, Mom. Not now."

"But honey, tell me—"

Henry clears his throat. "If it's all right, Mrs. Nadira, I can explain. Okay, Azra?"

Whether they see me nod my head in response or not doesn't matter. I keep going, heading for my room. I hear Henry say "accident" and then "horses" and "Nate" and shut my door to the rest.

I don't want to hear it again. The younger parking lot attendants found the stash of warm beer and filled their bellies. They wandered away from the bonfire and started messing with the horses at the farm near the entrance to the beach. One of the preteen boys crawled through the wooden post-and-rail fence and opened first the barn door and then the fence gate. Chasing the horses, they pushed the scared animals into the dark street just as Nate's parents were coming around the bend.

Yanking my down comforter over my bare legs, I inhale. The lilacs are strong tonight. The flowers should be long gone, their season usually confined to the spring. But they're my favorite. My mother's magic keeps the blooms lasting all summer so I can fall asleep breathing in the familiar scent, the scent I associate with the comfort and safety of home.

I inhale over and over again. But the increasingly deep and long breaths I take bring only the strong, fruity fragrance. This day that has stripped so much from me takes one more thing.

35

THE BARKING DOG RUINS MY PLAN TO SLEEP THROUGH THE NIGHT. For which I am grateful. My dreams quickly morphed into nightmares that only retreated with my waking up. Before I fell asleep I would have said nothing could be worse than reality, but my subconscious mind combined with Nate's grieving residual anima had other ideas.

I tug on my comforter, but it doesn't budge. As my eyes adjust to the darkness, I see what's holding it up. Or down.

Curled like a cat at the foot of my bed is Henry. Even tucked as compactly as he is with his chin and knees greeting each other at his belly button, he's still too tall to fit horizontally across the full-size mattress. The sight of him makes me want to laugh as much as cry. I'm betting it wasn't all that difficult for him to convince my mother to allow him to stay with me. Though he'll be sore tomorrow if he sleeps the entire night in this position, I know he won't say a word. I don't deserve him. If I tell him about Jenny, that likely won't be a problem. How could he ever forgive me? But can I really not tell him? Can I really keep this a secret from him?

Yes, I can. And I will. And this, above all else, lets me know I really have become a Jinn.

Unable to look at the framed photo of me, Jenny, and Laila, I place it facedown on my nightstand. I ease out of bed and fold my end of the blanket over Henry. My bonfire clothes smell faintly of smoke. I check to make sure Henry's asleep before I change into jeans and a light sweater.

It's very late, or really early, depending on how you look at it. Though my stomach growls, I feel guilty for thinking about something as trivial as food. It seems a betrayal to Nate to think anything but sad thoughts. To think of anything but granting his wish. I'm fortunate that I can do more to help Nate and his family than bake a crumb cake.

I lift the cantamen and a notebook off my desk. My bedroom door squeaks as I open it, but Henry remains in his little ball. I slip through and gently close the door behind me. Across the hall, my mother's bedroom door stands wide open. I start down the stairs and catch a few words spoken in her hushed voice. Light from the kitchen filters into the living room.

I lower myself onto a step and crouch behind the railing. It's a familiar stakeout position. Eavesdropping on my mother and one of her Zar sisters, usually Lalla Sam, who'd apport here for late-night gossiping was a staple of my childhood. The railing did a better job of concealing me back then.

"Maybe the Nadiras are cursed," Samara says.

"Sam, that's not helping," my mother says.

"Well, really, Kalyssa, who has this much bad luck?"

My mother sighs. "That poor boy, that poor family."

My stomach churns, rejecting even the thought of food.

Part of me wants to rush down the stairs and ask for help granting Nate's wish. But a bigger part stops me. Because *I* have to figure it out. Not my mother or Samara. Because it really is intimate, granting a human's wish. My connection to Nate's anima went so deep—it's still so deep—that I'm consumed by the need to protect it, to protect him and his wish, to be the only one privy to what's in his soul. I've finally done this to the best of my abilities, just like my mother's been trying to teach me to do. Just as we Jinn were meant to do.

All well and good, but my suddenly gooey center doesn't do squat for actually helping me grant the freakin' wish. This will require logistics, planning . . . like I should have done with Ms. Wood. Mrs. Pucher, Zoe, Lisa, all those wishes were easier because they could be granted in the moment.

Cantamen clutched to my chest, I retreat to my mother's room and stretch out on her bed. I lie on my stomach and pull one of her pillows toward me. A splash of red appears. Red leather. Underneath the pillow is my mother's diary. An uncapped pen sticks out from in between pages near the end, pages that are still blank.

My mother said she used a spell to hide the writing on those seemingly empty pages of the cantamen. The diary must be masked by the same spell. As I leaf through the codex, I keep my eyes open for both a way to grant Nate's wish and a spell to reveal the hidden ink. I find the spell first, thanks to a huge drawing of a pair of purple eyeglasses.

I touch the title next to the drawing: "Make the Seen Unseen." The spell that follows has it all: rhyme, foreign words, magic gobbledygook. Now all I need is a talisman. This I do not have. But my mother does. And I know what it is.

When my mother appeared at Ms. Wood's house, she was wearing her emerald signet ring. She doesn't wear it often. I always thought it was because it was large and a bit showy, but I now suspect there's another reason. The ring is her talisman. She needed it that day in order to use spells to fix my mess. Since Yasmin's been wearing and using Raina's ring, I'm pretty sure my mother's talisman will work for me.

When I found out about the car accident, my priorities shifted. But as I near my mother's jewelry box to search for her ring, my suspicions about my *A* pendant and what it means if they are true rise up again.

Stopping a few feet short of my mother's dresser, I focus on the jewelry box and the emerald ring resting inside. The lid opens, and the ring lifts, levitates, and moves toward me. I extend my middle finger, letting the emerald slide down. It's a perfect fit.

I walk to the dresser to return the ring to where my powers found it and dig the duplicate *A* pendant out of the bottom drawer. Either I'm wrong about all this, or everything that happened earlier distracted my mother from finding a new hiding place.

Holding the *A* in one hand, I step back until I'm in the exact same position I was in moments ago. Though I'm doing exactly what I did the first time, the jewelry box doesn't open and the ring doesn't float my way. Still focused, I drop the heavier *A* pendant to the floor. The emerald ring flies at me so fast I need to duck to avoid it colliding with my forehead.

Damn, I was right. *I was right.* The magic running through my Jinn blood doesn't need a bangle to unleash it. When I turned sixteen, my mother must have replaced the *A* pendant that she spelled to block my magic with the lighter one I'm now wearing. Her smooth actions allowed me to continue believing the lie: that because of my scar I needed a bangle to release my powers. Now I'm sixteen. I'm allowed to use magic. Why not tell me the truth? What is she afraid of? What should I be afraid of?

The fact that Samara's here stops me from confronting my mother. I kept Henry a secret from Laila because I didn't want to put her in danger. Knowing what I now know about the Afrit, I wouldn't be surprised if my mother has been doing the same thing with Sam. I've waited sixteen years to learn the truth, another day means nothing to me. But to Nate, whose deepest desire is to take care of Megan, another day must mean everything.

This is when it hits me that I should have done something to grant at least a portion of Nate's wish in the moment. How could I allow him to leave the parking lot without somehow letting him know that he already has all he needs to take care of his sister?

Logistics, legalities, that's what came into my mind when he said "take care of." But those words encompass much more. So much more, my lungs seize and I fall onto the end of the bed. Nate lost his father tonight. His mother is hurt, bad. His deepest desire is to know that his sister will be okay.

And I have no idea what I'm doing.

When Jenny died, all I wanted to do was stop being Jinn. But tonight, all I want to do is be a model Jinn. I have to do this. I have to do this *right.*

I squeeze my eyes shut and try not to crumble under the massive weight on my chest.

My skin prickles and a purring fills my ears. Smooth, warm hands rest on my cheeks.

"Oh, Azra, honey, what is it?"

Hana. Red hair tied into a loose bun on top of her head, a white goopy mask covering her face, toothbrush clutched in her hand.

"What . . . ?" I blink. Twice. "What are you doing here?"

Hana shoves her toothbrush in the pocket of her pajama pants. "You tell me. I expected to find you staked or something."

"They stake vampires, not genies."

"Could've fooled me with the way it felt like my heart was being impaled."

We stare at each other. "The link," we say at the same time.

I stand up. "You felt . . . felt, like, *me*?"

"Did you feel like you were having a heart attack?"

"Just about."

"Then yes."

"Cool," she says at the same time as "creepy" leaves my lips.

Her laugh instantly lightens the weight on my chest. Her hand that holds mine as I tell her first about Laila and then about Nate relieves it even more. Her words that guide me through what she expects I'll need to do, pulled from memories of her flash cards, combined with the secret to using the cantamen allow me to breathe again. Her encouragement that I can do this makes me hope I can repay her one day. I'll even wear her genie costume if she wants (which I think but don't actually say).

As she's getting ready to leave, she hesitates. "You know what you did to Laila was wrong, I don't have to tell you that." Her skin flushes a light pink as she looks me in the eye. "But I understand, in a way. We all have Jinn we wish were in our lives. Even if we don't talk about it, it doesn't mean we don't feel it."

Her brother. My heart pulls like taffy and I feel her longing.

"I'm so sorry, Hana." Instinctually, I wrap my arms around her and the ache in her heart—and then mine—fades.

After she wishes me luck and makes me promise to text her when I'm done, she sticks the toothbrush in her mouth and disappears.

I don't know—or care—if it's my own feelings or Hana's, but confidence fills me as I climb into my mother's bed. I set the diary aside and pull the cantamen into my lap. With my mother's ring on my finger, I draw on all the elements of nature and put my own spin on what Hana told me to say.

"Come on, Grandma, Great-Grandma, Great-Great Grandma, help me grant Nate's wish to take care of his sister." As I wave my hand over the open book, the light shines off the emerald ring I'm wearing. "*Please.*"

Wind whips my hair as the book's pages furiously flip. The green gemstone on my finger glows. When the pages stop turning and the exact entry I need, written in my mother's neat hand, stares up at me, I understand why this beast doesn't require an index.

I app myself to Nate's backyard. All the lights are out, which means, luckily, everyone's still sleeping.

Following the detailed instructions my mother entered into the cantamen after granting a similar wish, it's no surprise that accomplishing the logistical part of Nate's wish wasn't anywhere near as hard as I expected.

It also didn't hurt that his parents had most of the necessary things in order. But just in case Nate's mother . . . just in case, I made sure Nate, his sister, his family would be protected.

Life insurance, bank accounts, mortgages, wills, I apped to the home of each, conjuring paperwork, changing entries in computer databases, and using spells to do wild (and what I fear could turn out to be addicting) things like make me invisible to alarms and video cameras. The more spells I used, the more in awe—and frightened—I became of what I can do.

The hardest part was remembering to say *"izza samhat"* before using my powers. Would the Afrit know if I recited the words? The ones meant to release my magic? The ones I don't actually need? I have no idea, but keeping up the pretense my mother started seems like the safer play.

With my bolstering, there will be enough money to cover the most advanced medical techniques and rehabilitation Mrs. Reese could ever need. Grad school, medical school, and whatever else Nate and Megan might want to do short of buying a small island will be covered. And if . . . if circumstances require it, when Nate turns eighteen in a few weeks, he will become Megan's legal guardian. Nate will be able to take care of Megan, financially and legally. Wish granted.

Technically wish granted. Because if I left it at that, I'd be employing a bit of a genie trick. Which is why I'm at Nate's house.

Though I'm sure Nate can do the rest of what "taking care of" entails all on his own, I need to make sure he thinks so too.

I say *"izza samhat"* and magically unlock the back door. Tiptoeing into Nate's kitchen, my heart leaps to my throat when I see him slumped over the table, asleep. Mere hours have ticked away since his father died, and here Nate is trying to take his place, trying to take care of his family.

Unopened folders labeled "financial" and "will" and "mortgage" lay spread out in front of him. I silently move forward and look inside. A smile grows wide across my face. The spells worked. All the paperwork here matches the doctored ones I stashed in each official location.

Feeling the force of the talisman and . . . something else . . . *Hana.* Feeling the strength of my Zar sister, I draw on my powers and recite one of the spells I marked in the cantamen. A spell to boost someone's confidence.

Nate should now have everything he needs to take care of his sister all on his own. But he doesn't have to do it alone. I know how lucky I am to have Henry as my best friend, and, right now, I can't risk anything that might change that. So official wish or not, I'll grant Nate's desire for me to be with him. It's not like it's a hardship. I'm positive the whole "making the hurt less" goes both ways.

36

When I app back to my mother's bedroom, my adrenaline has me wide awake despite the late hour and all the apporting, conjuring, and spells I've done. Again, my mother was right. Drawing on nature allowed me to do magic without expending as much of my own energy. I can't help but wonder what'll happen when tapping into my full Zar.

I'm sliding my mother's ring to the end of my finger when I catch the splash of red out of the corner of my eye. The diary. For anyone tracking my magical energy, they'd see it activated all night for official Jinn business. If I don't do this now, I may not get another chance. At least not anytime soon.

I push the talisman back down and open the diary to the page bookmarked with the pen. Confident in my use of spells by now, I recite the "Make the Seen Unseen" spell. Nothing. I work through it three times without a single blot of ink appearing. Maybe I'm wrong. Maybe the writing isn't concealed by magic or maybe this is the wrong spell to reveal it.

Or maybe I'm an idiot. This makes the *seen unseen.* I need to do the opposite. I read the spell again. Though it's a mishmash of ancient languages, like all the spells I've used tonight, its roots are in Latin. Which is why my mother insisted I start taking the dead-for-a-good-reason language in junior high. Yet another part of my life dictated by becoming Jinn.

Wonder what she'd say if she knew how I was about to employ all I've learned.

Calling on my memory of the Latin words I can ferret out, I sub in ones that seem more appropriate for making the *unseen seen*. I rearrange some of the other ones I don't know and recite the spell one more time.

Ink spreads across the open pages of the diary. I lift the small, red leather book from the pillow where it was perched and gently turn pages. In blue ink, in black ink, in the occasional green, words written in my mother's elegant handwriting fill three-quarters of the journal.

It's only now that the words are able to be read that I consider whether they should be read. This ranks as a pretty serious invasion of my mother's privacy. I'd be furious with her if she did this to me.

Maybe just a peek to see where she left off. Considering I was fine with eavesdropping, how different is this, really?

I lay the diary in front of me and open to the last page with writing. As I skim through the entry under today's date, my pangs of guilt recede. I know all this already. She's simply reflecting on having told me the truth about the Afrit. When I hit the emotional stuff where she blames herself for not telling me sooner, it seems the too-personal line is being crossed. I avert my eyes and go back a few pages.

An entry from the day before the Zar initiation seems to be the first one in a long time.

Dear Diary,

Years have passed since the last time I wrote those words. As my pen touches this page, I realize the hole not keeping up with you has left in my life. Especially now. Now that my Zar has been broken. They've taken Raina.

We don't know why. We can only assume it has to do with her increased involvement in the uprising. But how was she discovered? Sam insists this is proof of why we need to act now. Doesn't she realize it's proof of nothing but the opposite? Yes, the Afrit need to be overthrown. The revolt is a worthy cause, and I want my family to be whole again. But at what cost? Should Azra and Laila lose us the way Yasmin lost Raina? They'll never see each other again. I cannot do that. Not to Azra and not to myself. I cannot lose anyone else.

But I need to tell Azra the truth. Sam was right about that. She needs to know what's at stake. I thought not telling her would protect her, but she's going to get herself into trouble even if she doesn't intend to. She's got too much of her father in her.

My father. I scan the rest of the entry, but there's not another mention of him. There's also nothing else about whatever this revolt . . . this uprising . . . against the Afrit's all about. Would an uprising stand a chance? And would it really mean my family would be whole again?

All of a sudden it's like a five-year-old has grabbed both sides of my Jinn world and is shaking it like a snow globe.

As much as I want the Afrit ousted from power, my mother's

right about what we all have to lose. The question is how it compares to what we have to gain.

I start leafing through the diary, scanning entries, until I find one that appears to be the longest one in the book. I check the date. It's from a few months before I was born.

Dear Diary,

I need to write this down. I need it here in case something happens to me. I'm too afraid to put it in the cantamen. But my words should be safe here, hidden until this little one growing inside me is old enough to both read them and discover how to read them. I need her to know this history so she'll understand. And it is a she. I know it's a girl. Xavier wants to name her "Azra," after my mother. We're certainly not choosing a name from his family. We don't want her to have anything to do with them.

Xavier. I fly off the bed and yank out the bottom drawer of my mother's jewelry box. I dump the contents onto the dresser. The photographs land facedown. There it is: the "K+X" written in the bottom corner of the later one. "K" for "Kalyssa" and "X" for "Xavier."

I flip the photos over and search for a resemblance in each of the two faces before me: the face of the boy in the tux, arm wrapped around my mother in her prom dress, and the face of the man whose cheek my mother's lips are attached to. My olive skin, my long, dark hair, my slightly turned-up nose all come from my mother. I push out my chin. It has a delicate heart shape. I move it from side to side, finding the light. Is that his? I pucker my lips. What about them? Are they his?

I touch the photograph. It's not my chin, it's not my lips, it's not anything I can put a name to, but it's something. This is my father. *My father.*

My head spins. This simple fact changes everything. This fact cancels out the fiction I've written of my mother's life. Of my life. My mother loved my father. My heart breaks imagining what it must have felt like to be torn apart.

When I pick up the diary again, my hands are trembling.

Little one, bear with me on this history lesson. To know how things came to be, you need to know how they were. We always had a council of elected Jinn—a cross between the human world's government and police. We were subject to the council's decisions, but today's types of controls and monitoring were basically nonexistent unless a Jinn was in danger of exposing magic to humans. If that happened, and it did and still does on occasion, the council was responsible for doling out punishment. But the other, more important job of the council has always been selecting humans in need of a wish. The idea of the greater good is ingrained in our species.

The difference is, in the past, Jinn volunteered for assignments. Only the best of the best were accepted as volunteers, and Jinn trained for years to achieve such an honor. Granting a wish for one of these specially selected candidates garnered much respect.

If Jinn did not volunteer for assignments, they selected their own wishees at will. Some did it randomly, some did it according to special criteria they devised on their own, some didn't do it at all. Jinn had the freedom to use their powers however they saw fit. That's not to say there weren't any rules or any consequences for inappropriate behavior. It's not like they could roam the streets doing magic for all the world to see.

When Jinn went too far, the council stepped in. Punishment was having one's powers stripped for a certain period of time, or if the crimes were that heinous, for life.

At some point in the long history of our world, it was discovered that certain earthly compounds conflict with a Jinn's ability to use the powers that are literally in our DNA. And, since every action has an equal and opposite reaction, other compounds do the opposite. Kind of like how magnets can attract some metals but repel others.

Therefore, the way a Jinn's powers were stripped, at least for the past couple of centuries, was by affixing an unremovable object to a part of the Jinn's body that blocked and prevented the use of magic. But that's not how it's done anymore, not since the Afrit came into power.

The Afrit took the science and perverted it. They created a compound that blocks our magic and injected it into every living, breathing Jinn. Then, the females were issued a bangle and the males a necklace. The mix of compounds inside the jewelry draws out our magic. The Afrit's advanced powers allow them to spell the jewelry to ensure we wear them until they say otherwise.

I stretch out on the bed. So that's why the bangle can't be taken off by me but can be removed by them.

These enforced injections that now take place shortly after birth render our powers inert until we are given the jewelry that releases them. The Afrit can take away our magic any time they like by simply removing our bangles and necklaces. This is how they have managed to maintain their control over us for so long. We are dependent on them for our magic.

I touch my bronze bangle realizing what my mother didn't—couldn't—know as she wrote these words: I'm the exception. Sweat soaks the back of my shirt. Surely if the Afrit knew, they wouldn't allow it. That's why my mother kept it a secret. Despite the tightness in my chest, I continue reading.

The Afrit came to power at a time when the human world was experiencing its counterculture movement. In the late sixties, young people began to question the world around them. It was liberating for many humans and a lot of Jinn too. But some Jinn started going too far. The abundance of drug use among Jinn certainly played a role. But that's no excuse. These Jinn wanted to return to a time when they didn't have to hide their magic. They started granting too many people too many wishes without using cloaking enchantments. We came close to being exposed. Centuries ago, humans believed in magic, but not even the culture of the sixties and seventies was going to tolerate true knowledge of magic existing.

The rebellion these young Jinn embarked on hurt and even killed people, humans and Jinn alike. It was ugly. The community was afraid, but it was also outraged. They rightly blamed the young Jinn who started it all, but they also blamed the council for not clamping down on the troublemakers sooner. The change those young Jinn were pushing for? Well, it came. Just not in the way they wanted.

The Afrit family is—

Family? Afrit is a last name? I thought it was . . . I guess I have no idea, but I didn't know it was a family.

The Afrit family is one of the oldest Jinn families in existence. Their magic is strong, more powerful than that of most Jinn. And they work to keep it that way, to keep their bloodline as pure as possible. But they were always a bit too conservative for the Jinn community as a whole. They were desperate to have one of their own elected to the council for decades but could never amass enough support—until the youth rebellion gave them their opening, and they took it. They used the fear that was so pervasive to overthrow the old elected council. The family assumed control and issued a sort of martial law.

Jinn were terrified. Fear is the most powerful magic there is. They lined up for the injections. My parents did. For years, it was considered a positive change. When I was born, my parents injected me willingly, happily. They had no idea what they were doing would result in our family being one of the last to live together. That allowing the Afrit to curb our magic would enslave us to them, leaving them free to invent punishments as vile as tortura cavea.

A revolt is what the Afrit fear most. Over the past few decades, they've instituted reform after reform out of pure self-preservation. Even with the rules we are made to abide by, coups have been attempted. But each one has failed. The Afrit punish these Jinn harshly, stripping them of their magic, taking them away from their families, and, sometimes, sometimes, killing them. The last insurrection was so strong, so close, that they are now mandating that all male Jinn leave the human world. They want to keep us separated, to prevent us from being able to plot another rebellion that could usurp their power. And they also want to punish us.

Keep in mind, the Afrit have strong magic. They have powers most of us don't, like mind control.

Mind control . . . like the mind control I have? My mother said Jinn can't do mind control without spells. But Samara said the Afrit can. I lift the photos of my father off the bed. My thumping heart threatens to break a rib. Was my father . . . *is. Please let it be* is. Is my father a . . . ? Is he one of them?

"Always," your father repeats to me as he caresses my round belly. "I'll love you both always." He insists when he goes back to his family, as he must do, he'll be able to convince them he's on their side. "This will be for now, but not forever," he says. He believes his loyalty will allow him to eventually help us fight against them. But his family, your family, the Afrit family, I'm afraid they'll never let him get that close. And I'm terrified for all our sakes that they will.

I drop the diary.

My father is an Afrit.

I am an Afrit.

That's why my powers are so advanced. That must be why the Afrit pounced on my first candidate so quickly. They were probably eager to see what I could do. I must have been quite the disappointment.

Bile rises in my throat, and I race to my mother's bathroom, but dry heaves are all that I can manage. Hugging the bowl, I press my forehead against the cool porcelain.

A Jinn trick to top all Jinn tricks. This is what I get for wishing not to be a Jinn.

Suddenly both mentally and physically spent, I'm barely able to concentrate enough to draw on my magic and cover my tracks. Working slowly, I recite my mother's spell and the words in her diary disappear. It looks as though I never read a word. Part of me wants to pretend I didn't.

But I know I won't be able to conceal the fact that I know about the Afrit's sordid past. It's too much to hide. My mother had said I could read their history in the blank pages of the cantamen. Once I tell her how I granted Nate's wish, she's going to find out I used spells anyway. I locate the blank pages in the codex and recite the unseen/seen spell I wrote. The pages fill with an abbreviated version of the history my mother wrote in her diary. The account in the cantamen leaves out all mentions of me and my father and our connection to the Afrit.

I try to arrange the bedsheets and the diary as I found them. I reassemble my mother's jewelry box, returning the emerald ring, the *A*, and the photos, though I don't quite remember where each piece is supposed to go.

Creeping back into my room, a deep voice carries up the stairs. It's a man's voice, but it's not Henry's.

"It's time, Kal. If not now, when? How much longer does she have, really? They'll come for her, you know they will."

I freeze as I picture the face that goes along with this voice. It's older, more fleshed out, maybe, but it's still a dead ringer for the one in my mother's photos. I'm not sure how I know, but I feel it in my Jinn blood, in my Afrit blood. Somehow, impossibly, my father is in my house, right downstairs, right underneath where I am standing.

I've imagined this moment over the course of my life more times than I can count, but it has never played out like this. Not with me backing away, retreating to my bedroom, and closing the door.

Henry stirs. "Wha . . . Is it . . . morning?"

"Shh, no, go back to sleep. I didn't mean to wake you."

Henry groans as he uncurls his body. He swivels his neck, which makes a disturbing cracking sound.

I return the cantamen and notebook to my desk, my hands shaking as I lay them down.

What am I doing? Nate lost his father, but mine's finally here. My whole family is here.

And I'm missing it.

With a start, I turn and rush to the door. My hand's on the knob as Henry sits up.

"Is that what woke you?" he asks.

The sound of the barking dog sends chills down my spine. It's the same bark that woke me up earlier. I'm now convinced it's the same bark that woke me the morning of my birthday, months ago. I move to the window. Walking across our front yard is a large, chestnut-colored dog with beautiful, shiny fur and thick, strong legs. It stops and turns its snout toward me.

It's eerie, the way it appears to be staring at me.

"Az, is something wrong?" Henry asks.

"No," I lie.

It can't be. The eyes simply remind me of his eyes, eyes I've never actually seen in person. Besides, it just . . . it just can't be. I turn away from the creature outside and shudder.

Can't be? After tonight, do I really think there's anything that can't be? They are his eyes. It's him. How, I have no idea, but it is. Guess the book of spirits was right about the shape-shifting. I look back out the window, searching for him, but he's gone.

"Come here," Henry says. "Try to sleep."

Since reality has become worse than my nightmares, I crawl under the covers that Henry's holding in the air. As I place my head on the pillow, Henry starts to return to his perch at the end of the bed. I stop him. He gently lies down next to me. I move my head to his chest and wait for his warmth to overcome the chills still coursing through me.

I'm still waiting hours later when the sun rises.

Awkward is the only word to describe breakfast.

On one side of the table sits Henry. Having cereal with Henry is awkward because we spent the night in the same bed and because my mother knows Henry and I spent the night in the same bed. On the other side of the table sits my mother. Sharing a pot of coffee with my mother is awkward because I'm ninety-nine percent sure my father was in this very spot last night and because I'm ninety-nine percent sure my mother plans not to tell me my father was in this very spot last night.

We are as screwed up as any normal family.

"Do you know when the funeral will be?" my mother asks.

I drop my spoon. Of course there will be a funeral, and of course I'll have to go. I sent Nate a text this morning asking about his mother. He answered immediately as if the phone were glued to his hand, which made me kick myself for not checking in with him sooner. His mother's condition is still listed as critical. He didn't mention a funeral for his father, and I didn't think to ask.

I shake my head. I've never been to a funeral before. I didn't even go to Jenny's. I am no longer hungry.

"Does everyone do that open-casket thing?" I ask nervously.

My mother squeezes my shoulder. "I don't think so, but even if they do, you can pay your respects without approaching the casket. It's okay."

"It is?" Henry asks, sounding as relieved as I feel, making me wonder if Jenny's casket was open.

My mother smiles weakly. "Yes, especially for you kids. Just be there for your friend. That's all that's important."

She returns the milk carton to the refrigerator and places her bowl in the dishwasher. She could use magic to clean up since Henry knows about us, but I can tell she's not in the mood. As she refills her coffee mug, I notice a slip of paper peeking out of her back pocket. Henry, whose parents don't allow sugary cereal in the house, has his head buried in his second bowl. Before my mother turns back around, I pickpocket her.

My chair scrapes against the floor as I excuse myself to get a tissue from the living room. Written across the front of the small, folded note is simply *"Kalyssa."* Instantly I recognize the slant of the letters. It's the same handwriting that was on the note, also addressed to my mother, that was waiting when Samara and I returned from Ms. Anne Wood's house. I unfold the paper. *"Always. But not forever."*

My hand grips the arm of the sofa. Those conflicting words wouldn't make sense to most. Then again, most have not read my mother's diary.

He *was* here. *My father was here.* And he's been here before.

Perhaps being an Afrit, he's able to come and go as he pleases. How could he visit my mother and not me?

I close my eyelids against the tears begging to come. My fingers begin to curl into a fist, and the note crinkles.

Wait. My eyes snap open and focus on the handwriting once again. My father's handwriting. My mother said whoever warned her about Ms. Wood was "someone with both our best interests at heart." My father.

I have to trust there's a reason, aside from my recent questionable secret-keeping abilities, why my mother and father haven't let me see him. I have to trust that, in his own way, my father is doing everything he said he would. Infiltrating the Afrit. Loving my mother. Loving me.

When I return to the kitchen, my heart still beating fast, I down my coffee and hold out my mug. "More, please?" I say to my mother.

Risking the minute amount of energy it must require, I cause Henry's spoon to slip from his hand. As he bends to the floor to retrieve it, I return the note to my mother's back pocket.

Taking my coffee, I needle my mother to see what, if anything, she might reveal about last night. "Sleep okay?"

"Not really," she says. "Samara came by. She was worried about you."

So she's not going to lie about that part.

"You two?" My mother is unable to conceal her slight grin.

I cut Henry off. "No, that dog was barking again. And you're right, it's definitely not Mrs. Pucher's Pom-Pom."

"Really?" she says. "I didn't hear anything."

So that part she's going to lie about.

We have achieved stalemate. We'll never know which one of

us might have blinked first because it is at that moment that my bronze bangle breaks in two and falls in my half-eaten bowl of soggy cereal.

My mother rushes over. She wiggles the dish but doesn't touch the bangle. "Azra, what did you do?"

"I was just sitting here!"

Her eyes narrow, and she takes my wrist. "Are you sure? Not even subconsciously?"

"If it was subconsciously, how would I know?"

My mother looks at Henry, who has pushed back his chair and is sitting with his mouth hanging open.

"They'll come for her." The words the man . . . my father . . . said last night pop into my head.

"Should Henry leave?" I ask. "Is this . . . dangerous?"

My mother cannot rid her face of its stunned expression. "I don't think so."

"But you don't know?" I stand up and point across the table. "Henry, go!"

He scrunches up his face, eyeing me as if I'm crazy. He doesn't know what I now know about the Afrit. About my family.

"Seriously, Henry, now."

My harsh tone works. He stands, but it's too late. Something else is already happening. The bronze bangle vanishes into the cereal milk. I take my spoon and swirl it around the bowl.

"It's gone," Henry says. "How could it be gone?"

A silver bangle identical to the one I first received on my birthday materializes in the center of the table. It rolls toward me. I stop it with one finger before it spills into my lap. At my touch, it pops open at a very visible hinge.

"I'm guessing this is for me?" I know I don't need it. My mother knows I don't need it. But she doesn't know I know. So I play along. "My probation is over, then?"

My mother shrugs, but seems unnerved. "Apparently so."

I lay my forearm over the table and line up my wrist with the bangle. It hops up, encircles my wrist, and snaps shut. The hinge seals itself.

Henry claps his hands. "That was awesome."

Eyes fixed on my wrist, my mother has still not said a word.

"Mom? What's wrong?"

She shrugs again. "Nothing, I guess. It's just odd. I've never seen it happen. I heard about it from Nadia, but you know how she exaggerates. There's usually a formal application process to have a bronze bangle removed. And it takes time, months, years even. It's quite rare. You must have impressed them, Azra."

She says this with sadness, and I know why. Impressing my paternal grandparents isn't something either of us wants me doing. The question is, what do they know? What are they impressed by? My use of spells, my granting Nate a wish properly, or my ability to use magic while wearing the bronze bangle? After what I read last night, I'm certain they wouldn't be rewarding me if it were the last one. They'd . . . *come for me.* But since they haven't, the secret about me being an evolutionary anomaly seems safe—for now.

Henry moves closer and touches the bangle. I wince slightly, but he doesn't notice.

"That's great," he says. "Now you'll be able to visit me." He gives my mother a sheepish grin. "That is, with your permission, Mrs. Nadira."

"Visit?" I say, confused. I then realize what he means. "So New Hampshire's happening?"

Henry rounds his shoulders. "Seems like it. It sucks, but it sucked worse yesterday. Do you know how many connections it takes to get from there to here on a bus?"

The hug from Henry and the fact that he's already researched bus routes cannot take away the pit in my stomach. I feel like I'm waiting for that Jinn trick to kick in.

Maybe it already has. Maybe being an Afrit has its perks.

It's been three days since the accident. Three days since I've seen Nate but two nights that we've spent together. On the phone. On this third day, I'm standing in a newly purchased bra and underwear (not a thong), ripping clothes off hangers. Though full of black, nothing in my closet seems appropriate for a funeral.

It's been two days since I lowered my wrist into the silver bangle that I don't need. Don't need because apparently the inhibitor injection I received was a lemon. Or maybe because my father is an Afrit, his strong powers supersede or counter the effects. Doesn't matter. With or without a bangle, I'm not using magic unless I absolutely have to. I don't want to give my father's family any more opportunities to discover my secret. Plus, if I don't use magic, I figure I'll be less likely to become one of them.

Maybe that's not really a danger considering my bloodline is muddled. I'm half Jinn, half Afrit. A hybrid. Still, I'm not taking any chances.

It's been one day since I made the decision to keep all the questions I have about the rebellion, about my mother's diary, about my father to myself. For now, the answers I have—about my mother, who'd go to any lengths to protect me, and about my father, who'd risk his own life to ensure my safety—are enough. *Always, but not forever.* Enough for now, at least.

Because right now I have higher priorities: Nate, Laila, Henry, and Yasmin. Yes, Yasmin. She must feel utterly alone without Raina. She doesn't have any human friends. She's clearly threatened by me and my role in our Zar, and the rest of our sisters don't know the truth about her mother. Ironic as it is, that the two of us know means we share a secret all our own. I might be the only one who can help her through this.

I give up on my closet and check my e-mail for the millionth time. The only new message is from Farrah, whose string of exclamation points follows Mina's winky smiley face, the latest in the thread started by Hana congratulating me on getting my silver bangle back. Nothing from Laila. Even though, for the past three days, I've been sending photos of the silver tinsel to her. Levitating in front of the framed picture of me, her, and Jenny, in my hair, dangling from my ear, around my pinky toe, between my front teeth, the locales keep getting weirder. Still, not a single response.

Last night, I finally got up the nerve to app to her house to deliver Mr. Gemp. I left it outside the back door, the photo of all six of us rolled inside along with another from the night of our initiation. Not wanting to pressure her, I waited, even apping in and out a few times, hoping she'd sense me and come out on her own. Too soon, I guess. That's okay. I'm pretty sure one trait I've inherited from the Afrit is persistence.

As I dash across the hall to find something in my mother's closet to wear to the funeral, I'm caught by my, at least currently, third priority.

"Henry!" I cover myself with my hands as I fly into my mother's bedroom. I poke my head out from behind the door. "Don't you knock?"

"I did. Your mother let me in." He grins. "*Thank you, Mom.*"

It's the first time I've laughed in days. It feels good and bad, right and wrong, all at the same time.

"I'm going to miss you," I say suddenly.

Summer's coming to an end. The school year will be starting soon. For the first time in years, it was something I was looking forward to. I'd be starting off with a best friend and a boyfriend. Now, the best friend will be gone, and the boyfriend, if that's what Nate will even become anymore, will be dealing with a tragic loss, afraid that his mother's injures might make that two.

"Maybe it's for the best," Henry says. "You'll be there for Nate and not have to worry about me."

"No, it's not for the best. How could you even think that?"

Henry's jaw drops as I say this, and I realize his words weren't spoken out loud. I read his mind without knowing I was doing so.

"Holy sh—" he starts.

"Shh!" I grab Henry's hand and drag him into my mother's bedroom. "Don't say anything. And turn around. All the way."

I hurry to my mother's closet and push back the hangers.

"Azra! How could you not tell me you can read my mind!"

"I said 'Shh!'" I look back to find him staring at me. "And I also said, 'turn around!'"

Long-sleeved wrap dress or suit with the pencil skirt? Dress. I don't want to be fussing with tucking anything in.

"For how long?" he says. "And how come you didn't tell me? Can you read minds other than mine? It's not just me, right? What . . . what else have you heard?"

I pop my head through the opening of the dress and wrestle it down. In front of the mirror, I adjust the neckline. I've been keeping my long hair down lately. I figure enough time has passed that no one remembers my shorter cut. If they do, whatever, I'll say it's hair extensions.

"See," I say, "this is why I didn't tell you. I haven't told anyone, not even my mother. It's just easier this way." I smooth the fabric over my hips. "You can turn around now."

Henry stuffs his hands in his front pockets. He's wearing the pants whose pleats I erased.

"They look good on you," I say.

"Yeah?" He looks down. "Something seemed different when I put them on, but I guess it's just your mending."

"Uh-huh." I hide my smile. "Must be."

"But Azra, seriously, don't go reading my mind without warning me. That's not cool."

I roll my eyes. "I didn't mean to. I'm still getting the hang of it. Believe me, I don't want to be reading teenage boys' thoughts any more than you all want me reading them." He blushes as I face him. "Well?"

He doesn't say anything.

"Henry? Is it okay?"

Still nothing.

"Will you please answer me?" I whine.

"I am," he says.

You look like the most beautiful creature I've ever seen.

"Stop that," I say, feeling my own cheeks burn. "And thanks."

"LET ME JUST GET MY BAG," I SAY TO HENRY AS I OPEN MY BEDROOM door. "I'll meet you downstairs."

Even from the doorway, the stupid gold envelope perched on top of my pocketbook can't be missed. The paternal side of my family is having too much fun toying with me. They can't drop it for a single day. Not even for the day of a funeral.

"Bring it," I say.

After everything I did the other night, there's nothing I can't do, there's no wish I can't grant, and, more importantly, there's no wish I won't grant. I'll do whatever I have to do to keep those I love safe.

I tear open the envelope. I curse and smile at the same time. You've really got to hand it to my family. They've got some *couilles*. That's French for balls. Henry taught me that.

Megan Reese. Nate's twelve-year-old little sister is my next assignment.

Henry takes my hand as we cross the threshold into the Reese home. We were both anxious to leave behind the cloud of gloom that hung over the funeral parlor. The years of sadness that oozed from every dusty curtain, every worn velvet chair, every piece of dark wood molding was to be expected. I was naïve enough to think this reception at Nate's house would be different. But the only thing lighter here is the paint on the walls.

Maybe I've been sorting through some weighty topics of late, but it's nothing compared to what's going on for the people in this room.

The last time I was in Nate's house, I didn't have time to take a tour. This time, I don't want to. The hand-knitted afghan draped over the back of the sofa, the model sailboat on the dining room buffet, the photographs on the mantel of a family of four reduced to three make me long for the funeral parlor. Where the cold is expected. Like the bright winter sun, all the things here that should exude warmth lure you in only to bite with the bitterness of a sub-zero New England day.

Just as Henry and I find Chelsea and the rest of the beach crowd, Nate's grandmother glances our way. She lifts her chin and smiles warmly as she pats Nate's forearm. He tugs on the collar of his white dress shirt and gestures for me to come over.

I leave Henry's side and walk self-consciously across the room. Everyone's eyes follow me as I approach the stars of the funeral, because that's what Nate and Megan are, no doubt about it. They are the main players on this perverse stage.

Nate grasps my hand and draws me to him. Megan leans against him, holding his other hand with both of hers. I feel like a fraud standing with them, but each time I try to excuse myself, Nate assures me he wants me to stay. So I do.

People flood the room, floating in and out, asking about Nate's mother, saying how sorry they are about Nate's father. Variations of the same themes dominate: "He was so young." "You are so young." "You're the man of the house now." "God works in mysterious ways."

It's clear that everyone means well, but it's not long before I'm numb. The words bounce right off; nothing sticks. After a while, nothing seems sincere. Maybe it's different for Nate and Megan, but I doubt it. They look vaguely distracted, like they are present only in body, not in mind.

The stream of people slows, which makes me nervous. With all those people filling the silence, the odds of me inadvertently reading Nate or Megan's minds were low. I don't want to hear their thoughts, especially Megan's. I don't want to know what she's going to wish for. Not now, not in the midst of this. It can wait. The 10 on the back of her candidate card means finding out what she wants can wait.

Nate's grandparents call to him. He turns to me and asks, "Can you stay with Megan?"

"Of course," I say, though every fiber of my being is telling me not to. I try to block Megan's thoughts, but the instant Nate's gone, Megan wobbles and I have to wrap my arms around her to keep her from falling. She buries her head in my chest, and her body deflates as it uses mine for support. Megan lets the tears that she's been so bravely fighting all morning come.

I rub her back and brush her hair out of her face. She *is* young. Too young to be dealing with this. And then, that's it, I'm in her head, I'm hearing every horrible, painful, tortured thought. Not since my first time with Mrs. Pucher has reading someone's mind been accompanied by feeling their emotions. And this skill, like everything else, has progressed.

The intensity of Megan's hurt overwhelms me. I clutch her hand, dragging her toward the stairs, which I practically carry her up. Her emotions are consuming her. And me. I have to stop it. I have to help her. Reaching for the nearest door, I pull us both inside what turns out to be Nate's room.

I take in the slate blue on the walls, the lacrosse stick propped in the corner, the medical dictionary on the desk, and in an instant, it all happens: the incantations, the cloaking enchantment, Megan in a trance-like state, the wish-granting ritual under way. She's in so much pain, and I'm so invested that I can't hold back my own feelings, and the words spill from my lips. "I'll make it better. I can take the pain away. Just wish for it. Just wish for it, and I can do it, I promise. You don't have to feel this. Let me help you."

And that's when she makes her wish. It's like a hammer has pounded a six-inch nail through my heart, in one side, out through the other. And it's my fault. What she's wishing for is my fault. My words encouraged her. Of course they did. How stupid, how very stupid I was. I shouldn't have rushed into this. I should have known this is what she'd want, this is what she'd wish for. And she's adamant that this is what she wants. That this is the only thing she will ever want. It is only when I envelop Megan in an embrace that I truly understand why.

After easing her out of the ritual and wiping away her tears, I force myself to bring her back downstairs, to bring her to her grandmother, explaining she was momentarily overcome. Her grandmother thanks me for helping and squeezes my hand. I'm dying inside. I manage to excuse myself, saying I need the restroom.

Halfway to the kitchen, I turn around. No one's watching me but Henry. I run out the back door, knowing he will follow.

I'm in the Reese's backyard, leaning against the wooden post of a weathered-gray swing set. Dizzy, I bend over, putting my head between my knees.

Henry's at my side before I know it. He grabs me by both elbows, asking what's wrong.

"Paper bag," I say.

"What?" Henry asks, confused.

"Paper . . . *bag.*" Isn't that what you're supposed to use when you feel like your lungs have collapsed? "Can't breathe. Can't see."

Henry lowers me to the ground, propping me against the splintering cedar. He crouches in front of me, saying soothing things until my eyes focus again. We stay that way as I do the thing I promised myself I wasn't going to do: load more weight onto Henry's shoulders. In this selfish moment, I pile it all on, telling Henry everything, starting with the Afrit's ability to take away and hurt everyone I care about, including him, flowing into the revelations about my mind control, Mrs. Seyfreth, my father, and who I really am, and ending with Megan being my next assignment. There's only one thing I leave out. Jenny.

Henry lands his butt on the grass and wraps his hands around the nape of his neck. He bobs his head up and down. "Okay, okay, wow, okay, okay, wow."

Though everything's come out in a stream-of-consciousness muddle, Henry understands. Henry always understands me. He gets it. He gets the danger of refusing. He gets that I have to grant Megan's wish. He gets that I don't have a choice unless I want to lose everyone I care about. He understands I'm going to have to do whatever it is that Megan wants.

I make sure of this. I make sure he gets it before I tell him what it is that Megan wants. He shouldn't be surprised. It's not that I was surprised by what it is she wants, it's what I'll have to do in order to accomplish it that has sent me into this spiral. Because, really, Megan's a twelve-year-old girl. A twelve-year-old girl who just lost her father, who's terrified of losing her mother. What else could she want?

"She wants her family back together," I say, sliding up the wooden post and circling to one of the two swings. I grasp the metal chain and wait until my heartbeat no longer pulsates in my temples. "Her wish is for her family to be whole again, her entire family. She wants her mom, her dad, herself, and Nate to be together again."

Henry rises. He runs his hand through his hair and starts pacing in front of the swing set. "But Azra, you can't do that. You've told me. Genies can't bring people back from the dead. Can't even heal people. It's not that it's forbidden, it's that it's impossible, right?"

I watch him as I lower myself onto the small, green plastic seat. I say slowly, "As far as I know, it's outside the powers of even the strongest Jinn."

Henry stops in front of me. "But what then, Azra, what are you going to do?"

"What do you think? How would you accomplish it?"

He moves closer, staring into my eyes with such intensity, I get chills. I hear his mind reach the same conclusion I did. The only conclusion there is. Hot tears fill my eyes, but I blink them back. I need him to reach this conclusion so he'll understand.

"Seriously, Azra? That's what you're going to have to do? You're going to have to . . . have to . . . *kill them*? You're going to have to kill Nate? That way the family will be together again?"

I picture myself in Nate's shoes, people consoling me because my mother is gone. I hear Henry's thoughts. *Don't worry about me, Azra. You can't do this. Whatever happens to me, happens to me. But you can't do this. It will destroy you.*

Henry, always thinking about me, first and foremost. Not a single thought as to his own safety. As to what might happen to him if I don't grant Megan's wish.

And so if that were really her wish, her deepest desire, I'd . . . I'd do it. Fortunately, my mother taught me well. While connecting with Megan's anima, I didn't stop there. I kept going, delving deeper, until I uncovered her true wish.

"Yes," I say, pushing my heels into the soft ground and starting to rock myself gently, "that's what I'd have to do. If that were truly her wish."

Henry's puzzled eyes stare into mine as he settles himself on the swing next to me.

Swallowing hard, I use my powers to give him a push. Just one. The soft breeze of his swinging sweeps the hair off my shoulder.

My voice is calm, steady. "But the real reason she wants her family back together is because she doesn't want to see the pain in Nate's eyes anymore. That's her true wish."

It's not that granting this wish is easy. It's not that granting this wish is without risk. It's difficult. It's risky. But as I needed to make sure Henry understood so he'd be onboard, it's certainly better than the alternative.

I wiggle my heels out of the dirt and use my magic to swing higher.

Yes, if I do it, I may hurt, maybe even lose, someone I hold dear, but if I don't, I will lose even more. Life, after all, is compromise. If becoming Jinn has taught me anything, it's taught me that.

Up and up.

Higher and higher.

Until I'm flying.

And so there's only one thing I can do to grant Megan's wish. My mother's done it, with varying degrees of success. Fortunately, I have something my model Jinn mother lacks.

Afrit blood.

Using my magic, I slow my swing, bringing it to a gentle stop. I look past Henry at the Reese's house.

"I'm going to have to erase memories. I'm going to have to use mind control on her," I say. "On them both. Make them feel their family is perfectly whole as it is."

See, when genies are involved, there's always a trick.

Acknowledgments

Behind every book and every writer is a pom-pom–wielding cheerleader. As time goes on, if you're lucky, you may look over your shoulder and realize you've gathered an entire high-ponytailed squad.

Turns out, I have been very lucky. My squad begins with my agent, Lucy Carson of the Friedrich Agency, whose editorial instincts turned *Becoming Jinn* into the book you are now holding. Thank you for supporting my voice and vision, for assuaging my fears and anxieties, and for somehow finding enough hours in the day to answer my every question. Thanks as well to the Friedrich Agency's Nichole LeFebvre, who has cheered Azra on since day one.

I am especially grateful to Jean Feiwel for her belief in this series, and to my editor, Liz Szabla, for asking the questions that pushed me to dig deeper. This book and these characters exist because of you. Thank you to the entire Feiwel and Friends/Macmillan team who work so hard and who have been gracious enough to give me and my book a most welcoming home.

Thanks to my beta readers, all incredible authors in their own right, who are masters at knowing when to say "rah, rah" and when to say "nuh-uh." My early readers, Georgia Clark and Aubrey Cann, helped shaped Azra and the Jinn world, and my later readers, Jen Malone and Chelsea Bobulski, helped fine-tune it. Thank you, Jen, for having a wealth of knowledge (seriously, how do you know so much?) and for being so willing to share it. And Chelsea, I could (and one day plan to) wallpaper a room with your beautiful, encouraging words. What can I say except you, my dear, are most definitely my sister. Finally, thank you doesn't seem to encompass what I need to say to N. K. Traver, the kindhearted, enthusiastic cyber-stalker who demanded to read my book and then did so in one day. You made me believe, Nat. I am forever in your debt.

Thanks to my fellow 2015 YA debut authors, the Freshman Fifteens, for all of your support and friendship. And don't forget your promise to slip on harem pants, ladies.

A special thanks to Anna Banks, whose generosity, guidance, and friendship are only surpassed by her ability to make me laugh.

Thanks to all the friends who have supported me (and refrained from telling me to can it with the book talk already) and to my family, the Montemurros and the Goldsteins, whose enthusiasm often surpasses mine. Thank you, Martha, for reading, listening, and cheering me on. Thank you, Dad, for always reading to me, turning the pages before I was able to do so myself. Thank you, Mom, for faking it so well, and reading every school essay with a red pen in hand to push me to do better.

That's one impressive squad, but I wouldn't have any of them if it weren't for the team captain, my husband, Marc. The day he told me to write changed my life. Every step of this journey we've taken together. Thank you for telling me "there's something here" and for not letting me give up. Thank you for reading revision after revision until you could recite my words by heart. Thank you for every Saturday night plotting session. Thank you for laughing where I hoped you would, and crying where I knew you would. Unlike me, you always knew this day would come. Thank you, my soul mate, my best friend, for being right—for once. Now, don't let it go to your head.

Thank you for reading this
Feiwel and Friends book.

The Friends who made

Becoming Jinn

possible are:

Jean Feiwel
publisher

Liz Szabla
editor in chief

Rich Deas
senior creative director

Holly West
associate editor

Dave Barrett
executive managing editor

Nicole Liebowitz Moulaison
production manager

Lauren A. Burniac
editor

Anna Roberto
associate editor

Christine Barcellona
administrative assistant

Follow us on Facebook or visit
us online at mackids.com.

OUR BOOKS ARE FRIENDS FOR LIFE